THE FATAL F

ALSO BY LYNDSAY FAYE

Dust and Shadow
The Gods of Gotham
Seven for a Secret

G. P. Putnam's Sons
New York

The

FATAL
FLAME

LYNDSAY FAYE

G. P. PUTNAM'S SONS
Publishers Since 1838
Published by the Penguin Group
Penguin Group (USA) LLC
375 Hudson Street
New York, New York 10014

USA • Canada • UK • Ireland • Australia
New Zealand • India • South Africa • China

penguin.com
A Penguin Random House Company

Library of Congress Cataloging-in-Publication Data

Faye, Lyndsay.
The fatal fame / Lyndsay Faye.
p.   cm.
ISBN 978-0-399-16948-9
1. Irish Americans—New York (State)—New York—Fiction.
2. Police—New York (State)—New York—Fiction.
3. New York (N.Y.)—History—1775–1865—Fiction.   I. Title.
PS3606.A96W37   2015   2014008958
813'.6—dc23

Printed in the United States of America
1   3   5   7   9   10   8   6   4   2

BOOK DESIGN BY AMANDA DEWEY

For my great-great-grandmother Katie,
whose true surname was lost after she traveled here from Ireland—
and for Grandma Meg Fay,
who told me the story

SELECTED FLASH

TERMINOLOGY*

A

ARTICLE. A man. "You're a pretty article." A term of contempt.

AUTUMNED. Married.

B

BAT. A prostitute who walks the streets only at night.

BESS. A pick of a very simple construction.

BLEAK-MORT. A pretty girl.

BOARDINGHOUSE. City prison.

C

CAVED. Gave up; surrendered.

CHAFF. Humbug.

CHAFFEY. Boisterous; happy; jolly.

CHANT. To talk; to publish; to inform.

---

*Excerpted from George Washington Matsell, *The Secret Language of Crime: Vocabulum, or, The Rogue's Lexicon* (G. W. Matsell & Co., 1859).

CHINK. Money.

COLE. Silver or gold money.

COVE. A man.

CROSS-COVE. A thief; any person that lives in a dishonest way.

CRUMEY. Fat; pockets full; plenty.

D

DARBIES. Handcuffs; fetters.

DARBY. Cash. "Fork over the darby" (Hand over the cash).

DIMBER-MORT. A pretty girl; an enchanting girl.

DOXIE. A girl.

DUSTY. Dangerous.

F

FADGE. It won't do; "It won't fadge."

FARMER. An alderman.

FIGNER. A small thief.

FLAM. To humbug.

FLY-COP. A sharp officer; an officer that is well posted; one who understands his business.

G

GAMMY. Bad.

GIGGER-DUBBER. A turn-key; a prison-keeper.

GRAFT. To work.

GRUEL. Coffee.

GUNNED. Looked at; examined.

H

HAMLET. A captain of police.

HASH. To vomit.

HATCHES. In distress; in trouble; in debt.

HICKSAM. A countryman; a fool.

HOCKEY. Drunk.

HUSH. To murder.

K

KATE. A smart, brazen-faced woman.

KEN. A house.

KINCHIN. A young child.

KIP. A bed.

KITE. A letter.

KITTLE. To tickle; to please.

KNOCK-ME-DOWN. Very strong liquor.

L

LACE. To beat; to whip.

LAG. A convicted felon.

LAND-BROKER. An undertaker.

LAY. A particular kind of rascality.

LEAK. To impart a secret.

LEERY. On guard; look out; wide awake.

LENTEN. Having nothing to eat; starving.

LION. Be saucy; frighten; bluff. "Lion the fellow."

LOOBY. An ignorant fellow; a fool.

LULLABY-KID. An infant.

LUNAN. A girl.

LUSH. Drink.

M

MAB. A harlot.

MANDERER. A beggar.

MAZZARD. The face.

MILL. A fight.

MIZZLE. Go; run; be off.

MOLL. A woman.

MOLLEY. A miss; an effeminate fellow; a sodomite.

MOUSE. Be quiet; be still.

N

NIX. Nothing.

O

OAK. Strong; rich; of good reputation.

ON THE MUSCLE. On the fight; a fighter; a pugilist.

OPTIME. Class. "He's optime number one as a screwsman" (He is a first-class burglar).

P

PAP LAP. An infant.

PEACH. To inform.

PECK. Food.

PECULIAR. A mistress.

PEERY. Suspicious.

PHILISTINES. Police officers; officers of justice.

POLT. A blow. "Lend the pam a polt in the muns" (Give the fool a blow in the face).

PRIGGER-NAPPER. A police officer.

Q

QUARRON. A body.

QUEER. To puzzle.

R

RABBIT-SUCKER. Young spendthrifts; fast young men.

RIG. A joke; fun.

ROPED. Led astray; taken in and done for.

S

SANGUINARY. Bloody.

SKINNERS. Small lawyers who hang about police offices and figuratively skin their clients.

SKY BLUE. Gin.

SLIM. A punch.

SLUICE YOUR GOB. Take a good long drink.

SNUG. Quiet; all right.

SPICER. A footpad.

SPOONEY. Foolish.

SPUNG. A miser.

SQUEAKER. A child.

STAG. One who has turned state's evidence.

STAIT. The city of New York.

STARGAZERS. Prostitutes; street-walkers.

STIR. A fire.

STOGGER. A pickpocket.

T

TAP. To arrest.

TO RIGHTS. Clear. "Oh! Then you are to rights this time" (There is a clear case against you).

TUNE. To beat.

W

WARE HAWK. Look out; beware.

WHIDDLER. An informer; one who tells the secrets of another.

WHIPSTER. A sharper; a cunning fellow.

WOMAN'S RIGHTS

It is her right to watch beside
The bed of sickness and of pain,
And when the heart almost despairs,
To whisper hopes of health again.
Her right to make the hearth-stone glad,
With gentle words and cheerful smile:
And when man is with care oppress'd,
His wearied spirit to beguile.
It is her right to train her sons
So they may Senate chambers grace—
Thus, is she with more honor crown'd,
Than if herself had filled the place.
It is her right to be admir'd
By ev'ry generous, manly heart,
When with true dignity and grace,
She acteth well a woman's part.

. . .

What would she more than to perform
On earth, life's holiest, sweetest tasks
When you a perfect woman find,
No other rights than these she asks.

—MRS. N. P. LASSELLE, 1850

Prologue

DUNFHLAITH Ó DUFAIGH, as she had been called in the green mother country, where the rocks pierced the grasslands the way gaunt collarbones pierced the peaceful slumbering corpses in the streets, recalled what it felt like to be hungry. To long for thick brown bread with salt, to taste pipe smoke on her tongue as if it were solid charred beef. To find mushrooms in a tree stump and sell them for whiskey—not out of recklessness but because mushrooms could barely touch her appetite, while a pint of whiskey might help her forget her ravenous belly for an entire day. With care, maybe two.

Dunla Duffy, as they called her in New York City, remembered Ireland with a fondness that lingered like the mists which used to flinch away from the doorstep of her hovel when the stern sun rose. Because Dunla Duffy wasn't hungry anymore.

These days Dunla was starving.

When I was a younger version of Timothy Wilde, not copper star 107 of the New York City Police Department but a kinchin

1

running feral through the streets, I knew hungry like I knew my own name. But I've never known *starving*—and if my brother, Valentine, had never done me a single other good turn in his mad life, that would have been enough.

He did more for me than that, of course. But if I get ahead of myself, I'll never manage to put any of this on paper.

Just before dawn on the day we met, Dunla and I, she sat in the corner of a ground-floor chamber in Pell Street, listlessly hemming ankle cuffs in the rented room she shared with other molls who did manufactory outwork in their living quarters. Trousers were heaped into ziggurats throughout the room, waiting for the brutal sunrise and for the women to rouse themselves. Both the workers and their wares were on the splintering floor, furniture being a luxury. Both were, by Manhattan standards, worthless, because the year was 1848 and the British Isles hadn't glimpsed a potato that wasn't blackly leprous since 1845. At daybreak others like Dunla would arrive. Such women were similar to the piles of garbage heaped on our street corners.

No one wanted to look at them. And there would be more the next day.

"You thief," snarled a crone's voice from the opposite corner.

Dunla, distracted by a rash that had recently bloomed along her limbs like frenzied spring wildflowers, didn't reply.

"You're a *thief.*"

The room's twelve other residents stirred fitfully at the noise. Dunla managed, with an effort she found frankly unfair, to raise her head.

As Dunla informed us later, she was fourteen years old. Her huge eyes shone out pale green from straggling locks of equally green and greasy hair framing her round face. She'd once owned pale copper tresses and couldn't recollect quite how they'd faded to the color of rotting corn silk—I worked out the mystery of her seaweed-bright curls for myself eventually, of course, as I've a tendency to unravel puzzles. For all the meager good it does my acquaintances. Dunla did remember that, with her sweetly blank expression and her unnerving eyes, the villagers had given her wary glances when she was a child. But her mother had once lifted her high in the air toward the full silver moon and called Dunla her brightest light, brighter even than the *gealach lán* above their heads. Whenever Dunla's imagination attempted to reproduce fresh butter and failed, she thought about being someone's moon.

Dunla, to be truthful—because Christ knows the tale is too grim to be anything but true—was simple. But she managed in spite of the fact.

The moon seems far off and all, she told me on the day she watched my heart break, *but the tide still comes in. Don't it, now?*

From Dunla I learned that people, like deities, can move in mysterious ways.

"*Thief.*"

"What?" she said toward the rusty voice.

"I say you're a whorish, no-good, shit-eating *thief,*" the old woman snapped.

Dunla blinked in surprise.

The Witch continued sewing. She stitched quickly and without finesse, her iron hair massed in thunderstorm billows under a disintegrating scarf. The others whispered that the Witch was mad. Dunla had never seen cause to disagree with them. Anyway, she'd glimpsed the Witch before they shared this stifling Pell Street purgatory—she'd been conjuring flames out of a cauldron, Dunla was sure of it.

Dunla had crossed herself, terrified, and hurried away.

"There are laws in this country," the Witch declared.

The Witch had moved into the front room the previous month, carrying seven vile candles she'd made from rancid lard and twine contained in clay cups. When alight, the contraptions reeked of smoldering entrails. One burned now, and Dunla was using the devilish dregs of its glare by which to sew. She'd woken the instant the glimmer touched her eyelids. Mistakenly thinking it dawn.

"Laws, ye say?" Dunla repeated, frightened. She'd never broken a law before.

"I *do* say. Laws against stealing light."

Twelve other pairs of eyes narrowed, appraising. The young mother and her daughter. The two sisters. The stargazer and her very close friend, the other stargazer. The three German women who were always weeping, staring at the walls and clutching one another's hands. The pregnant lass curled on a pile of newspaper. The girl from the House of Refuge with her hair shorn off. The eleven-year-old kinchin mab.

"It's *my* light," the Witch hissed. "You want to use it, you pay me. What can you pay me, little rat?"

When Dunla saw the other women staring, her spine began to quiver. Some looked vexed, some pitying.

All looked afraid of the Witch.

A knife appeared in the Witch's hand. It shimmered in the glare of the sputtering animal fat.

"Pay up now, precious," the Witch whispered, "or I'll carve my dinner out of your backside."

"Tomorrow," Dunla squeaked. "I can sure enough pay ye tomorrow."

"By tomorrow I'll have every last one of you roasting over a spit."

"Please—"

"Pay up now, or suffer the consequences."

A minute later, maybe less, after screams and chaos and cries of *Get out, for God's sake*, Dunla found herself on Pell Street—shoeless, as she'd been for months—with her arms full of unfinished trousers. A thin, miserly rainfall heralding her arrival.

4

Huddled half under the clothing, Dunla remained on the front steps until the feeble clouds expired and the April sunlight glared dully down at her, illuminating the hordes of Africans and emigrants bustling through Ward Six—the neighborhood known worldwide as a ripening lesion on the face of New York.

It's my ward too, of course. So I don't mean that *personally*.

Tottering through horse droppings and far worse, Dunla staggered past the unconscious drunks with the flies buzzing about their grog-stained shirts, past the drooping wooden houses parroting her own imbalance, past a legless veteran returned from Mexican glory, propped against a porch. We all refer to them as the "returning volunteers," which makes a pleasanter time for us than saying "ruined men." This one had tied his uniform into knots at the knees and sipped steadily at a bottle of morphine. The veteran made a bitter grab for Dunla's skirts. But he was nearly as weak as she was, and so she lurched with her armful of pantaloons onto Chatham Street and turned south.

On Chatham Street it's impossible to tell where the shops end and the road begins. The borders fluctuate, as porous and fickle as our laws. The storefront of WM. DOWNIE'S HARDWARE EMPORIUM gushed into traffic in the form of tool-burdened tables and a dozen open boxes of carpentry nails. Dunla nearly overturned a precarious pyramid of hats stacked before HABERDASHERY BY P. J. COPPINGER but avoided it when the shop attendant shoved her aside and she fell into the fragrant spring mud.

The next thing Dunla remembered was standing before the foreman of the manufactory in Nassau Street for whom she did "outwork." That's a new market, modern as the telegraph, meaning "work without the sordid taint of decent wages."

"You're daft," Mr. Simeon Gage said, incredulous. "I'll have to *charge* against your next batch for these materials. They're ruined."

Dunla looked down at the mud-soaked pantaloons and couldn't think of a single word to say.

On her way out of the manufactory, past rainbow rows of flashily dressed Bowery girls at tables doing the more difficult cutting, one familiar face hurried up to her. A pretty peaches-and-cream face with clear, defiant amber eyes, framed by the palest shade of ash-brown waves.

"Oh, Dunla, thank heaven," the cutter said softly, pressing a folded paper into her hand. "I've been looking for you. Here's four bits. You can pay someone to read this note and then have enough left for some real peck. Lord, but you're lenten, my girl. Run along now! And you mind what it says!"

Of this dialect, spoken by our criminal element and our rowdier gentry and called flash patter, Dunla comprehended little. Just then she understood it precisely as well as she did the note in her hand, which was not at all.

Thanks to my downright bizarre thirty years of informal education surviving here in New York, I can both speak flash and read English, so I know that her friend had said, *You can pay someone to read this note and then have enough left for some real food. Lord, but you're starving, my girl.*

And I know that the note said:

I fear that my friend means to set your house aflame and burn you all alive.

Dunla did understand the fifty cents, however, and soon found herself shoving a fried-oyster sandwich into her mouth, weeping as she did so, salty juices and tears running down her chin and fingertips while the world flowed soundlessly around her like a cold river eroding a stone.

I

*It is impossible to go a rod in any of the more thickly
frequented thoroughfares without meeting some apparently
miserable supplicant for the bounty of the charitable. All
kinds of deformity and suffering are put to use in this
business; mis-shapen children, pale and pining infants,
wretched old age. . . . Many of these objects are shocking if
not disgusting, and ought to be strictly excluded by the
authorities from the public streets.*

—*NEW-YORK DAILY TRIBUNE*, AUGUST 17, 1847

I AM NOT THE HERO of this story. I don't suppose I ever was the
hero of any of these stories I set down to make some sense of the
senseless. At least I've been writing of the hero all this while.
Even back when I'd supposed my brother little more than a
flaming plague on the surviving Wilde household.

Admittedly I played a role in the war between the manufactory
girls and the men who'd wronged them so savagely. And I managed to be clever and discreet, which is why Chief of Police George
Washington Matsell trusts me with solving his most controversial
crimes in the first place. Though I always take justice as far as I
can, I've hushed up many a shame-stained scandal in my time as a
star police.

I'd stand up and applaud myself if I deserved it. So I'll sit here and keep writing.

Despite my former bartender's attention to detail and the fact that people tend to press their darkest secrets into my palms like razor-edged love tokens (neither of which qualities I can even take credit for, as they come naturally), I'm not particularly bright. Clever, yes. Oh, I've found myself so very, *very* clever at times. But as my brother, Val, frequently mentions, I am also dim as dusk. And when I think about that now, about how much more I could have done and what others were forced to do in my stead, something in my chest begins a deliberate downward tear.

Oh, not that yet. That part of the story will come all too soon.

I am not the hero, as I mentioned, but I was playing at one when it began.

I stood huddled in the doorway of a sail-repair shop in plain view of the lumbering East River, jostled by leathery first mates placing orders. I'd a fine vantage point of the James Slip, just at the corner of Oliver and South Streets—briny April wind in my face, a pickled seaside sun in my eyes. Birds wheeled above, screaming for scraps. There are plentiful dregs to be found along the waterfront.

We were after the human variety.

"When can we expect this coldhearted villain to make his appearance?" my friend Jakob Piest asked, ducking into his gruel-speckled muffler.

My closest police comrade has a tendency to wear what he eats. I think of Piest as my partner-in-whatever-it-is-we-do, since I don't know the name for hunting down criminals after the fact rather than stopping crimes in progress, as the roundsmen do. Somebody should conjure one up. The police have existed for three years now—that's plentiful time to have figured out a title for my job. Most of the copper stars walk in circuits, eyes peeled for mayhem. Thanks to Chief Matsell's esteem, I decipher unsolved mayhem.

Whenever I can borrow Piest, I do—it's keener sport with a mad companion beside me. His eyes are invaluable, and he's honest as the frayed cuffs on his frock coat. I likewise appreciate that he resembles your friendlier breed of barnacle and talks like a knight-errant. It's a good job there aren't many windmills left in Manhattan and that jousting poles are similarly scarce, or Mr. Piest would never set aside the time police work requires.

"According to the shipping wires, they're smack on schedule, so he should be here any minute now," I mused. The vessel before us rocked and groaned in protest, lashed down like a frothing wild creature. The gangway was rising, and swarthy stevedores with tobacco in their cheeks leaned against dollies, waiting to grapple with the huge ship full of luggage and dry goods about to be disgorged.

"I hope that I am neither a vicious nor a petty person, Mr. Wilde." Piest's stringy grey hair waltzed in the spring breeze. "But I relish the thought of Ronan McGlynn passing his days in a Tombs cell, watching the mice cross the great mountain range of his belly as he attempts to lull himself to sleep."

I smiled at my friend's quixotic turn of phrase, eyes skipping across coal-stained enginemen and the chalk-and-rouge-smeared whores who survived off their nickels. Piest's tone was pure poison, but so was our target. We'd recently learned that for months Ronan McGlynn had been turning a tidy profit in plucking comely Irish virgins straight from the gangways and welcoming them to worse than hell with a smile. And nothing scrapes either of our tempers thinner than the exploitation of wide-eyed innocents.

Before us, reporters from the *Herald* and the *Tribune* gathered, salivating over the freshest news from overseas. Beyond, the water lapped at the tugs and the sloops and the freighters, striking in lacy plumes against the docks.

"Ah," breathed Mr. Piest.

"Bully," I agreed.

The great ship, hull glistening, had commenced hemorrhaging first-class passengers. Fine-featured ladies, feet invisible under the great swaying bells of their skirts, once-careful curls harassed by the ocean wind. Gentlemen at their sides, nodding vague approval beneath their black hats and checking the time and generally congratulating themselves. In ten minutes they'd have disappeared with their steamer trunks piled high behind the hacksmen, gliding away to make vastly important decisions about proper hotels and appropriate restaurants and the writing of letters back to wherever they came from.

We didn't give a damn about them, though. Another figure had materialized, bouncing on the tips of his boots in anticipation, carrying a sign tucked under his arm. It read APPLICANTS FOR MANUFACTORY WORK WANTED. Which is true enough, now that these eerie mass workplaces have begun cropping up like dry rot.

Ronan McGlynn, however, didn't mean a word of it.

I set McGlynn's age somewhere north of fifty, for while his blue eyes remained clear and his ruddy skin hale, his shoulder-length hair was white and his legs sticklike beneath a jolly round belly. He wore perfectly cut doeskin trousers—not the ready-made slops New York has begun vomiting out, but sewn to measure—and a white vest beneath a violet frock coat. A snowy beard and a grey top hat completed the benevolent picture. But he was only a pantomime of a prosperous businessman. McGlynn owned a thin gash of a mouth and the stare of a born slave trader, the outline of a flask marred his jacket, and his nails where they gripped the pasteboard sign were dark with grit.

I notice that sort of thing, though. When the Irish lasses poured off the boat, dazzled and hungry, they'd be lucky to notice a twenty-one-cannon salute. Not that they'd get one.

"If it isn't the ugliest pair o' copper stars this side of Connell's arse," came a gruff Irish voice to my left.

"Me arse is widely considered comely, truth be told. The shape of it, the heft and all. Are ye blind, Kildare?" a still-thicker Irish brogue questioned, amused.

"Welcome to the festivities." I smiled crookedly beneath the brim of my broad black hat.

Maybe I ought to have objected to the greeting, but Mr. Piest's bulging blue eyes and absent chin admittedly resemble a carp's. As for my own appearance . . . the Fire of 1845 had replaced the upper right quarter of my face with skin like a poorly cobbled thoroughfare. No one to my knowledge found me unbearably ugly previous, but I hadn't exactly taken a survey. People find Val plenty spruce in appearance, and we could be twins apart from the fact he has me beat by six years of age and eight inches in height. We've deep-set green eyes and a little downward half-moon stamped in our chins, clean features with a slender nose below double-arched dirty-blond hairlines. Youthful faces for all that we've both seen too much, his marred only by weighty bags beneath his eyes and mine by a scar ugly enough to pickle cucumbers.

So I wasn't going to argue with Connell. Not when I enthusiastically agreed with him that neither Piest nor myself belongs on a facial-tonic advertisement.

As for our fellow copper stars, Connell has a pleasantly boxlike head, rough-featured and approachable, with flaming red hair he ties back with a short ribbon. Mr. Kildare, the taller and quicker-tempered of the two, rubbed at his wiry black side-whiskers. They joined us in the sail-repair shop's shadow, leaning with indolent nonchalance against the brick wall.

"Where's the pimp, then?" Kildare wondered.

"I'll be after thinkin' ye really are blind." Connell nodded toward where McGlynn preened. "Will you look at the airs and graces o' the scum."

"Shit'll fly, if ye hit it with a stick," Kildare reminded us.

The last of the first-class passengers descended. "You hired McGlynn?" I asked quietly.

"Yesterday, 'twas. We're meant to be the muscle for a goosing slum in Anthony Street," said Kildare, whose beat had bordered mine when I'd spent sixteen hours a day trudging in a circle as one of the first New York police.

"A real brothel or an imaginary one?" Jakob Piest asked, brow askew. He doesn't speak much flash, but we deal with so many brothels it would have been absurd for him not to recognize *goosing slum.*

"O' course a real brothel. Don't be insulting," Connell said mildly. "Paid the madam five dollars in case McGlynn wanted to check up on our sincerity, didn't I now? She's a motherly sort to her stargazers, more than game t' help flush out the likes o' this rat."

"An unnecessary and ungallant query on my part, Mr. Kildare," Piest apologized.

Prostitution, I should mention, is illegal. Not in *fact*—merely on paper. When women resort to the practice due to hunger or cold, I mourn for them. Arresting them, though, all the many thousands of them, would be a bit of a wrench, since testimony from the gentlemen who'd bought their kindnesses would be required to convict them. That doesn't mean, however, that *forced* prostitution is a form of commerce we're willing to tolerate. We calculate there are enough slaves south of the Mason-Dixon without treating Manhattan women like the cheaper sort of broodmares.

"We ordered a great bloomin' lot o' fresh dells, plump virgin dells fit to break yer hearts and raise yer flagpoles," Kildare explained, smiling. "Dells with small knubbly titties, dells with great pillow titties, dells with perfect round peach titties to make ye praise the Maker fer—"

"He's to bring in six new girls for us special like." Connell pulled out a small notebook. "To be viewed directly, at a quarter past twelve."

A thick stream of respectable dull greys and browns and maroons seeped from the boat as the second-class passengers, faces hopeful and wary, descended the gangway, their plain woolen traveling costumes thrice mended. Shabby young unmarried men who'd carefully brushed their hats, bespectacled women with the addresses of female boardinghouses clutched in spotless gloved hands. The one thing more disgraceful than being poor, I've found, is *looking* the part. A penniless but chastely dressed woman is graciously allowed to beg for a stale crust. A slovenly dressed one with a cache of gold in the flour jar from her midnight admirers is widely considered better off dead.

McGlynn, still hopping a little in expectancy, stilled when the steerage passengers—no better than ambulatory cargo but treated less tenderly—began to stumble blinking from the bowels of the ship onto American soil. I was peering with grim intent at the older man when the flash of a blue hat and a sweep of black hair passed the corner of my eye.

Before I knew my legs had made a decision, they'd taken two quick steps toward James Slip.

"Mr. Wilde?" Piest questioned, instantly alert. I must have looked like a greyhound quivering at the starting gate, electric shimmers gliding along my skin.

I forgot to answer him.

And it was all nonsense, of course, because *that can't have been her, the last of the second-class passengers. That can't possibly have been Mercy Underhill.*

Mercy Underhill, an old friend and correspondent of mine who held my heart in her hands when she imagined she was merely embroidering with them, or doling out beef tea, or writing her darkly magical short stories, lived in London. Not New York. Not since she'd left it, in 1845, three years back.

But it was just the way she held her head, exactly so, inky hair and papery skin. Since I was a boy, I've been studying the way Mercy carried herself at the slightest of angles, as if reading a book held in one slender hand, as if she were always looking for someone who'd disappeared round the corner, just out of her reach.

"Mr. Wilde?"

I stepped back, embarrassed. "I fancied I saw someone I used to know."

Nothing remained of her. Only swarming Irish, emaciated to the point of weightlessness, some bloodlessly pale and others burned nut brown from outdoor labor, coming thick and fast as petals blown from fruit trees. That was sensible, though, because Mercy had breathed not a word of returning to the city that had treated her so poorly in her last correspondence to me. And anyway, I love her. I see echoes of her everywhere. I could probably find her face in tea leaves and collapsed puddings, as if she were my first and forever saint.

"We had him pegged, all right," Connell said, eyes fixed on our true prize.

I shook my head in considerable self-disgust, though that didn't go far toward clearing it.

"Manufactory work for the healthy and willing!" McGlynn rang a small chiming bell, sign in hand. The lettering wasn't meant for the emigrant Irish, since nary a soul of them could read it, but for our colleagues—roundsmen passing with a curious eye. "Skills taught upon hire! Fair pay for dependable and virtuous females! Women only need apply, to preserve the safety of our workplace!"

"D'ye find it more disgusting he's speakin' o' workplace safety or virtue?" Mr. Connell growled.

A nicely plumpish Irish lass who'd apparently survived the voyage with occasional meals, though God knows how she'd come by them, approached McGlynn. *Is there yet work to be had, sir?* I saw her ask. Her voice was soft, but if you can't see the difference between *champagne* and *whiskey* in a deafening saloon, you make for a poor barman. The trick had remained handy when I became a copper star.

"Work aplenty!" McGlynn crowed. "This is New York, my girl—the most commercial city in a rich nation. Welcome, welcome! Manufactory work for the chaste and diligent!"

Within three minutes, dozens had lined up. Girls with midnight-black tresses and blue eyes like cornflowers, girls with locks the pale orange of a sweet September leaf. Eyes latched onto McGlynn as if he were a lifeline.

"Give us the plan, then, Wilde," Kildare demanded.

"Take off your copper stars," I answered. "You and Connell split off to meet McGlynn at the designated address. Which is?"

"Northwest corner o' Rose Street and Frankfort. A brothel called the Queen Mab."

"Best to turn up early so he doesn't suspect you. Meanwhile, I'll track these girls with Piest, make certain McGlynn doesn't drop off any human deliveries before he arrives there."

"I'd nary think it likely, for by all accounts the Queen Mab is a clearinghouse," Connell reported icily. It's a personal opinion of mine that buildings where women are systematically violated for commerce should have a worse moniker, and if I ever find one to express the proper feeling, I'll employ it. "Screams at all hours, curtains sure enough plastered over the windows, though 'tis a weight off my mind—don't let 'em out of your sight fer love or money."

"And when the pair o' ye arrive at the Queen Mab?" Kildare put in, cracking hoary knuckles.

"We linger outside until you're being shown the main event, then burst in and cry inspection," I answered. "Keep McGlynn from escaping out any rabbit holes. Simple."

"It's never simple, Wilde, y' brilliant little tit," Kildare chided, not without affection.

"Ye've titties on the brain, Kildare. Leave off the resident genius until something goes sideways," Connell chuckled as they set off for Rose Street. "Then we can blame him, don't you know. Won't that be nice."

They never did any such thing, of course. Even when they ought to have done.

Piest, meanwhile, was jutting his inadequate jaw toward McGlynn's bevy of unwashed beauties in a pugilistic manner I found alarming. He's a passionate man, but never a violent one. Then I glanced back and felt something thickly furious turn over at the bottom of my stomach.

There were far too many girls for McGlynn to take.

Of course there are, I thought, repulsed by my own surprise.

And so, naturally, McGlynn was standing with elbows akimbo, calling out regretful dismissals in a fatherly baritone. Sending skinny, heartsick maidens and pregnant widows away in tears while he selected the prize lambs for the slaughter. The ones with long lashes and tender little mouths. The fair ones and the rosy ones. The ones gratefully gathering off to the left of a massive pile of parcel post, stroking one another's shoulders in the depth of their collective relief.

I ought to have expected McGlynn to have his pick. We city dwellers were all of us standing on the tip of Death's scythe just then, arms flung wide with terror and the sharp point sinking through the boot sole. It was a pretty universal sensation. The young New Yorkers and the old, the Irish and the blacks, the natives and the emigrants, the Protestants and the Catholics, the men and the women. None of which sets got on with each other too amicably. The year 1848 was not, by any standard, a comfortable one. We'd just finished a war with Mexico, and the houses of Congress's newest hobby seemed to be waging a new one against each other; the country was tearing itself apart at the seams, our rancor poker-black and spiteful. Meanwhile, here in my arrogant young port town, folk were clawing for supremacy like distempered street cats. Nearly half a million of us. The newcomers had proved too plentiful. Too frail and too numerous to live.

I might have mentioned already that the potatoes in Ireland were rotting. It seems worth mentioning again. There was a problem regarding the edible nature of the tuber on Irish shores that directly affected our general welfare.

So of course there were too many girls lining up to be raped to accommodate the man who wanted to rape them. But generally when circumstances set my blood stewing so hot, terrible things happen.

That day was no exception.

"Ready to lock this worm underground?" I questioned.

"Always a pleasure, Mr. Wilde," the eccentric Dutchman replied.

When our grandfatherly Pied Piper had assembled his elite band, ignoring the pleas of those left behind, he set off, and we followed at a good easy distance. We weren't any too leery that he could speedily change direction with so many girls in tow. Nine of them, by my counting, six special-ordered by Connell and Kildare. He turned left on Cherry Street, which curves into Pearl as the nautical-supply stores fade along with the smell of sharp vinegar blasts from the billowing water.

I'd figured McGlynn for chaffey enough to parade the whole merry troop right through the main door at Rose Street, but I underestimated him. Sliding the sign beneath his arm, he started making a god-awful racket. This is New York—that's the way to instantly stop people from listening to you. I made a show of pulling a newspaper from inside my greatcoat while Piest pretended interest over the advertisement I pointed at.

"Applications for manufactory work with mandatory sewing skills, speed test this way!" McGlynn boomed, beaming at the women as he waved at the more discreet service entrance. "Step right through! Training is provided at all aptitude levels, ladies!"

"I'm going to feed this man his own bollocks," I mentioned behind the paper. Meaning the sentiment, if not the literal activity.

"We've only to wait until they are cloistered with Mr. Kildare and Mr. Connell, and then I will gladly assist in the . . ." Mr. Piest's voice trailed off as he spared a glance above the page.

"What?" I whispered. Not daring to look up, when from the rigidity of his limbs I knew that Mr. Piest was staring intently.

"Erm, very likely the most innocent of misunderstandings and nothing that ought to cause you the remotest alarm."

"Jakob," I said forcefully.

"It's just that your brother . . ."

My attention snapped like a whipcord up to the front door of the Queen Mab.

And yes, there was Val, walking tranquil as you please up the front steps of a clearinghouse. My brother, Valentine Wilde, the captain of the Ward Eight copper stars and the neighborhood's Party boss, the legendary hero of more fires than I care to ruminate over and the undisputed bane of my existence, carrying a leaded walking stick twice as dangerous as his tongue—and that is saying something—shut the door of the Queen Mab without a backward glance.

"Did—"

"He didn't see us," I assured Mr. Piest.

"Then what—"

"Oh, Christ," I interrupted him for the second time.

For Val wasn't the only visitor I recognized entering the Queen Mab just then.

The man following close after my brother—not a sinister shadow, just a fellow arriving at an appointment—was also known to Piest, for he stiffened again. The newcomer was tall and superficially dashing. I didn't know him well, and I didn't want to know him better. At all. In fact, I'd once known him only as Pocket Watch. That was on the occasion, of course, when he'd volunteered to kill me. His real name was Robert Symmes.

I might as well have introduced him, though, as Tammany Hall.

2

. . . an old lady called, asking aid in reclaiming a grandchild who had been led astray at the age of fourteen, by a married man, a father, Superintendent of the Sabbath School to which she belonged! She had been under his deadly influence for more than a year. . . . They fear, young as she is, she is so contaminated, that nothing but coercion and a long confinement will avail anything. The House of Refuge was recommended as the most suitable place for her.

—THE ADVOCATE OF MORAL REFORM AND FAMILY
GUARDIAN, 1852

JAKOB PIEST AND I STOOD outside the Queen Mab on the languidly brightening morning of Wednesday, April 19, 1848. Wondering what was best, or in fact possible, to do.

Briefly, I assured myself that Val's personal roster of less-than-desirable habits—which so far as I was definitely aware included narcotics, alcohol, bribery, violence, whoring, gambling, theft, cheating, extortion, sodomy, spying, forgery, and lying—could never lead to the sort of debased vice indulged in that place. He'd always been especially infuriated by the notion of the gentler sex being bullied, come to that. I pictured his bold, cynical, morphine-strained face when he discovered just where he was and realized we were in for a hearty serving of warm trouble.

As is pretty usual practice for me.

Folding the paper, I peered at the Queen Mab. Three stories, some of its windows ominously boarded over. Built before the population explosion and thus sturdy if obscenely crumbling. Carpenters these days will lean a pair of uncured planks against each other in the wildwoods north of Chelsea, spread a welcome mat in front, and call it a town house. That would be amusing, supposing humans didn't actually *live* in such places.

"It's to do with the election, it must be," I conjectured.

"I question this choice of meeting place in the strongest terms," Piest replied gloomily.

Robert Symmes was about to be reelected, which meant he needed my brother. Val is a police captain by virtue of wit and nerve, a fireman by virtue of tragic history, and a deity to countless Irish by virtue of feeding them. Or if not feeding them directly at the Knickerbocker Engine Company Number 21 on charitable Sundays, then setting them up with the work enabling them to buy cabbage. They'd have plenty to palaver about, the Tammany politician and the Tammany legend who'd deliver him the election on a scrollworked platter. Especially considering the recent splintering of the Party along Hunker and Barnburner lines. But whatever was afoot, it muddled our own ploy.

"I don't like this at all," I confessed. "Trust Kildare and Connell to keep the girls safe in the meanwhile . . . but we can't very well start a raid in the middle of a Party meeting."

"I cannot see that we have any alternative choice in the matter," Piest observed worriedly. "We ought to tip a hat to our betters, take the lay of the land, and then I propose it's on to McGlynn."

He was right to be anxious. The neophyte police force has always been loathed by the Whig Party, which makes us a pretty squarely Democratic affair. Thus, copper stars who cross Tammany tend to be summarily transferred to the bottom of the Hudson. Grasping this fairly relevant principle had proved one of the nastier lessons of my none-too-peaceable lifetime.

"Right, then," I said, and we strode across the street.

I eased open the unlocked door. We found ourselves in a dank hallway decorated in the style typical of bordellos inhabited by the semistarving. Someone had taken a pornographic magazine, the sort one seeks in dusky alleyway racks, framed all the moldering pages, and hung them from the plaster. It was not an inspiring display, in light of circumstances.

Voices drifted through a crack in a nearby door. This time I did knock. Though I didn't wait for an answer.

"... the reason I knew you could be counted on," Symmes continued. "Oh, here's your brother. I'd no idea you wanted to bring him in, Captain. But it's genuinely rewarding to see how Party-minded you're becoming over time, Mr. Wilde."

Had Symmes seen my true mind, he'd have read printed along the inner circumference of my skull the motto DAMN POLITICS, DAMN THE DEMOCRATS, AND DAMN YOU FOR THE LOW WEASEL YOU ARE. But admittedly I've spent the past few years at intensive training in keeping my mouth closed when necessary. The hard way. So I touched the edge of my broad hat and nodded, saying, "This is my colleague, Roundsman Jakob Piest."

Robert Symmes sat with a glass of brown liquor in his hand, smirking at nothing specific. He seems always to be wishing he could be better occupied or in flasher company, compulsively checking his heavy silver pocket watch. This might flam the foolish into thinking he's powerful, but to my mind he's impressive only in the way inert solid-gold bars are. He's tall and broad-shouldered and blue-eyed and blond, with fairer hair than my brother and a sharper face—all angles and edges in a way that makes him look strong, even thoughtful. He isn't thoughtful, though. He wears an artful moustache, brilliant waistcoats, turned-down white collars, and a smug expression, and if he's ever done a good thing for Ward Eight other than to leave it alone, I can't imagine it.

Meanwhile, my brother was fighting the lingering effects of a spree. His bright green eyes shone feverishly, and the sporadic twitch of his chin meant nothing good. I'd used to spend my nights wondering with a spear in my belly whether, if Val survived the amount of morphine he'd swallowed, it would merely mean he'd die fighting a fire the next day. Rendering the lucky recovery moot. The man thinks he killed our parents in the leaf-crisp brown autumn of 1828 when our home in Greenwich Village tragically went up in cinders. Thus the firedogging, and the narcotics, and the not-very-bearable fact that I can't change any of it. I'd have better luck requesting in a stern note that the British Parliament stop shipping us Irish peasants than I would persuading my brother to forget what happened the year he turned sixteen and accidentally dropped a lit cigar end in our stable. Or so I assume. There are things, 1828 foremost among them, that we absolutely do not discuss in English. Occasionally in blistering silences. In quick-shuttered looks. Nothing more.

But lately Val, though he hasn't changed, has mellowed. He's more inclined to break a scoundrel's nose than his leg. Lose consciousness in a dazzling white fog of liquor and opiates on the floor of the Liberty's Blood saloon rather than in a ditch. It's . . . nice. Sort of *domestic,* I suppose. If baffling. He wore the same cut of rich Bowery duds as Symmes did, tailored black trousers and a tightly fitted emerald jacket over a morning-glory-patterned waistcoat that was equally expensive as laughable.

"Tim," Val grunted, electing not to be surprised. "Mr. Piest. Well, since you both savvy what I do already, the podium's yours, Alderman. Keen to report a crime in a private way, I take it?"

It was smoothly done. The pair of us sat on the molding settee across from my brother and his alderman, by now plenty fretful over our own designs. I reached down to tug at a bootlace and tapped at Mr. Piest's skinny calf en route. Understanding me, his scarecrow limbs popped upright again.

"Alderman Symmes, I wished merely to pay my sincerest personal respects, since I've another, unavoidable engagement. Rest assured that my esteemed, nay, my *renowned* colleague Mr. Wilde here will inform me in the greatest possible detail how it is we may assist you, and to that end may I wish you a very good day."

The door clicked shut behind us. Which muffled the direction of my friend's clamorous boot soles, thank Christ. I leaned forward with my fingers linked, all attention. Val ran a finger over the semicircle etched in his chin.

"Well," Symmes sniffed. "To begin with, Mr. Wilde, as you may know, I am the owner of a considerable amount of property, ranging in description from housing for our newest voters to estates north of Thirty-fifth Street to modern textile manufactories."

My brain readily translated, *Slums, rectangles of woodland, and human gristmills.*

"You could call me a rich man without being a liar, Captain," Symmes continued. "And I've earned it too, every chipped penny— my manufactories are the universal pride of Ward Two. It's to do with one of them I called you here."

The manufactory girls who work downtown and populate the Bowery are the least terrible sight in a legion of piss-poor vistas of late. They're bizarre creatures, to be sure, outlandish as elephants. We've never seen their like. They live in all-female boardinghouses empty of fathers and husbands, walk to work sharing secrets and grainy ripe apples. They wear scarlet vests over yellow frocks and cry "Bully!" at the drop of a hatpin when they're pleased. Their hours are long, I hear tell, and the labor both difficult and tedious. But they throw "check-apron" dances at the Red House come January. Feast on charred pigs and hot cider. Smile when a fellow like me dares to look them in the eye and then laugh at me when I nod back. It's disorderly, confounding, and—for a man who sees starving women on an almost daily basis—downright pleasurable. The Bowery girls own a frankness that looks like pride, and it's mesmerizing.

The outworkers, though, the emigrant women. The ones who aren't whores and aren't American and still sew clothing. They're another story entirely.

"Rich man, you say. By Christ, can you imagine I'd guessed as much? And just which bit of velvet is feeling coarse against your delicate bits, Mr. Symmes?" Val inquired testily.

Symmes drew a much-folded piece of paper from his frock coat. "As a boss who manages many sets of laborers, I've identified certain . . . *types*. Malcontents who are only satisfied by dissatisfaction, for instance—eager to slander authority but sluggish over actual exertion. Of course you must have combated such slow rot yourself, Captain, within your copper stars."

My brother showed a lightning glimpse of canines that has never boded well for anyone. "Truth be told, I've a pack of fly-cops posted under me, and the only hicksams honest heavy lifters."

"In English, if you please, I refuse to endure common flash cant."

"I trust my men, and I like them," Val drawled. "So you'll have to touch on the specific."

Lifting an eyebrow, Symmes offered the crumpled document. Valentine took it without any theatricality whatsoever and spread it on his thigh. Something in his face changed from dismissive to intrigued.

"Specific enough?" Symmes sniffed as the pocket watch made an appearance.

"Not that Tim here can always tell east from elbow, but he might help shine a lantern on this." Val snapped the paper against his knee, passing it to me.

The scrap of foolscap read:

> *Women across the nation are on the rise. As strikes don't move you, we'll see whether vengeance might. Improve the hateful conditions of those who wield the needle as a sword or watch your outwork go down in flames. We will not be cowed by those who think us less than human. You might not weep over the martyrs we will create in the name of justice. But you will mind about your lost pantaloons when they burn.*

This was enough to give pause.

Our gunpowder keg of a local workforce has been shrieking itself dumb of late over multiple thorny questions, two topics trumping all the rest for volume and bristling hostility. First, I don't think announcing a "right to work" and then proceeding to slaughter one another as they're currently doing in France is a very sensible proposal. But reading about the catastrophic scope of dead Frenchmen in the *Herald* excites the appetites of our equally ravenous laborers, their callused and empty hands itching for doughy capitalist necks.

Second, I don't suppose targeting female workers—who constitute the next ax on the workingmen's grinding stone—any too practicable, since they haven't any wealth to redistribute in the first place. Though the Married Women's Property Act just allowed them marginal safety as regards inheritance, they're still about as well-off, legally speaking, as your more pampered stock of Georgia house slave. When once married, they don't own their kinchin, they don't own their wages, they don't even own their own hides if the master of the house is inclined to regular doses of the belt.

As women have recently begun to point out. To vigorous and near-universal ridicule.

So the note was genuinely worrisome. Meanwhile, Val had indirectly asked me to play my little saloon-keeper's parlor trick with it. So I set to.

"This was wrapped around a small brick or stone. The wrinkles radiate from four points. Thrown through your window, maybe?" I asked, eyeing the alderman.

Symmes blinked in surprise and then shrugged the insight off. "It was, at that. I suppose next you'll pinpoint the perpetrator?"

"I'm not a magician. But the author probably has access to a printing press. Maybe an apprentice at one of the smaller journals, though a man who does small batches from home isn't impossible. Whoever made this wanted it to resemble a major newspaper, but that's hocus. The *Herald*, the *Tribune*, they're all printed double-sided. This is printed on one side only—a special order, then. From the tone I'd figure the writer for educated and plenty familiar with foreign politics."

Symmes sat with a smirk hastily scrawled over his face, trying to decide whether to be mocking or bored. Valentine merely coughed in contentment, running a pugilist's knuckles down his costly waistcoat.

"Threats of this sort are common enough," I reasoned, keen to escape upstairs. "People borrow wild language from the morning editions, lay ideas that never hatch."

"Granted, I suppose many locals are corrupted by the writings of foreign anarchists and Yidishers," Symmes owned, yawning.

Not caring to address this topic, I returned to the previous one.

A man can own the deftest tongue on the planet, but I've found if his audience lacks ears, talk is ineffectual. Anatomically speaking.

"I suppose we burn the letter, then?" I hazarded. Knowing the Party's ways.

"Oh, no, not when it's clearly of such *use* to you." Symmes sighed pettishly, staring now into the middle distance. "That document will be further proof against the culprit, who has been threatening to incinerate me in my bed for weeks."

My black boot stopped inches from the fireplace, a reddish haze gleaming hungrily over its toe.

A mad correspondent was one thing. We've both local and imported religious radicals, utopians in pristine white uniforms, half-witted screeds in the place of journalism, and a national congressman who insists that the solution to the slavery dilemma is to slit the throats of all blacks and chalk the experiment up to an honest mistake. Hell, Hunkers within the Party are calling for Barnburners to hang for traitors to Tammany, and vice-versa arguments are screamed with equal bloodthirsty enthusiasm.

But a mad correspondent who actually acted—I've dealt with such vipers' nests before. As for a genuine incendiary, exactly nil words in the English language ketch me quite the way *fire* does.

I needed out of that room.

Valentine shifted in his chair. "In that case just give out the guilty party's moniker and we'll—"

"Who do you imagine wrote this, then, Mr. Wilde?" Symmes demanded of me lazily. "Make use of your . . . faculty, whatever it is, and identify the perpetrator."

I've lived for thirty years on this unfortunate planet, six years less than Valentine. And the only person I have ever heard interrupt him without fearing for his health is me. My brother's eyes were sparking like the Harlem line train's iron wheels.

"A tailor, obviously," I grated out. "They think the seamstresses lower than fleas for stealing their livelihood, and the unemployed ones breathe in air and breathe out inflammatory articles. You're after one with an idle needle and a busy press."

"Wrong." Symmes checked his pocket watch again. "What a disappointment you are in the end, Mr. Wilde. I'm after a bumptious wench with a busy press and a busier mouth. A Fanny Wrightist harlot by the name of Sally Woods, whom I was forced to sack from one of my aforementioned manufactories. You can find her at one-thirty Thomas Street."

I blinked.

My abnormally patient brother at last stirred. "You're being threatened by a *bluestocking*, Alderman?"

"Yes, to my profound annoyance. I've so very many demands on my time during this eventful elec—"

Val sat forward with such abrupt force that Symmes stopped midsentence. My pulse quickened uncomfortably. But at least the world as I knew it had returned the north to its pole.

"You mean to suggest to me," my brother said in an undertone dark as coal dust, "that you called me here, wherever here is— during, I need not remind you, the height of *your* election season— to ask me to muzzle a moll who sent a kite through your window for a lark. Because this doesn't go very far toward guaranteeing an actual fire. *Sir.*"

"I asked you to speak plain English, and I meant it. Of course she'd never dare to go through with her threat, but—"

"But since you're not up to controlling your manufactory wenches, you summoned me. Notwithstanding the sprees I've yet to plan nor the spungs I've to wring for campaign funds nor the manderers I've to dress like Democrats within a fortnight for you. *Sir.*"

"Captain Wilde—" Symmes sputtered, furious.

"Do you honestly think you're the only man in this room with starch in your collar and time at a premium? Or can't you lion a Bowery gal at all? They need ginger management, I'll own as much, spitfire creatures to the last of them, and if you've a weak hand—"

"Valentine!" I exclaimed, aghast.

"Treat me like a spicer," my brother growled to Symmes with a positively voracious smile on his face, "and I will—"

Several thumps and a muffled shout emanated from the cracked ceiling, sending my hackles skyward.

"Enough of this posturing, Captain!" the alderman cried. "Show a modicum of respect. Of course I'd thought to make the errand, and I'll admit an errand of sorts it is, albeit likewise a civic duty, worth your while. Why do you think we're *here*, for God's sake?"

"Try me," I shot back, glaring upward at the plaster dust drifting onto the brim of my hat.

Seeing my expression, Val pushed to his feet. "You've ten seconds left to jaw, Symmes. Make them bleed for you."

"Oh, for Christ's sake, don't act the innocent, Valentine," Symmes snapped. "It's ludicrous on you. You're a man of appetites, and everyone knows it. This afternoon is just a small token, a gratuity if you will, for settling this little matter of mine—fresh as they come."

"Val," I hissed, stomach knotting, "we're—"

"Just what in the name of the devil," Valentine said tenderly, advancing toward the politician with his mother-of-pearl-topped stick firmly in hand, "were you planning to *tip* me with, Alderman?"

A sharp scream sliced through the thin flooring. I was off like a hare, my brother audible at my heels.

Whatever was happening needed to end. Instantly.

"Do I want to savvy why you're really here?" Val demanded from the stair behind me. He's quicker, but there wasn't space for him to pass.

"No," I admitted, swinging myself up and into the hallway by the newel post. "Should you have insulted—"

"No," he snarled, "but I've been keen to for *years*. And if what I suspect is true—"

I skidded to a halt in an open doorway, my brother towering behind me.

It was a spare room with six straw mattresses in it. Filthy and lice-ridden as their scores of temporary occupants, pooled with tallow-colored stains that didn't bear scrutiny. The floor was achingly bare, the two windows boarded over, the room's only light emanating from a set of brass kerosene fixtures attached to either wall, leering like rotten teeth. Pondering what had been done in that room countless times over would have been hard enough going without a set of nine frightened Irish girls herded inside, suffering torments.

But that wasn't quite the case either.

Carefully, I took in the scene.

Ronan McGlynn had his dirty hands up in apparent shock. Mr. Connell stood in the corner with his burly arms spread wide. Mr. Piest murmured soothing words from a spot near the door. The nine Irish lasses did indeed look frightened, pale skin waxy in the jaundiced light, huddled into a pack with their backs together and their teeth bared.

And one of them—a blazing redhead with a face freckled as if she'd been lovingly splattered by her ancestors with a tiny paintbrush—held a makeshift knife point-up against my friend Mr. Kildare's throat.

3

Woman's Rights, or the movement that goes under that
name, may seem to some too trifling in itself and too much
connected with ludicrous associations to be made the subject
of serious arguments. If nothing else, however, should give
it consequence, it would demand our earnest attention
from its intimate connection with all the radical and
infidel movements of the day. A strange affinity seems to
bind them all together....

—*HARPER'S NEW MONTHLY MAGAZINE,*
NOVEMBER 1853

As with most situations ending in life, death, or arrest, the arrival of newcomers garnered a healthy percentage of the room's attention. Piest fell silent, Connell speared me a canny sidelong look, and the Irish girls as one organism inched farther into the back of that beastly room. Kildare suffered a tensing of the knife at his throat and murmured an appeal in his own language. Whether to God or to the redhead more immediately deciding his fate, I couldn't say. His face was chalk-drawn in the way only a man with his life taken out of his hands can look.

Meanwhile, I'd been having a chat downstairs with a politician. I will never lose the ability to surprise myself. And I don't mean that as a compliment.

"All right. Let's have a short palaver, and then we'll all be on our way. Except for that man," I added, pointing a finger like a pikestaff at McGlynn, "who will be going to jail."

McGlynn's eyes narrowed into snake slits, white beard jutting in defiance. I feared a hidden exit but suspected there wasn't one—any molls incarcerated to be broken there might have found it. Unfortunately, I've rich experience with girls being abused as men please. My very young friend Bird Daly, who'd provided not only my first crime of citywide significance but my first friend after the fire had scarred me, was once imprisoned in a chamber with cleaner bedclothes but an identically rank purpose. One finds few escape routes built into dungeons, whether they belong to the absent-hearted Madam Silkie Marsh, who sold mere kinchin for pleasure, or to dockside kidnappers.

I stepped ever so carefully aside. For the single reason that I wanted my brother to have a clear sight line more than anyone else in the room.

Mr. Piest's brow was damp, but his voice emerged calm and reedy as ever. "I was just saying the same, Mr. Wilde, and also that these two fellow Irishmen you see here, madam, as well as myself and the two noble gentlemen who have just arrived, are star police of New—"

"Liar!" she hissed. Her blade seemed to have been honed from the end of a cheap pewter soup spoon, the bowl of which was clenched in one hand, Kildare's hair fisted in the other. "These ten minutes and all they've been a-standin' there, ogling, arguin' our price."

"I know." I advanced a single step more. "It's part of our—"

"Saints have mercy, what call d'ye expect me to trust a *policeman* fer, even if 'tis gospel yer speakin'? Pigs," she added, spitting at us.

There was a point that I couldn't rightly argue. We're not all of the same stripe, we copper stars. Oh, we wear the same badge and we work under Chief Matsell, who, for a political man, is a shockingly decent one. But none of us are quite meant to be here, after all. Some of us are meant to run a distillery or own a haberdashery or till a farm. Others are meant to keep a gambling hell or host a bear-baiting ring or rob headlong midnight stagecoaches. Plenty are a little of both sorts, like my brother, both ruthless and pastoral, and skirt dangerous boundaries. But we've all been blasted by something that scored lasting marks. Not a man of us woke up and said, *May I one day be a policeman of New York?*— because we simply didn't exist. Who could imagine such work as keeping a city safe?

And that makes for a wide, wavy ribbon of light and dark.

"'Tis from the docks themselves we've been tracking ye this past hour," Connell pleaded. "When y' came off the gangway, that bonnie lass wi' the dark hair and the blue shawl there was on your arm, and us watching, a-fixed to trap this rat in his—"

"That proves a great barrel o' nothin' as I figure it." She angled the knife higher, shining wide grey eyes on each of us by turn. "Could have been spying fer any reason, and none of 'em decent."

"What if—" Piest began, advancing.

"Get back afore I cut his bollocks as well as 'is worthless throat!" she cried.

We did. Posthaste. Kildare glared daggers at Piest, who blushed crimson and then promptly continued, dogged as ever.

"They've copper stars in their pockets, madam, the identical ones that we wear," Piest repeated. "Show her, Mr. Connell, that you are a stalwart vessel of the—"

"I. Hate. Pigs." The emigrant woman jerked at her captive's scalp. I couldn't muster the energy to fault her for it.

"Please tell us, just what is your plan here?" I begged, palms forward.

"Now, that's the right question," Valentine said pleasantly from behind me.

The Irish girls swept eyes made all the brighter by dint of dirt and tear tracks toward us. It was like being stared down by an ancient, many-headed creature in the gloom of its echoing cave. Downright uncanny. And my lungs were already strapped tight with fear.

"Do you *want* to kill that man?" he inquired. As if asking after the likelihood of rain or location of the closest apothecary.

If the panicked huddle knew what to make of the giant who'd stolen the spotlight, they didn't let on. Propping his stick against the wall, Valentine pulled something from his waistcoat, which act violently alarmed both sides. But it was only a cigar stub. He smiled, a real one, with teeth that weren't meant to rend, and lit the cigar with a vesta struck against his thumbnail. The instant the tobacco aroma began to drift, soporific and familiar, the charged atmosphere shifted.

"I did actually want to know," Val objected when the lass holding the shiv stood glaring wordlessly. "You can want to kill him or not, as long as you tell me which."

What in hell is wrong here, I thought, *other than the obvious?*

I realized in another clock's tick that my sibling wasn't speaking flash. And that—after long wondering—I at last knew whether or not he could tell the difference. It was the right lay to make, to be sure. How could a green girl from a green island understand our blackest speech? And so he was talking plain English. As I'd not heard him do since . . . I could scarce remember.

"What's yer part in this?" the girl demanded. "Boss o' the place, are ye? Or just a *patron*?"

"I'm another star police, same as these." Val waved the cigar in a cordial arc. In every direction save McGlynn's, whom we'd trapped in the corner when we crowded the entryway. "This is my brother here, the small one. Ever seen a family work that way? All the height, brains, and good looks to one brother?"

"Don't forget vices," I couldn't help but retort.

But he had the girls, if not remotely in the palm of his broad hand, at least listening. Part of his appeal to them was the charm he can gush as if he's a Croton pump fitted for the purpose. But the rest was simpler far—he was the only man in the room not exuding a rank musk of dread. Deliberately, I lowered my shoulders. One or two faces at the other end of the room, meanwhile, almost smiled at the thought of their siblings.

"I'd still appreciate knowing what you plan, miss." Valentine blew a fat smoke ring as if reclining on a veranda.

"Gettin' out o' this den of whores and pimps alive," she snarled. "What else?"

"A very fine goal, and may I—" Kildare began before his speech was stopped by the pressure of an exceedingly sharp spoon.

The other copper stars froze, statuelike. All save my brother, who leaned against the left side of the doorframe with his arms crossed.

"Do you want to *kill* that man, though?" he insisted. "It would be messy for everyone, all that mopping up blood and filling out paperwork, and you'd be a murderess, you see, and we'd be forced to lock you up. Not that Kildare here is so very inspiring. He isn't. I hardly need to tell you that—you're the one netted him like a butterfly. It's just the principle of the thing. Anyhow, I've a suggestion. You can take it or leave it, but hear me out?"

By then I was on a kinchin's merry-go-round, reeling inwardly. Not having heard Val speak actual English since, say, around 1830. It was like watching him whisk his own face off to reveal a second one, but one I recognized from childhood.

"D'ye need my permission t' speak, or shall we mill about till yer ready?" Kildare's captor returned.

Two of the girls giggled, several smiled. Valentine dropped his head backward and laughed, flinching as if he'd a cracked rib.

"Right, yes," he agreed. "I'm going to offer you a trade. I will remove any man you please from the present situation. Take your pick. One of us I eliminate for you as a gesture of good faith."

"And then?" she prompted defiantly.

"And then you march Kildare here or whomever else you like downstairs at the end of your blade, me if you fancy, and when you breathe the fresh air, you let the poor bastard go. You've won, you see. This is me negotiating the terms of our defeat. I like my plan better than your plan, and I figure you do too. So I'll just wait until you've picked a fellow, and then I'll get rid of him."

Piest stared at Valentine with eyes wide as chowder bowls. Kildare appeared, as was only to be expected, less than pleased with this lay. Connell glanced heavenward as if praying for it to work without killing anyone.

I searched my brother for a signal. None seemed remotely apparent.

Valentine returned to smoking, pointedly not looking at anyone, leaving the girl to her choice uninterrupted. Then, quite by accident, he studied the gritty floor beneath the doorframe, and his boyish, careworn face turned hard as exposed bone. I followed his gaze and saw along the cheap pine a pattern of nail gouges from previous attempted escapes. Just as a frothy tide of rage washed over me, Val snapped back into focus.

"Well?" he asked in a friendly tone. "Any ideas?"

She'd already nerves of sheer Irish cliffside and a heart to stand up for her friends—even if they weren't her friends at all. That would have been more than ample, for my money. But the girl thought it over, and she gave it time.

"That one," she determined, her eyes staking a claim on Ronan

McGlynn. "Give me the dog who dragged us t' this den and call it even."

"Thank Christ." Valentine shoved his cigar in my direction. "Hold this. For a moment there, I thought we'd all have to witness something unpleasant."

My hand had scarcely moved before McGlynn hurled himself at my brother with a knife snatched from within his boot, swinging wide and wishful. Val, pivoting on the instant, blocked the strike with his forearm. Snarling, McGlynn tried his luck with a back-handed stab, twisting all his weight onto his opposite foot to lend more strength to his gnarled fist.

It didn't work.

Valentine caught McGlynn's wrist with a little circle that looked like a waltzer's flourish and tethered it, the knife now pressed against the hollow of the villain's spine. With his other hand gripping McGlynn's shoulder, Val took four quick steps forward with his shorter, weaker antagonist and sent his head through the wall.

By saying *through* the wall, I mean literally. For the walls were crumbling back into forest sod, and the upkeep was nonexistent.

One speechless moment passed, everyone staring at the hole with McGlynn's motionless pate resting inside it. A fragile bird cradled within an inhospitable nest. Then Val uncurled his hands and Ronan McGlynn slumped to the floor. Breathing, as I could see plain in the swells of his swollen belly. As oblivious as an unborn babe, fresh blood caressing his eyebrows.

I traced my mouth with my fingers introspectively. Wondering just how Val expected me to drag a fourteen-stone villain to the Tombs. And certain as the Party is crooked, he wasn't going to be helping.

The girls burst into spontaneous applause. All except their

ringleader, who was still shoving honed metal into my friend Kildare's neck. Exchanging a look with Piest that was equal parts relief and exasperation, I lowered my hands.

"Everyone back flat against the walls save Kildare, who doesn't try anything exciting." I hoped she remembered he had a name, however much she mistrusted him.

Val strode in my direction and plucked his cigar from my fingers as the others retreated. I'd forgotten I'd been holding it.

"Victors first," he announced, winking.

The girls, Kildare, and his lovely freckled captor foremost, headed for the stairs. Connell raised a ginger eyebrow at me as if demanding to know what abominable alchemy had created my only sibling and what in bloody hell we were doing with our lives.

I'd have given him an answer or two. But I hadn't any.

When the girls had filed out, we waited to give them a nice, amiable head start. Connell, worried over his closest mate, followed them first. Mr. Piest nudged McGlynn's temple with the blunt toe of his weighty Dutch boot and, finding him incapable of further atrocities for the time being, turned to my brother with palm outstretched.

"Always an absolute pleasure to work with a man of your caliber, Captain Wilde," he announced happily, wringing my brother's hand.

He would say that, though. Mr. Piest is crazier than a sack of river rats.

"You want a rough on the muscle, I'm your scrapper." Val turned to the wall, grinding his cigar out on the peeling paint. "I've seen you fight. It looks like a chicken after the ax has come down."

Laughing, Piest marched for the door. It was true, after all, and Jakob Piest owns the rare virtue of not allowing true remarks to unsettle him.

"I didn't know you spoke English," I informed Valentine. It sounded ridiculous even to me.

"You . . . I *what?*"

We headed in Piest's thudding wake, Connell's flaming head just visible entering the front foyer. Unfettered light streamed into it from the open door beyond. It gladdened my heart as nothing had that morning.

"You've been palavering flash more or less nonstop since I was five," I said to the back of Valentine's neck. "I didn't know whether you savvied the difference any longer."

I didn't add, *And it sounded good to me, old and familiar, as if we were about to feed the horses and then give them the sour apples from the crooked tree by the fence. Do you remember that, how we'd collect the fallen ones? Do you remember that tree, and do you remember their hot teeth against our fingers?* Because that is just the sort of thing we absolutely do not mention. Whether by unspoken agreement or purblind cowardice, I couldn't possibly say.

"Of course I savvy the difference," Val retorted. "Hell on horseback, I can *read*, can't I? Do you use that pate of yours for anything other than decorating your neck? You do know what flash is *for*, yes, my Tim?"

"To keep respectable people from understanding a word you say."

He half turned to look up at me. "Yes, and to prevent mace coves and canary birds and idiots like the alderman from realizing I'm educated and can outbrain them in jig time."

"That's . . . extremely clever," I owned reluctantly. "And never occurred to me."

"Pissing away from the wind doesn't occur to you," Val muttered as we passed through the miserable pornographic hallway and into the greater world of Ward Four.

The spring breeze carried manure along with the sharp salt, but it struck our faces like a benediction nevertheless. Five steps with an iron rail on either side led to the Queen Mab's entrance, and our colleagues had arranged themselves on the stairs as if playing a child's game where to touch the street meant losing. All save for Kildare, of course, who stood with a spoon to his neck in the middle of the cobbled road. Beginning to look hopeful. The girls surrounding him were boneless with relief, one or two openly weeping and the others smiling in wonderment at a miracle. As for their leader, her bright, speckled face was flushed with triumph.

"*Sláinte chuig na fir, agus go mairfidh na mná go deo!*" she cried, and pushed Kildare away.

A roar of merriment went up as the molls started cheering and embracing. Connell barked a laugh and yelled something I understood equally poorly, while my brother swept his black silk hat off in salute. The curve of a smile tugged at my lips, and Mr. Piest shouted, "Welcome to America, patriots all!" at the top of his concave lungs.

"Any lass who wants good cheer and stout Irish company, come to the Knickerbocker Twenty-one Engine Company of a Sunday in Ward Eight, and don't forget to bring your menfolk!" Val called out, returning his hat to his high brow. "Real employment for your beaus, rum and hot stew gratis, all courtesy of the Democratic Party!"

I sighed. "Will you ever stop politicking for as much as five seconds?"

"I'll be croaked one of these days, and then likely a good deal quieter," he returned cheerfully.

Nine girls waved to us, turning back toward the waterfront. The sight of all those dark and brassy heads striding away from the Queen Mab was a considerably spruce one. I was about to demand that Val help me with the unconscious blackguard upstairs whether he wanted to or not when a hoarse shout prevented me.

"Wait!" Kildare cried. "You wi' the spoon and all! I don't even know yer name!"

One by one, the lasses glanced at one another.

And then, as was only fitting, exploded into laughter again.

"Dear heavenly saints on high, have mercy upon the mad and likewise upon the merely stupid," Connell prayed, chuckling heartily.

"Oh, my God," I said.

"Well, can you blame the man?" Val grinned, leaning against the railing like a card sharp at a table. "I'd split that doxie like a fence post, given an invitation."

"Valentine."

"Oh, come off it, just look at her!"

"The course of true love never did run smooth!" Mr. Piest cackled.

Kildare stood at stark attention, almost leaning after the moll who'd just spent a solid ten minutes threatening to kill him. She returned to the front of her ragged band, red-gold curls dancing in the wind, staring with hard but amused grey eyes at a genuinely pathetic batch of star police.

Then, grinning broadly, she cried, "Caoilinn!" and threw her slender arms wide into the air as if about to take flight.

More cheers went up, a "Bravo!" from Mr. Piest as Kildare made a low bow. But recalling with a queasy sensation our unfinished business, I plucked at my brother's coat sleeve and we returned to the front parlor, away from the shrill whistles and the friendly insults and the most disturbing courtship it has ever been my sincere privilege to witness. The alderman, of course, was long gone. Val raised his agile eyebrows expectantly.

"Symmes," I said.

"Ah," he said.

"That was . . ."

"Necessary."

"Couldn't be helped."

"Seeing as I can't diary the last time I was offered a free rape in lieu of a thank-you note and I've wanted to put that looby's head in my chamber pot since he went into politics, no, it couldn't," he growled.

"He tried to kill me once. It isn't as if I'm fond of him."

"I have not forgotten the occasion," my brother said in a voice I can describe only as knifelike.

"But what are we going to *do*?"

The Party works on a system. If you have chink, buckets and barrels of it, and you give plenty to Tammany, and you own the flexibility of a Chinese acrobat when it comes to morals, you can be a politico with a smile on your mazzard and your thumbs tucked into your braces. If you're dangerous and hardworking and intelligent and loyal, you can be a ward heeler or a copper-star captain.

Trouble is, the hierarchy is inviolable.

"I don't know yet," Valentine answered.

My lips parted in dismay.

"Dry up, bright young copper star. I said *yet*. Meanwhile, Symmes is an ambulatory sack of mouse droppings and a goddamn Hunker to boot."

The nigh-successful bloodbath over Texas, combined with the highly contested condition of Oregon—both of which might as well be their own continents they're so bafflingly immense—has started up a bare-knuckled regional battle. Whig or Democrat now makes no difference. It's North versus South in the Capitol, and it's Southern sympathizers versus Northern ones in the free cities above the Mason-Dixon. The Hunkers, in brief, are of the mind that the South should be coddled, or we'd face a devastating war rather than regular fisticuffs in the Senate. This position is not unrelated to the fact that plantations produce cotton, and New England produces cloth, and our manufactories produce slave clothing out of the cloth, which the South purchases in bulk. Like a poisonous snake biting its own tail. The Barnburners think the new territories should be kept slave-free and that the Hunkers are a pack of yellow-livered cowards with their pebbly capitalist arses hanging bare in the wind for the South to wallop as it pleases.

The Wilde brothers, for once in concert, believe the latter. I don't tend to have political opinions. Other than that politics is a pretty ripe joke. But I have plenty of antislavery opinions, and Val thinks of Hunker complacency the way sharks think of bleeding minnows.

"Stop looking like a sheep caught in a bramble patch," Valentine ordered irritably. "I'll think of something."

"Symmes had a point regarding your reputation. You could be more careful about your person."

I once thought my brother would sleep with anything that breathes. But that isn't true. He sleeps with gorgeous free black women, beautiful emigrant molls with lusty appetites, high-spirited Bowery girls, and an aristocratic male English pianist by the name of James Playfair, with whom he practically lives, though they maintain separate residences and double sets of keys. So far as I know, I've listed those in ascending order of frequency. It's no wonder the man is infamous. His trousers are as often open as shut.

"Where would be the fun in that?"

I shook my head. "Are you going to help me carry the pimp you laced to the Tombs?"

Val chuckled, wincing. "Of course not. Afternoon, brother Tim."

He turned to go. I have often suspected with a queasy tingle on the underside of my ribs that something terrible is going to happen.

That circumstances recently set in motion are heavy—crushing, really—and they will now roll momentously toward a sharp dip in the cliffside. I'm usually right about such things.

Unfortunately, that doesn't go a very long way toward preventing them happening.

"Are you going to keep campaigning for Alderman Symmes?"

"Fuck no," Valentine scoffed, throwing wide the door and slamming it behind him.

4

*We view it as a most insane and ludicrous farce, for
women in the nineteenth century to get up in a public and
promiscuous assemblage and declare themselves "oppressed
and fraudulently deprived of their most sacred rights,"
when, if they really knew what belonged to their true
position, instead of stirring up discontent and enacting
such foolery, they would be about the sober duties and
responsibilities which devolved upon them as rational
beings, and as "helpmeets" of the other sex.*

—*THE LIBERATOR*, SEPTEMBER 15, 1848

TRANSPORTING THE FRAGRANT LUMP that was the concussed
Ronan McGlynn proved simpler than I'd anticipated, since
Ward Four thrives on shipping and my colleagues are resource-
ful men. By the time Valentine departed, the girls had gone and
Mr. Connell was returning from a freight yard with a rickety
wooden handcart. He'd obtained permission to use the device
by offering not to inspect their premises for unreported—and
thereby untaxed—cargo. Which was big of him.

When we'd dumped McGlynn in the most swamplike cell we
could find, roaches fleeing in pretend and temporary fright, Mr.
Piest offered to return the cart in exchange for my making out the

police report. It was a hard bargain, since I loathe that particular task. Writing police reports flattens living people into headstones, erases motives, erects paper monuments to dark errors and cruel whims. But I've never told Piest as much, so no malice was intended on his part.

"All right?" I asked Kildare as he made to exit. Only half joking.

"It's the queerest o' things, when it happens," he replied dreamily. "Caoilinn may not ha' slit my throat, but she stabbed me through the heart sure as—"

"Stop afore ne'er Wilde nor Piest is able t' keep a meal down fer the rest o' their natural lives," Connell ordered, escorting his friend forcefully out of the lockup.

I could have told Kildare I knew what he felt like. But it wouldn't have helped—nothing about love can be helped—so I let Connell drag him off to be hosed down or fed whiskey or whatever the Irish do in extreme situations such as the one in which Kildare found himself.

I lit for my office, a two-minute trek down one of the Tombs' interminable echoing corridors, rolling my stiff neck to coax McGlynn's deadweight away. Reaching it, I unwound a notch. Not that my office is comfortable exactly—I think of it in good humors as a whitewashed mouse hole, in bad ones the benign sort of coffin. Admittedly I've equipped it well. Bookshelves of local directories and codes of law, drawers that lock and pens that flow. A carved pine desk and an armchair upholstered in dark green preside, both given to me by a friend who moved to Toronto. A better-than-decent lamp painting an incongruously civil glow over the room. Two plainer chairs, ones I scavenged, wait for colleagues and crime victims. Finally I've a little table with Dutch gin and glasses resting on it, for whenever my colleagues stop by to ease the aches from their wearisome rounds.

Dipping the steel nib in my inkpot, I wrote:

Report made by Officer T. Wilde, Ward 6, District 1, Star 107. Upon investigating the activities of one Ronan McGlynn, now incarcerated under prisoner number 52640, discovered that claims of manufactory employment were a front for abducting female emigrants and forcibly ruining them. As witnessed with Roundsman Jakob Piest, Star 341, nine women were led . . .

My handwriting—always perfectly legible when recording human indecencies—steadily filled the foolscap. Which never fails to disgust me.

When I'd finished, I chewed my pen and debated warning George Washington Matsell over the Symmes debacle. After some unfocused staring at the watercolor-coded map on my wall found my eyes uneasily tugged back to Ward Eight, I concluded that disclosure was the better part of valor and pushed to my feet to visit the chief. Not on my life would I have confided in anyone else ensconced in the Party's upper echelons—but Matsell trusts Wildes and makes plentiful use of us, so we trust him and occasionally request assistance in return. Up and up I went through the Tombs' vaultlike stone halls, finally knocking at the chamber with the plaque reading GEORGE WASHINGTON MATSELL: CHIEF OF NEW YORK CITY POLICE.

"Come in," he called in his flat, sober baritone.

Chief Matsell wasn't doing anything I'd expected him to be doing. He wasn't working, for one, nor was he fiddling with his lexicon. Matsell finds flash patter both fascinating and necessary, and thus, for copper stars yet damp behind the ears, he's compiling definitions of street slang. The dictionary is like his kinchin—he dotes upon the project, lends it every spare minute. Which is why I was so queered at finding him idle. He was merely sitting. All three hundred robust pounds of him, face deeply scored in inverted

V-shaped lines from the edges of his noble nose straight through to his porcine jowls. Looking neither at the framed portrait of his hero, the original George Washington, hanging high above him, nor out the massive barred window sending dark, scarlike lashes across his polished floor.

"Wilde," he grunted. "Have a seat. Whiskey?"

"Thank you." Dropping my hat on the chair back, I hesitated. "Is something the matter?"

"Plenty." He poured neat golden drinks into two tumblers. "But why don't you talk about what's in your hand first, so I don't spend any more time trying to guess at it."

I set the dubious report on his desktop, tapping it. "Ronan McGlynn, newly in custody. He's a rapist and a fleshmonger who deceived nine emigrant Irishwomen into accompanying him to a clearinghouse this afternoon. And they were far from the first, God help us. Piest was on hand to assist, of course, along with Connell and Kildare."

"Your usual complement, then. Any snags?"

"I think Val gave him a concussion, but that's hardly a snag. The man is a fiend."

The chief scowled even deeper than his perennial frown. When a man's neutral face appears already highly displeased, some find that man difficult to read. But I could see urgent business *tap-tap-tapping* within his huge pate.

"So you wrote out this report and delivered it personally."

"Yes, sir."

"And for some reason that is inexplicable to me when discussing so simple a task as arresting a rapist, your brother was also present today."

I took a sip of the whiskey. For bravery, not flavor. It seared my empty stomach nicely. "We encountered Valentine there. He'd been summoned by a Party man to partake of the merchandise, as a gift to secure a favor. My brother . . . didn't take it well."

"No." Matsell pressed at his temples. "No, he wouldn't. What unfortunate Party man would that be?"

"Alderman Robert Symmes, sir."

I was prepared for diverse reactions to this information. Including but not limited to stony silence, sanguine discussion, and being ordered out of his office while he dealt with more important matters. I did not expect his meaty fist to come crashing down like a judge's gavel. Startling me and the whiskey alike. I nearly flinched, and the liquor quivered pitiably.

"Sir?"

"Apologies, Mr. Wilde." The chief downed his drink, rose, poured another, and left the bottle between us. "What time is it?"

"I have twenty to four."

"It has already been a long day."

Matsell pulled open his desk drawer, removing a document and spreading it open. The foolscap looked as if a chart had suffered a bout of hysteria and dissolved into inky delirium. It appeared to have begun as a complete list of Democratic-versus-Whig candidates, the vote on which would be decided in ten days' time (the Liberty Party was also running, but talking about the actual plight of Africans is a deft form of political suicide). These predictable camps had splintered into frenzied subfactions to show the Hunker-versus-Barnburner candidates pitted against each other in their own ward elections.

I've never voted for anything in my life, finding the whole process farcical. But if I were a political man, it would have looked like the anatomy of a nightmare.

"Behold," Chief Matsell announced, "the collapse of Tammany on paper. Ever since the Barnburners convened to choose their own delegates for the Democratic Convention, our local Party has been dissected into rancorous cliques. You see listed by ward a number of candidates for office whose names I will not speak aloud, because it would depress my spirits so much as to alarm your sensibilities. And now you are telling me," he continued, pressing his long finger against the only straightforward part of the page, "that the boss of Ward Eight has been deeply offended by the Ward Eight candidate for alderman."

It wasn't a question, so I held my tongue.

"Do you have an impression whether your brother will continue to campaign for Symmes?"

"I have an impression," I confessed.

"And?"

I shook my head.

We drained our drinks. Matsell refilled them. I've never been fond of, friendly toward, anything other than disgusted by the Party. They're a corrupt propaganda manufactory that strives to make their followers feel righteously patriotic for voting for an organization no better than the amoral businesses lining their pockets. But they also feed starving Irish who've nowhere to turn, employ countless able men, allow them to sweat in exchange for commodities like edible stew and snug roofs. Men like me and my brother. So the concept of our safety net fraying into so many flimsy threads was . . . distressing.

Chief Matsell drew a ponderous question mark below the name Robert Symmes. He didn't enjoy the task. But our chief is about as calm as bedrock, which goes a long way toward herding the purblind scoundrels who populate his police department.

"Any insights?"

"I only wish." I finished my drink, standing. "Save for life-or-death circumstances, I don't know that Val's ever crossed the politicians who give him orders before."

A smile lurked behind Matsell's teeth. "I notice you didn't say his 'superiors' or his 'betters.'"

"No, I don't think I did," I realized, raising my brows quizzically. "Surprising."

"What was the alderman after, anyhow?"

I explained about the note, terse but duly sober.

George Washington Matsell folded his hands over his wide belly and his spotless grey waistcoat, nodding. Weighing mighty risks the way the great dockside scales weigh freight tonnage.

"So you're after an incendiary," he said slowly.

"No," I pointed out. "I'm after a slightly too enthusiastic correspondent."

"Whose topic of choice is deliberate firestarting. And you'll be . . . comfortable with that, Mr. Wilde?"

Willing myself not to bare my teeth, I contemplated Chief Matsell. Daring that mountain of a man to say, *You're a whey-spined coward when it comes to fire, and I'm aware of the fact,* or, still worse, *Would you like someone better suited to settle this?*

"Supposing you're ruminating over an answer, I've all the time in the world," he drawled, eyes twinkling with both impatience and amusement. "Make yourself comfortable."

"I'll handle it," I answered, jaw tight. "Worry about your elections."

"Oh, I will, trust in that." George Washington Matsell sighed. "Steer well clear of Alderman Symmes until I've had a chance to speak with him—the man enjoys disproportionately crushing opposition. Alert your colleagues of the situation and learn whether the threat of an incendiary is genuine. And tell your brother not to do anything drastic, foolish, or impulsive."

A frown crooked my lips. "He's never yet in his life listened to me of all people."

Matsell shrugged, replacing the deformed chart in his drawer.

"Then embrace change, Mr. Wilde. I certainly intend to, if only to keep myself from resignation and the idyllic forests of New Jersey."

"You truly think we'll live to see retirement to the countryside?"

Chief Matsell didn't answer me, returning his attention to his whiskey glass. An action for which, in retrospect, I cannot fault him in the smallest degree.

Walking the easy distance home to my rooms above Mrs. Boehm's Fine Baked Goods, constellations hung close as paper lanterns above me, I wondered whether Val had worked out an angle yet. Seeing as Robert Symmes was as likely to beat a problem to death as to negotiate with one. When the anxiety had well curdled my stomach, I forced myself to picture the Irish girls—finding real manufactory jobs, or work as serving girls pouring white-capped beer mugs, or as housemaids. Those being their three options other than *voluntary* brothel work. Recklessly, I envisioned them fat grandmothers who'd grown particular about keeping fresh flowers in their wallpapered front halls. I'd nearly made myself cheerful again by the time I'd entered my rented residence on Elizabeth Street and was assaulted by aromas of eggs and cherries and nutmeg.

Hanging my broad black hat on its peg, I ducked under the hinged countertop and into the downstairs kitchen. Elena Boehm—widow, baker, and a single year my junior—didn't glance up when I entered. She never does. That's a compliment meaning I'm part of the house, like her windowsill or her mixing bowl, an inventoried item with as special a place indoors as her best teacups. But her thin sickle of a mouth perked at the corners. She was playing solitaire, the remains of a dish of rabbit stew with currant jelly before her.

"What on earth is cooking, and are we eating it for breakfast?"

I removed my frock coat. My cravat soon followed. Which was certainly not my typical habit in the presence of ladies, particularly ones I was heartily fond of. But as with every rule, there exist exceptions, and Mrs. Boehm was mine.

"*Bielefelder schwartzbrotpudding,*" she answered, all innocence.

Mrs. Boehm is very thin, far too thin for a baker, for all that her hips are wide and winsome. She has a clear, broad Bohemian countenance and eyes of a grey-blue no easier pinned down than a cloud formation on the distant horizon. There's such a frank presence of mind in her unusual face that I liked her upon introduction, three years back. Her lank, silvery blonde hair was coiled loosely atop her head, and she'd thrown her apron over the knob of the pantry door, leaving her in a loose white blouse and navy skirts.

"You know I don't speak whatever that was."

I fell gratefully into the chair. Elena is half German and half Bohemian, and she wields both languages at me as she pleases.

I like when she does as she pleases.

"Black-bread pudding," she replied. "And tomorrow by the slice I will sell it, but yes, we can have it for breakfast."

Standing up, she abandoned her card game and crossed to my side of the table.

Oh, I thought as trickling warmth pooled in my belly. *One of those nights.*

Elena rested her skirts against the edge of the flour-spattered table in front of me, casting steely eyes—they were grey just then, the grey of eight in the evening in March or the more melancholy Chopin nocturnes—from my boots to the swooping twin arches of my hairline.

"So early you come home." Her grainy voice husked against the consonants.

"I solved it."

"Oh, did you?" She smiled.

"Right down to the ground."

"I like when you solve it."

She kissed me, and I breathed in the warm bready scent of her before catching the back of her head with my fingertips and chasing the hint of brown sugar I always suspect lurks on the underside of her tongue.

I'm always right, too.

Some New Yorkers would disapprove of the fact I try to make myself useful to my landlady. From help with squeaking door hinges to help with fastening (or unfastening) intractable buttons. But oh, how much less lonesome she makes me of all the undeserving people she could choose—a copper star with a fragmentary face. She's unpretentious and open and strangely pretty, and she loves nothing more than scandalous literature, which means that she readily tolerates my eccentric profession. We both are fiercely attached to one Bird Daly, whom we encountered three years ago at age ten, running from her madam, Silkie Marsh. We keep to ourselves unless we don't, and I always make certain she initiates matters, because I never want her to think me either ungrateful or demanding. Then I end them in as many inventive ways as I can think of, as many times as possible. And the afterward ever finds her smoking tiny hand-rolled cigarettes in my bed of a Sunday morning, light playing off the downy skin of her inner thigh.

In short, when she's lonesome or suspects me to be, her generous lips find my collarbone. And I can feel the imprint of her smiling there for days afterward.

"I'll try to solve everything quicker, in that case."

Mrs. Boehm seated herself in my lap, arcing forward when I traced a thumb over the line where her shirt ended and milk-colored skin began.

"Quicker you can be at solving crimes," she agreed in my ear, my other palm flattened against the affable ridges of her lower back. "But right now, if you want, you should take your time."

I did want. Rather badly.

Rap-rap-rap.

Elena pulled back. I chased after, catching her laughing lips for a moment longer before she escaped me.

"More work for you?"

"God, I hope not." I tugged my jacket on again as I went to the door. "At this time of night, it's either a riot or a murder or a—"

When I'd unlatched the door and pulled it open, I stopped speaking.

Because Mercy Underhill was standing in the moonlight on the other side.

From what I can recall of the moment, which hung suspended in a dew-drenched web of spider's silk, spinning into ever more complex patterns, my brain kept functioning. Even when my heart stopped.

So I registered that Mercy was standing there, wearing a fawn traveling costume trimmed in jet beads and the little sapphire hat with the black feather I'd apparently caught a glimpse of at James Slip. Her pale face, with its lovely arched half-English features and the distinct vertical cleft in her chin, was so familiar but so unexpected that I felt as if a character in one of her own well-thumbed fictions had walked off the printed page into Ward Six to shake my hand. Widely set eyes of pastel china blue formed the upper two points of her triangular face, ending in a too-small bottom lip that takes refuge beneath the bow of her top one when she's ruminating.

Mercy was ruminating. And something ferocious too.

Around then I realized I'd opened the door and commenced not saying a damn thing.

"How are you here?" I marveled.

"Oh, Timothy," Mercy said, nearly laughing. "How do you think?"

I asked her in, I must have done, and Elena made gentle clicking sounds as she helped Mercy with her hat and matching blue gloves. But I think I can be safely excused from complete comprehension just then. My Past and Present had just collided like freight trains on a single track. There Mercy stood, flushing along her stark cheekbones, complimenting Mrs. Boehm on the smell that flooded the room when my landlady pulled two trays of bread pudding from the ovens. Elena set them on flat cooling stones, glancing behind herself as if she'd been caught out at something.

"I didn't know you were coming back," I said. Because it needed saying.

"No," Mercy agreed sadly.

It isn't that I'd believed I would never see Mercy Underhill again. But I'd stopped allowing myself to think of it. Mercy knew I'd idolized her since childhood—unfortunately resulting in my viewing her as a picture postcard of a perfect creature, to be smothered under the best glass and kept in a thickly carved frame. When I'd learned she was just like me, all walled-off secrets and raw longings, I hadn't acquitted myself well. And too much had happened to us for me to wonder what would happen next. The mathematics didn't bear scrutinizing. I only wrote to her, and read her letters, and grew to know her better. And allowed myself to wish that she was happy.

She wasn't.

Elena Boehm, after setting her baking out to cool, filled three tumblers with a better-than-healthy measure of gin. Pale eyes friendly and cautious. She knows I write letters to an eccentric girl in London whom I've adored since I was fourteen. And I know she's in love with her dead husband. Thus we treat each other well. Like comrades trudging through the filth and darkness of the same war. To boot, Elena knows Mercy's mind in a certain sense, because Mercy, before all fell to pieces, used to write a lyrical and macabre series called *Light and Shade in the Streets of New York*—published under "Anonymous," of course, since Mercy's style was far too voluptuous to allow pride in her own work—which both Elena and I used to read voraciously. All unaware that the companion of my tender years was penning them. Those stories owned a grisly sensuality, as perfect and desolate as broken seashells. I may have been the only person in the room that our society condoned reading them, but they brought us together in a way, the three sets of eyes all absorbing the same tales. And the single set of hands responsible for creating them miraculously present, now pressing hard into the edge of the table as Mercy waited for someone, anyone, to say something.

"How was your journey?" I asked.

Idiot. You could ask Mercy anything. She's sitting right in front of you. And you want to know about weather and cabin space and the relative efficiency of porters.

I expected a question in return, that being Mercy's curiously roundabout way of communicating. But she only lifted the gin and raised it in Elena's direction, a silent toast. She'd been so long absent, every gesture felt like a minor miracle. If I didn't pull myself together, I realized, I'd forget to trust in realities like gravity and sunrises.

"I know I'm descending on you terribly late," she said. "I was desperate to see a familiar face. The journey was nicely uneventful, but I spent hours finding rooms that wouldn't ruin either my reputation or my bank account."

"And a clean proper room you managed to find?" Elena sat down on Mercy's side of the table. Taking over the questioning rather than indulging my fish-mouthed bafflement any further.

I'd have been grateful. Had I the mental capacity.

"Are there any *proper* rooms for unmarried females traveling alone?" Mercy mused. As if catching herself at an old trick, she nodded. "It's just east of Broadway, at a theatrical boardinghouse. Meals appear to be based upon another species of clock than the one in this world—they're prepared at sixes and sevens precisely. So I have to wonder if I've truly returned to New York or happened upon Someplace Else." I could hear the capital letters in her voice clearly as I could see the feather-pale back of her hand three feet distant. Almost within reach. "But the tenants are lovely. No one asks prurient questions when I pass the parlor where they're all banging out music-hall tunes on the pianoforte and I slip away alone. They're very kind, actors," she added more darkly. "They spend rather less time hating people than do the general population, don't they?"

"But the room?" Elena prompted.

"Oh. Four walls, papered in fern print with only a score or so of smashed mosquitoes, quite a tolerable little sanctuary. And of course I needn't stay if I don't like it," she hastened to add.

"Very difficult it is, for a woman alone to find a space," Elena commiserated.

"I've only ever thrown myself at family and hoped they'd put me in a jewel box. I'd never had to seek one out for myself before. Is it always so terrifying?"

"My husband, he dies," Mrs. Boehm said evenly, tracing the lip of her cup. She didn't mention that her son had been taken as well, in one of the all-too-common cattle drives up Broadway that devolve into chaos and tragedy. "So. I say to myself, why must I suffer so deep? Then Franz's ovens and his flour sacks and his loaf pans, I begin to see them. Notice through tears. And I think, I have everything. Space, work. I am rich. I am forever unhappy. But unhappy in my home, never unhappy I will be on street corners."

Mercy tucked a stray piece of hair behind her ear, leveling a particular look at Elena. I was staggered at seeing it again. It's the one she adopts when she's admiring but doesn't wish to offend the source.

"I'm very sorry for your loss," she offered.

Elena shook her head, for some inexplicable reason giving me a small smile. "It was a long time ago. If one is to lose everything one loves, one might as well be comfortable about it, yes?"

To my shock, Mercy laughed heartily. Elena, chuckling, refilled everyone's gin.

"Are you going to ask me?" Mercy inquired, eyebrows quirked in my direction.

"Are you going to answer me?" I returned. Much harsher than I'd meant to. "I'd never press you," I hastened to add. "But—"

"But I didn't warn you before arriving on your doorstep." Mercy took a mouthful of gin that could hardly be called delicate, even in Ward Six, and cocked her head at me. "There isn't a polite way of saying I'm suddenly much wealthier than I was. That is, however, what I ought to have done. I apologize. Just because I don't know where my efforts will bleed into offense, doesn't mean I shouldn't try them out first. I have a backbone—I ought to make use of it occasionally."

"You have had an inheritance?" Mrs. Boehm questioned.

Mercy stared deep into her glass, reflecting. "I've been staying with my kin, running their curiosity shop. Antiquities, books, that sort of thing. An old gentleman whom I'd often helped knew of my work in the East End soup kitchens, and we struck up a— I'd say a friendship, though there may possibly have been more to it on his part. I found him books on botanical subjects. He seemed to feel as if flora was God's living art crafted specially for him, you see, and one day I gave him a fern preserved in glass that someone had sold us. He said it was just the sort surrounding the tiny cottage where he grew up. He was always very shabbily dressed for all that he was well spoken, and when he passed away, I discovered that he was the richest old miser who ever slept on his pile of coin."

"That's amazing." I shook my head, smiling at last. "Congratulations. It sounds like something from one of your stories."

She smiled in return. "It does, doesn't it? I think of late that the difference between what is real and what is not real isn't so stark as we suppose it to be. I dream electric thunderstorm squalls, cataclysms if I'm honest, and somewhere in other worlds I know the tempests exist in truth, because I wake gasping as if running for shelter from howling winds, and my sheets are like ice, and I can taste the sweetness of the lightning still on my tongue. Have you ever felt that way?"

I wedged a hand over my mouth. Concerned—deeply concerned—about whatever would come out of it next.

"Hasn't everyone?" Elena attempted.

Mercy sighed dreamily. "I thought so. Though what was I just saying? I can't always recall when I'm tired. And the journey was so long. There were angels, good angels, keeping the monsters clear of the ship this morning. Under the water, of course, their wings covered with the most beautiful fish scales rather than feathers. But it was still quite exhausting. Sea voyages always are, don't you think?"

"Yes." Elena cast me a worried look. "Yes, I do."

It bears mentioning that my letters from Mercy had grown . . . *erratic* is too light a word. She's a poet, always has been, but the imagery had turned wildly abstracted of late. Worse even than in the months immediately after her father died. Sonatas and star systems and demons and birds of painful flaming brilliance rising from charcoal.

I likewise found it distressingly relevant that—by the end of his life, before he hanged himself—her father was wholesale insane.

"Why did the inheritance compel you to leave London?" I inquired when I was capable. "You've always wanted to live in London."

"I did, yes," Mercy whispered, pulling her fingertip along the tabletop. "But I didn't want to *die* there. The ground there is too ancient. It was far too old, the ground in London. Already filled with corpses. No one should die there. It would be so *crowded*. You'd never get any rest."

She stood up, finishing her drink as she smiled at us once more. "Thank you for the company. I'm . . . too tired to be here, I think. I apologize if I've been too tired. Have I been very tired, does it seem to you? I hadn't quite realized how much the journey taxed me. I'll get a hansom on Broadway back to my rooms. It was a welcome homecoming, and I'm grateful."

Mercy rapidly donned her hat and gloves while we stared, dumbstruck.

"Should I take you back?" I asked, rising.

"Oh, no, I'll be fine—I was raised in New York. Don't you remember?"

I did remember. I remembered every detail, from the cherry-printed dress she wore at the dinner celebration her father threw the night she turned eighteen to the exact proportions of her elbow as I'd helped her avoid a noisome patch of Canal Street.

And I'd loved every second of her. Even the ones that had been hideous for us both.

"I'll call again, if you like?" Mercy questioned. Suddenly uncertain.

"Of course I'd like," I vowed.

"Oh, good. Here is my address, should you want to find me. Calling for reasons is much more generally accepted, I think. But I've always preferred calling for no reason at all, so you are more than welcome to treat me in kind."

Handing me a card with the details of her new lodgings scribbled nearly illegibly upon it, she smiled wistfully once again as she shut the door.

"What was that?" Elena asked. Sounding as dazed as I felt.

"I'm not completely certain," I replied, studying the card. "But I suspect it might have been my worst nightmare."

5

*If woman under the present system of female servitude can
exercise so much influence, what more do they want?*

—*OHIO STATE JOURNAL*, NOVEMBER 19, 1850

THE NEXT MORNING only sheer sheets of spring fog beyond my
windowpane greeted me, as no one slumbered in the crook of my
arm. Lacking Elena there, I found I missed her. But no matter
how unattached you are, floating like a kite torn from a kinchin's
hand, introducing the woman you love to the woman you are making love to is a curious affair. Because it had never been distasteful,
what was between me and Elena. It was warm as the skin just behind her ear.

I'd kissed her thoroughly and said I needed to think. She'd
nodded and poured another gin. And I'd taken myself off to my
room, unease flickering like a tremor under my ribs.

Blinking at my chamber, sun seeping through my curtains in
a waxy haze, I appreciated the mere fact I had a sanctuary. Women
who find themselves similarly alone, as Mercy and Elena had done,
were expected to procure magical establishments where they could
genteelly refrain from all corrosive male contact, including such
perverse activities as *eating in male company* and *living off the same*

corridor as a man. Small wonder that Mercy had found such a stroll through the wolf's maw terrifying. After the strain of her voyage and her housing search, maybe it was only natural that . . .

Stop thinking about Mercy's mind before you lose your own, I admonished myself sternly as I sat up in bed. I'd been half sick over it for hours the night previous.

If she's here and she's financially secure, then by God you can fix the rest of it.

I've arranged my upstairs rooms atypically. The walled-in "sleeping chamber" I use for a library, not being overkeen on sleeping in matchboxes. But it hasn't proved quite sufficient. So I've supplemented with shelves in the main room, the one with the window essential to my sanity, and the place thus resembles a library of tomes young and fresh and used and cracked and bought and received as gifts.

But with a bed in it.

The rest of the walls, unfortunately, are obscured by my charcoal drawings. I say "unfortunately" because ever since the worst fire, the first fire, the one that stole our parents, I've sketched vistas and portraits and eager flames and lashing storms when my mind is uneasy. I've a certain facility for it, actually. And it helps order my thoughts when a crime needs untangling. But there are . . . scores of them, and those only the ones I keep.

If I could manage a happy enough month to scribble only ten charcoals, that would be a sun-gilt, face-skyward occasion.

Elena, I discovered after a duck in my washbasin and a shave, was out making a delivery. So I snatched up my usual day-old roll rather than molest her bread pudding (which was half gone by then, and it barely seven) and elected to pay a call on Miss Sally Woods. The bluestocking whom Symmes had accused of itching to turn firestarter.

What sort of woman would write such a threat?

A bitter, dry-lipped spinster, I supposed, or an actress whose petals were drooping. Both desperate for a spotlight.

I could only have been more wrong about Miss Woods if I'd surmised that she was probably a performing bear.

Walking up Greenwich Street through Ward Three, I was suddenly enveloped by springtime. Springs and autumns aren't given more than a finger snap around here before fleeing from blazing jungle summers and frigid moonscape winters. But that day, after the clouds broke, gleamed vivid as the inside of a watermelon. A lovely colored woman with a berry-bright head scarf brushed past me, her basket teeming with muddy carrots and a fresh-killed chicken slung over her coppery arm. Our streets seemed alive as they hadn't been seconds before, omnibus drivers now free of the bone-chilling mists shrugging off oilskin capes to feel the daylight on their necks. I wasn't fussed by the discarded leaky kettles in the gutter or the trimmed-off rotting lettuce leaves or the brownish laundry suds underfoot as I drew nearer the East River.

I didn't even mind the squat ruffian pasting up posters that screamed BARNBURNER TRAITORISM MUST PAY THE ULTIMATE PRICE! And that's saying something.

The house at 130 Thomas Street proved to be damaged by salt spray but far sturdier than the reeling shanties of my ward. My knock was soon answered by a stooped, lantern-jawed woman with a bad case of the mumps, for she'd wrapped a long flannel rag several times beneath her jaw and tied the bow over her head.

"Yes?"

"Does a Miss Sally Woods live here?"

"Oh, yes," she agreed, adding a small humming sound I wasn't sure she knew she was making. "But not *in* the house, you understand me."

I didn't.

"In the cellar?" I hazarded.

"Oh, mercy no, dear, I'd not subject anyone to my cellar, the house is that large. Hmm."

"But she . . . doesn't live in it?"

She cast red-rimmed eyes over the woefully unpolished copper star pinned to my chest. "Are you a policeman, then?"

"Yes, ma'am."

"Aren't you ashamed of yourself?"

"Sometimes," I agreed. "Where can I find Miss Woods, outside the house?"

"Oh, yes, straight down this hall and into the rear yard, and do behave yourself, dear. Hmm. Policemen are never to be entirely trusted."

"Not even the best of them," I said with a sigh, pulling my black hat off as I stepped into the hall.

Somewhere above me a bugle was being practiced in the usual manner—that is to say, unpleasantly—and the rusted-gate smell of a ripe sheep's liver frying filled the corridor. The once-delicate pink wallpaper was peeling in shreds as if the foyer suffered from leprosy.

When I stepped into the back area, expecting an anterior shack erected by the unforgivably greedy, I entered a strange and wondrous new world.

I stood in a tiny meadow. Not the sort you'd have seen on the huckleberry hillsides of my youth in Greenwich Village, and not the sort at the tiptopmost edge of Manhattan around Fortieth Street. No, it was only a small rear yard. But it had been allowed to blossom into a paradise. I trod through thorny grasses and dandelions big as cabbage heads, scuffed my boots against wild roses. Most of our parks are either cesspools or walled-in odes to money. This was Nature, and Springtime. This was exploding columbine spring, spearlike violet lupine spring. Plants I couldn't name and had never seen survive our boot soles bursting with tiny white flowers. It was bred of pure laziness, not keeping chickens in the back area or the yard trimmed.

It was marvelous. And just at the far end of the tiny tanglewood was a large, mud-smeared greenhouse.

Fortunately for courtesy, the glass was filthy enough to be opaque. And I'd seen *far* stranger living arrangements in swollen-to-bursting New York—people live in derelict train carriages, there's an Irish tent community or twelve in the woods, folk are flooding to Brooklyn of all places, and I once arrested a man who lived in the meat cellar of a chophouse. Even had his mail delivered there.

This was . . . unusual, however. I knocked.

"Come in," a brisk voice answered.

I'd expected a cot, plus maybe a stove or a washbasin. At most.

Instead I discovered a large room, glass spotless on the interior side, with a wooden plank floor covered by two knotted rugs. A neat bed in the corner, lamp and newspaper resting on its side table. A writing desk. Three tall bookshelves half collapsing with volumes. A few pictures atop the furnishings, propped against the glass walls, mainly popular woodcuts of opera stars and concert vocalists. Four mismatched armchairs surrounding a dinted hardwood table, where one could sip and chat as if in a coffeehouse.

But the chamber was dominated by the printing press.

A dwarfish metal contraption by comparison to some, but still it loomed large, with its great wheel and the thick arms through which the paper was fed, its heavy tray and the pervasive clean, inky smell of the previous typeface project. A pile of blank broadside sheets rested compactly next to the thing, awaiting the whim of their owner.

An uneasy feeling stirred.

Sally Woods looked up from her writing desk with an efficient smile. "Copies of 'A Digression Upon the Subject of the Female in the Book-Folding Workforce' are a penny apiece. Two bits will get you thirty," she announced.

I'd have pegged Sally Woods, with her artlessly brazen gaze and her straightforward speech, for a Bowery girl of about twenty-five. The manufactory sort, and Symmes had admitted to firing her. Except that she wasn't one. She'd a large-featured face with a rounded chin and a flat nose that suited all well. Most would have justly referred to her as "handsome," and her hair, which was a thick chestnut brown with an arresting silver streak at the right temple, was loosely piled as if she didn't own quite enough hairpins—unlike the molls of the Bowery, whose curls tend toward the scientifically impossible.

Meanwhile, dark brown eyes can often seem coaxing; hers were rifle sights. Sally Woods's entire appearance would already have been remarkable for its complete lack of inhibition.

Even if she hadn't been wearing trousers.

I'd glimpsed such women before. One being ticketed for public indecency as I dragged a killer to the Tombs, and I'd cast the un-practiced copper star a dark look. We've better tasks to be going about. One at the Minerva, pretty face powdered into oblivion, singing and strutting for errant nickels in dress blacks. One in a private club, the variety where my sex is neither useful nor desirable, posing in a panorama as an unlikely Davy Crockett.

But as for one sitting at a writing desk like a businessman—that hocused me pretty thorough. The trousers were striped in charcoal and black, tucked inside well-worn black riding boots, the ensemble complemented by a crisp white shirt, buttoned about as carelessly as Val's tends to be, and a black velvet waistcoat. Over all she wore a grey ladies' monkey jacket, the sort that falls in a graceful curve down to midthigh, cloth cut as tight against the waist and shoulders as if the garment had been plastered to the wearer.

It was enough to give a man pause.

"I'm not here to buy a broadside. But I'd like to ask you a few questions."

"Oh, you're a copper star. Sorry, the light in here is dreadful. Are you arresting me for my taste in fashion?"

"Like I said, only questions."

"No objection here to questions." She rose, nodding at the configuration of chairs. "Step into my parlor. You want a drink?"

"If you're joining me." I selected the armchair done in faded red brocade, setting my hat on the table.

"Oh, bugger all, I'm out of scotch. Um. Whiskey, gin, or pine beer?"

"Whatever you're having," I replied, smiling.

She returned with a pair of whiskeys and sat opposite me, crossing her trousered legs. "To your health."

Our glasses clinked optimistically. "Cheers. That's what I would have chosen, by the way."

"Oh, I can tell."

I cleared my throat and lifted the tumbler. The whiskey was excellent, even dare I say costly. "You have good taste in spirits."

"And in absolutely nothing else," she returned, grinning.

"Well, your living arrangements are pretty spruce."

"Thank you. The old bat who owns the place found herself in hatches after some bogus investments didn't pan out. I needed new digs around then, and though she wouldn't let me stay in the house with her men boarders, she agreed to let me fix this place up. It's cold as anything in the winter, and once I left the door unlatched and ended up with a raccoon in my bed."

"Wait, you made all the alterations?"

"Flooring isn't that difficult." She shrugged. "Getting the fertilizer smell out was, but I'm not bellyaching. It's a nice place to entertain."

"I take it you're a printer, Miss Woods?"

Her chocolate eyes gleamed. "I do odd jobs—particularly the ones nobody else will touch. Socialism, anarchism, anticapitalism, anti–Mexican War pamphlets. A good many articles on the rights of women."

There was such a candid way about her, easy leaning posture and sweetly unkempt hair, that it was almost possible to forget that Sally Woods was dressed like a man. Almost. But I suspected I liked her anyhow. Which only charged my anxiety over the threat I'd guessed came from a printer—one named by Robert Symmes, one whose social causes were scandalous if not obscene.

"Where did you come by the press?"

This question likewise kittled her. "It was my dad's. I learned typesetting before I learned needlepoint. Never did learn needle-point, come to that. Mum was more of a gardener than a seam-stress. I lost them to smallpox five years back."

"I'm very sorry."

"So am I. All I have left of them is this press. I grew up on Stone Street, in a printing shop with our rooms above—seems old-fashioned now, with all the giant houses and the outwork printers. These days you have to be either enormous or particular. God, I haven't thought about Stone Street in months. Not that anything that was there is still standing."

"I used to live in Stone Street," I said, surprised at the coinci-dence. "Before . . ." I gestured to the rippling burn scar she couldn't have missed. Not being dead blind.

"Oh. I'd never have asked, but . . . Well, sod that fire anyhow, we're still standing." She leaned forward for another toast. "To your good looks."

As I raised my glass again, I thought, *This is bad.*

This is very bad, and about to get worse. It doesn't matter that you like her—you have to accuse her of threatening to set the city aflame.

I wasn't attracted to her, had nil desire to reveal the flesh under the shocking trousers. And something about her even then, if I'm honest, scratched a pinprick of alarm in my sternum. But she reminded me of my former stargazer friend Bird Daly, the way she speaks her mind because she doesn't know how to stop, because the latch guarding her lips was long ago broken irreparably, and I felt a similarly protective urge arising.

"Before you were a printer, what did you do?"

"Are these really the questions you're meant to be asking me?" She smoothed her hand over the arresting white streak in her chestnut haystack of hair, a worried gesture. "If not the togs, it's the press, isn't it? I break obscenity laws two or three times a week. You're fining me?"

"No." I spread my hands. "I grew up here too, on the streets sometimes, and I'm not often ketched by things that aren't worth being ketched about. As for your press, I'm a copper star who loathes Tammany and is a rampant abolitionist."

"An abolitionist?" Sally Woods chuckled, wriggling in her seat. "I love those. Though more than half of them are as useless on the topic of women's rights as any old Whig. As I said, I grew up learning my dad's trade, and when I turned eighteen, after I'd begged hard enough, he and Mum sent me to Mount Holyoke Female Seminary."

"Really?" I quirked a brow at her. "That's dead flash, Miss Woods. What was it like?"

Mount Holyoke was opened eleven years ago. By a woman, no less, not a man with the temerity to suggest that females would not become emotionally unbalanced upon learning Latin, that they could possibly even manage astronomy without developing hysteria, and that a smattering of Homer would fail to explode their crystalline minds. Its detractors—which includes nearly everyone, male and female alike—protest that since women can't be doctors or merchants or statesmen or lawyers or businessmen, otherwise perfectly contented future wives are being rendered unfit help-meets, sullied with the heavy drag of superfluous information. By this they mean information apart from how best to ensure the cook buys the freshest, cheapest produce and whether baby vomit can be scrubbed out of satin. Its five or six apologists protest that educated women will produce wiser, more upstanding kinchin, thus raising keen and strapping boys and thereby finer senators. It's true enough that apart from manual labor like straw-hat making or bookbind-ing or manufactory drudgery, women can't work. And therein lies the crux of the argument that one may as well teach a duck to speak Spanish as teach a woman geology at Mount Holyoke.

I can picture Mercy Underhill there easy as I can close my eyes and see her face.

"It was grand." Sally Woods's eyes took on a dreamy watercolor cast. "We couldn't afford it, but Dad said he figured I'd as much right to education as anyone, since I'd been doing print work start-ing at four years old. Neighbors thought he was cracked, of course—what possible use could a hen make of algebra? I was meant to tell them I'd find a husband who'd be proud of what I'd learnt, but when I didn't bother, they gave up on my prospects altogether, and that was bully by me. Sorry. What's Holyoke like, you asked? It's red brick, crawling with ivy, a chapel with a real rose window, a library with a ceiling so vaulted you'd suspect you were in church. I studied natural history there, architecture, physics."

"I'm jealous," I confessed with a rueful twist to my lips.

"You sound sharp enough."

"I read whenever I've time, that's all. Nothing to boast over."

"I was boasting, wasn't I? I'm sorry, pax."

"No, no, it's a remarkable achievement."

"That doesn't mean I have to bounce about it."

"You must have learned flash patter in the manufactory," I inferred aloud without thinking. "It sounds oddly well on you."

Her face instantly hardened into a frozen granite stare.

Oh, excellently played, my brother's voice drawled in my head. *You, my Tim, are an intellectual lamppost.*

"How in *hell* do you know I did manufactory work?" she snarled.

"Your former job is relevant to the questions I need to ask you," I admitted.

"Are the girls all right?" she demanded, voice shaking.

I was confused by the question. Then I remembered the sort of building in which I'd last encountered Alderman Symmes, her former employer. And began to suspect that something may have happened—something very old and impossibly twisted, like the root of an evil tree.

"I'm afraid I don't know. But I will go direct to the manufactory after we're through to ask them personally. And if they aren't all right, I will arrest the bastard who led them to that state. Is that a deal?"

Sally Woods finished her whiskey in a bolt and topped up our glasses, her comely face grey with disgust. "If you mean it, it's a deal."

"I mean it comprehensively. Who should I ask after?"

"Ellie Abell." Miss Woods recrossed her legs, slumping dully back in her secondhand armchair. "She'd not string you, you can trust what she says. And everyone adores her, talks to her, so she'll know if the others are well." Another expression flitted across her features—just as repulsed but much harder to read.

"I'll visit her as soon as I've asked you a few questions."

"The relevant ones now?"

"Yes. What is your relation to your former employer, Robert Symmes?"

Her face went as pale as the streak in her hair. It was a look of mingled loathing and fear so rarefied that it could have cured hide. Not just a disquieting expression—a dangerous one. And my heart started up its usual inconvenient habit of trying to exit my chest cavity for fairer climes as I remembered the wording of the threatening note. Most of its content could have sprung from any halfcracked socialist revolutionary. I'd seen the like in *Working Man's Advocate*—calling for the roads to run red with the blood of tyrants, et cetera. But one phrase, amid so much that was predictably impotent and enraged, stood out to me now.

We will not be cowed by those who think us less than human.

"Are you all right?" I asked.

She wasn't. That much was obvious.

I sat back, trying to make myself even smaller than I already am. I've terrified copious people due to the disreputable star pinned to my coat, but this was different. Something infected lurked in her marrow. Waiting. Poisoning her—poisoning others, I suddenly feared, should the venom escape her slender frame.

"Can I help?" I attempted when she made no answer. "I'll fetch water if you tell me where it is. Would you like—"

"I would like," she hissed, "to see Robert Symmes tortured, drawn, quartered, and his head stuck on a pike in the middle of City Hall Park. Can you arrange that for me?"

"While not in my job description, Miss Woods, speaking from personal experience of the man, that seems a pretty worthy goal."

She relaxed fractionally, her face losing its death-mask pallor.

"All right." Her dark eyes glimmered like stones in a deep pool. "You want to know my relationship to Robert Symmes? Robert Symmes is a man who pays his girls too little and treats his emigrant outworkers like pests. He's rich as Astor but doesn't use any of his chink to improve the city. He's convinced that he is the greatest politician since Jefferson, but he's mistaken about that. And he is, in addition to all this, the cruelest human being you could possibly imagine."

Carefully, I studied her. Her engaging snub nose and teak-colored eyes and active mouth. Wanting to ask a hard question. Because if what I suspected had happened was the truth, she deserved mountains more from the star police than a gaping houseguest who depleted her whiskey supplies.

Not that there was any guarantee I could deliver it to her. On the contrary.

"Is there anything you want to tell me? Anything. At all."

Shaking her head bitterly, she pulled herself up. "It's personal, and can't be helped anyhow. But you don't strike me the way copper stars generally do, and you should know it."

"Granted, I'm considerably smaller."

This earned me a dry chuckle followed by a sigh.

"Can you tell me why Symmes sacked you?"

She stared at my wide hat on the table. "No, I cannot do that. I've been told if I speak of it . . . Well, it doesn't matter. Now, what is this all about?"

Pausing, I read the note again in my mind. I tried to imagine Miss Woods lobbing a brick through a window to unsettle a vile man. I succeeded. She'd the will and the arm to play with the alderman's mind, though he seemed with a rat's cunning to have put his finger on the culprit almost at once.

Then I tried to picture this uncannily dressed, gorgeously *present* woman actually setting fire to a building full of innocent outworkers.

Despite the wholesale malignancy of her expression seconds previous, I failed.

Not a single brushstroke of that image could I picture. And yet a small pull like the tug of a thread wrapped around my finger reminded me that something about her was unnerving. Even downright frightening. Whether the togs or the naked stare or something more noisome below the rest, however, I couldn't be certain.

"You threatened Symmes, didn't you?"

"Of course not."

Angling an eye at her, I waited. It's generally not a long preamble before people start showering me with every acid secret they can think of and then searching their minds for more. It's exceedingly useful. No matter that the tales leave burns in my flesh.

"I did not threaten Alderman Robert Symmes," she grated out. But I knew better.

"Supposing I already savvied that you did?"

Sally Woods's hands began to shake. I didn't care for that, so I pressed on.

"I'm not threatening you. I'm *asking* you."

"Yes," she growled at last. "He told you, didn't he? That *filthy* man actually set the star police on me. I'd cause, you have to know that. I'd—" Her voice broke. "I'd *such* cause, and now you're going to carry me off to the Tombs and—"

"I don't think you'd much like the atmosphere, though I could arrange a tour." Rising, I returned my hat to my head. "I need you to stop toying with his mind from now on. This kind of threat . . . it's a serious matter."

Miss Woods stared at me, dumbstruck. Then she levered to her feet and stuck out her hand. I shook it, finding her grip every bit as firm as mine. I liked that, though. I liked her, considerably. Even though something about her prickled the nape of my neck.

"Where am I bound?"

"Nassau Street and Cedar. It's called the New American Textile Manufactory. Symmes owns at least four others I know of. Maybe more. But that's where I worked."

"I'm on my way there, then. Thank you for the whiskey."

"Come back if you like, Mr. Wilde." She followed me to her

door. "We'll have a drink and talk abolition and dirty politics. I mean it. You're welcome here."

"I'd love to," I assured her, meaning it just as heartily.

I would be returning, of course, all too soon. Just not for any so charming a reason. Meanwhile, I pointed my boots south in the direction of the Second Ward, the affectionate April sun giving me no indication whatsoever that I was on a direct collision course with a hurricane.

6

*The first event engraved on my memory was the birth of
a sister when I was four years old. . . . I heard so many
friends remark, "What a pity it is she's a girl!" that I felt
a kind of compassion for the little baby.*

—ELIZABETH CADY STANTON, ORGANIZER OF
THE 1848 SENECA FALLS CONVENTION

THE STROLL FROM THOMAS STREET down to Nassau wasn't taxing, so I walked there. Soon enough nearing what we'd used to
call the Burnt District. And the teeming hive of manufacturing
there, as if an industrious honeycomb had been cannonaded and
splattered its sweet commerce throughout the once-charred First
Ward.

If I could choose between a fire that destroyed our family and
a fire that destroyed a patch of my skin . . . there isn't any question
which I'd erase from the record. But the Fire of 1845 brought its
fair share of consequences. One was that my life was ruined, and
thus I became a reluctant—very reluctant—star policeman. One
was that people died. Too many of them. One was that about three
hundred buildings at the busiest tip of Manhattan surrounding
Wall Street burned down to their basements.

Another was that industry has popped right back up again

from the soot. Startling and sudden and garish as a jack-in-the-box.

Brick buildings and board buildings. Brownstone buildings and even some strange few painted iron-faced buildings. Grey-trimmed buildings and whitewashed buildings and marble buildings and granite buildings. I can't describe the vertigo of it. The sheer scope. Three-story buildings, four-story buildings, fives and even neck-craning sixes towering above the fractured pavement, where the speckled pigs still roam free in search of sex and cabbage scraps. It's a heady business. Absinthe-rich, delirious. I'd made the mistake of nearing that newborn rumpus of a district at about half past twelve. And striding down Broadway, no less—the more fool I. So I was jostled continually by stockbrokers and hot-corn girls and stoggers with their hands half in my pockets before I'd slapped them aside like so many flies. My nostrils full of horse manure, and fried clams, and the sweet neutral aroma of stone simmering in the sun.

Quick as was possible, I turned off kaleidoscope Broadway down Cedar, in sight of my goal.

Nassau isn't a street I much frequent. It's being rebuilt with manufactories where the business-residences and coffeehouses had stood before the flames licked them to rubble. That is, I knew as much, but it must have been six months since I'd set foot in it, and I confess . . .

I was not a little bustled.

It was a cluster of manufactories all right, regardless of the irregularity of the architecture. Interrupted only by the newly famous American and French Dining Saloon, where the merchants gather to shake shrewd palms, its sign advertising TURTLE SOUP FOR EXPORTATION. Tradesmen bustling, their shabby custom-cut coats mended on a dozen occasions and cheap cuff links shining, doing business. Colored men delivering goods and picking up orders—though none are allowed to be official stevedores. Several boy kinchin asking after prices and running them back to Wall Street with unlit cigars marinating in their mouths.

And finally, the girls of the Bowery.

Dozens of them. Scores. More females eating their midday dinners on stoops and stairwells so as to soak up the sunlight than I'd ever dare to count.

The New American Textile Manufactory, a strange iron fabrication, proved to be unlocked. The front hall was as spacious and aloof as a bank, doubtless to accommodate the molls arriving en masse at six in the morning. Its lower levels were offices, so I climbed up an equally disconcerting—but thankfully solid—set of cast-iron stairs to the second floor.

Stepping over the threshold into the manufactory proper, I took a moment to stare. Scores of women were dining in the huge room before me. It was occupied by very long aisles, large bolts of extremely cheap unprinted fabric in blues and browns and greys, tall enough ceilings to give one pause, and dozens of long tables at which the Bowery girls worked. Curled and ribboned and flounced and colorful as peacocks. Their scissors and measuring tools sat idle before them while they ate, laughing as they shared boiled peanuts and pickled radishes.

I paused just beyond the entryway. Reading conversations on their lips, as the echoing din prevented my hearing them clearly.

Many were chatting of beaus, but most were talking practical matters. That wasn't in the least shocking. Women are required to be practical the way fish require water. What was surprising was that they were talking practicality to one another not in shuttered-off nooks filled with silver-edged portraits. Nor in the sweat-sweet kitchens of rank hovels.

But in public. In a workplace, no less.

In New York as in other cities, the fair sex falls into pretty particular categories—categories that dictate behavior the way species decides fur versus feathers. Women with enough money to be termed ladies aren't meant to be seen in the open, not unless being put through their paces along Fifth Avenue, or tasting cordials at the Astor House, or taking the air in an open four-wheeler. And they're not meant to be aware of mud, or sweat, or labor—so if one did start up chatting pothole repair with a gentleman friend, she'd be dosed with a headache powder and sent to sleep off the strain. Women lacking the funds to be called ladies can talk domestic concerns over tea with thinned milk within bare walls if virtuous. If unvirtuous, they can say whatever they damn well please, as ruination doesn't visit by degrees but rather once and forever after. And if emigrants, they can shriek what they will from street corner to street corner, as they're already about as high in the social strata as our feral cats.

This wasn't the same. This was healthy kates with coin in their pockets and blood in their cheeks. Discussing how they lived their lives.

Come time for the roof to be mended, 'f I don't ask Jeremiah to fix it and no one else, I'm the biggest flat as was ever taken for a—

Did you see Kitty's new straw bonnet, she only paid three bits, and it's worked like a craftswoman's showpiece, you simply must go to Bowery just north of Spring and ask for—

Don't be a ninny, Mexico isn't the question any longer, it's about whether or not they'll demand Oregon follow along in the vile trade despite its latitude, and then we're sure enough—

Striding past the working girls and their rows of open tin dinner pails, hinges gleaming, packed with leftovers of jugged hare and cocky leeky and baked goose, I made every effort not to cast dark looks of concern at them. I'm pretty sure I was a fantastical failure.

"Can I help, sir?" came a cutting American tenor.

The foreman greeted me in the wide center aisle. He was fifty, maybe, nearly as short as I am, bald as a frog, with a prim mouth and a pinched, nickel-counting look about the eye.

"Simeon Gage," he announced as we shook hands.

"Timothy Wilde. I'm from the star police."

"I can see that. What's it to do with us?"

"Might you take me to your office? It's a private matter."

His mazzard congealed in the way that means, *If it's bribes you're after, please be sane about the figure.* But he led me into a room at the back of the giant workspace, indicating a chair across from a desk with a messy stack of ledgers and time sheets and insurance forms resting on it. We sat.

"Busy day?" I angled my eyes at the paperwork.

"I take care of some of the alderman's more tedious filing," Gage replied, chest ballooning. "He is a personage of great importance. You might call me—as a trusted overseer, you understand—one of his secretaries. Accounts payable, contracts, policy renewals, and the like. I can barely keep up at the moment. Let alone manage those witless hens out there."

I smiled. Not amiably. "Are you familiar with a former employee of this establishment, a Miss Sally Woods?"

He shifted his priggish lips. "Aye."

"What can you tell me about her?"

"She's trouble."

"What variety?"

"The worst I can think of." He scraped backward in his chair dramatically, tugging his waistcoat down. "I was a tailor before this modern system unmanned me. When I was down on my luck, with no orders coming in and otherwise respectable people thinking nothing of wearing ready-made slops, Mr. Symmes gave me a boost out of the mire. So by trouble I mean the sort of trouble every fellow fears most—the sort that'll strip him of his dignity. No respect whatsoever for the natural order, for authority, for rules, for Mr. Symmes. She worked hard enough, for a girl anyway, but she's ruinous otherwise. Educated, you know," he added, picking at one of his fingernails.

I made a hare-quick decision to spend as little time as was possible with Simeon Gage.

"I need to speak with an Ellie Abell. Is she here?"

"Sure enough." He narrowed his eyes, measuring.

I waited.

That went on for a spell.

"I'll just bring her in, then?" he sneered.

"Aces, I'd appreciate it."

He departed with an audible level of annoyance in his footfalls. When he returned, it was with an apple-cheeked beauty with light ash-brown hair, full lips, and a pair of golden eyes that radiated fear.

"Thank you for seeing me, Miss Abell," I said. "Mr. Gage, I'll show myself out when I'm through."

An eyebrow as bushy as his pate was hairless reared upward. "If it's to do with Miss Abell here, then it's company business, isn't it?"

Miss Abell's mouth twitched, the door of a safe slamming shut.

"You'll probably want to give us some privacy," I objected, "unless the manufactory is after a hefty fine."

"What in hell would you *fine* us over?"

"I'm a pretty imaginative sort. I'd puzzle it out."

Purpling with vexation, Gage made an effort to slice me open with his eyeballs. He wasn't any too successful. But his heart was in it, bless the man.

"*Much* obliged for your cooperation, Mr. Gage. I'll make sure Tammany hears of it."

I wouldn't. But that tipped the scales into Simeon Gage's exiting his office, yanking his door shut so hard than a pen on his desk toppled out of its stand. Reaching, I returned it to its home.

"Please sit down, Miss Abell." I took my hat off and gestured at Gage's chair behind the desk. She sat as gingerly as if requested to perch on a fence post. "My name is Timothy Wilde. You're in no scrape here, I promise. I just want to ask a few questions for your own safety."

"For *my* safety?"

"I was sent by a Miss Sally Woods."

Her fetchingly ample cheeks paled, followed by a look of dull horror she smothered so quick it might never have been there. "What's Sally up to now, then? What's she keen to bring on our heads *this* time?"

Taken aback, I shifted elbows in the straight-armed chair. "She wanted to know if you were faring well here."

"Oh, she's scheming something again, that wicked little cat, I *knew* it."

Conversation appeared to have made a sharp turn. So I adopted an understanding look. Ran my fingers along the edge of my scar, which was burning in the usual futile alarm. Annoyed myself and dropped my hand.

"I'd like to hear what I ought to look out for, in that case."

"Oh, I couldn't possibly speak about Sally to a policeman."

"Miss Abell, I'd sooner cross Tammany Hall than an honest woman. On my honor."

Ellie Abell licked her rosy lips, cogitating. She wore a dress of sage green and, in typical Bowery fashion, had belted it with a yellow shawl. Her intricate little straw bonnet perched at the back of her head, clinging as if to a cliff's edge, festooned with fabric buttercups and a ribbon of brighter yellow still. First impressions told me she was the brand of good-hearted that verged on gullible. The layer of ice that keeps city dwellers safe from one another was lacking. Intuition told me she had the brains to combat that deficiency, even if her face was the picture of a tea rose in midbloom. So *honor*—and God knows I make every effort in that direction— seemed the right tactic.

"I spoke too soon, Mr. Wilde," she fretted, pulling out a handkerchief and twisting it. "I don't *know* that Sally's planning any lay. We haven't spoken. Not for ages. Not since she was sacked."

"She seemed mightily concerned over you."

"Well, that's stemming from the wrong source *entirely*. Oh, I'm not the sort to hold a grudge, Mr. Wilde, but sometimes I could just . . ." She fluttered a hand vexedly. "Just spit on that girl's shoes."

I frowned. "You tell me the story, and I promise I'll keep an eagle's watch over this place, Miss Abell. It's important, for reasons I can't discuss just now."

Seconds passed as she did sums in her head, adding the columns over whether trusting me or sealing her plush mouth was the better course. As had already happened once too often that day, I was faced with a moll who'd turned sea green with fear.

Miss Abell reached a decision and drew a steadying breath. "It was . . . let me see." She counted on her fingers. "Probably six months ago now since Sally started ruining *everything*."

"How long have you known Miss Woods?"

"Oh, I went to seminary with her, you know. Mount Holyoke. We were thick as anything there—went to picnics and concerts, played Schubert duets half the night long. We were practically sisters. But she's always been . . ." Miss Abell sampled words on her tongue, made a careful selection. "Headstrong. And of *course* I think women ought to study, and work, and maybe . . . maybe even vote someday. Only if we're schooled well enough in politics, naturally. An ignorant vote is as undemocratic as an absent one."

She stopped. Checking whether I was shocked at the concept

of females stuffing ballot boxes. The answer was that Frederick Douglass wasn't and neither was I, never mind that most New Yorkers would figure both myself and Mr. Douglass for legally insane. So I crooked my mouth up and leaned forward with my elbows on my thighs.

Miss Abell blew out a little gust through her lips. "But she's . . . ugh, I can't stand *shocking* decent Christian people to make a point, it's . . . undignified. No, *indecent*. Who does she think she *is*? She isn't helping the cause in the smallest by making people *hate* her. After school everything changed. It was as if all the radical principles she'd heard there had . . . *stuck* to her somehow. It was bad enough when she wore petticoats and stirred up trouble, and now I hear she's printing all manner of freelance trash and dressing like a *man*. It sets the female-rights movement backward in the public eye every time she leaves her house."

"Can you tell me why she lost her position here?"

"The strike, of course!" Miss Abell lurched upright, bosom heaving as a dawn blush rose over her cheeks. "*Everyone* savvies that."

Here was a point of interest. Manufactory work hasn't been common in these parts for long, so neither have strikes. But the Lowell girls struck in 1834, and again in 1836, and the entire state of Massachusetts called them plentiful ugly names, *whores* being the most popular, before they trudged back to work following threats of blacklisting and far, far worse. The newspapers warned us all uneasily that a shameless "gynecocracy" threatened. I'd never lit eyes on the term before, and damned if I fully comprehended the dire consequences of a gynecocracy, but it didn't take me long to determine which side should actually be diagnosed with hysteria and dropped in an ice bath.

"Tell me about it," I requested.

"She went and made up a workers' manifesto, didn't she, Lord knows that must have been what gave her the notion to go into printing after she was fired . . . she tacked it on the door of the manufactory as if she were Martin Luther. Oh, so many of us went along with her lay that I blush to think about it, I really do. She's always been that silver-tongued."

"She struck me so too."

Ellie Abell gazed at a memory rather than the wall. "We were all out in the midsummer torrents last summer, marching in circles with painted signs. Caroline has the best voice, so she organized the choruses, and Patience made badges, and I even wrote a *poem* to contribute to the local papers. None of them took it, of course. They thought us all noddle-headed for demanding higher wages when the tailors detest us working in their field at all. But Sally wanted rates closer to the male cutters and double the chink for the outworkers, so there we were with rain in our boots."

"And how did you fare?"

"How do you think? Poorly." She glanced at her lap. "It was awful. Just . . . I felt like such a goose for joining Sally, picketing and all. That little minx even convinced a good many of the out-workers to join us, and God knows they can't afford to lose so much as a penny's wages. When I think of people jeering and throwing rotten food at us and the outworkers *actually picking it up* to eat . . ."

She waited to see if I was shocked. I'd like to have been.

"Sally swore that they'd never hold out against all of us together—the cutters *and* the outworkers. But they'd no intention of raising wages." Her pale brown eyes glinted with betrayal, hurt. "I just . . . It was *selfish*, Mr. Wilde. She meant to make a name for herself. Well, she did, and may she have the best of luck with it."

Miss Abell sat back, tugging her sleeves down emphatically.

"Is she dangerous?" I asked. I'd suspected so myself, after all.

"Socially, perhaps." Miss Abell refolded her kerchief and re-turned it to the pocket of her dress.

"Lawbreaking?"

"God, yes. *Enthusiastically.* Did I mention the trousers?"

"Violent?"

Her face tightened. She shook her head. "I don't . . . Oh, I couldn't ever tell you for certain. I pray not, Mr. Wilde."

That was about as comforting as a spilt basket of snakes.

"And what is her relationship to the owner of your manufactory, Mr. Robert Symmes?"

She was out of her chair as if launched from it, hands smoothing her skirts. "Oh, that's none of my business. None whatsoever. Heavens, think of the time, and I've not even washed my lunch pail, the whistle will blow at any—"

"Miss Abell, I must insist that—"

"No, no, no, you've already sent Mr. Gage into a temper, and I was a *bit* slower than usual this morning, but I can make it up—"

"I want you to answer the question. Please." I rose to my full if inglorious stature.

"And I'll never put myself at risk for *her* again!" she cried.

Clapping a shocked hand over her mouth, she stumbled backward, her other fingers over the V of bright yellow shawl tied at her waist. "Oh, Mr. Wilde, I'm sorry. . . . I believe you, you know, that you're honorable. For the love of mercy, leave it alone."

Ellie Abell fled. Minutes later, yet lost in sinister reflection in Simeon Gage's office, I heard the shrill one-o'clock whistle signaling the employees to return to their stations until their shifts ended at six, and the girls of the Bowery streamed out into the lengthening evening shadow play. Figures casting scarecrow-thin silhouettes upon the pavement, swinging clasped hands as they walked north and home.

"Bugger," I said decidedly, putting my hat on after giving my scar a mean-spirited squeeze.

When I quit the manufactory, all the molls cutting cotton and

Simeon Gage looming over them like a stone-lipped gargoyle, I spied out where Miss Abell sat. Her lowered face was writ thick with prophecies. Anxious and expectant. As if cruel events would follow upon the heels of my visit.

She was right. I knew it even as I stepped back into the afternoon sunshine. I still made every fool's effort, meanwhile, to suppose that she was wrong.

I strode north, approaching my workplace at around two p.m. It's a monstrous hollow rectangular building with an open gallows yard in the center. Worthy of ancient pharaohs who'd as soon kill as pardon, a gloom-draped monument to punishment, with Egyptian detailing and double-height windows set deep in the massive stone walls. The place is horrid on every level. But although horrid it's also *mine,* mine in a way no other place of occupation has ever been, which strangely endears it to me. Rapacious skinners with neat frocks and smart cravat pins stood on the wide steps at the southern Leonard Street entrance, passing coins to the colored men who run within the lockup to question whether any fresh arrivals can afford a lawyer. Several of the flint-eyed barristers nodded to me as I approached, though whether due to my familiar if grotesque face or to the fact that I admittedly deposit a great many profitable rogues in that dungeon, I couldn't say. Nodding in return, I gained the front stairs.

I'd take a sip of gin in my neat little office, I thought. And put my pen to paper. And think it through.

It seemed a fair enough plan. Except that someone familiar was hurtling out of the prison-courthouse on skinny crab's legs, bug-eyed and frantic, a tattered red muffler flapping behind him.

"Mr. Piest! My God, man. Where's the fire?"

He scraped to a halt, gasping. "Thank all the stars! When you were not in your office, I was *most* distressed. But how did you hear with such speed?"

"What *happened*?" I demanded, gripping the noble old crack-brain's coat sleeve.

"Well, you've heard, obviously," he returned. "The fire is in Pell Street. Come along with me, or Robert Symmes will suppose we've much to answer for!"

Fires lend me the sensation that electric eels reside in my pelvis. And by the time we'd reached the leering nightmare of Pell Street—leaping over the manure-heaped iron path that was the New York and Harlem Railroad tracks, skirting the rum-drenched netherworld of the Five Points, ducking into a despair-tinged corridor three blocks east of the Tombs—I'd learned a bit more about this stir in particular.

Robert Symmes, as he himself had boasted, owned buildings that could be characterized as "highly saturated with tenants" and might better be called slums. One of them had burst into flames at about twelve-thirty that day—and its immediate proximity to the Tombs meant that Chief Matsell was able to alert Mr. Piest as he walked his Chatham Street rounds.

"Is the fire out, then?"

"To my knowledge, yes, Mr. Wilde, thank Providence and the ready assistance of a redoubtable fire company. But Symmes was apparently furious—that ignoble brute told the chief he held the star police personally responsible for its failure to protect his private interests. Thus I would gather the damage is palpable."

"Casualties?"

"I cannot say, Mr. Wilde," the mad Dutch roundsman gasped, nearly breaking his neck when his boot met an eroded pit in the roadway. "We'll know soon enough."

Pell Street leans inward from both sides, like knob-boned

crones hunched over soup bowls in a workhouse dining hall. It's all topsy-turvy pine structures divided into innumerable apartments, with rear buildings erected in the anterior yards to serve as fertile generators of misery and sewage. But even through the twin stenches of poverty and overflowing school sinks, I could smell brimstone by now.

It clogged, greasy as bad porridge, in the back of my treacherous throat.

A fire engine and hose—beautifully maintained but covered in soot—sat before a building sending a noxious miasma of white steam and black smoke from its exposed bowels. The tall spoked wheels of the chassis rocked, as the dappled mare didn't much care for its situation. I could sympathize. The contraption was of very modern design, as most of the hose carts are. This one must have arrived with explosive speed. It had been attached to the nearest pump, the long arms of the engine's pressure device shining with wet black paint, its leather hose uncoiled, its pair of brass lanterns and great brass drum gleaming through the reeking haze.

NEPTUNE ENGINE NUMBER 9 was inscribed in ornate characters on the side of the carriage. Apart from the presence of fire, the pretty apparatus didn't quite belong. Not surrounded by grime, gawked at by the rag-clad Irish.

Craning my neck, I examined the building.

All the while thinking, *It isn't a fire anymore. Now it's a heap of charred wood that can't hurt you, your scar is only burning because you belong strapped in a strait-waistcoat, you liverless addle-cove.*

The structure had been gutted something ferocious. Thankfully, the surrounding houses were untouched. There didn't appear to be any rival firedogging gangs on the prowl, so the Neptune Nines had accomplished their objective without the added felicity of brass-knuckle brawling. If there's one thing that kittles the fire rabbits more than walking into charnel houses, it's beating one another crimson over the privilege.

My stomach writhed a bit more. Recalling the words:

As strikes don't move you, we'll see whether vengeance might. Improve the hateful conditions of those who wield the needle as a sword or watch your outwork go down in flames.

"Stout work, fellow defenders of the metropolis!"

Mr. Piest addressed a pair of rascals in red flannel shirts and fitted black trousers, patent belts pulled tight as corsets, emerging from the soaked front steps. The rest of the gang swept smoldering rubble into piles, sharing swigs from rum flasks.

"Would you be so kind as to tell us what you can about this conflagration?" my companion continued. "It seems that the building's owner has been the target of scurrilous threats."

The taller of the two, a thin-faced rascal with a long white scar at the edge of his eye, stopped short and grinned. "Well, I'll be ketched—look, Archie, it's Val Wilde's kid brother. Drake Todd, at your service." He slapped me on the arm hard enough to leave a friendly purple reminder.

"I'd heard Valentine's brother had turned pig, but damned if I believed it." The one called Archie, squatter and burlier, with a twice-broken beak, repeated the limb-numbing gesture. "Archie Vanderpool, a pleasure. A copper star, my God. What, Wilde, all the sewage-inspector jobs full up?"

They cackled, pulling congratulatory cigars from their shirt pockets. I thought about being annoyed and found I couldn't be arsed. Unfortunately, these were the sort of dusty thugs Valentine ran with.

No, I corrected myself wearily, *this is the sort of dusty thug Valentine is.*

"Fine work." I cast my eyes over the grim husk. "Any dead?"

"Two." Drake Todd's mouth twitched. "Couldn't get ladders to the third level in time. A pair of stargazers, already carted off to the land-broker. I'm guessing sixteen if not younger, and we almost had them too. Sodding death-trap tinderbox," he added, spitting.

He meant it religiously. All the firedogs do. They rove in feral gangs, by turns giving each other knife wounds and practicing filthy politics and pulling folk from incinerators. It's the maddest breed of human on earth. And Val is their goddamn king.

"Occupancy at the time?"

"We were lucky there," Vanderpool answered. "A hundred or more at night, God knows, but only about thirty at midday."

"A most fortuitous chance." Piest angled a weathered hand on his hip. "The residents consisted mainly of female outworkers, I imagine?"

"By a Texas-sized margin, aye. Threatening letters, you said?"

"Precisely so. Did you discover anything of note?"

Drake Todd coughed meaningfully. Archie Vanderpool, shrugging, bent to scrape charred material from his boot with a pocket-knife.

A cold feeling ran down the length of my arms.

"Who sent you here?" Todd wanted to know.

"Chief Matsell," I answered.

He inclined his head, satisfied. "White phosphorus, and plenty of it from the burn pattern. You can probably smell it." And yes, something harsher stained the woodsmoke aroma, scraped my nose like the reek of concentrated urine. Grinding out his cigar on his belt buckle, Todd took a step away. "Come see for yourself, lads."

An alarming moment transpired when no one spoke. Or moved. I swallowed hard, my throat attempting to close to a thread's breadth.

Move your worthless feet. It's a smoldering skeleton, not a goddamn fire, and if you're keen to prove an actual man *at the ripe age of thirty, you'll—*

"I wonder if you might escort me within whilst my colleague Mr. Wilde questions the neighbors?" Mr. Piest interjected. Not even sparing me a concerned glance, proving him the most compassionate man on Manhattan Island. "He is a master at gathering anecdotal evidence, none finer, and I've an excellent pair of eyes. No objections? Quick march, in that case! If there is aught within to see, sirs, by the good old streets of Gotham, we shall see it!"

After the three had vanished, I felt less like I was being garroted. An enthusiastic surge of self-loathing and a hearty yearning to send my fist through a wall promptly followed.

It was distracting.

So when I discovered that a girl stood gaping goggle-eyed at the ruins, mouth working like a trout's, I confess myself taken aback.

The young moll facing the wreck of Symmes's hellhole was so emaciated that a breath could have shattered her. Her face was pie-round and pasty, with flaking lips and royal violet semicircles under her eyes that reminded me of Val after a positively operatic morphine spree. She was too tall to be a child, too lost to be a woman full grown. Starving to death as she was, dressed in rags and filth, the poor wretch looked as if she were already decomposing. She was in considerable distress.

"Is this your home?"

She blinked mechanically, gulping in air. Her much-pinpricked fingers clutched a piece of paper. Her state reminded me painfully of another seamstress from what feels like a very long time ago, when I first started police work, a mother I found in a closet starved for light and air whose senses had tragically leached away into the grime surrounding her. Gently, I reached for this new stranger's closed fist.

"Do you know someone who lived here? Tell me how to help, and I'll—"

After prying the note from her hand, I lost my train of thought.

Because it was fair to state that reading the words *I fear that my friend means to set your house aflame and burn you all alive* made a powerful impression on my mind.

7

*It is ridiculous to ascribe this sentiment to the jealousy of
the stronger sex. It is not from fear of competition, but from
fear of losing the charm of the world; from love of woman,
not from jealousy, that man so earnestly contends she is
now in her place. He knows himself and the world well
enough to thank God that woman is not like him, or
exposed to his lot. It is tenderness to her, and an
enlightened self-love, that unite to make him disgusted
with the first signs of a metamorphosis of women into men.*

—NEW YORK CHRISTIAN ENQUIRER,
NOVEMBER 2, 1850

FOR A MAN WHO TYPICALLY culls information from his subjects
like sap from a swollen maple, the next interview I conducted
was mightily vexing.

I'd told Dunla Duffy—her name, she'd managed to recollect
following serious effort, was Dunla Duffy—to stay put. She froze.
I'd called into the burned house, telling Piest to meet me at Buttercake Joe's a few blocks east on Pearl and Elm. He agreed. I'd led
Miss Duffy to the cellar eatery, unmarked streetside save for a
camphor lantern sending delicate black soot flakes down its iron
stand, expecting her to liven at the scent of fresh biscuits. She did.

Thus I sat elbow to elbow with Mr. Piest across from Miss Duffy at a low wooden table, its surface scraped with zodiacs of initials and obscenities and discourteous sentiments regarding strangers' mothers. Between us reposed three chipped mugs of steaming black coffee and a plate of threepenny buttercakes, which are dense biscuits with a generous dollop of butter wedged between flaking halves.

Miss Duffy, now that she was silhouetted in the smoky gloom of Buttercake Joe's, had lost her grip on speech entirely. She kept reaching for the refreshments, glancing up as if I'd thwack her hand with a cane, and then eating after I'd smiled encouragement. When I comprehended I was ravenous myself, I tucked into a buttercake.

"These objects are strangely addictive for the . . . ah, hearty nature of their consistency," Mr. Piest observed, smearing glistening fingers on his trouser legs.

Toady—the taciturn and porcine proprietor—winked at me when I signaled for another platter. I'd discovered the establishment during my first investigation and frequented it thereafter, because there exist precious few twenty-four-hour grog shops in Ward Six offering baked goods garnished with butter and not thrice-used lard, a glass of rum a man can trust not to render him snoring and penniless, and a mug of coffee made with coffee beans rather than roasted acorns and potato peels. It was mostly empty in the yolk-yellow spring afternoon. But by midnight it would be swarming with newsboys. Fresh kinchin newsboys of five years to hardened ruffian newsboys of fifteen, keen to lift a well-earned glass before sleeping beneath the rubbish and starshine of City Hall Park.

When the second heaping pewter plate had landed with a salutary belch from Toady, I tried again.

"Whereabouts in Ireland do you hail from, Miss Duffy?"

She startled backward. "And how did ye know I were from Ireland, now?"

"Call it a lucky guess."

Dunla Duffy aimed wonderstruck eyes at me. There were depths to those eyes, however, depths that the open, crumb-strewn lips couldn't negate. Reaching up, she twirled a piece of mossy hair, which might have been blonde if clean. It wasn't clean, though, and hadn't been for months. I didn't blame her for that. But Miss Duffy was just the sort of emigrant our charity workers—Mercy Underhill always excepted, ever let there be an exception for her raving, raging, radical compassion—would have declared the just casualty of God's wrath against brute laziness and stubborn pope worship. (Charity in these parts isn't pretty. It's rarely even charitable.) Recalling that Mercy was less than a mile away rather than an ocean's distance didn't aid my concentration, meanwhile.

"Yer a lucky sort, all right," Miss Duffy agreed, awed. "I could always tell."

I severely doubted this remark's value. Unless she meant I was lucky the way the Irish were lucky and could look forward to forever improving my strength of character by serving as Dame Fortune's personal slop bucket.

"I come from . . ." Her eyes screwed tight with effort. "Clonakilty. Aye, that were the name. But there was naught to eat there. Here there's victuals but no money t' buy them. Ye have a *money famine.*" She nodded, convinced. "By rights ye should make more money fer everyone—'tis only paper, after all, not like tradin' work for food back home."

It held water like a sieve, speaking economically. But, God, when I thought of the lengths to which people go for sustenance, selling bits and pieces of themselves, I half agreed, and when I thought of Bird Daly, around thirteen years old now and living at the Catholic Asylum learning theology and arithmetic from Father Sheehy and growing prettier by the second, no more than a year distant in age from this Dunla Duffy if that, nearly an adult and yet so piercingly young, a familiar cold fear gripped my sternum. Just what was Bird meant to do when through schooling, without a cent to her name or walls to keep the wind away? Sew, as this near-skeleton so obviously did? Work twelve hours daily hunched over bookbinding until faint from the rabbit glue? Marry someone approaching tolerable in exchange for meat and cutlery? As Mercy had once forced me to question, is there any difference between trading offspring for security and trading mere copulation for the same? It can wake me in the small hours, the odds against Bird hewing a path for herself through the forest.

Terrible, I've always thought it, the way fierce enough love can make the future seem to ripple with nightmare.

"Eating is a bad wrench in these parts. I've suffered it myself," I replied with feeling. "Miss Duffy, I need to know . . . did you *live* there in Pell Street?"

Miss Duffy swallowed the last of her fourth biscuit. "Aye. But I were told to live somewhere else. That's sure enough less trouble now, seein' as 'tis burned down."

"An eminently practical sentiment, and I applaud your optimism," Mr. Piest approved.

"Will you show my friend here the note you were holding?" I inquired.

I'd given it back, as she'd seemed off balance—well, more off balance than she was already—with the thing in my pocket. But she readily drew it from her skirts and passed it to Piest, whose bulging turtle's eyes widened at the single line.

"Most disturbing," he muttered.

"You were told to live elsewhere, you said?" I prompted.

Miss Duffy ducked her chin. "The Witch, she'd ha' skinned me sure and certain else. So I ran, but then I'd nary other lodgings, y' see."

This was less than enlightening.

"You were . . . threatened by a witch who lived in the building?" I attempted.

She wrapped her arms around herself, shivering. "It were me own fault. But I ne'er meant offense, on the Holy Cross I didn't."

"Fear not," Mr. Piest commanded gallantly, flapping his frayed sable coat lapel with its woefully bashed star emblem. "We police are here to provide you with protection, citizen."

Dunla Duffy's perfectly spherical mouth widened in a horrified gasp.

That's torn it, I thought, shoving a thumbnail into the edge of my scar. For of course she hadn't any notion of what our copper star badges meant.

"Police?" she squeaked, eyes flooding with tears. "*I'll pay her back.* I ne'er meant to steal it. Oh, Mother Mary, the Witch must ha' told ye the whole story, but I didn't mean it, *I didn't—*"

"We know you didn't," I cut her off, thinking, *Facts be damned.* "All right, Miss Duffy? You never meant to steal . . . ?"

"The light," she said on a helpless sob.

"The light?" Piest repeated, baffled.

The poor girl's entire frame shook with choked-back tears, making her seem a far younger kinchin trapped in midnight terrors. "I stole a wee dram o' her light clean away, sittin' near her candle . . . and I'm sorry. I've money t' pay her back now."

"And this witch, the one whose . . . light you stole. By *accident,* yes, I know. Someone who feared she might harm you all wrote the note?"

"I don't understand, sir."

Mr. Piest placed the communiqué delicately before her. "This scurrilous witch you've mentioned meant to wreak darkest vengeance upon you? And an ally in the house gave you this message?"

The rocking worsened. "Nay. That were from t'other lass. She'd stars in her eyes, before."

"Can you tell us her name, miss?"

"The manufactory lass. She's the one give me the note and four bits, the one as used t' have stars in her eyes. Not any longer, though. I took the light sure enough, but I *didn't* steal the four bits," she whimpered, fresh moisture threatening to spill down her pale, round cheeks.

"No!" Piest exclaimed, holding his hands up in surrender.

"I never stole the pantaloons neither, *never*, not though they was trod i' the mud and all and the foreman threw them out. It weren't *my* fault they was trod in the mud."

"No," I protested, equally alarmed.

By this time she was gnawing her thumb bloody as she stared unseeing at the table. "They said not to trust star police. Said as police would fine us for bad women if they saw us on the streets wi'out a purpose. I never meant to steal the light, and now I've nothing to sew and the building burnt and all, and I know I were just standin' there looking. But I'm *not* a bad woman," she pleaded.

"No," I said again, emphatically. "You're not. Now, listen—"

"I'm a good girl. Me mam raised me proper."

"Of course she did. I can see that for myself. But this note, Miss Duffy . . . what did the giver *mean* by it?"

Our distraught guest spared the note a quick flick of her eyes. Went back to rocking, gentler this time.

"I couldn't tell ye," she murmured. "What does it say?"

Biting my lip in frustration at my own slowness, I answered, "It says, 'I fear that my friend means to set your house aflame and burn you all alive.'"

"It *does?*" Miss Duffy rocked faster.

"I'm afraid so. What—"

"Oh, wicked, *wicked!*" she cried. "Do those letters there tell ye who meant us harm? They must do. Read the rest o' the note, sir, for God's sake read the rest."

Instead I tucked the paper into my black waistcoat, edged the buttercakes toward Miss Duffy, patted her hand, caught Piest by the sleeve, and retreated to the rear of the murky room. We wanted fast answers and weren't getting any. None that could ease the cramp at the back of my brain insisting, *Sally Woods is a radical and an educated woman, not a mad incendiary, and, unlike most, you actually savvy the difference.* Anyhow, I was engaged that fast-approaching spring evening, upon a matter I fervently hoped could combine workplace efficiency with personal obligations.

"We need a less threatening interrogator," I suggested when we'd ducked partly behind a dust-festooned burlap curtain. A group of newsboys done with selling their afternoon editions flowed through the cellar door beyond, their acrid cigar smoke trailing like proud parade ribbons. "But we *cannot* lose track of her."

Piest frowned thunderously. "She'll never trust us, and for excellent cause if we arrest—"

"God no, we'd neither of us dream of clapping her in the Tombs." I pulled a pencil and a notebook from my coat. "Take her to this address and see whether the occupant is willing to assist us in housing her. On a *very* temporary basis, and she'll be repaid for any expenses by Matsell. If Miss Duffy dissolves into the ether, I don't like to think where this investigation is going."

I didn't like to think of that anyhow. But minus Dunla Duffy, I knew we were in a coffin with the lid half nailed shut—I'd no notion who passed her the warning, no clue who the girl with "stars in her eyes" could have been other than that she likewise performed manufactory work. So I handed Mercy Underhill's new theatrical address to Mr. Piest and requested he take Miss Duffy there. I didn't mean any harm by that—it was merely the best of all possible shit-poor decisions, and yes, I wanted to see Mercy again, and yes, I adore that she's generous to a fault, and yes, *I wanted her to have a task.* Tasks, I know from personal experience, are remarkably fine bulwarks against an eroding mind.

"By all means, Mr. Wilde." Piest took the address.

"I'm sorry about the burned house, earlier."

"Why would you be—"

"Stop playing the slubber when you know perfectly well what happened back there, and tell me what the evidence inside suggested," I snapped. Within a heartbeat I'd realized I was ragging the man who'd just rescued me from severe public embarrassment and experienced another warm wash of shame. "I apologize," I added instantly. "God, Jakob, I beg your pardon, it's not—"

"Mr. Wilde?"

"Yes, I know, I'm—"

"Allow me the freedom to speak, if you please, my esteemed colleague."

Mr. Piest smiled in satisfaction after I'd managed to keep my trap shut for over five seconds. Admittedly, I'd have placed the odds against my managing the ordeal.

"It must have been planted previous." He coughed, pulling out his worn linen kerchief. "The phosphorus accelerant whereby the blaze ignited so quickly, I mean to say—it seems to have run through the crumbling walls in places. Nowhere anyone would have noticed it day to day, however, or so I was assured when the firemen described to me the condition the building was in prior. Holes in the plaster, floorboards missing, the usual inhumane squalor."

"Does the technique used help us?"

"According to Messrs. Drake and Todd, any villain who looked up phosphorus in the encyclopedia could have accomplished as much. It isn't as if there's a science to these foul deeds. We would do well to question the survivors regarding any recent repair work, suspicious characters entering the building, et cetera. But I fear, though the despicable crime was undoubtedly the work of a deliberate and cold-blooded incendiary, knowing *how* does not directly lead us to *who*. The ignoble coward simply set match to tinder, as it were, and walked away."

"Surely someone would have noticed as much."

"If so, it is indeed unfortunate that by now the residents must have scattered to the four winds." Mr. Piest passed a hand over his brow in thought. "We can expend our energies in the search for them, of course, but you've seen as many of these ghastly rookeries as have I—no real names given when dastardly landlords even bother with names, no registries, no locks on the doors, windows broken, casual lodgers and casual intimacies being exchanged at all hours. We've no guarantee whatsoever the culprit was observed."

I rubbed at my eyes, ruminating. About fire and its consequences, mainly. About the fact that New York resembles a kicked anthill. About Alderman Symmes and his vices. About the fact that I'd left Miss Sally Woods well before noon and that if she'd quit her queer greenhouse home minutes afterward, newly infused with righteous brimstone over the fact that Symmes had set a copper star on her tail, supposing she'd already planted the necessary inflammables, nothing would have prevented her from—

"The suspect Symmes named," Piest mused. "Have you spoken with her?"

"Yes. She has cause to hate the bastard, even admitted to threats. But anyone could have set that fire."

"Nevertheless."

"I know. I'll confront her again, this time with more arrows in my quiver. Whatever we're digging up here, I warn you, its roots are deeper than we'd supposed."

A fresh spill of newsboys washed down the stairway. Spying one I wanted, I squeezed Mr. Piest's shoulder. "You hide Miss Duffy safely away, I'll have a word with our friends of the local press, and then I'll speak with Symmes himself at the Knicker-bocker Twenty-one Tammany benefit this evening, yes? I strongly suspect he'll show his face, if only to keep my brother in line. It's for his own blasted campaign after all."

"The alderman will certainly attend, as he is part of the pro-gram, I take it. But that sounds . . ."

"Deeply problematic, I know," I confirmed, giving him a light push.

Mr. Piest strode away with the heart of a warrior and the legs of a langoustine and escorted Miss Duffy out. Meanwhile, I timed my return to our table so as to catch one of the newsboys via a firm tug of the earlobe. That made me look in charge, so later he could bounce to his pals about how he'd lioned his way out of a scrape with a copper star. I didn't think he'd mind a quick patter session, though, not when I'd plentiful buttercakes remaining.

My friend Ninepin landed with a hearty grunt of protest in the seat Miss Duffy had just vacated. But when I swept my hat off and he saw all three-quarters of my mazzard clear, he stuck out an ink-stained hand.

"Well, if it ain't Mr. Wilde, gentleman fly-cop."

Ninepin, bless the lad, is a garrulous, deft, cunning newsboy of about fifteen years with sunflower-yellow locks falling into his eyes. The eyes are obscured behind a pair of delicate gold ladies' reading spectacles that he imagines accentuate the forcefulness of his arguments. On this occasion he was resplendent in checked fitted trousers, a striped waistcoat, a secondhand blue velvet jacket he'd cleverly purchased too long in the arms so as to make the greater use of it, and a cravat I am reasonably certain was previously a purple curtain sash.

"Buttercake?" I offered.

"Cheers. Who's gruel is this one?"

Miss Duffy had failed to touch her coffee, in fact had seemed not to know what the substance was. "Yours. Should still be hot enough."

My young companion sipped studiously, smacking his lips together. Ninepin, along with his profound love of boxing, cockfights, and theatrical productions, the last of which he generally stars in himself at the newsboys' theater company, owns a particular affinity for coffee.

"How's the newspaper business?" I asked.

"Plump. How's the prigger-napper lay?"

"Policing took a fresh turn for the unpleasant this morning."

"Only thing as we can count on certainwise in this life is trouble and then more of it, Mr. Wilde."

"Too right you are." I hazarded a philosophical query. "What do you think of the female-rights movement, Ninepin?"

His nose contracted in thought. "Personally or professionally?"

"Both."

Pulling his spectacles off in a manner I'd call foppish if I didn't know the boy thought street brawls one of the mellower leisure activities, Ninepin rubbed the spotless glass lenses on the drapery around his neck. This activity continued as he expounded, though he paused periodically to sip his coffee. It was artful pageantry. He might as well have been sitting behind a desk at New York University, wearing hose and a soft cloth professorial cap.

"Well, Mr. Wilde, I can't say as all my feelings are of the same color on the problem. Chink is scarce. So supposing the molls had their shake at the same grafts—what, we want half the jobs in this stait to dry up when there ain't enough now? And anyway, who's left to fry the bacon of a morning, supposing you do end up autumned, with the wife and the three squealing pap laps and all? I can't picture it, and I'd not court a lady dockworker either. I like 'em soft and I like 'em sweet."

Doubtless by the advanced age of fifteen, he'd begun his collection of amatory experiences. But I refrained from picturing Ninepin, who now whisked at the spectacles with the tasseled end of his makeshift cravat as if it were a feather duster, courting anyone at all. Fearing that my resulting expression would strain the cordial relations between us.

"But then there's this wild little rabbit as used to hawk papers with Zeke the Rat's gang," he reflected. "Pumpkin, he went by, on account of his hair. And *was* he ever a pumpkin. Could sell stiffs faster than fresh doughnuts, and I once saw him in a mill with Seven-Fingered Sam, and Pumpkin floored him with a rib-bender after eighteen rounds. Then one day Zeke found out the truth. He never leaked how, though I'm betting it was weaselish—you savvy Zeke the Rat is a waste of a good body with a rotten pate tacked on top."

I nodded. Knowing this for fact.

"But Pumpkin was a lunan. No, I swear, she was every bit of her a girl! You could have kept cozy all January standing next to Zeke, he was that hot about it. Chucked her out, left her to begging outside Barnum's American Museum. But then Pumpkin took up with Cottonhead Mike's gang in Ward Three after she bet Mike he couldn't hold as much whiskey as she could without taking a piss and he ruined a new set of trousers. She still runs with that crew. And here's what I want you to tell me, Mr. Wilde . . ."

He leaned right up against the tabletop, poking me twice in the chest. *"Why. Not."*

Smiling, I shook my head. "I couldn't tell you."

"Thought not. Don't want to class ourselves with the likes of Zeke the Rat, now, do we?"

"May death come sooner."

"You're an optime number-one cove, Mr. Wilde—best of the copper philistines, and that's gospel. Now, what do you want me for?"

"Did you hear about the fire in Pell Street?"

"Hadn't finished selling my stiffs till half a bloody hour ago— what with the Hunkers and Barnburners fixed to polt each other in the muns, you'd think they could scratch out a decent headline. Give me the chant."

I explained to my young mate the lay of the land.

Ninepin whistled through his front teeth. "An incendiary? Say it ain't so, Mr. Wilde."

"It's true. I need to know if you lot hear of anything queer to do with Symmes, his buildings, that fire, who might have started it. And if you discover any reporters are investigating the matter, hike straight for the Tombs and find me, all right?"

The lad tapped his fingers against the table. "There's a reporter at the *New Republican* as wrote a rum piece on Symmes and his needle molls last year. I sold out of the lot in an hour. Bugger if I know what it said, not being the reading sort myself and all, but they told me the headline was 'Rights for Females, Sewing Girls a Busted Flush.'"

"Who wrote it?"

"Goes by the moniker of William Wolf. We just call him the Wolf, on account he's that canny—we're in gravy every time he prints. That, and we're pretty sure he's an Indian."

I let this intriguing detail go unexamined. "Tell him something's afoot for me."

"What's in it for Ninepin?"

As if floating above the table, I heard myself saying, "A dollar. And I'll bring Mercy Underhill around for buttercakes if you find anything."

A small spray of coffee emerged from the newsboy, garnishing the remaining two biscuits. That was fine, as they'd gone cold and thus resembled our daintier paving stones. I don't suppose I've ever flummoxed Ninepin so thorough. The kinchin is a genuine insider. But when you adore Mercy Underhill and she's suddenly returned from abroad . . . well, I wasn't in any difficulties imagining how the lad felt. Suggesting the rendezvous had set my heart sparking like a Fourth of July firecracker.

"Bleeding Mary on a donkey, she's *back*?" Ninepin slouched into a dazed posture. "Miss Underhill. *Here*. In New York City. It's like the whole island's back to rights, isn't it, Mr. Wilde?"

I counted out dimes from my waistcoat pocket. "That's *precisely* what it's like. Do we have a deal?"

"What kind of hicksam do you take me for? Of course we have a deal. Funny coincidence, though."

Lifting my hat, I paused. "What coincidence?"

"Oh, we've been jawing over Alderman Symmes all day, me and Matchbox and Fang and Tommy Two-Fist and Dead-Eye, on account of tonight. As many of us as can be there will be, bet your bollocks on that."

"At the Knickerbocker Twenty-one benefit? Why?"

"Bob 'Bonecrusher' Symmes hasn't fought in the ring these five years, has he, not since he was elected. Bulliest notion he ever hatched, staging a fight for Party lucre. You lot will be raising the wind something spectacular—I've got a ripe sum of chink on the match myself. Would have figured you'd have a stake it in too, considering."

"Considering what?"

"Considering the odds are dead even since Thundering Tom

dropped out this morning and they announced his replacement. Been a booker's nightmare, you can imagine."

"Can I?" I asked. This time with some asperity.

Ninepin studied me as a man of the world will regard a pitiable hayseed who has missed items of weighty public significance. "Christ Almighty. You might not follow boxing, but Valentine Wilde *is* your older brother, ain't he?"

8

BEFORE QUITTING BUTTERCAKE JOE'S, I was informed that Thundering Tom, pugilist and breeder of thoroughbreds, had suffered an accident when the pleasure trap he'd been racing up Third Avenue encountered a truck transporting two hundred live chickens. While Thundering Tom was thrown from his seat and his arm broken in three places, the horses, chickens, and farmer were thankfully unharmed. Valentine had volunteered that morning to take Thundering Tom's place.

I wanted a strong word with my brother. And to harm him in painful yet nonpermanently damaging fashions.

But assuming Val was readying himself for a boxing match, not to mention a Party function, he could have been in any of a dozen places. So instead of shaking him until his vision blurred enough he could see sense, after finishing my reports at the Tombs, I stopped at the Catholic Orphan Asylum to collect my companion for the evening.

The orphanage is on the corner of Prince and Mott in Ward Fourteen. The Sisters of Charity run the place, which goes more formally by the Roman Catholic Benevolent Society. But some of the priests, like my kindly and astute friend Father Sheehy, teach courses there as well. I sat on a bench outside its sturdy grey walls, awaiting Bird Daly. Twilight leaked slowly over the dwindling clatter of carriage wheels; distant gas jets flared to life as the Bowery lurched awake two blocks to the east.

In the mullioned windows above me, shadows danced like moths flirting with candle glow. Scores of shadows, an energetic blur of vague shapes, hurrying to evening mass and scuffling forward for portions of parsnip soup and soda bread. The building is so crammed with parentless kinchin it practically hums, so Archbishop Hughes wheedled permission two years back to build a mammoth new facility, between Fifty-first and Fifty-second Streets along Fifth Avenue. An amusingly backhanded concession from the Common Council, to my way of thinking. They get the Catholic orphans out of Manhattan—out of earshot, out of sight, and out of mind—and all they've lost is a useless patch of schist and brambles. Fifth Avenue isn't even paved that far north.

Five minutes later Bird skipped out the main entrance, dark red hair flowing and a pair of tiny braids making a circlet around her head, tying a cloak over her shoulders. The orphans' togs are secondhand, so their attire is at best eccentric. But this was a cloak made for a short woman draped over a tall thirteen-year-old, done in pale lilac with a hooded cowl. It made her seem a spirit from her ancestral home, come to shower leprechaun gold and mischief in equally lush quantities.

"Mr. Wilde!" she called, grinning.

I'd not seen her in two weeks, so I caught her one-armed round the waist and spun her in a circle before offering her my elbow and setting off as if nothing had happened. She laughed, then subsided into the quiet we favor—a quiet like lazy lemon-hued Sunday mornings and balmy August firefly nights. We watched the passersby in Prince Street as we traveled westward, knowing things about them—I because I'd taught myself to pay attention, she because she'd been *forced* to teach herself to pay attention. We spied dandies in factory trousers on the brink of financial ruin hastening to further ruin on the Bowery, respectable clerks with the dragonfly sheen of laudanum on their brows rushing home with their briefcases and secrets.

"How's school?"

"Better than my room anyhow." Bird had grown like a dandelion that past winter. Her square face was squarer, grey eyes deeper set and cleverer, mahogany hair reaching her waist, her limbs elongated, and her gait easier than I'd ever seen it before. In short, she was at any second about to be monumentally arresting. It comprehensively terrified me. "It's like a cranky-hutch in there," she muttered, using flash for *madhouse*. "There were already six of us. I'm meant to kip with another girl *in my bed* now."

"Really?"

"It's all bob, but it's awfully tiresome. I mean, she hasn't anywhere else to go or she wouldn't be there. I don't grudge her the space, Mr. Wilde. But her feet are *cold*. And she naps my stockings whenever she hasn't any clean ones. And she thinks Liberia is the answer to the Negro problem. I don't know which end she's talking from half the time."

A smile tugged my lips at the implied obscenity. Bird noticed, of course—she notices everything—and thereby robbed me of an opportunity to implore her not to be coarse. She's rapped on the knuckles for it at school and thoroughly indulges in flash patter whenever in my company. It seems to kittle her, though, so I can't object too strenuously. Besides that, I've started to notice her talking abolition and female rights and (Christ have mercy) politics. I'd be a turnip not to mark that she tends toward my views a touch. And simultaneously be delighted and horrified over it.

"Duck into the kitchens and borrow some hot pepper powder. A little at the fingertip ends of gloves does wonders."

"Mr. Wilde!" she exclaimed, gently slapping my arm.

I inclined my head to her ear. "Listen quick, now. It's flash of Father Sheehy to let you come to the benefit, seeing as you and Val and I are mates, and I'd never miss a chance to see you."

"But . . . ?" Bird asked, glancing quickly up at me.

It was still *up at me.* For now. I wondered what I would do when I was staring her right in the face and then wrenched myself back on topic. We'd been a mere three blocks from the Knicker-bocker 21 at the orphanage, and now I could see it down Mercer Street, its great doors thrown wide like the mouth of a volcanic cave. The engine itself had been polished to a high gleam and moved outside. It looked like a vision of a mechanical future, a weird and glorious contraption. The thing was crawling with tattered kinchin while two of Val's firedogs looked on, calling friendly gibes and drinking from hip flasks, occasionally swatting an urchin away from a sensitive mechanism.

"There's nothing to fear, all right? These are all dyed-in-the-wool Party rabbits who know where their bread is buttered. But apparently my brother is boxing with the alderman. And my brother is . . . not on good terms with said alderman."

Bird examined me worriedly. "You think there's to be a dustup even beyond the match? I heard Billy tell Liam the odds are dead square since Mr. V threw his hat in the ring, and even if it were weighted toward Bob the Bonecrusher, I'd still—"

"You savvy more than I did this afternoon," I complained. "How?"

"Billy heard it from the boys who rake the grounds, who heard it from a news hawker, who—"

"Right, bully. What's our lay to be, then?"

She lifted her face, the brightening glow tracing fine hairs at her temples. "Keep close and keep leery. Any way it ends, if we listen keen enough as we walk about, we can be whiddlers for Mr. V when it's through."

"Aces. It's a plan."

As we entered the Knickerbocker 21, Bird's liberally freckle-dotted china complexion flushed pink with pleasure.

"Oh!" she exclaimed, pausing in the door.

They'd done a princely job turning an engine house into a dance hall. They always do, and it always awes me. Silk ribbons in red, white, and blue swooped from the half floor high above our heads, where the firedogs bunk. Democratic posters screamed from every wall not hung with leather helmets and hoses and polished brass nozzles, assuring attendees they supported GOD'S AVENGING RIGHT HAND FOR THE FREE CITIZENS OF NEW YORK and THE TRUE PARTY OF THE PEOPLE. Every corner of the room save that reserved for a small orchestra was crawling with dead rabbits, Bowery girls, firedogs, Irish, Germans, natives, convicts, news hawkers, leeches, panderers, and stargazers, the stargazers wearing marginally more clothing than was typical. All drinking knock-me-down from giant crystal punch bowls. Every so often a sparkling tumbler would drop. But they'd carpeted the cavernous place in a noxious cacophony of Turkey rugs, which diminished glassware casualties nicely.

"It's beautiful," Bird whispered.

"It's something akin," I amended.

The center of the room boasted a raised, square, roped-in

area—presently employed for dancing, a rainbow array of skirts swirling and spotless black boots gleaming in jig time. As for its later use, I didn't want to cogitate over that yet.

"Where's Mrs. Boehm?" Bird wanted to know.

"She was meant to be here, but she sent me a note at the Tombs to say she couldn't make it."

"Damn and blast."

"No swearing." I willed myself not to smirk. Unsuccessfully. "Flash is fine, but no swearing."

"Anything else?" she questioned, rolling grey eyes to the gaudily beribboned ceiling.

"Leave my sight for so much as five seconds and I'll get plenty anxious over it."

"Don't worry, I won't," she promised, face softening.

"Mr. Wilde!" exclaimed a familiar voice. "Best out-and-outer your kin's produced yet! Introduce me to the dimber-mort on your arm, if you please?"

Ninepin sauntered up with a pair of half-full punch glasses. He passed one to Bird, bowing nearly to the floor. He'd made the addition of a gold-painted temperance-pledge pin to hold his cravat in place. It was aesthetic if not sincere.

"Oh, for God's sake," I sighed.

Bird cast a pleading look toward my mazzard.

"One cup," I answered. "One only. Do you hear me, Ninepin?"

"Like trumpets, Mr. Wilde."

"Ninepin, may I introduce Miss Bird Daly."

She smiled, curtsying. Then she took a sip of the lush and suppressed a cough.

"Might I take your cloak, Miss Daly, and introduce you to a few of my sundry associates?" Ninepin inquired.

I studied Bird for signs of reluctance. Not wanting to fret her if she was disquieted. Ever. Nor smother her if she was keen. Ever.

She stared up at me, the prettiest silvery question marks flitting across her irises.

"Have a good time," I said.

She started off, grinning from ear to dainty ear. I seized Ninepin by the elbow as he turned to follow. Hard enough to mean it.

"Behave like a spotless gentleman or I will tell Zeke the Rat who chalked the drawing of him and the donkey in a romantic interlude on the side of the *Herald* offices."

"That's as much as my life's worth, Mr. Wilde," the kinchin whispered, aghast.

"Think about it."

The orchestra crescendoed to a mighty flourish and ended the jig, prompting a savage roar of laughter and curses. It took me only half a minute to discover my brother's whereabouts during the break, for he's distressingly large. He'd seated himself next to the pianist on the polished oak bench, facing away from the instrument as the musician idly ran his fingers over the treble clef. Laughing with his tawny head thrown back and his face in its familiar glad grimace. He didn't seem any too amused, though. It looked like a laugh to stanch a hemorrhaging gap in sound.

"What in the name of Holy Christ were you thinking?" I greeted Val. "Hello, Jim, how are you?"

James Playfair, or Gentle Jim as my brother often calls him, delivered me a fleeting but warm smile. He's a slim, chiseled, impeccably handsome fellow of London extraction, with arches everywhere a face can produce them, black hair, and deeply blue eyes. Deeper even than Mercy's, though it shames me to say so, eyes just about as blue as his blood. He wore a subtly cut swallowtail coat, every muted sartorial detail contrasting with Val's aggressively turned-down shirt collar and ludicrous rose-patterned waistcoat. To my eye—and after arduous practice I can read Jim pretty fairly—he'd something on his lips he was busy not-saying. Of a quarrelsome nature. Jim has every reason to quarrel with Valentine, since they've been sleeping together for three years. But I suspected this was a specific complaint, not *You are a profligate miscreant.*

"Timothy, what an unparalleled pleasure," Jim drawled. Then I knew him for peppery. Jim is as arch as he is clever, but he doesn't often play the visiting earl for my health—I know him to be banished from his homeland for his bedroom habits, so it wouldn't be fooling anyone. "As to your first question—'What in the name of Holy Christ was Valentine thinking?'—I have not been able to determine the answer to my personal satisfaction and thus cannot advise you."

"Ah," I answered.

"As to the second, I am at the peak of good spirits and *thrilled* to be present for this occasion. A *boxing* match. Next we ought to chain a bear to the back wall and set the mastiffs on it. Oh, wait, that distinctive pleasure can be had a quarter of a mile east of here, so carry on with the pugilism."

Valentine scowled. "Timothy, he's been like this all night. You tell him."

I nearly laughed. It was a close thing. "Tell him what?"

"That I'm as prime on the muscle as any professional milling cove."

"Do speak English, my dear man. My regrettably limited vocabulary can scarce follow you," Jim suggested in a voice narrow enough to turn coal into jewelry.

My brother, I thought, was in for a bad night of it. "Val wants me to tell you he's as good a boxer as any."

"Which is why his odds are precisely even against a man who enjoys the sobriquet *Bonecrusher.*"

"For God's sake, Jimmy, this is sport, not assault. Besides, how many back-alley squalls have you seen me walk away from?" Val pushed his fingers through his hair in considerable annoyance.

"Apologies, I was not aware that liquor-fueled daybreak tussles with men who either admire you, are afraid of you, or are your physical inferiors were quite on a par with a public match *against our alderman.* I shall subside at once."

"I wish to Christ you would," Val snapped.

James Playfair ceased softly teasing at the piano, turning his body toward Val with a smile that could have kept butter solid through July. "Do you mean to win, in that case? Or do you mean to adhere to Tammany's wishes, and later I can congratulate you upon *throwing the match?*"

Valentine's jaw spasmed, rage mingled with offended honor pressing his mouth into a line like a crowbar. Then his active green eyes lit upon something behind me. He stood, pulling the ridiculous waistcoat down neatly.

"If you were anyone else, I'd fight you for that," he said to Jim clearly. "It's a dirty thing to ask a cove all the same, and if you meant it, I can't imagine why you'd tolerate my company."

My brother departed. Leaving behind him two deeply dissatisfied individuals.

"God, Timothy, please kill me and thereby spare me future trials," Jim moaned, collapsing against the music-stand portion of the grand piano. He didn't need it for any other purpose, certainly not for sight-reading. Every ditty I've ever heard Jim play lives in his capacious head.

"I take it he didn't consult you over this plan?"

"It's a *plan?* No. And you?"

"Ditto."

"Good heavens, what are we coming to?"

My lips tilted up in sympathy. Some might suppose I'd be sore at the chap who spends the lion's share of his days—pardon, nights—indulging in alarming sexual practices with my only sibling. However, Jim is an honorable, artistic, quick-witted individual, and my brother is a narcotics fiend for whom "scruples" apply only to rules such as keeping fish alive until seconds before frying them or never adding unheated milk to coffee. Apart from culinary practices, my brother is inexcusable and James Playfair is . . . James Playfair is a molley.

It occurred to me, like turning a page to reveal an illustration, that Val's steadiness of late—the livid sacks under his eye sockets shrinking and his new tendency to end up with his boots off when he loses consciousness—might be Jim's influence. The theory was worth examining further.

Then I saw who Valentine had targeted across the room, and icy claws bit into my spine.

"Oh, *bugger*," I breathed.

Robert Symmes had entered the ballroom-cum-firehouse, top hat in hand and pale hair neatly oiled back, moustache waxed to a merry flourish, laughing like a new-elected senator.

"Have you any idea how dangerous that man is?"

I glanced at Jim, who was chewing his lip in consternation. And yes, I did. I remembered being tied to a chair in a library in Tammany Hall, after having been given the twin gifts of chloroform and a concussion, and Symmes's reaction when his fellow Party officials suggested relieving themselves of my pesky convictions.

One of us should get rid of him the quick way, the powerful man— the reasonable if implacable one, the one I'd called Scarred Nose— had said.

I'll take care of him, Symmes had answered. As if murder were on a par with a trip to the Patent Steam Ice-Cream Saloon in Chatham Square. Jim had no need of reminding me what Symmes and his cronies were capable of; the alderman's lackeys had slit his throat because he objected to their kidnapping me. I'm not very likely to forget that occasion. He has a picaroon-worthy white streak of dead tissue slicing along his body from left shoulder blade to opposite collarbone. I've had nightmares about it. Repeatedly. It generally snakes itself into a thin ivory cord and strangles him to death.

"The only person I can think of with fewer virtues is Silkie Marsh, and that's only because I know her better," I admitted.

Worriment etched a line above Jim's patrician nose. "You don't want to know him better. Symmes is a degenerate. A preposterous assessment coming from the likes of me, I realize, but—"

"Sons and daughters of liberty, welcome to the Knickerbocker Twenty-one!" bellowed the voice that I imagine insults me whenever I've done something dense. "Thank you for being here—on my behalf, on that of my engine house, and on behalf of Tammany Hall!"

We shifted to view the dance floor, where my brother now stood with his mast-thick arms spread wide. His high brow was beading with sweat, his posture a mix of *Welcome to our shores and to our very bosoms* on behalf of the Irish and *I can lace a man down to ruby ribbons* for the Party thugs. Not that Val needed to win over his own station house—every firedog there would have walked in front of a cannon at my brother's lightest suggestion.

"You all imagine we're here to raise some cole for the Party that's given us so much in return for our mere support—our jobs, our kens, our comrades, even our dignity," Valentine called out to the captivated assembly. "You suppose we're after a bit of your chink—as well as your votes a fortnight from now, when the Whigs will remember the meaning of the word *trouncing*." He flashed the gleaming shark's-tooth smirk that makes sane men follow him into burning buildings and women drop their frocks to the hardwood. "Well, I *would* like your votes, sure as gravity, and donations boxes are set up in all four corners of the firehouse."

Laughter eddied across the room in a gleeful ripple as the scoundrels tugged their wasp-waisted sweethearts to their sides.

My attention was on Symmes, listening with his hands in his pockets—smug, impatient, inscrutable.

Underneath the rest, furious.

"But there's another reason you've been gathered here," Valentine continued, accepting a tumbler of punch from a stunning fair-haired Bowery girl with breasts I was concerned might pitch out of her candy-pink gown onto the carpeting. He bent to kiss her hand, prompting a profusion of wolf whistles. "As you know, in February the Barnburners picked a pack of stout coves to send to the Democratic Convention. And as you know, there's those who are fixing to fill Texas with slave plantations."

Hisses erupted. I couldn't tell whether the sound was produced by the revelers or the viper that was suddenly coiling round my stomach.

"I want you all to think on the state of this country," Valentine boomed, eyes tracking slowly across the assembly. "About Albany, and the Capitol, and the way the North has been showing its tender white belly to the tyrant South every time they flap their tear-soaked kerchiefs and kick up a fuss. 'Our slaves have escaped—find them for us and ship them back,' they tell us. And we fold. 'Abolitionists keep mailing us tracts that prick our tender feelings—police the post office for us,' they demand. And we fold. 'We've made a shit-arsed mess, and there are too many slaves now, and we're afeared of them—give us more land so's we can spread them around,' they suggest. And we fold."

A slim hand gripped my forearm. Jim, now cotton-white and breathless. "This isn't happening. At any moment this will cease hap—"

My gaze flashed to Symmes, and my liver gave a weak flip of dismay. He'd unbuttoned his frock coat and stood with his hands in fists upon his torso. The surface of his face, the polish on the cauldron, openly jeered at my brother. The interior bubbled over with Hunker rage.

"Well, when I look out over this crowd, do you want to know what I see?" Valentine cried. "I see a pack of honest working coves—working molls too, by God—taxpayers who take their lumps along with their wages and would *die rather than show the white feather.*" Unabashed applause erupted. "I see steel-spined Party loyalists sick enough to hash their guts out over being told, *We're too occupied shaking hands with slaveholders to hoist you out of the mud when you fall.*" Louder cheers and the stomping of boots. "I see a brotherhood of patriots who would take up their rifles rather than surrender to a tribe of fat parasites who derail our Northern government, shit on our proposals, offend our good graces, and think hard work doesn't merit decent wages—*or any wages at all!*"

The atmosphere, stifling and roaring as a breaking June thunderstorm, registered its approval. Jim had a vise grip on my arm by then.

"Don't," he said tightly, and not to me. "Don't, please, stop—"

"And that is why," Valentine concluded, "I hereby announce my candidacy on the Barnburner platform to humbly serve my betters as the alderman of our very own Ward Eight!"

Blithe shrieks erupted from the women, shouts of approval from the granite-eyed men. Jim released my arm with a horrified slump against the piano while I shoved my knuckles against the cracked fault line of my scar.

This, I told myself unhelpfully, *is a very unfortunate development.*

As the cacophony increased, my brother delicately removed his frock coat and passed it from the raised dais down to the wonderfully plump blonde creature in the pink dress. He next proceeded methodically to remove cravat, collar, waistcoat, shirt, and undershirt, as most of the attendees hooted in wholesale enthusiasm. By the time my brother was bare from the waist up and walking in the soundless steps of a tiger with meat on its mind toward the other edge of the platform, Alderman Symmes had turned faintly magenta.

"Thanks for coming. I'm throwing down the glove, Symmes," Val declared. "What say you?"

Robert Symmes smiled—an incensed baring of teeth beneath a bristling moustache. But he made no move to join Val. He pulled out his pocket watch and studied it as if it were an oracle.

"As your present and future alderman," he called out, "I cannot endorse a farcical bout that would only serve to confuse my ward."

"They don't look any too queered to me." Valentine made a fist of his right hand and idly examined it.

The laughter grew, if anything, bolder. Symmes made a bow toward the small, quivering herd of Hunker loyalists. "I beg your pardon for departing in haste, but this proposed match is a direct affront to Tammany! To legitimize it by complying would—"

"I'll *be* Tammany in two weeks' time, you sorry son of a bitch," Valentine snarled with both hands on the rope guard.

The room exploded into a caterwauling bedlam of sound. It occurred to me that Symmes, with his lofty wealth and low wages and priggish disinterest, was something less than popular. He won his ward perennially because of the man ridiculing him. Fleshy male fists clenched. Women booed openly. Pithy insinuations were made as to the nature of Symmes's character, the marital status of his parents, and whether his genitalia were entirely intact.

Symmes stood there, quite still. Maroon face swiftly paling. It was a stillness like a cocked pistol on a table.

"What's it to be?" my brother demanded. "Do you think you have the stuffing to serve me out?"

"You want a war, Valentine?" Symmes growled. "A war's what you've earned yourself. May you enjoy it as much as I will."

He turned on his heel and departed. Maybe a dozen guests followed him. The rest of the firehouse screamed ovations in a congratulatory display I'd never dreamed possible. Not barring the return of George Washington from the grave, that is to say. Valentine threw his shirtsleeves back over his muscled shoulders but went no further, in fact failed to even button the garment, swinging down into the welcoming embrace of his fire gang, sweeping the blonde with the pink gown into a low dip and kissing her. To the vocal approval of all who bore witness.

Save for two.

"Fuck," I said. Meaning it.

"There are no words." Jim actually sounded frightened. "But that one approaches the point better than any I can think of."

Troubled beyond my capacity to describe it, I made for Bird Daly. She was in a cul-de-sac where the newsboys hovered like summer gnats around a punch bowl. Bird watched the proceedings with eyes like pewter platters, dividing her attention between my kinfolk's sobering follies and being doted upon. Ninepin held her lavender cloak as if he'd been asked to help lift the train of a queen crossing a swampish roadway. It endeared him to me.

And then again, it didn't.

"Ninepin," I said, "if you've given her more punch, I'm—"

I stopped. Having glanced toward where my brother's back was being heartily slapped by his allies.

And there—gazing upon the triumphant revelry in the mouth of the wide engine-house door—was Madam Silkie Marsh.

9

Shall we yield? NEVER. God forbid! Are we so tame, so servile, so degenerate, that we cannot maintain the rights of a free soil, and a free people? Where is the spirit of our fathers? Are we slaves, that knowing our rights, we dare not maintain them?

—DAVID WILMOT, BARNBURNER, 1847

I DIDN'T THINK when I saw Madam Marsh. Her lips fragile as peach blossoms. Her flawless frame in its black silk dress with the beaded wrap over her shoulders. Her pale champagne-spray corona of hair. Her expression, which tends to read like a polite invitation to stick my neck under an ax. Considering the company I was keeping, I didn't think when I spied Silkie Marsh at all.

I moved.

My arm was around Bird's shoulders before a single second had etched its mark, and I swept her cloak out of Ninepin's arm.

"Mr. Wilde," he protested, "I were—"

"Ware hawk," I mouthed back at him.

Ninepin turned to the doorway at my warning, and a stifled gasp sounded—him knowing Silkie Marsh by sight, as I've made sure he does. Madam Marsh doesn't hire kinchin as mabs any longer, no more than she still sells their hushed corpses to anatomists or enjoys being Valentine's mistress, all of which deeply needle the woman. Child whores were a lucrative business for her. Both alive and dead. And to the desiccated extent she can love anything, she's in love with my brother. But better safe than deceased when it comes to Selina Ann Marsh. I couldn't fathom what had possessed her to enter Val's station house. Silkie Marsh has her hands in up to her shoulders where graft, cronyism, and Party politics are concerned, granted. But she isn't stupid. And showing her angelic face at Val's unofficial headquarters seemed sure enough witless to me.

"Mr. Wilde!" Bird exclaimed as I bustled her across the crowded room. "What the devil—"

"It's been a brief evening, and Lord knows I'm sorry for it. But Alderman Symmes is a menace, and my brother might be objectively insane."

"Mr. *V*?" she protested, nettled. "Mr. V is twice the man of anyone in this room saving yourself, Mr. Wilde. That lily-liver was *afeared* of him and ran like a spooked hare—"

I dropped to one knee behind a small knot of roisterers and took Bird's face lightly in both hands. She peered back, startled.

"Do you trust me?"

Hot anger flashed over her freckled skin. "How could you ask me—"

"Pax, please," I said. "But you're leaving. Now."

Fuming, she allowed herself to be towed in my wake. I strode arrow-direct for the piano, that object now standing forbiddingly silent. And for the pianist, his cutting blue eyes scraping furrows down my brother's back even as Jim finished a monumental tumbler of knock-me-down.

"Bird, you remember Valentine's friend Mr. Playfair. James, you know Bird."

Jim wrenched his attention off my brother. When he did recognize Bird, he rallied admirably, making an efficient bow.

"Miss Daly, what an unexpected pleasure. Are the gentlemen behaving to your satisfaction?"

"They're bully, Mr. Playfair. Ready with the rum punch, and . . ." She smirked at me when my ears flattened against my skull. "And I said no. The first drink was pretty flash, but I didn't much like the taste of it."

"No lady possessed of a civilized tongue could possibly enjoy the taste of knock-me-down," Jim said smoothly.

"Take Bird back to the Catholic Asylum. I'll owe you worlds over," I requested softly.

"No, *don't* take me back," Bird protested.

Jim's lips twitched in stifled displeasure. "I hadn't actually planned to—"

"Jim," I said, pulling him aside as I palmed him a dollar, "please take her out the back exit, and *now*. Go to a late-night concert, an ice-creamery, a bowling hall, so long as she ends up at the orphanage. I'd not ask unless—"

"Timothy," Jim interrupted, returning the money with a resigned nod, "say no more."

He approached Bird. Far more gracefully than anyone she'd encountered that night. When she took Jim's hand, he leaned down and murmured, "I don't believe these fellows are paying sufficient attention to us. Do you?"

Bird tossed me a smoldering glance and shrugged.

"Let us no longer force our society upon those who fail to appreciate our charms. Have you ever bet upon a dog race, Miss Daly?"

"Never!" she gasped, square face brightening.

"Never? How shocking. We must lose no time in remedying this regrettable oversight in your cultural education. Good night, Timothy," he added, before setting off at a pleasingly brisk pace toward the rear alley exit.

Breathing again, I made a slow turn. Coral and jade and daffo-
dil frocks danced across my vision, near blinding me. But no onyx
gowns with the hard glimmer of polished jet slung across white
shoulders, no stony hazel eyes with a queer circle of blue in their
centers floating above a slender neck. I imagined she'd been and
gone already.

That was before the rich scent of violets met my nostrils and a
warm hand touched my elbow, and I spun to face her.

"Mr. Wilde." Silkie Marsh looked me up and down as if hailing an old acquaintance returned from abroad. Curious, enthusiastic.
"I gather that Valentine has just taken rather extraordinary political
measures against Alderman Symmes."

"You could call them extraordinary. You could use several other
words."

"Valiant?" she suggested, dimpling. "Audacious?"

"Madam Marsh, what in hell are you doing here?"

She pressed her rosy lips together in a striking combination of
smile and pout. Lacking natural human expressions, she feels free
to invent new ones, and the results are occasionally spectacular.
"Mr. Wilde, simply because the two of us embarked on the wrong
foot years ago, must you be so *very* uncivil? Mustering such outrage
whenever you see me must be quite exhausting to your constitution."

"Not really, no. Not when you hushed your own stargazers,
sent free blacks to live as slaves, tried to see my brother hanged,
tried to have me deported, told Tammany that I was running an
illicit—"

"You hold such grudges." She sighed, adjusting the sparkling
wrap. "It isn't precisely Christian of you, nor does it look well on an
officer of the law."

I waited. Not eager to waste more air on the woman who has
sworn to ruin me before dispatching me like a prize turkey. And
almost managed it on multiple occasions.

She slowly passed her tongue over her lower lip. "Have it your own way. I shall be brief, Mr. Wilde."

"Too late for that. What do you *want*?"

"You," she said calmly. "If you'll escort me back to my establishment at Greene Street, we can have a discussion. Can your Valentine spare you for as much as ten minutes, Mr. Wilde?"

It wouldn't take ten minutes to reach her gorgeously appointed brothel, which was on Greene Street a mere three blocks south of the Knickerbocker 21. It would take two. But she was right—Valentine had no need of me. He lounged on the staircase, the buxom moll perched on his lap, declaiming with his shirt open as his lackeys treated him like a gilded demigod. They ought to have brought grapes and palm fronds for the occasion. The pink-clad girl seemed an amiable sort, for all I'd ever see of her again. I don't think Val has ever bedded anyone twice, save for Silkie Marsh and James Playfair—the former because he didn't understand her and the latter, I think, because he does.

Meanwhile, I was achingly curious. Silkie Marsh is a chess player in a world of dice burners, and she owns fewer sentiments about shifting human pieces than a master strategist would in lifting a brass pawn.

"After you," I said, gesturing.

Madam Marsh swept away. I followed. A few heads turned, curious—any donor with her level of chink would be infamous, even if she hadn't seduced half of the Democratic Party's insiders. Seconds later we'd passed the fire engine, still crawling with emigrant kids as the volunteer engine men looked impassively on. We turned south under a moonless sky—blank as a slate and strangely expectant. Ward Eight is one of the best in the city. It's mostly sedate residences of brownstone, hedges and trees, quiet brick chophouses. And a line of discreet brothels in Greene Street, amber windows aglow and violet curtains drawn nearly to, where women ply the only profession open to them not requiring a sixteen-hour workday.

"It comes as no shock to me that Val rebelled against Robert's leadership, for lack of a more apt term," Madam Marsh began. "Robert's . . . presence? He is hardly a commander of men."

I wasn't surprised that she knew her own alderman intimately, nor that she'd mapped out the battleground between Symmes and the object of what passes for her affection. "Tammany won't be best pleased."

"Perhaps not. But between us, though I know there is neither trust nor regard lost in that chasm, Robert is not a good alderman," she reflected, the sullen glower of a gas lamp outlining the picturesque waves of her pinned-up hair.

"Is this about Valentine running for office, then?"

"In a sense. Your brother is a remarkable man, and one whom I have been proud to call my friend, even if a former friend. I passed some of the best months of my life in his company." She dipped her chin, as if girlish humiliation cowed her.

"I'm not in a box seat at the Astor Place Opera House. Spill."

Madam Marsh raised her head, annoyed. "You really are the most obnoxious creature ever to sully an otherwise charming family, you know. Robert Symmes is my landlord."

My stride actually broke rhythm. Which kittled Silkie Marsh enough to provoke a pretty, trilling laugh like a cut-glass perfume bottle filled with vitriol.

"Now do you see the landscape plainly, Mr. Wilde, or shall I draw a better map for you?"

"No," I said, understanding. "You've all ten fingers in the Party's pies. So in the midst of this Hunker-Barnburner feud, it's all you can do to back the right ponies. Symmes owns your ken, and thus your livelihood is in his pocket. Meanwhile, everyone knows you're really in Val's corner, at least when you're not framing him for murder or trying to kill him yourself. Have I got it down fine?"

"Regarding about half the story, yes, you show an admirably apt comprehension of my unique difficulties."

"What else is there?"

"The fire in Pell Street, for one. I know that Robert was the victim of a threat naming his properties as targets, and that said threat has unfortunately come to pass. My residence thereafter lost a significant percentage of its comfort."

My thoughts darted hither and thither like mice. "Know anything else? Who Symmes might have hurt, who wants him hurt in return?"

Madam Marsh shook her head, the blue circles within her hazel irises glinting like ice shards. "Robert is a man who takes what he wants simply because others prefer *not* to give it to him. I cannot begin to imagine the enemies he has engendered. Though up until now he has been wealthy enough and powerful enough to erase the trail of his trespasses."

"Plenty of these reprobates hide dirty deeds under American flags."

A corner of her mouth curved ironically. "Do you know, I readily admit that you are a man who can string words together, Mr. Wilde. Though it is likely the only quality you possess other than a profound knack for barging in where you are unwanted."

"Just why are you palavering with me, then?"

"Because I want you to barge in where you *are* wanted for once in your petty little life," she hissed, showing the bile beneath the elegance.

"You're trying to convince me to protect you," I realized.

"No, I *know* you'll protect me." She gestured at the brothel we were fast approaching, its sedate exterior belying the perverse events that had occurred within. "You won't *want* to protect me, as uncomfortable as that fact might be when placed alongside your tiresome notions of chivalry. But protect me you *will*, nevertheless."

"Whyso?"

"Because you'll be protecting fourteen other girls, Mr. Wilde, not counting me nor the servants, who make the total eighteen. And for one other reason."

"There's nothing in the world you're capable of bribing me with, Madam Marsh."

"No," she agreed, laughing softly. "Quite right you are. By the way, who was your companion of the evening? Comely young thing, very poised. Potentially an unparalleled breaker of hearts, if you ask me."

I didn't answer her. My tongue reposed behind my teeth, a useless lump of flesh.

Silkie Marsh pretended to ruminate, affected the hazy-eyed middle gaze of a woman reflecting on better times. "She resembled . . . a frail sister of mine. One who was unrepentantly stolen away from our establishment. Why, they could have been cousins, the likeness was so uncanny." Frowning, she adjusted the expensive jet wrap draped across her white shoulders. "I wonder whether she's in want of ready coin—the poor girl's clothing seemed *very* well worn."

Stopping cold in the roadway in response to Silkie Marsh's barely veiled threat at Bird Daly wouldn't have served me. Where Silkie Marsh is concerned, best to keep one's sentiments tight under the vest. As well as three or four jackets and a greatcoat for good measure. But I'd be lying if I said I didn't feel a hatchet lodge in my gullet at the merest mention of my small friend being used as a bargaining chip. I gripped Madam Marsh tight by the elbow, and she stopped in exaggerated startlement.

"Why, Mr. Wilde, whatever—"

"There aren't a lot of things I'd kill in cold blood over," I grated out. "That doesn't mean the number stands at nil."

Surprise shifted to amusement as we fell back into step. "And here I've been wondering all this time just what your hands on me would feel like, Mr. Wilde," she said in a low purr. "You're just as . . . forceful as I imagined."

Repelled beyond words, I dropped her arm. We had reached her doorstep. The two blond brick stories above, the basement below that frankly didn't bear meditating over for reasons I'd prefer not to delve into. Strains of fiddle music spilling from the door-jamb, punctuated with peals of feminine laughter, laughter produced by fallen girls who by no means deserved to perish in flames as some of the more righteous among us argue they do. For the first time, looking at the building that had spelled disaster for so many, I didn't know whose side I was on. That was terrifying. Like surviving a shipwreck only to find myself alone in a lifeboat. Albatrosses above, sharks below, adrift on a moonless sea. Madam Marsh drew a small silver key from her handbag.

"News of the fire in Pell Street could have come from plenty of channels, and you're nothing if not well informed," I reasoned, regaining control of myself. "But how did you learn of the written threats to Symmes's buildings?"

"From the alderman's property manager, of course," she answered, silhouetted by the faintly orange shine of the hearth in her parlor. "I deal with him regularly, although I admit he could not possibly have spilled for altruistic reasons, as the man is a brute beast—that scrap of gossip was more likely a slip of the tongue. He is prone to them, I daresay."

"Give me a name so I can question him?"

"Oh, his answers are never to anyone's liking." A toxin-laced lilt had corrupted her velvety voice. "But supposing you can locate him—and I'd suggest the Queen Mab bawdy house, though you may not appreciate the ambience, Lord knows I fail to see any redeeming qualities—please do ask Mr. Ronan McGlynn any questions your heart and mind desire," she concluded, shutting the door behind her.

I stared stupidly after Silkie Marsh, pulse racing like a trapped fox's. Then I set off at an equally high-strung pace for the Tombs.

Hailing a hack two blocks east on madcap, moonstruck Broadway would have taken more time than I had at my disposal. Anyway, I wanted the clarity that comes with long strides and deep breaths. So I marched down sparsely populated Greene through puddles of lamplight and gusts of spring air teasing at the furled leaves of the elm trees.

Can you trust a single word Silkie Marsh says? I asked myself. Considering the shocking possibility that one answer might be yes.

No, I concluded in three more steps.

Does it fuddle you much that the proprietor of the clearinghouse Val was invited to is also Symmes's property manager?

No, I thought grimly, recalling McGlynn's red-rimmed jackal's eyes.

Setting the question of Bird aside, as she'll not come into this, can you abandon not merely Madam Marsh's stargazers but all the many residents of buildings Symmes owns, to the mercy of a mad firestarter?

No.

Drastic, immediate action was required.

The Tombs was largely deserted, its new-washed stone steps empty of the dregs who had haunted its entrance during the day. Hurrying past the odd star policeman escorting a bloodied drunk, I located the key to my office in my waistcoat pocket.

Once at my desk, I wrote another terse, emphatic note to Chief George Washington Matsell, ending with the instruction that if he could manage the favor, he send a runner to alert me early the next morning regarding a time and a place for my desired rendezvous. After I'd sealed the letter with blue wax, it took me six minutes to traverse the echoing stone halls and tack it at eye level—Matsell's, not mine—to his door. That put the hour at half past eight in the evening, for I'd stayed only briefly at the Knickerbocker 21. I made a left turn when I'd regained the cavernous entrance hall like a giant's sepulcher, cutting across the yard under wisps of steely clouds. Then I trotted down a dank, mossy flight of steps into the men's wing of the jail cells.

A spotty blond star police sat before a partition of iron keys hanging from hooks. He'd a single wall-mounted lamp for company. But it hardly illuminated its own metal sconce, let alone the double row of cell blocks. He'd augmented the light with a squat bull's-eye lantern, its faint tinny scent near drowned in the underground reek of Ward Six's sewage runoff. Beyond, I heard snatches of an old drinking ballad meant to lead men through times of trouble.

The song had its work cut out for it.

"Evening, Mr. Wilde," said the guard.

"Evening."

I was growing gradually used to being recognized by then and had stopped berating myself over disremembering my associates. Not when it became obvious I'd never met the new yearly hires who'd heard tales of a bantam copper star with three-quarters of a face.

"Mind if I have a word with one of our boarders?"

"Not a bit. Did you really nab a picklock on account of his right shoe?" He spat a stream of brown into a tin pail at his feet.

"Yes, actually," I admitted sheepishly.

"How so?"

"He was left-handed, and when he knelt to crack the lock with the bess, his right foot would scrape the ground. He'd scratches all over the toe."

"God bless us, but you're keen on the sharp. Which prisoner?"

"Ronan McGlynn."

The guard winked happily. "Enjoy yourself. Need the key?"

"No," I said, puzzled.

"Just as well. Wouldn't stop sniveling the last time someone tuned him, and it's loud enough in here as is. *Shut your holes!*" he screamed, and all the noises save for those made by the uninvited creatures ceased of a sudden.

"We've been beating him? Who? When?"

"Day he arrived, twice. Then again this morning. No harm done, a few kicks, a knuckle or two in his mazzard. I thought they said you was the one arrested him—do you even need to ask who?"

"Apparently."

"It's Maguire, O'Brien, and Murphy so far. Word got out as McGlynn was in the forcing-Irish-virgins line of work. They wanted to pay their respects. So have plenty of other copper stars— the redheaded ones, if you follow me—who stopped by to say a few words and raise a middle finger."

"But the three you mention figured he needed punishing. And you gave them the key."

"Course I did. The sick coward. I made sure it was just a few lumps—a minute at most, I timed them with my watch. I've only been at this post six weeks. Is there a problem, Mr. Wilde?"

"I honestly don't know. Might I borrow your bull's-eye?"

Spitting again in agreement, he nodded at the lantern, and I caught up its handle, heading for the cell where we'd deposited the wretch. It was hardly uncommon practice for some of my colleagues to leave our prisoners' flesh mottled with their signatures. And God knows I've had to fight my way out of trouble with claws bared myself on plentiful occasions. Our work is dangerous even when it's dull. And the Tombs is nothing if not a bleak place, and a violent one.

Still. I'd not often heard of multiple visitors lacing the same stranger.

Hisses underscored my footsteps, whispered taunts to *come closer.* I knew the bars for sturdy, but I felt backside frontward—as if I were the caged tiger and they the spectators taunting me with sharp sticks. Slender rivulets of condensation trickled down the uneven corridor, sparking reflections like darting minnows in the stone. I reached McGlynn's seven-by-fifteen-foot chamber and cast my beam of light within.

A pair of baleful eyes above a now-bloodied white beard blinked malevolently at me. McGlynn's lip had been split, and I wondered whether he'd as many teeth today as he'd owned the day previous. His togs, so carefully arranged to make him seem a man of importance instead of a bloated species of leech, were crusted with the hellish concoction that makes its home on the underside of New York boots.

My Irish colleagues, apart from doing an adroit job of smashing McGlynn's suave façade, had decided that his cell needed decorating. This was apparently what the junior guard had meant by a quick chat and a flip of the bird—the floor surrounding the mildewed mattress and the dripping iron water closet was littered with orange peels, chicken bones, cheese rinds, an oil-soaked newspaper of the sort to house fried potatoes, several cracked and emptied lobster carcasses.

When I realized their goal in tossing these gifts through the bars, I couldn't help but admire their ingenuity. If there hadn't been roaches and rats sufficient to their liking sharing McGlynn's lodgings yesterday . . . well, there certainly would be tonight.

"Come to attack a defenseless prisoner like those filthy Paddies?" the pimp snarled.

My brow quirked as I parsed this statement.

Ronan McGlynn had almost certainly been born in New York—his accent told me as much, if not his glib willingness to abuse fellow humans. But I'll never comprehend how we Gothamites manage to divorce ourselves so completely from our pasts. As for mine, I know that our great-grandparents had come from a rural English hamlet and settled outside Manhattan in Greenwich Village to farm, and Henry and Sarah Wilde died before I'd thought to ask them more. But if McGlynn's parents weren't Irish, I'd eat my hat. And here he was whinging about Paddies as if he were Paul Revere's nephew.

It riled me enough to wish I'd brought a stale bread crust or a gnawed husk or two of buttered hot corn as a housewarming present.

"I don't need to kick you, though you deserve worse," I answered, slinging my hand around one of the grainy bars as the other held the lantern steady. "I have a few questions, though."

"What makes you think I'll give any answers to a runt pig who locked me in a dungeon?"

I smiled. Digs at my height are simply tedious.

"You've heard from your employer Symmes by now? He must have been here to see you, even if your bail is set too high for comfort."

The sullen set of McGlynn's jaw beneath the blood-crusted beard tightened. "So he hasn't come around yet, the alderman. So what? He has plentiful things on his mind, after all. He's probably lacing Thundering Tom's quarron black and blue right this very moment."

I blinked at the flash, but I shouldn't have done. The veneer of the gentleman entrepreneur had been stripped away from him with boots and ripening fish heads, leaving a twenty-four-karat thug.

"Probably so." I tapped my fingernail a few times against the metal barrier. "He'll be along tonight, then, you'd wager? After the bout at the Knickerbocker Twenty-one?"

"Yes."

"Or maybe in the morning, first thing. If he's wearied overmuch by the fight."

"Maybe so, maybe that's more likely."

"Or by tomorrow night at the very latest, if he has Party appointments." Snapping open the case of my pocket watch in a gesture meant to conjure Symmes's presence, I checked the time.

"What's it to you?" he growled.

I returned my loose grip to the bar. Reminding him of the solid impediments between his cell and the outside world. "I'm the one who has to investigate the incendiary, whether I'm endeared to you maggots or not."

"You're a purblind fool to talk about an alderman that way, and one as powerful as Mr. Symmes," he sneered. "He never wanted you on the job in the first place. He wanted your *brother*. It's not Mr. Symmes's fault you barged in like some sort of Sunday-temperance warden."

"You're pretty untroubled by your side profession. The Queen Mab is yours, I take it. An alderman wouldn't exactly want his name gracing the accounts ledger."

"He owns the land," McGlynn growled, kicking an impressive Jamaica Bay clamshell my way. "But you're right, the Queen Mab is mine. No use denying it when the alderman will have me clear of this shithole by tomorrow, as you say. He needs me."

"In that case I suppose we'll have no choice but to let you walk. Even though you deserve to be strung up in the middle of Broadway for—"

"Oh, don't make me laugh, you puny prig. Those Irish lasses are born whores. God just went and turned their potatoes as rotten as their muffs. They all become mabs sooner or later anyhow, once they arrive here. Why should you care if I help them along? The way they take to it after a day or two and a few licks with a belt, you should see them—begging for it."

My stomach entered into an argument with my brain over whether spitting fresh bile into McGlynn's cell or calling for the key from the pimple-faced guard would be more satisfying.

"And don't look so disgusted just because you've a wee little pencil between your legs," he scoffed sulkily, linking his arms over his sore, swollen torso and wincing as he did.

That wasn't remotely true. But I stayed dark about it. Some lights are best kept hidden under bushels.

"It was a low trick, sending those two-faced Paddy bastards to catch me out," he muttered balefully. "Alderman Symmes wanted your brother, and it's your brother he should have got."

I managed a nod, forcibly altering the mood. "I've no love lost on either of you, but I'd hate to cross Symmes direct, you understand. That's why I'm here. I've nothing to go on and figured asking you about it while he's busy politicking would be better than waiting. I might not be Valentine, but I'm not lazy."

"Asking me about *what*?"

"The fire at your slum in Pell Street this afternoon, of course. The building was destroyed and two women killed. Symmes must have sent you word?"

He hadn't. And I'd figured as much.

Watching folk absorb momentous information is a curious business. Most react instinctually, then school their features. Some few, like my brother, who have already lived through about the worst that can happen to them and thus developed leathery dispositions, show only the smallest tics. Fewer still, like Silkie Marsh, can channel startlement into new expressions, create artfully painted puppetry effects from horror. As for me, I have a grisly enough time keeping my head shut even when I do know the lay, let alone when I don't.

McGlynn, though—McGlynn was like watching the Wall Street freaks scribble stock prices in the steamy pits they call trading floors. Transparently, immediately shocked. Silkie Marsh, for all she was evil embodied and sheathed in a sublimely cut dress, had him pegged dead to rights—brainless slips of the tongue seemed to me well within the pimp's repertoire.

"Surprised?" I asked.

He swallowed a few times, took a deep breath.

"There's nothing left. The place is rubble."

McGlynn approached the bars. "It . . . it was only threats!" he cried. "Christ, I . . . I never expected it to go this far. She'd threatened us, threatened Mr. Symmes I mean to say, but never— I never thought . . ."

"And by *her* you mean?"

"Sally Woods, of course. She . . . My God," he whispered, seemingly addled over the prospect of his buildings on fire. He paced, shoes nudging up against the pork ribs that had been tossed at him as if he were a mastiff.

"Can you tell me anything useful?"

He stopped. Seemed to grow bone-weary.

"Fuses were found, traces of energetic materials," I prompted with less patience. "Any idea how someone might have placed them there?"

He shuddered. "How should I know?"

"Have you met Sally Woods personally?"

"Of course I have. She's a nasty bluestocking with a passion for trouble."

"The Nassau Street pantaloon manufactory property is likewise your responsibility," I mused. "So you met her when Symmes was quashing the protests."

"Sure. Then. Other times. Saw plenty of her, and when the boss finally managed to shake her loose, the letters started coming. He showed them to me. Uppity wench."

"You think she's dangerous."

"I think she's an unbalanced bitch."

"Is she an incendiary, though?"

"Well, she must be, now, mustn't she?" He glared at me, showing yellowed teeth framed in a humorless rictus of a smile. "Talk to the alderman—he's the one who was sharing her sheets. If you ask me, Robert Symmes keeping the likes of Sally Woods as his mistress for all those months is about the most foolheaded decision in the entire history of New York, even if she's a pretty little piece. But I don't have to tell him as much, and neither do you. He's paying for it dear enough now. Isn't he?"

IO

"What, a little sewing girl, eh? The very game I like—go
away, boys, and let me talk to her—I spoke to her first, and
by Jupiter, I'm the one to see it out!"

"No—not quite so rapid, if you please," replied the one
who had spoken second—"we'll toss up, Harry, who shall
have her!"

—NED BUNTLINE, MYSTERIES AND
MISERIES OF NEW YORK, 1849

BY THE TIME I'd trudged the stone's throw back to Elizabeth
Street and my cozy residence, with its front left shutter that rattles no matter how often I adjust the hinges and its relentless
aroma of clove and butter, I felt about as witless as possible for a
man with his skull still attached.

Physically speaking, Robert Symmes, with his dashing airs and
careful blond moustache, would look very well indeed next to Sally
Woods's boldly drawn features—her shapely afterthought of a nose
and her radiant chocolate eyes. So long as she was wearing female
attire, that is.

Spiritually speaking, I might as well have imagined a snake
bedding a beautiful winged Sphinx with lion haunches and Miss

Woods's arched brow and defiant gaze. So wrong that the mind made a balking, donkeyish halt. But human affection is a capricious affair.

Sally Woods detests Robert Symmes with a sweeping purity like a famine or a drought. And there is no deeper hatred than that engendered by someone you loved once, and were hurt by, and can love no longer, I realized.

I'd never managed to hate Mercy Underhill, as the blame for not having her rests on me. On eyes that never saw she wanted men's company and took it when possible. On ears that didn't hear her when I discovered the fact and left her, frightened and mortified, in a rented room in Silkie Marsh's ken. On a tongue that never mentioned *I love you* and instead phrased it, and I quote, *you aren't stupid, the last fucking thing you are is stupid, you've watched me for years trailing after you, the way I look at you, it's obvious to the entire goddamned world, you can't stand there in front of me and claim not to have known it,* and somehow supposed that a civilized observation.

No, learning to hate Mercy when I've such plentiful practice hating myself would have proved a wash.

I've come close, though. Before she started writing me, before she admitted she'd allowed me to fashion her into an irresistible cipher. I'd done the lion's share of that work, built a towering, ornately bejeweled pedestal when what was wanted was a goddamned *bed.* And she'd every right not to love me—I'd never asked her to. But knowing I'm to blame didn't go far toward cheering me in those early days of her absence, staring at my ceiling in the thin grey hours. Imagining her laugh as a stranger drew his fingertips across her navel, crooking an arm and pulling her higher up onto his spread thighs.

That was generally the juncture when I'd send my fist into my headboard, where it wouldn't reverberate through the wall.

The wind had picked up, scattering torn scraps of local ward flyers and the smell of horses and a few mild drops of rain, when I turned north onto Elizabeth Street. I was skirting by long habit the toxic fissure in civilization called the Five Points, so troubled I could scarce see my feet before me, when the door to the house next to Mrs. Boehm's Fine Baked Goods flew open and a booming laugh barreled down the street.

A family of Germans live packed into the building next door like smoked oysters in a tin-lined can. Flooding the road with the sounds of drinking, brawling, and music-making, often simultaneously. We buy rye beer from them, and whenever the clan is either mourning or celebrating, they hire Elena Boehm to bake the identical white, almond-dusted "joy and sympathy" cake. They're boisterous people, equal parts coarse and kind.

My landlady stood in their doorway, wide mouth cracked in an answering grin, on the arm of Herr Getzler, who either had consumed about a dozen mugs of ale or had managed to sunburn his nose on a mild spring day. He's one of the better of the goodhearted if disorderly mob, with a round belly and a thick brown beard and a laugh like a tuba. He was regarding Mrs. Boehm as if she were a particularly tempting pastry display. That was typical.

He was also patting her hand where it rested on his forearm. That was new.

"Oh, *tch*, and here it seems about to drench you," he tutted in his pleasant guttural growl, holding a hand out to measure the rainfall. "One moment wait, I will get my coat."

"Don't be silly, I have to walk only five steps from here," Elena said with a chuckle. "Look—an escort appears from the shadows. What luck. Good night, Josua."

"Gute Nacht," he answered, sweeping her hand up for a kiss before waving curtly at me as he returned indoors.

Elena took my arm. She wore one of her better frocks, of a rich ivory cotton and a flatteringly worked pattern of layered flounces that made her too-thin waist nearly ample and her too-fair hair shine beneath the flecks of spring rain. It occurred to me that we both work such long hours I can count the number of times I've seen her outside the house without removing my boots. To me she's a thin-lipped smile across a warm kitchen and a dough-smeared table, that or a carefree gasp in the dark of my room when my thumb glides lightly between her legs.

"Did you have a good time at the—"

"Why were you speaking English with Herr Getzler?" I questioned, apparently annoyed. Though I certainly shouldn't have been. "You speak Bohemian and German fluently, and his English sounds like a rusted hacksaw."

"Practice." She angled a look at me with water-blue eyes. "Josua wishes to become man of business, not petty seller of small beer. Have for himself and his two sons a brewery. Considerable money he has saved for this future. When I see him, now that he wants title and property like a real American, we speak together English."

We were at the door by then. My key slipped for the second time. Elena dropped my arm, setting her palms on the spots where I knew amiable hip bones jutted beneath the soft fabric, amused at my struggle. Her mirth didn't render me any less peppery. An incendiary was keen to raze bits of the city, I'd practically signed on as Silkie Marsh's new champion, and my brother had just torpedoed his own ward. It was hardly *my* fault that the lock needed oiling.

"The day Herr Getzler sounds like an American will be the day America transplants itself to Prussia," I decreed uncharitably as I finally thrust open the door. Setting my hat on its peg blind, I lit the lamp that always rests on the three-legged table with a match from my waistcoat pocket. "And if you're correcting his grammar, he should pay you."

The oil flared to life and sent a glow spilling through the dark bakery. Elena smoothed her hands over her damp hair. "What's a word of advice between friends?"

You aren't friends with Josua Getzler, I thought as a petty sting bit at the edge of my scar. *You trade him fresh eggs for good beer and open the windows when he's singing Faust because you love the story and he has a fine tenor.*

Lifting the hinged countertop, I carried the lamp in search of a much-needed whiskey. After pouring two generous splashes without thinking, I recalled I was irked at Mrs. Boehm and grew still more irked. "Bird asked after you."

"My sweet girl. I miss her during the school year."

"I was surprised you'd missed her deliberately. Though that was before I was surprised my brother announced he's running for alderman." I pulled a chair away from the worktable. "Oh, and before I was surprised Silkie Marsh arrived."

Elena's horrified intake of breath wasn't a bit satisfying, and I cursed myself for being in a uselessly foul mood. Instead of taking the seat, I set the liquor down and stepped to where she leaned against the floured wood, her other fingertips tracing her prominent collarbone.

"It's all right. Well, no it isn't, but Madam Marsh— Bird is fine, they never spoke. She's sore at me, but that's nothing special. I sent her off with a friend."

I failed to mention that Silkie Marsh had spied Bird all too clearly and correctly identified a fit crowbar to pry my ribs open. That would have added injury to insult, the way I saw matters, and anyhow I'd never let affairs come to such a pass.

"Which friend?" Elena asked hoarsely.

"Jim Playfair. She's snug in bed by now and none the wiser."

Elena's eyes closed as the fingers at her throat curled in on themselves. I brushed my hands across her shoulders in apology. She sighed, stepping in closer. And my arms fit around her instantly, because I like her better than I do almost anyone, far better than I did myself just then.

"That awful woman, at your brother's firehouse," she said to the edge of my cravat. "What reason could she have?"

"She was troubled by incendiary threats against the buildings Alderman Symmes owns. Her brothel is one of them. I'm taking care of it."

"Your brother, then. What will come of him running for office?"

"Nothing whatsoever to the good."

"So seldom Bird leaves the orphanage." The downy center part in her hair tickled along the underside of my jaw. "I should have been there."

"You couldn't have known, and there isn't any harm done."

"Still."

A thought occurred. A belated thought, one that ought to have been obvious, and my grip tightened fractionally.

"You'd wanted to see Bird tonight, you'd said as much. Were you keen to avoid me at the fund-raiser?"

She raised her head without haste, though the sweep of her mouth had turned stormy. "No," she declared. "I was making it easier for *you* to avoid *me*."

Shifting my hands farther down her arms, I studied her from brow to narrow chin. "What sort of call would you have to say that?"

"You treat your friends well, do you not, Mr. Wilde?"

I twisted my lips. "I hope I do. I'm sorry about—"

"A good man you are, a man with principles," she continued without minding me, her tone casual, as if she were asking me to pass her the morning copy of the *Herald*. "Important, you think it, to be a gentleman. Yes?"

"Yes. I never meant to—"

"You respect me, and you respect where we live." Her spine where I'd slid one hand round her waist was fast petrifying. "You respect feelings. You respect *privacy*. So respectful, always, so careful to leave what you found where you found it, unchanged. Never taking away without permission. Never leaving a mark. I think, *this is Timothy*, very deeply he has been hurt, so has his family, this is a way he has. He takes care. And then I see you with this woman from London. The poet."

She brought her hands up and linked them where the hairs were prickling along the back of my neck, her usually soft gaze piercing. "A very great surprise, her returning here, and I am curious. How could I not be curious? I have never seen her before, but I have read her *Light and Shade* stories until in my heart it is like I know her—I understand why you love her, and it is another sad story like all the many sad stories in the world, and I think, Timothy, *such care* he would take with Mercy Underhill if he saw her again. And then I am wrong."

We were locked into each other by this point. Fused. Cruelly mimicking a dance or a prelude to lovemaking when what it felt like was a crossed pair of dueling swords.

Elena pressed her hip against mine, about as close as two people could be and remain clothed. "This woman Mercy, who is so troubled in her mind, you look at her, and then you look away because it is too much, and you do not want to take *any* care with her. Oh, no. You think you want to make her happy, but all of that is to convince her to *look at you* and never stop looking. With her you actually want to take a hook and sink it deep in her chest where she will feel you there and where she will bleed if she moves away from you."

"Elena, please—"

LYNDSAY FAYE

"Try to deny it."

My heart was pounding. I wanted to say, *That's a lie.* I didn't. I couldn't. Because it was merciless and it was shameful.

But it was true.

"You do not like it, you do not like it *at all*, but it is so, and I know, I remember how I looked at Franz before he died," she hissed. "I fell in love in Danzig in the slow summer, with a German merchant who had stopped at the port to buy a ship from my father. My father, he wanted to marry away my three older sisters, find them good matches, and half the time he could not see me at all. Forgot my name and called me *słoneczko*, 'little sunbeam.' For a week Franz was there, negotiating. I was sixteen. He could do anything with his hands—comfort frightened horses, fix my clock that wouldn't chime. When the ship he bought from my father sailed, I was on it. When he lost the ship in a storm on its way to Odessa, I had already married him. When we boarded the ship for New York, heavy I was with little Audie. We had fifty thaler, no relations in America, and whenever Franz looked at me, I wanted to dig my hands in his chest and feel his heart pumping."

I could feel her own heartbeat, having bent down to measure it, the way it leapt from her throat against my lips and tongue. Even as I belatedly realized that all the care I'd taken only told her unequivocally I didn't need her, not in that way.

"I pictured you at the fund-raiser. You being careful, you being *courteous*," she gasped, arching. "Worrying about her and hiding it. Trying not to hurt me. I did not like thinking about this. It was disgusting. I went to Herr Getzler's and spent the evening with a man who wants to brand his name in my arm."

"*You* don't want *him*, though." The low growl that emerged shocked the pair of us, I believe.

Pushing me, she stepped away, her chest with its tiny points of bosom heaving. "No, I don't."

156

"I don't give a damn how much chink he's saved so he can swill more of his own product—he doesn't deserve you."

"No." She laughed in a short burst. "No, he doesn't deserve me."

"Nor do I, for that matter."

Elena shook her head, exasperated. "You are my friend. Qualities you have, that I have mentioned. Stop, *bitte*, the being ridiculous."

"But it's the truth. What do you want from me?"

Elena returned to the table, still keeping a safe distance, and drained her whiskey. Touching her fingers to her slender curve of a mouth, she shook her white-blonde head once more.

"I visit your room sometimes," she said in a faraway voice. "We share things. Secrets. Skin. A gift you have, you realize, for listening, for making people feel they are *heard*. Never have you knocked at my door, wanting, greedy. Sinking into me uninvited. This is the sort of care you take with a woman you do not love. I admire you—I should not have mocked that you are kind. But I think you would prefer to find new lodgings than to stain my bedsheets."

She turned to go, and that was . . . ruinous.

"I won't apologize for not being more cruel," I rasped.

"I won't apologize for not being more kind. You do not live here, you see, not really. You live for your brother, and for police work, and for Bird, and for your memories of this girl as she was before. If I cannot make you feel anything . . . what, then, is the point?"

"You do make me feel things!" I cried, following her to the base of the stairs, where she was gliding upward in the gloom without a candle. "For instance, at the moment you're scaring me half to death."

Elena stopped, hand on the banister rail. She turned to peer at me. Her cloud-colored eyes were barely visible in the thickness of the enveloping dark.

"Good," she concluded, continuing on her way.

I passed a night of cold sweats and bone aches in an unhappy in-between where Mercy and Elena stood before the Tombs holding torches. Flushed with righteous approval as the enormous blaze burned criminals and copper stars alike to good clean ash. I'd no sooner awoken from that vision than, drifting fitfully, I was treated to another—Valentine being crowned King of the Rats whose realm prevails beneath the Tombs and appointing McGlynn as prime minister, the long-tailed rodents shrieking their cheers.

After that dream brought me awake, after turning up my lamp while gentle rain pattered against the shingles, I pulled out my charcoal and paper and sat at my desk, meticulously rendering Elena Boehm from memory. She'd been lying on her stomach with her arms crossed over the edge of my bed, smoking a tiny cigarette with her left hand, while I did nothing more complex than to read the *Herald* cross-legged with my back to the wall and my fingertips occasionally exploring the lush landscape of her lower half. She's distressingly thin but constructed like a ripe September pear, and she was dead wrong. She made me feel many things. I'd just slid the portrait under her bedroom door, the one I don't allow myself to knock on for reasons both well intentioned and apparently terribly selfish, when the banging commenced.

Elena appeared at the bottom of the stairs after answering the knock, staring up in surprise to find me awake and dressed. Seeing that there was no need to rouse me, she nodded at the half-open door, pulling a basket of chicken feed farther up her arm as she headed for the rear yard.

I liked her watchful silence just about as much as I liked my next task.

Thus it was that, at six in the morning on April 21 and having followed the chief's courier, I found myself next to George Washington Matsell in a pair of emerald velvet armchairs so overstuffed as to verge on the ludicrous, seated across a continental expanse of desk from Robert Symmes, one of two candidates for Ward Eight's alderman. Symmes appeared to have passed the night stewing in the vat of his own hot rage. His neat moustache and dapper togs were well in hand, but he wore a volcanic expression, neck knotted with tension and eyes rimmed in a vengeful red.

Meanwhile, I was severely grateful for the chief's elephantine presence, calm and collected in his grey sack coat and striped trousers. Symmes needed interrogating further. But that didn't mean I was eager to end up croaked for my thoroughgoing professionalism. So we were questioning him in tandem, in his positively opulent mansion in Varick Street, with the warm apricot light of a spring dawn streaming through the giant pair of bay windows in his study.

A portrait of Symmes hung behind the desk, which was so typically self-obsessed a choice of décor that I found it nearly humorous. The Symmes of the painting looked down with a benevolent smile gracing his manly features. The Symmes of flesh and blood glowered at us, positively bilious with the force of his pique.

"Your family," the latter Symmes said in a poisonous undertone, "has been proving a *great* disappointment of late."

I didn't bother denying it—I was wracked enough over the two deaths at Pell Street without his assistance, and as for Valentine's candidacy, I couldn't rightly argue with the man.

"Captain Wilde alerted me via letter yesterday stating his intentions and expressing wishes that the alderman race be conducted with as little collateral damage to the Party as is possible, a sentiment I'm certain you share," Matsell observed in a voice equally dry as it was exhausted. "Your disappointment, as you term it, must be expressed in the spirit of republican fair play."

"Oh, I plan to smash Val Wilde at the polls, if not literally," Symmes hissed. "In fact, Chief Matsell, I confess myself surprised you haven't already sacked the traitor."

Matsell only smiled coldly, tapping his broad fingertips together in a habitual gesture. "Were I to sack every copper star who owned strong opinions in either the Hunker or the Barnburner direction, Alderman, I'd have to replace my entire staff."

"When I'm reelected, I'll see to it Captain Wilde is dismissed in disgrace."

"When you're reelected," Matsell answered with the glint of gunmetal in his eye, "you're welcome to. Meanwhile, an incendiary threatens and the younger Mr. Wilde is one of those tasked with finding the culprit with all possible speed."

"I can't say that bolsters my confidence," Symmes sneered as his pocket watch made its first appearance. I don't know how his pals felt about the timepiece, but I wanted to shatter the thing. "He is hardly even the intellectual equal of his turncoat brother. My warning was crystal clear, and nevertheless I am now the owner of a pile of soot where was once a thriving rental property. *Disgraceful.*"

"Ronan McGlynn sends his regards," I interjected, determined anew not to let my chief suppose I was inadequate to the task of chasing after a firestarter. "I'm not fool enough to pretend to like you, Alderman, but I'm not fool enough to let a crackbrained incendiary run amok through Manhattan either. So I questioned your employee last night. He thinks you're en route to the Tombs to post bail."

"Oh, I fear I couldn't conscience posting bail for Mr. McGlynn. He served me well enough as a property manager, no doubt, but while a man is entitled to, shall we say . . ." Symmes drew his tongue across his upper lip, considering. ". . . recreational female company, I was unaware McGlynn's establishment took such an *aggressive* recruitment line. And on property rented from me, no less. I need not even bother with dismissing him but shall merely allow justice to take its natural course."

Smirking, he linked his fingers. I recalled Symmes's mentioning *fresh as they come* to Valentine and actively detested him an additional dram for lying through his teeth to me.

"McGlynn likewise pegged Sally Woods as the incendiary," I continued. "Mentioned previous threats as well. I need to see them."

Symmes traversed his sumptuous Oriental rug, opened a squat but prettily worked English Chubb safe in the corner, and returned with a small bundle. Dropping it before my nose on the desk with a loud smack, he regained his chair and regarded me and the chief with the same respect he might expend on a spat lump of phlegm.

We began to sort through and read them. The format, to my stifled alarm, was identical to the threat against the alderman's buildings: the same heft of paper and typesetting printed on a single side with neatly aligned margins. Before we'd been reading long, Matsell and I had a graphic impression of the mental state of the author.

I think my favorite was:

> *You soulless fiend whom once I cherished, may you suffer exquisite torment in hell's eternal fires for your crimes. May I be there, with all the water on planet earth at my disposal, and never lift a finger to ease the bubbling of your seared flesh.*

That one was . . . compelling. Though the chief, I recall, coughed when he encountered:

> *Not a day passes when the dream of murdering you by my own hand fails to bring solace to this husk of a human, this empty vessel you drained so utterly dry.*

So maybe the latter had better claim to literary merit. Anyhow, they were certainly of a *theme*.

"These are pretty . . . personal," I suggested.

A flash of feeling sharper than his usual umbrage appeared and disappeared. There and gone in a heartbeat, but informative nevertheless.

Sally Woods frightened Robert Symmes more than she frightened me.

Recovered, the alderman regarded his fingernails with perhaps unmerited interest. "Miss Woods is violently hysterical, and now she is a murderess to boot. Surely it's small wonder that her monomania is passionately expressed."

"My impression of her—"

"My impression of *you*, Mr. Wilde," Symmes snarled, "is that you are so blinded due to personal dislike that you refuse to arrest a threat to this entire city. Had you imprisoned Miss Woods before now, my property would be intact and two dead people would be *alive*."

Since my hand was already wrapped into a fist, I settled on tapping it against my knee. "That isn't quite what I meant. Or wasn't Miss Woods your mistress? Matters must have ended about as badly as possible for her to want to kill you after you parted ways."

"How *dare*— My private life is *not* the concern of a stunted copper star with . . . with delusions of competence," he spluttered.

"It is, though. Under the circumstances."

"*I* am the *victim* of this heinous crime!" he cried. "What about this are you failing to grasp?"

"Just what your relationship to Miss Woods was prior to the threats starting," I answered dryly.

"Oh, I was bedding her on a regular basis, Mr. Wilde," he growled, leaning forward. "I wonder, though, whether ending a trivial affair with a saucy little manufactory wench quite merits *death threats*. And I wonder what steps I can take to protect myself, my property, and my city when you appear to have discarded your masculinity altogether and joined the ranks of murderous anarchists and bluestockings."

I'd have delivered a poor response to this if Matsell hadn't prevented me.

"So there's a long-standing dispute between you and this Miss Sally Woods. Setting firestarting aside for the moment, bedding your garment workers was never going to end well, was it?" Matsell sniffed, seeming as much disappointed as galled. And truly, Symmes's blend of arrogance and peevishness begged for a swift cuff to the ear. "Of all the multitudinous ways it *could have* begun and ended badly between you, just how *did* it begin and end badly, might we ask?"

"That's a personal matter." Symmes waved his hand as if shooing a gnat.

"Alderman, while I sympathize with your desire to protect both your holdings and your privacy, I'm considerably more motivated by the former. You're the one who dipped your wick into your own payroll. Answer the question."

Symmes and Matsell exchanged lethal volleys with their eyeballs. It brightened me considerably. Then, as if a line in the sand had been smoothed over, the alderman's fury was replaced by an almost pleased-looking moue of distaste. I wondered what on earth it meant and then realized that part of Symmes was glad at being forced to discuss his conquests—that he was as kittled rosy to brag about Miss Woods opening her legs for him as some would have been over displaying a rare species of butterfly drugged senseless and stabbed to a corkboard.

It was, quite frankly, repellent.

"Very well, if I am to be interrogated, let it be by the chief of police rather than an inept underling," Robert Symmes whined, physically shifting in his chair to face Matsell. "From the moment my foreman hired her for the pantaloon manufactory we established in eighteen-forty-six, Miss Woods made every effort to catch my eye when I appeared on routine visits. Eventually she approached me directly after an inspection, bold as any heathen, to discuss the plight of the outworkers and better wages for the cutters. She's a striking woman, and needless to say an immoral one—it took me all of a week to seduce her. Appalling. She argued, I listened or pretended to, and for all her factually absurd cant about *equality*, she was an inventive little slut between the sheets."

Eyes burning like embers in my skull, I stared back at him. I wasn't certain he'd wronged Miss Woods at all beyond dismissing her from the manufactory, but when I recalled her saying in a lifeless tone, *It's personal, and can't be helped anyhow* . . . Between Woods herself and the Queen Mab, and even Jim's hushed words of warning regarding the alderman's reputation, a definite suspicion had formed.

Rape is criminal and despicable. And about as easy to prosecute as it is to reach out and pluck the chime of a bell from midair. A rich woman attacked by a low brute was nearly sure to see justice done if she took the reputation-killing step of admitting to the assault in the first place, and I could convict McGlynn on brothelkeeping charges without violation even entering into the matter. But a woman of Sally Woods's station against an alderman? When she was a trouser-clad deviant? And had already given herself to him more than once? He could have kept her locked in a garret and tormented her for weeks and I could still never punish him for it this long after the fact. Every lawyer in Christendom claims "lack of feminine virtue and salacious signals led to confused circumstances" when defending a client against rape charges. In the case of Miss

Woods, the crueler and more religious among us—who are sometimes the same people—would have said she deserved no better.

So I simply stared at Symmes, the sickeningly happy tilt to his lips and the callous mirth in his eyes, and thought, *Whatever you did, I will see that you pay.*

"Something ended it," Matsell said flatly. "What?"

"She went so far as to organize a strike for higher wages, the jezebel. I fired her so fast her pretty head must have spun. Oh, I showed mercy to the dim little sheep who'd followed her, but I could hardly have extended Miss Woods the same generosity. She is a completely unprincipled woman, the sort who is not only infamous for wearing obscene clothing in the amoral cause of destroying the balance between the sexes but is apparently capable of setting my property aflame."

Matsell arrowed a grey eye at me.

"She's a radical who favors unconventional dress," I admitted.

"She's an offense against the natural order and thus presents an active threat to our system of values even if she weren't a crazed firestarter," Symmes shot back.

"As if you have any idea what values look like," I snapped.

"Mr. Wilde, control yourself," the chief growled.

The alderman half rose, showing his teeth. "The good people of New York have chosen *me* to represent their interests, their principles, and yes, their *values*, you unbearable prick. Keep a civil tongue in your head when addressing your betters and arrest that madwoman before she can do any more damage to the metropolis and to *my life*. I've an election to win."

Best of luck with that, I thought acidly as Matsell stood to depart.

"All necessary steps, including arresting Miss Woods should her arrest be what's called for, will be taken without further delay if my staff knows what's good for them," Chief Matsell said, stab-

bing a riled finger toward my nose. "If we require further cooperation on your part, Alderman, I trust we have it. Wilde, you're
settling this business and settling it now."

"I need to keep these." I reached for the stack of letters.

"Take them and be damned." Symmes sighed as the pocket
watch made yet another appearance.

"Do you have some other appointment at bloody six-thirty
in the morning?" I demanded, having expended my small store of
patience.

"Yes, including but not limited to ruining your disloyal worm
of a sibling."

"We're through here," the chief called, flapping a flipperlike
hand as he lumbered out the door. I'd pocketed the evidence and
taken two steps after him when Symmes rounded the desk and
gripped me by the arm.

"A word of warning," he said in my ear. His classically handsome features had twisted into a dog's brutal snarl. "If your brother
withdraws his candidacy by the end of the day, publicly apologizes,
and throws his support behind my own election, I will consider—
consider, mind—showing him clemency in thanks for his previous
years of service."

He returned behind his desk about half a second previous to
finding himself punched in the jaw.

"And if he doesn't?" I wanted to know. "What then?"

Descending into his chair, Symmes looked up with a smile. "If
Valentine Wilde doesn't withdraw, I will so utterly destroy that
arrogant, ungrateful sodomite that he and everyone close to him
will wish they had never been born. Think carefully on that, Mr.
Wilde. And a very good morning to you."

I I

The spirit of opposition between the barnburners and
hunkers waxes warmer and warmer every day. So
great has the gap between them become, that they have
entirely forgotten the principles for which they have been
fighting, and are each trying now to oust the other from
Tammany. . . . The barnburners go in strong for free
soil, and are determined they will not yet give up old
Tammany, where they have so long reveled in the pride
of their physical strength.

— *THE NEW YORK HERALD*, JULY 27, 1848

I DIDN'T SET OFF TO arrest Miss Woods. Though I should have. Instantly.

No, I marched straight for Val's lodgings several blocks away from Symmes's residence, selecting choice words for him as I traveled. It was too early for him to occupy his police captain's office at the station house in Prince Street, and considering the way they'd left matters, the odds were against his having slept at Jim's elegantly furnished digs near Washington Square. By then the sun had risen, illuminating the dress buttons of prim Irish housemaids walking to market and the lacquer of sweat on the brows of black laborers hauling bricks. Sure enough, when I reached the trim row house in Spring Street, there was movement in the parlor window of the second story, the floor that Valentine has kept for more than a decade.

Making double time up the stairs, I knocked twice at Val's door. Upon entering, I discovered that I wasn't the first person to conclude my brother needed immediate sense pounded into him.

"What in God's name is going on?" I questioned.

James Playfair stood in my brother's kitchen amidst the shining glass jars of dried herbs and spices and the pot of Harlem honey and the dish of rendered pork fat for egg fry-ups. He glared into my brother's mazzard with the expression Alexander the Great might have worn when he decided that acquiring more personal property might make for an engaging hobby. Jim could have been sitting on the back of a war elephant. He sported a neat claret cravat and a matching wine-red waistcoat, and his wiry chest heaved in anger. I'd never seen his graceful features twist so. Nor seen Val so alarmed by a mere facial expression.

Val was in the state he usually endures following Party sprees— haggard, half dressed in an undershirt and trousers with braces hanging, eyes bloodshot above bags that might have carried a month's post across the Atlantic. He sat in the kitchen chair he uses when peeling potatoes or plucking a fowl, and if Jim had just kicked him, he'd not have looked any less pleased.

"What do you *think* is going on?" Jim snapped, and then paused, shaking his head.

"How's Bird?" I ventured with better caution.

"I apologize, Timothy. Good morning. How are you faring? Bird is fine, and four dollars richer thanks to the greyhound which won the final contest at Vauxhall Gardens."

"Oh, aces, you'll apologize after you mouth it at *him*," Valentine noted cuttingly, slouching as he uncrossed his legs. Size being a natural advantage to the activity, no one can sprawl like my brother. Even when his complexion is the color of sperm-whale wax.

"Do you know something, you're right, Valentine, I am more than happy to apologize to you," Jim hissed. "I sincerely apologize for suggesting that you intended to lose a boxing match for the benefit of Party solidarity, and I hereby express my sorrow that I did not sooner reach the conclusion you meant to risk your entire career upon an egotistical whim. Forgive me."

"You're about *this close*," Val reported, holding up an unsteady thumb and forefinger, "to actually angering me. I don't calculate that's a goal you'd feel chaffey over achieving."

"If it wasn't a whim, then what was it?" I dropped my wide hat on the kitchen table. "Because it sure as hell is summery wasn't a good idea."

"Symmes has been a thorn in my hindquarters for long enough," Val spat. "He's as gammy a politico as he is a fund-raiser, the Hall will ignore me if I lose and slap me on the back if I win, and anyway, the notion I'd go in for abusing a poor Irish chit in exchange for lioning some kate he sacked was the last straw."

"Symmes offered a carnal reward in exchange for Val's assistance," I explained to Jim's baffled eyebrows. "Not the . . . ah, mutually agreeable variety."

"He's a barbarian," Jim concurred, appearing neither surprised nor any less livid. "I was playing for a benefit given at the Astor House and discovered Symmes meddling with one of the chambermaids when they sent me in search of more champagne. She'd obviously been struggling, and when I deliberately knocked over a mountain of soup tureens, she ran, and I departed with similar haste."

"So he's a barbarian, and you're still keen to vote for him and not for me as alderman?" my brother protested.

"Yes, because now he is a barbarian *who loathes you*, Valentine."

"Flash." Val yawned luxuriantly. "I'd hate to think my feelings were one-sided. Hell, I've wanted to torch his property myself."

"Well, now you needn't," I retorted, "because by all appearances our Miss Sally Woods has that task firmly in hand. Energetic materials were used to destroy one of his houses in Pell Street yesterday. Two people are dead."

"Oh, my God," Jim gasped.

Pulling the letters from my jacket, I shoved them at my infuriating sibling. "Look familiar?"

Valentine sifted through them quickly and whistled. "Two people croaked, you say? For the love of Christ, Tim, any reason you're not off clapping her in darbies?"

"Because Symmes wants me to tell you that if you back him for alderman again by the end of the day, he'll refrain from destroying you."

Jim shifted from foot to foot. "Valentine—"

Val aimed a finger jab at his friend with such vehemence it would have broken skin had it made contact. "You're about to suggest I hand over my bollocks to a peacocking prig who thinks slave states will disappear if only we shower them with enough commerce and compliments, and when I've already announced before the free republicans of the Eighth that their ward boss—who is also their police captain and the senior engineman of the Knickerbocker Twenty-one—will serve them better than a reprobate landowner who thinks shoving his cock where it isn't wanted makes for a spruce hobby. Save yourself the breath."

Reaching into his coat for his small pipe, James sensibly turned on his heel and retired to the parlor.

"*Jimmy!*" Val called after him in a voice equal parts fond and fuming.

I settled, half leaning, against the table. Val crossed his arms with an operatic flourish and shot me a green-eyed glare. It desired me to answer the question *How do you people expect me to tolerate your nonsense?* I'd no ready answer, because now, for the first time within the tempest of my anxiety over Val's sticking his neck out, I realized that he had a point. Which was unhelpful.

"You've always been good about women," I mused quietly instead. "Some of the rabbits you run with wouldn't know the difference between a rape and a dead flash night on the Bowery."

Val lapsed into thought, absently scoring his scalp with his fingernails. "Well, at the end of the day, there's coves as have served time in the House of Refuge when they were squeakers and coves as haven't."

Confused, I glanced at him. Many years ago—when our parents were yet living—Val had briefly disappeared. His devoted delinquency led to a stint at the House of Refuge, a remedial establishment for vagrant kinchin located in the untamed countryside at Twenty-fourth Street and Fifth Avenue, and one that favors hearty floggings as an aid to character development. My brother's character had not, I need hardly say, been improved, and when I think about the copper-wire smell of dried blood emanating from his back and the reckless smile he'd worn when he staggered home with his hair shorn off, visibly thinner after less than a week, a smoldering hatred burns in my gut.

This new information, though—when I'd managed to process the remark, my blood froze. Val noticed my horror and shook his head.

"Not *me*. Though right you are, my Tim, there's bastards there as fancied the young lads particular. No, but . . . there was a little miss. Thin face, blonde plaits, had a haunted look to her. When I told her I was fixing to escape, she asked me either to take her with me or cut her throat. She'd a piece of glass saved for the purpose. I couldn't manage either, you mark me. Bad business. I was only twelve, but I always wished I'd done the one or the other."

Eyes shutting briefly, I nodded.

I remembered in a flood all the many, many occasions Val had interacted with Bird Daly, brought her oranges and cast-off frippery from the Party's charity trunks, called her *little cat* and laughed, wincing, always wincing, as if the fact of his laughing at all were somehow a crime, when she either made an apt observation or ribbed me over my plentiful faults. I remembered when I'd yet hated him, first informing Val that Silkie Marsh kept ten-year-old stargazers. Morphine-crazed as he'd been, my own eyes blinkered with spite, I could still recall the warped spasm of revulsion that flickered across his face. Then I recollected I'd actually imagined that he'd sent Bird to the House of Refuge over Party obligations. And that he'd tried to have me permanently hushed for the same reason.

Unfortunately, my version of guilt is a bitter pill gracelessly swallowed. And so I needed in an urgent fashion to change the course of the dialogue. Before I'd nauseated myself any further.

"I need to know how serious you find Symmes threatening your candidacy and possibly your life. You're reckless and morphine-addled as a general practice, but hardly suicidal. Well, on the days when you aren't fighting *fires*," I couldn't help but add meanly.

It's a fundamental difference in logic. Val thinks of fighting fires as a holy penance set against the balance of burning our parents alive. I think of it as a self-destructive compulsion designed to remove the burden of living from his shoulders altogether.

Wanting an ally, I marched from the kitchen into the comfortable—if questionably decorated with framed Tammany propaganda—front sitting room. Jim's brooding pipe smoke had filled the air with clove and warm, bitter walnut. He angled clear blue eyes at me as I landed in the striped armchair. As I'd expected, Val followed me into the meticulously clean parlor so he could continue attempts to needle me into submission.

"How worried *should* I be over a goddamned Hunker when the hardworking men of this ward would sooner spit in a plantation owner's eye than shake his hand?" Valentine leaned against the doorframe. Jim resolutely ignored him.

"There are plenty of popular Hunkers in the Party," I argued.

"No, there are plenty of *rich* ones, and your knowledge of inner-circle Tammany dealings wouldn't top up a thimble."

"It isn't as simple as all that."

"Of course it is, and you are being a blue-ribbon horse's arse. Symmes and his ilk, all these new garment-industry bosses who pay their workers chicken feed and drive down wages, they manufacture *slave clothing*. The pantaloons, the cotton shirts, the linsey-woolsey gowns, the linen aprons, the pantalets thin enough to see your hand through—"

"The South sends us the cotton, the North turns it into cloth, then we turn the cloth into togs and sell it back to them. Yes, I'm not political but I'm not *stupid* either," I groused.

"You sure as taxes had me fooled."

"I'm not the one who deliberately called down hellfire and brimstone from his own alderman!"

"Can the two of you *hear* yourselves speaking?" Jim queried under his breath. "It's like a pair of schoolchildren scrapping over a marble."

"What the devil could that flea-brain Symmes *possibly* do to me?" my brother growled, hands now propped against his hips where the braces dangled like unanswered questions. "Other than bore me to death when he makes speeches about Southern conciliation? Because—"

"He might have mentioned that you're a molley," I fired back, thoroughly flummoxed. I stood to face him. "And that he could severely harm your reputation by implying such."

"Oh, of all the prattling nonsense," Val scoffed. "I'm *not* a molley. That was easy, wasn't it? Next?"

James Playfair, who was attempting to appear not even mildly interested and failing miserably, directed his attention to the light bleaching the edges of Val's white curtains. Sodomy is punishable by a decade's stint at the Tombs, I should mention—but only sodomy. So we copper stars arrest people for affectations about as often as we turn down illicit reward money. What would be the point? What if we did collar a slender-limbed aesthete, down where they loiter beside the defunct City Hall fountain that since March has forborne the giving of aesthetic pleasure in favor of dribbling green ooze from its spigot? Which partner sheltered in the shadows of the park's trees would be the witness to the crime and which the criminal? The one on his knees or the other? And who would give a damn?

That doesn't mean that news of Captain Valentine Wilde's extended amorous liaison with James Playfair wouldn't spell disaster of the highest order. On the contrary.

"Right," I retorted sardonically, "of course you're not a molley. Symmes actually said *sodomite*, but no, you're not breaking the law, you're merely canoodling *with a man* nine nights out of ten, perfectly respectable seeing as actual buggery doesn't enter into it."

No one answered. James continued staring through the gap in the curtains as a faint blush rose over the tips of his ears. Valentine didn't say anything either. Just pulled up his braces as if he'd not previously been aware he was wearing them. In fact, the pair said nothing at all so loudly just then that what they weren't saying was perfectly . . . audible.

My mouth dropped open and shut again.

"Don't tell me," I begged, closing my eyes and raising my palms in supplication. I did my best not to look unfriendly as I took a step back. It was only a signal. An *urgent* one. Nothing personal. "God, just *don't* tell me."

"Timothy," Jim attempted, sounding mortified, "I—"

"*Not* telling me is what you're doing. Right?"

"For heaven's sake, I didn't say anything!"

"I know, but now we're past that, keep cracking on with the not saying anything, would you?"

"Why in Christ's name are your *eyes* closed, you mutton-witted runt?" Val's voice demanded.

I opened them, newly furious. Then I strode up to my brother and got a good handful of his shirt. "Maybe it's so I don't have to watch you glibly dismissing my concerns when Symmes could try to *send you to prison.*"

Val, notwithstanding my grip, tossed his face ceilingward as he laughed over the top of my pate. "*I* am not the molley in this room. Nor the bright young copper star with the panic problem. I am equally not the nut-shriveled politician who doesn't realize that the Party will *never* allow a ward boss to be slandered as a lace-festooned debauchee. Your concerns are—"

"Justified," I snapped.

"Severely understated," Jim said in a low moan.

"Irrelevant," Val insisted. "I have an entire ward's worth of Irishmen in my pocket, rabbits that I see are fed and clothed and kept in brown liquor. Symmes smears me, we *all* lose them. He won't smear me."

"Right, I am going to depart before you lot start up the fisticuffs, and do recall that last time it garnered only a matched set of black eyes and was thus spectacularly unhelpful," Jim announced, rising.

"It felt good, though," I muttered, dropping Val's shirt.

"Damn right it did," Val hissed. "James, just where do you think you're going?"

"Oh, I don't know," Jim answered with a too-bright smile that wavered at the edges. "To the bathhouse to steam away my sorrows, to my flat to drown them in gin, to hell, it really isn't any concern of yours, and you can expect to see *very* little of me until after the elections."

"Christ on a mule, *why* are you acting like this?" Val groaned, pressing his forefinger and thumb hard into his ancient-seeming eyes.

"Maybe he's concerned Symmes might make public the fact you're fucking your best friend?" I posited.

"Wait, wait, *you* can say it out loud, but *we* can't say it out—"

"Well, there we have it, and I shan't take up any more of your time," Jim said desperately, making haste for the front door.

"Jimmy, to put it another way, it would kittle me muchly if you didn't swan off on the very day I'm about to start a run at the office of alderman and could use your wits, instincts, and company," my brother bit out when Jim's hand reached the doorknob. "Stop diddling about and come back."

Jim paused, huffing a laugh that sounded more like he'd been punched in the solar plexus than it did an expression of mirth. "Why?" he asked.

"Holy Lord, what do you mean *why*, you limp-wristed tit?"

"I should like to know the reason that action would please you, and I thus inquired."

"Because I want you *here*."

For an instant, Jim looked about ready to cry. He's in love with my brother, after all. But the brightness in his eyes might have been a trick of the light. I honestly couldn't say, since less than a second later he'd slammed the door behind him.

My business with my brother and his long-suffering friend having been conducted to the satisfaction of no one, I went south to Thomas Street to speak with and probably arrest Sally Woods. Natural inclination urged me to instead go straight to Mercy Underhill's new residence, both to question Miss Duffy further (a note from Piest assured me that she'd been readily welcomed by the object of my devotion) and to study the curl that refuses to be included in Mercy's hair arrangements and rests, a single whorl of feathery black, at the nape of her neck. Since that's what I wanted to do, rather than learn that Miss Woods was a murderess, my duties to Manhattan clearly lay in the opposite direction.

The Thomas Street landlady with the unfortunate mumps affliction appeared unsurprised to see me, merely making a humming sound when she answered.

"Might I go through and speak with Miss Woods again?"

She glanced at my star pin. "Police roaming the streets, meddling with perfectly decent folk. It's not Christian, dear."

"Agreed," I answered as I passed through into the hall.

The little greenhouse in its wild habitat had taken on a decidedly more sinister air since the Pell Street fire and the collection of violent threats in my frock coat. The grimy glass house I'd once thought charming now called to mind a sorceress's cottage, nestled in the depths of a wood where crooked paths change their patterns in the dappled sunlight, leading kinchin ever farther into the gloom of gnarled trees.

My knock was answered with an energetic "Come in!" and I entered. Miss Woods was at her printing press, setting type. When she saw me, she brushed her fingers together and pulled a nearby tarp over the machine.

"Liberal as you are, that's a right fiery piece written by one of my former classmates for the *Working Man's Advocate,* and I'm really not financially stable enough to be fined just now," she said, smiling nervously. She wore trousers again, but this time her chemise and matching fitted jacket were blue, and she'd added a mauve neck stock fixed with a small pearl pin. Her chestnut hair with its streak of white midsummer-lightning bolt was even more helter-skelter on this occasion, only the front half pinned up and the rest scandalously left falling down her slim back. "Morning, Mr. Wilde. What can I do for you?"

"I need to have a few more words with you, Miss Woods. There seem to be . . . conflicting accounts."

Sally Woods pressed her lips together, complexion fading to an uneasy ivory. "You've been plenty square with me, please don't suppose I can't savvy that. But it's . . . any angle you ogle from, it's a painful subject. Can I decline?"

"Not this time."

"Is Ellie all right?"

There was such fear in the rising plea at the end of that question that I couldn't help but feel for her all the more. "She's fine. But she painted an interesting picture of you, Miss Woods. Might we sit down?"

"I'll get the whiskey. Sounds like we'll need it." She sighed, nodding at the circle of chairs.

When she was seated across from me with the bottle of spirits between us, swirling pretty copper liquid on her provocatively crossed knee, I set to.

"Miss Abell mentioned that you were at Mount Holyoke together—that you were pretty thick there, the pair of you, like sisters."

Sally Woods looked sure enough heartbroken, glancing sharply away from me with her chin up as if telling herself to be brave, and

I hadn't even come to the *difficult* questions yet. That mightily troubled me.

"I adored Ellie. *Do* adore her. She's passionate and clever and warm, and God knows I'd seldom enough met a girl who shared my interests before the seminary. We're kindred spirits."

"She's charming."

"Ellie is plenty more than charming, though she's that as well. She's got an incisive mind matched with great gentleness. A combination of qualities I lack, so I admire her all the more. She can tell a rig sharp as any fishwife's, but with no one the butt of the joke—I've always been biting, aggressive. I thought that was what strength looked like. It doesn't. Strength looks like Ellie. She's oak as you please. I love her very much."

"She seemed well bustled over the strike business."

Miss Woods took a small sip of liquor, eyes downcast. "She lost her respect for me. I'd have done the same. She'd used to think me a pretty fine specimen before I flew too close to the sun. I'd grand ambitions and grander still intentions, Mr. Wilde, those of reshaping our society for the better, but failure leaves a stink. And then she blamed me for stirring up trouble, getting myself sacked, ruining it all. I don't blame *her* a bit for refusing to speak with me."

Tracing the ragged edges of my scar, I pondered tacks. Dive in too quick and she'd snap closed like a clamshell, even supposing she *was* innocent. Dip my toe in too slow and she'd likewise grow peery.

"Miss Woods, I don't relish asking you questions I know will pain you. But Robert Symmes has accused you of threatening him again, and it's come to light that you knew him . . . intimately?"

Her breath came fast and fearful through her delicate snub nose. When next she lifted the whiskey glass, I'm sorry to say her hand shook. But she swallowed, and looked at me as if through a pistol sight, and nodded.

"Robert and I caught each other's eye when I was hired at the manufactory," she bit out. "Remember how I told you I've superb taste in whiskey and in nothing else? Well, that goes for my taste in men too. Ellie was hired on day one, same as me, and she warned me to steer clear of him—I'd always been mooning after married professors and the like, the more untouchable the better. *Every morning I wake up wishing I'd listened to Ellie and not tried to bag myself a powerful alderman.* Though that makes me sound a brazen opportunist, and really I was halfway in love with him in about the space of a sneeze. I thought him handsome and aloof and mysterious rather than handsome and conscienceless. He's a complete smirk. It was my own blunder, and Ellie and I are paying dear for my mistake."

"You discussed the female-rights movement with him?"

"I thought, hell, why not use his affections for everyone's mutual benefit? Wouldn't that be civic-minded of me? Of all the stupid, self-obsessed notions. He was never fond of me, only fond of what we were about."

The phrase *inventive little slut* flashed through my pate against my will. Miss Woods carded her fingers through the tangle of hair lying over her shoulder. Talk of Symmes looked about as pleasant as cutting out her own tongue.

"You weren't afraid of children?" I wondered.

She paled still further, seeming almost faint for a moment, but shook her head. "I'm a modern and an educated woman, Mr. Wilde. I've a sponge I soak in vinegar. You'll be wanting to see it, I suppose."

"Of course not."

I tried not to sound scandalized. It didn't work. Mrs. Boehm has a similar pessary she washes in herbal tea, as she isn't remotely interested in bearing my kinchin. But Sally Woods was practically a stranger, and Mrs. Boehm was . . . not. I realized, as if a curtain had been swept aside, just what alarmed me about Miss Woods. I know formidable women, dozens of them, women who fight and who win, women who have killed in self-defense or deliberately died for their loved ones. Noble women. Heroic ones. But I'd never met a woman previous who was completely uncaring as to my opinion of her—who'd sleep equally well if her new acquaintances thought her a freak or a marvel. Even Silkie Marsh, for all she's a paper-doll version of a female, preens when she's raking me over the coals. Miss Woods—hair cascading in a tangle, trousers tailored, drinking whiskey with a deftly bent wrist—gave a damn how she looked and sounded. But she didn't care how she looked or sounded *to other people*. Only herself, maybe her loved ones or romantic conquests.

I wondered how deep the divide went, whether it could render her deaf to innocent screams.

"So you initiated the sewing girls' strike, which drew rotten vegetables instead of higher wages, and everything changed between you and Miss Abell," I suggested.

"Robert was not pleased." She winced, agonized. "I thought if he could only see the depth of my sincerity on the subject, it would overwhelm him, supposing he cared for me. . . . He'd never openly objected to my talk of female rights. I was a spooney little fool."

"And then?"

"And then he took his own version of revenge, and no, Mr. Wilde, I will *not* talk about it." Her head dropped, the silver streak in her hair glinting softly, as she struggled to regain control. "I can't say any more, except that he hired the other girls back and not me."

It's an understatement to say that I felt terrible. Drinking her whiskey, plying her with wretched questions. It was every bit my duty, but it felt like abuse.

"All right," I said slowly. "As you may know all too well, the latest letter threatening Robert Symmes came to pass—his building burned, two girls died, and both Symmes and Ronan McGlynn have you pegged as the incendiary. I've been charged with stopping the firestarter, and all evidence points plumb at you, supposing you had opportunity to plant energetic chemicals. So the question I need you to answer, Miss Woods, is—in light of everything you've told me—what am I to make of *these?*"

I pulled the packet of letters Symmes had given me from my frock coat and set them on the table before her.

Sally Woods stared. Pretty mouth gaping, the atmosphere in her greenhouse turned poisonous as the smoke that murdered the stargazers in Pell Street. Her tumbler crashed to the floor in a firework of glittering glass shards as she half rose, reaching out with a clawlike hand at the papers.

"You need to play straight with me," I insisted, also standing. "I've tried my best to help you. The truth, now, or by God—"

I didn't get any further. With an expression of animal terror I'd seldom seen the like of in a fellow human, only in panicked horses and hydrophobic street curs, she snatched up the whiskey bottle and bashed me over my pate.

Things got pretty quiet after that.

For a long spell.

There were no dreams in that place. No visions of Mercy lying on her back in the summer grass at Battery Park, lifting her fingertip to write words in the air, poetry shining golden as sunbeams before fading to a memory. No nightmares of Symmes triumphant, parading Valentine through the streets in a cage.

No, the two hours I spent unconscious on Sally Woods's greenhouse floor were about as absent as my good sense.

When I did wake up, I rolled to my side and hashed the scanty contents of my stomach onto her carpet. It didn't help. My head throbbed like an open sore, though when I set my fingers to it, the skin wasn't broken. Instead I found a lump the size of a bread roll and what smelled like dried whiskey when I pulled my fingers away. The heavy bottle hadn't broken—I could see it lying forgotten on its side. But it had been open when she'd wielded it, so I'd been splashed with the stuff.

When I managed after another minute to drag myself to a seated position, I was unsurprised to find the greenhouse empty and the trunk lid thrown back as if someone had frenziedly packed a carpetbag.

"You brainless little puppy," I said aloud.

Next I crawled to the whiskey bottle. Half its contents had bled onto the floor, but I did a man's work of shrinking the remaining supply. It didn't make my head feel any less of a rotten egg with a crack in the shell. But it improved my mood. I cast a muzzy look at the table where I'd set the bundle of letters.

Of course they were missing. The empty table seemed to level a barefaced leer at me.

Once I could stand, I staggered with the whiskey bottle to the printing press. Throwing back the tarp, I leaned over to peer at the mirrored letters. With my brains in that scrambled condition, making sense of the phrases was no easy matter, but manage it I did, and discern what Sally Woods had been keen to cover up when I'd arrived. They were neatly set in a typeface that was growing uncomfortably familiar, and read:

> *Don't imagine that the copper stars can save you. You will pay for what you have done, and pay at my hand. I will burn the very soul in your body to ash.*

1 2

Oh, isn't it a pity such a pretty girl as I
Should be sent to the factory to pine away and die.

—SUNG BY THE LOWELL FACTORY GIRLS
DURING THE STRIKE OF 1836

THE CIRCUMSTANCE OF having your head stove in by a crazed incendiary is more than moderately unpleasant.

Then again, the circumstance of having the injury fussed over by Mercy Underhill was one of the better experiences I've catalogued.

I'd teetered like a drunkard west and north, though God knows the whiskey I'd consumed had been insufficient to achieve that happy enterprise, sunshine lancing harpoonlike through my eye sockets. Broadway was a fusillade of pedestrian traffic. It was high noon in New York City in springtime on Broadway, and I was in the humor of the men who end up in the Tombs overnight for punching tourists in the mouth.

But he was standing in the middle of the pavement, the natives tell us earnestly, a crazed look to their pupils. *Not even looking at anything particular interesting or nothing, just up at the buildings. Not talking to anyone neither. Just . . . just standing.*

Mercy's new digs were in Howard Street between Broadway

and the railroad. Just north enough of Ward Six to be respectable but close enough that the theatrical types could walk to the Bowery. A brick building, plain but tidy, with flower boxes under the white shutters. After I'd rung the tinny bell to no avail, I cracked the door. Hesitant, hearing hearty applause and a melodic laugh but no approaching footsteps.

When I'd reached the first opening off the foyer, I discovered some half a dozen men and women in a parlor with tattered curtains but remarkably fine art on the walls. Four lodgers smoked and sipped coffee or brandy, and two flanked the piano. The performer to the left was shorter than me—nearly a dwarf if not well and truly one—with a style inclined toward the dapper and a set of gleaming red moustaches echoing his fiery hair. The other was a statuesque woman of perhaps sixty—tall, half smiling, and I suspected the source of the laugh I'd heard blithely echoing out the door.

"I'm terribly sorry," I said, hat in hand, "but I'm—"

"Don't be," scoffed a portly fellow with a fuchsia waistcoat. "These two just delivered a bawdy interlude regarding the lamentable inability of men's cocks to shift their proportions relevant to the . . . well, requirements of the new mother following her precious gift from God, shall we say. And to the tune of Rossini's matchless *Assisa a' piè d'un salice.* You, I am certain, sir, have nothing comparable to be ashamed of." He lapsed into a merry attack of coughing as the rest of the room suppressed similar fits of mirth.

It wasn't that I didn't like them. I did like them. It was that I couldn't see them very well.

"I just need to speak with Miss Mercy Underhill, and then," I said—perhaps a bit unclearly, and clutching at the doorframe.

"Oh, Miss Underhill!" exclaimed a young nymph with enormous blue-green eyes and a Cupid's-bow mouth almost as tall as it was broad. "We *adore* her so already, and the reading she gave us last night—*such* poetry, I'm still weeping in my kerchief, it—"

"Are you a friend of hers?" the distinguished near-dwarf cried in an agreeable basso profundo. "She's our best new recruit! Will you look at him—handsome as he is with that remarkable disfigurement? Of course she would know all the finest flash men in town. Oh, what *luck*."

"Look at the badge on his coat, Kindling," said the queenly woman on the other side of the piano. "He hasn't time for your foolishness. Are you all right, sir? We can take you up to her directly."

"Please," I managed. "That would be—"

"Better now?" Mercy's voice inquired.

The dizzy spell and the tiny man and the portly coughing fellow had presumably taken me up the stairs and into a combined sitting room and bedchamber. It boasted fern wallpaper as liberally dotted with mosquito corpses as Bird's face is with freckles. And that's saying something. I'd landed in the chamber's only visible armchair with my pulsating pate between my knees, a cool wet cloth over my neck, thinking, *Mercy's hand is resting against the cloth on the back of your neck, and you are in no fit condition to diary that memory.*

I've experienced myriad disappointments in my life. But that one stung.

A vague shadow edged past as I regarded the uncarpeted floorboards—spindly figure, girlish posture. Wearing stockings that had once been cut in half and reversed for longevity, the heel portion becoming the toe with the opening sewn shut.

"Miss Duffy," I managed. "How are you faring?"

When I looked up, Dunla Duffy was wandering toward the chipped windowsill. I marveled at the difference a day made. No, at the difference *Mercy* had made. I've spent years pondering what Mercy might taste like, but her charitable inclinations always petrified me. Her mother, Olivia, died of an ailment contracted from someone precisely of Dunla Duffy's ilk, and her father lived—grief burrowing through his soul like a ravenous parasite—to take his spectacularly misguided revenge. The emigrant's hair, now clean, was still a brittle greenish gold color I'd only ever glimpsed before in metal, but Mercy had braided it into a queue. She must have made a tincture for the rash as well, for my old friend has always been clever with potions, and the furious bumps had faded from scarlet to pink. In short, Dunla Duffy looked skeletal but rather less poised to die in any immediate fashion.

Delicate fingers felt at the lump on my head. I figured it for about the size of a smallish prize turnip and said as much, sitting up.

Mercy smiled at one side of her mouth, the smile where the other side tucks into a wry frown, the one that means, *Yes, yes, clever you,* and dropped the wet cloth into a bowl with faded flowers edging the lip. "Rather smaller than a prize turnip but bigger than an underdeveloped watermelon?"

"A minuscule ostrich egg."

"An extraordinarily large marble."

I smiled at her, feeling about twenty years old again. Back when being in love with Mercy was a blaze of unclouded constellations and not a diamond-bright stone in my chest. She wore the sort of gown she favors, with a very wide neck and wider sleeves, striped top to toe in yellow and grey. A few scattered strands of silver outlined her simply arranged black hair. I wanted, *needed*, to count them individually.

Then it occurred to me to wonder if I'd greyed myself. Since 1845 I haven't been any too friendly with mirrors.

"Will I live?"

She tugged my hand up and consulted my life line, cornflower-blue eyes narrowed. "Yes, I think so." She dropped it readily, but in an amiable fashion.

My breath caught at the whimsical reply. She seemed suddenly identical to the Mercy I remembered. Not the Mercy who hid her novel from her father for fear he'd burn it, which he did. Nor the Mercy who hid her assignations with men from the world because the world would judge her a harlot, which we did. Nor the Mercy who thought if her true self were ever revealed, all the lights and the shadows, she'd lose everything.

Which she did.

No, this was the thirteen-year-old Mercy who discovered a mouse nest in her garret and lost no time in collecting brick shards, lumber scraps, and glue, demanding we construct a fortress in the style of the Taj Mahal. The cupola was made of chicken wire, and though I was building it for mice ostensibly, I was actually building it for the same motivation as the creator of the original palace. Mercy cried for an hour when the cat devoured the occupants, cried as if her trust in the world were shattered.

"Who tried to take a closer look at your thoughts?" she wanted to know.

"A manufactory girl."

An eyebrow slid toward the ceiling in disbelief.

"A violently delusional manufactory girl."

"I should say so." She looked doubtful, lower lip taking refuge beneath her upper one. That expression had always broken my heart a little. "Are you going to tell me about it?"

I was brain-injured and in love. So I told her about it.

"How terrifying. And what a pity for the New American Textiles strikers it came to nothing," she mused when I'd finished. "Though frankly, the manufactory conditions in London's East End make our workhouses look like pleasure gardens. I toured one once with a reformer's association. A great, dark, overheated room like a circle of hell where the women worked mechanical looms. The place reeked of sheep's wool and sickly sweat. I was assured that lewd advances by the overseers were so frequent as to be expected and were borne with a sort of numb horror. Meanwhile, the poor creatures' wages wouldn't keep the breath in a gnat. Most were too tired for rage, but as for those who were not—I can picture this Sally Woods, how the system broke her."

"I couldn't, before today," I confessed. "Setting fire to a building full of innocents? It's inhuman."

"Oh, quite human, I fear." Mercy drew her fingers over her opposite wrist regretfully. "It is a mistake to imagine reprehensible acts inhuman when so many humans are capable of them, don't you suppose?"

I did. But it burned in my throat to know that Mercy agreed. That she was picturing her father strapping her in a strait-waistcoat, forcing her into an ice bath. Nearly killing her.

Brightening with an effort, Mercy angled an eye at Miss Duffy. "You sent me a friend. An eccentric housewarming gift, but then we never did go in for convention, did we?"

I studied Mercy over. She wasn't looking at me—hardly ever does when she's speaking, not with anyone. Her eyes are always listing to the edges, as if the mad world she'd spoken of night before last lived in the space between the wall and the window, or the cobblestone and the curb. She seemed rested. Focused. Altogether *better*. I could have lifted her in the air by the waist and twirled her in a circle. Of course I didn't, but even the craving felt better than the dull ache of anxiety.

"Thank you for taking her in," I said. "I could think of no one who'd dream of actually letting her inside, and . . ."

"And you thought of your old friend the madwoman, did you?"

My eyes snapped back to hers, startled. Mercy's are pretty widely set, and she uses them to level a gossamer-delicate gaze of incomprehension at people she thinks have just made confusing, stupid, or bigoted remarks. So innocuous it's devastating. And it was aimed square at me.

"Who is she, then?" Mercy inquired.

"She does outwork for New American Textiles and was given a warning note before her house burned. But it didn't identify the firestarter, and I can't work out who gave it to her. Might we all have a chat? I couldn't get anywhere alone."

"I can't imagine you struggling to maintain a conversation," she said, smiling. "But of course we can."

Mercy went to the window and touched Dunla Duffy's threadbare sleeve. "Dunla, dear, do you remember Mr. Wilde?"

Miss Duffy turned. Her face and eyes were both so spherical she looked quite void of sense. But then she said, "It's the one with the mark on his face. He ought to have jailed me fer standin'—'tisn't right to stand, they say, 'Move along'—but he bought me buttercakes."

"He's much more the sort to buy a girl buttercakes than to jail her for standing." Mercy cast a look at me, and for an incandescent moment I thought it appeared almost fond. She went to the bed and sat, patting the simple quilt. "Dunla, would you come talk with us?"

Miss Duffy's cracked lips dipped into a small frown. "I've nay talent fer talkin' as such. Even Mam said so."

"But you're so kindly and frank—that's all we require."

Dunla Duffy sat gingerly on the edge of the bed. "He's the one read me the note as said she wanted t' *burn us*," she whispered to Mercy. "But he nary said *who*. Can ye ask him, then, since yer his moon?"

"His what?"

"Me mam when I was low once lifted me and said as I was bright to her, brighter than the *gealach lán*, and later when she were gone away and the hunger grew past bearin', I'd think on bein' her full moon. So maybe he'll answer ye when he'd not when I asked him meself."

My hand lifted to push at the rubbery skin on my brow, it not being possible according to the laws of physics to sink through the floor.

"Unfortunately, the letters that spell the name of the culprit weren't on that piece of paper," I hastened to explain. "Can you tell me more about the manufactory girl who gave you the note? You said she had stars in her eyes?"

"Aye, she had, but not any longer." Miss Duffy stared into the middle distance. "'Tis maybe a blessing, I knew a lass in the village as died of it."

"Died of stars?"

"Sure enough, though some survive."

I traced my lips with my thumb and forefinger. Mercy seemed likewise riveted—this was half madness and half metaphor, and yet there was such *method* in it. For all we couldn't savvy her, Miss Duffy clearly imagined she was talking solid, straight-line sense.

"And you know her well?" I urged. "The girl who'd stars in her eyes?"

"Well enough from the spell, when they said as we'd be given more wages if we linked arms, singin' and marchin' in a circle, like."

"This spell . . . did they call it a *strike*?"

She snapped her fingers. "Aye, 'tis the very word."

Here was progress, the sudden lightening of my heavy bones told me. For strikes are rare enough, strikes by women practically unheard of. Dunla Duffy performed outwork for—of all places—New American Textiles. The picture in my mind, as yet the merest suggestion of an outline, gained a new brushstroke.

"It reminded me of a spell me cousin tried on the potatoes afore she died," Miss Duffy continued, "so I didn't favor it, spells bein' wicked, sir, and the potatoes as rotten after as before. But they said as it weren't the wicked sort o' spell, and I were that hungry, so I thought the saints would nay see the harm?"

"They don't see any harm at all in the strike sort of spell, Dunla, I assure you," Mercy said, a brittle weariness sharpening her tone.

"I trusted the starry-eyed girl when she said so," Miss Duffy agreed. "She'd nary lie t' the likes of us outworkers, she were always so gentle. We'd nay trusted her friend—the one as is marked by the devil, she frightens me—but we trusted her. It were that disappointin' when the spell didn't work after all."

My head pulled back, the motion echoing through my sore skull like a hammer blow against a great iron bell.

"Does the girl with stars in her eyes have a lovely complexion and very pretty ash-brown hair—about five foot two, plump, amber-colored eyes?" I asked carefully.

Miss Duffy's innocent face sparked with triumph. "That's her."

"And the one with the devil's mark—she has a handsome face and dark brown hair with a great white streak at the temple?"

Grinning, Miss Duffy nodded. "Just so."

"Timothy, are you all right?" Mercy asked urgently.

"No," I admitted, newly sick to my stomach. "If what she says is correct and I'm hearing it aright, Miss Ellie Abell attempted to warn Miss Duffy here of Sally Woods's desperate intentions. The note clearly indicates the house in Pell Street, since it was given to a resident. Then I handily allowed Miss Woods to bash me in the cranium and disappear."

Eyes wide, Dunla Duffy commenced rocking a little. I figured it for a fair reaction. She was young, I reminded myself, so very young yet, no older than fifteen, and navigating a faraway land with neither kith nor kin to guide her. Anyway, I was half set to try rocking myself, and the rest be damned. But Sally Woods wanted fast catching, so I sucked in a breath and carried on.

"Miss Duffy, can you remember any strangers visiting the Pell Street house before it burned?"

She only rocked harder. "Nary strangers."

"The other outworkers must have fled with or without their piecework. Can you think where any might have gone?"

"The Witch would ha' gone back to her tower," she whispered. "Back where they hover over their cauldrons. She said when I offered to pay her later fer the light, she'd have us all roasting over a spit by then, said as tomorrow wasn't good enough, and so the others chucked me out."

"She sounds terribly frightening," Mercy said soberly.

"She'd seven devil candles, just that 'twas enough to make you afeared o' her, sure enough."

"Right," I sighed. "Excepting witches in towers, did you know any of the residents well enough to help me find them?"

"I'd not lived there long. I'd been ousted from me old digs when I could nay pay them weekly, and the rent in Pell Street were by the night. I'm a good girl, I work honest. Some said as there were other ways o' bein' paid, but I wouldn't. They weren't my friends, those other lasses, though I'd ne'er want them burnt."

Mercy took her hand with an expression that tore a sizable hole in my chest, she having once been in the unspeakable position of facing ruin or exchanging intimacy for a hefty sum of money. I'd caught her at it and turned a private nightmare into a public spectacle, one I can't think of without wanting to eradicate myself. I can still hear her shouting at me three years later, still see unshed tears gleaming in the moonlight.

Stop looking at me like that, it's horrifying. I am the only thing I have, a man can't ever understand that, I have nothing else to sell, Timothy.

Wrenching myself out of the past, I questioned, "Can you tell us aught about your employer, Robert Symmes?"

Dunla Duffy stared, mute.

"The man with the pocket watch?" I attempted, faintly amused.

"*Oh.*" Miss Duffy made a frantic sign of the cross. "He's an awful bad man, sir."

"Can you tell us why you think so?"

"Because o' the girl with the stars in her eyes. After the strike she were gone fer another week entire, and when she came back, he'd smile every time he spied her. He'd touch her arm, her cheek. It weren't decent, sir, even after the stars had gone."

"What do you mean by stars, Miss Duffy?" I asked in despair.

She appeared offended by the question. A mulish cast suffused her features.

"I think I know," Mercy mused, touching her bottom lip introspectively with her teeth. "Miss Duffy, have *you* ever had stars in your eyes?"

"No," she gasped, scandalized. "I *told* ye, I were raised proper."

"You see?" Mercy asked me, smiling sadly.

For a moment I didn't. Then I did, and that was much worse.

"You think that Miss Abell was with child, Miss Duffy?" I questioned.

Dunla Duffy furiously clapped both palms over her ears.

"He's sorry for being so crude, Miss Duffy." Mercy gently reclaimed the nearer hand. "Can you tell me, between us womenfolk, and meaning her no harm, how you learned that she'd stars in her eyes?"

Dunla Duffy dropped her voice conspiratorially. "At work when I were after pickin' up more pieces, I stopped to freshen myself, and she were in the lavatory, nine sorts o' sickly, and I petted her hair and said as no matter what the circumstance, it were God's gift t' her, but the sickness were makin' her muddled in the head, fer I could nay understand her answer."

"What did she say?" Mercy asked as I leaned forward.

"Well, 'tis true enough that I don't always follow folk when they're speakin'," Miss Duffy replied slowly. "But this weren't the same, fer she looked me clear in the face and she said, *This is all Sally's fault.*"

I nterrupting Miss Abell inside the manufactory again seemed neither prudent nor profitable. At six o'clock when the sun sank westerly, I could catch her if I timed it well and discover just what razor-thorned entanglement had perhaps produced a child by another woman's doing—and a lost child at that. So after stopping at the Tombs to order an immediate guard set over Miss Woods's eerie greenhouse, I headed for the Catholic Asylum to patch up one of my few friendships.

My trek to the orphanage passed as if in a dream. Because I wasn't walking, not really.

I was cataloguing moments.

Moments of quiet glances at Mercy, her bird's-egg irises cupping black pupils that seem to stretch for miles in the distance. Me thanking them both, Mercy's *We will see you soon, in that case?* and how it left no room for refusal, only my *If you'd be so kind,* and then her *Can selfish wishes be kindnesses simultaneously?*—which was admittedly the enigmatic Mercy but her saying something marvelous, ending with a press of her hand, which I didn't kiss because it would have been too soon, too much, and far too little all at once.

I arrived at the orphanage during lunch hour, but I'd no luck in the dining hall, standing in the arched stone entryway searching the tables for a dark red head. Thankfully, though, I know a great many of Bird's pals. And they know me, because if I'm willing to compliment myself on any of my meager victories, it's this one: I'd put them there. Having found them somewhere else that doesn't bear writing about. So when Ryan and Neill and Sophia spied a copper star with a wide black hat standing under the keystone, they ran up to me.

"What the devil's happened?" Neill asked, in the brogue that's lessening every time I hear it. "Bird said she'd be in her room finishing a *love letter*."

"I—she *what*?"

"She won't even tell me about the ball," Sophia—who was eleven, and newly enamored of balls—complained. "Will *you* tell us about the ball, Mr. Wilde? Were there cakes? She was very pretty in her cloak, didn't you think so?"

"I did think—"

"She looked like an angel, she did. I ain't half surprised she's found a beau," Ryan added with a shy smile.

My mouth worked at speech. It failed despite thirty years of steadyish practice.

"There was a newsboy, this morning. *Loitering*," Neill said meaningfully.

"A *handsome* one," Sophia confided, "wi' fine manners and blond hair and spectacles—"

"I'll be back soon, and with more time to spare, all right?"

I clapped their shoulders and made for Bird's room as hastily as my pounding head allowed. Startled but optimistic as to my prospects. Continuing the established theme of my day, however, our meeting did not go according to plan.

"I *don't* want to see you," said Bird Daly when she opened the door, regarding me as if I were a less desirable species of bedbug.

"Bird, I'm sorry, but that benefit was getting downright dusty."

She'd stepped back from the threshold, so I walked inside. The nuns ensure their charges' sleeping areas are kept virtuously tidy, but this one seemed overpopulated beyond its occupants' control. Hats stacked atop trunks. Boot tracks crisscrossing. Crude rag dolls with woolen hair, limbs akimbo, keeping company in a neat line along the wall with a single horsehair pony that Elena had given Bird two years previous. Hair ribbons lurking under bed frames and dangling from bureau drawers. One too many pillows in Bird's bunk. And there it was—a letter in Bird's floridly dramatic hand, drying cool as you please on the desk in a barrage of midday sunlight.

Sidling closer to the writing surface, I sifted through and selected words for her. "You've every reason to be annoyed, but—"

Smash.

Bird stood before me, chest heaving, having just fragmented her own inkpot in preventing me approaching the desk.

I gaped in dismay. Not at the inkpot. She'd used to shatter things when she felt she was shattering herself, when the world around her tilted unbearably and she struggled to navigate the tempest, would test gravity by destroying ornamental knickknacks and mugs of tea and on one memorable occasion an actual window. It devastated me to think she could still feel that way, its being a year and more since the breaking things stopped.

"Bird—"

"You should have *told me!*" she cried, walking through ink to press a livid finger against my chest. "That she was there, that the *Madam* was there."

"Holy Christ," I managed, no longer concerned over profanity. "How—"

She reached into a pocket of her simple brown charity dress and thrust a poorly penned communiqué into my face.

Dear Miss Daly,

I write at the conveenyance of my frend Matchbox as hes learnd of his letters and I an unskooled News Hawker but plenty Rich for all that. Your pressense at the bennifit was much

wellcome and I hope later to see You maybe by the fountain in
this here cort yard maybe else wear but I'll be there to meet You
at seven of the clock every night till the nights stop coming. Don't
be ketched about Silkie Marsh at the fight or that you missed the
rest. There was no fight and its a damn shame Val Wilde wuld
have won that bout twenty ways from nohow it wuld have
been a particular smasher you bet your last dime. I love you.

—Ninepin

"Bird, I'm . . . I'm so sorry you found out this way. But why would I have wanted you to know that—"

"You wouldn't," she interrupted, tossing her head and pretending there wasn't ink on her shoes. "But I *ought* to have known. You ought to have savvied that I'd have cut out properly if you'd chanted the truth to me and not treated me like . . ." She lost English for an instant, fuming. "You thought I couldn't manage seeing—"

"That's not true, I didn't *want* you to—"

"I ought to have known!"

"I'd have been a cad to tell you."

"You don't savvy she's in my head anyhow?" she all but shrieked.

We were quiet for a few seconds. I didn't know what to say. And had I known, I wouldn't have been brave enough to say it.

Bird's small frame was practically thrumming with rage. "You don't think it matters to me whether or not *you* tell me the truth? Get *out*."

As I was pushed unceremoniously out the door by a thirteen-year-old girl, I attempted, "Bird, I'm truly sorry. Forgive me. I'll be back by later. And meanwhile please be careful about writing Ninepin love letters. He's a genteel sort but rough living, and he gets enthusiastic over beautiful—"

"As if I would ever write that silly newsboy a love letter!" she cried.

I took a moment. Caution seeming appropriate. "Neill thought you were writing—"

"Yes, indeed I was. It's none of *your* business, though, and it's *nothing* to do with that newsboy. I am writing a letter to Mr. James Playfair, and you've a great deal of nerve, and I'll thank you to *get out* and allow me to get back to my own affairs."

She slammed the door in my face.

As I exited the prettily worked stone corridors the way I'd come, I concluded with grim reluctance that I'd slender chance of success at any of the tasks Gotham's gods had seen fit to bestow upon me. Through an open streetside window, a baby was shrieking, as unwanted tiny creatures tend to announce their continued existence to the world.

13

Were she, scorning the opinions of that world which scorns her poverty, to cast herself into the hot-house of vice, she might get along very well as regards mere food and clothes, for a winter or two; but let us rather hope to see her freeze, starve, die in misery, with purity still in her soul, than to yield to the fatal step which would engulf all that is precious and beautiful in her character.

—NED BUNTLINE, *MYSTERIES AND MISERIES OF NEW YORK*, REGARDING THE POOR SEWING GIRL

AT FIVE MINUTES TO SIX O'CLOCK, daylight ebbing sluggishly into gunsmoke clouds, I lurked in a doorway in Nassau Street across from the New American Textile Manufactory. My hat pulled low, my head pounding like a brass band. The painted metal windows where the cutters labored over slave togs showed row after row of beribboned heads and Simeon Gage's stalking shadow.

When six o'clock pealed stridently from the church towers, the manufactory girls rose as if one. It took a few minutes to collect their belongings, store their unfinished efforts, don their bonnets of white chip and elaborately worked straw. Then they poured out of the great building, some arm in arm and some swinging tin lunch pails, a rainbow-hued stream of feminine labor.

Then a man who'd likewise been idling in a doorway burst out of it. He'd a bucket in one hand, a paintbrush in the other. And when the first of the Bowery girls drew near, he dipped the brush and slashed across the front of the moll's dress a lurid streak of blood-red paint.

She screamed, and quick as a viper he'd progressed to the next girl, swiping at her with a murderous look in his eye as she ducked away in terror.

"Harlots!" he was shouting. He was a small man, a sallow-cheeked and an underfed one, with clothes that had been perfectly cut to his shape but made from the cheapest possible cloth. A tailor if I'd ever set eyes on the breed. "You filthy, selfish, heartless—"

I was nearly across Nassau by then. Dodging hacks and wagons, half slipping on dung and straw, hands curled into fists. Other men stopped, turning to see what the shrieks were about. While several appeared plenty alarmed, a hatchet-faced brute started up whistling while a lout selling trinkets from a harnessed box clapped in approval.

"Stop that *at once*," I ordered, flapping the lapel of my coat with the copper star pinned to it.

"They're *vultures!*" he cried, wielding the brush in my face. The savagery of the gesture made it seem a bloodied knife. "Jezebels, the lot of them, stealing bread from the mouths of honest family men."

"You're an honest family man, I take it?"

"And a Bible-fearing Christian who respects the *natural* order. Get the hell out of my—"

He stopped talking after that. Mostly because, after a planted left foot and a short but merciless spin, I'd pinned him to the grimy sidewalk with his arm twisted behind his back and my shin against his spine, winding him. He spluttered, his face keeping closer company with bird droppings than usual, thrashing under my leg.

"If you don't want a lacing, you'll settle, and I mean *instantly*," I suggested, grinding my knee into his ribs. My temper had passed scorching into molten. The girls formed a half circle. Staring with white faces, a few of the molls paint-smeared and weeping softly.

"You've obviously never watched your kinchin go hungry so a pack of whores can live in sin, you pig!"

"I've also never been arrested for assaulting ladies in the street, so you'll have the advantage of me there too."

"You smug little—"

"Excuse me—sir!"

A chap with muttonchop whiskers—a tanner from the smell of him and the looks of his mottled hands, who'd been observing proceedings with consternation—stepped forward. "Aye?"

"There'll be another star police coming up Nassau on his rounds any minute now. Would you flag him down for me? Head south until you see the copper pin."

"Gladly," he agreed, striding away.

"Whores," the man beneath me moaned. "Bloody *whores*—"

"Shut it," I suggested with feeling.

"My work has dried up, my son hasn't eaten meat in a week, and all so these uppity bats can keep themselves in perfume and flounces. It's *wickedness*."

"My wages go to my mum in Connecticut," one of the paint-smeared women protested, her lip trembling, "and I've never—"

"Ma'am, this one doesn't merit your life story," I observed. "Are any of you hurt?"

Murmuring to each other, blinking damp eyelashes, they answered in the negative. Then Ellie Abell, her lovely features taut as a tightrope, edged her way to the front of the crowd.

"Oh, Mr. Wilde," she breathed. "Whatever are *you* doing here?"

"Just now, arresting a scoundrel. But might I speak with you? When my hands aren't full," I added, glaring at the villain's back.

"I, I really haven't the time," she stammered. "I must be getting to—"

Thankfully, the fresh copper star materialized, led by the tanner. Unsurprisingly, I didn't recognize him. Unsurprisingly, he recognized me. He was a burly fellow with a plug of chewing tobacco in his mouth and enough healed-over breaks in his face to qualify for state congress.

"Mr. Wilde," he grunted. "Post me."

"Deliver this to the Tombs and I'll owe you one?"

"I'd been yearning for a little exercise." He knelt, holding a Bowie knife before the bulging eyes of my captive. "Give me any trouble and I'll slit your nostrils. Savvy?"

I'd have harbored concerns over this remark had it not been both typical and beyond my control. So instead I watched the tailor being dragged off by his shirt collar.

"Are we in any trouble, sir?" one of the paint-smeared girls whispered.

"Of course not. You needn't even bring charges. I saw the whole thing. Good afternoon, ladies—Miss Abell, I need a word."

The trembling Bowery girls dispersed northward, casting curious looks at Miss Abell but keen to fly away home. It was a Saturday, I realized, and thus they'd just been paid their weekly wages. Dress pockets with dollars tucked into them muttered papery whispers, eager to be emptied at dance halls and oyster saloons after the bills had been paid and the cash sent home to kinfolk. A single night of pleasure before the treacle-thick drag of mending and washing and housework to be accomplished before Monday.

I offered Miss Abell my arm. "Might I escort you, wherever you're going?"

She took it, hesitant but smiling a little. "After that arrest . . . I reckon so. Thank you."

"My pleasure. Destination?"

"I'm going to Catharine Market for groceries."

So I turned us east on Maiden Lane, then north on Water Street, where the masts of the ships thrust skyward above the rooftops. Not speaking at first. Letting her grow accustomed to me. Women lit lamps in the windows of low public houses, wiping callused hands on their aprons, watching the swelling flood of workers. The edges of the sky tinted like a slow-rising bruise, shadows strengthening Miss Abell's cheekbones and dulling the soft curls of her hair. Sally Woods, warped as she clearly was, had been right about one thing—Ellie Abell was exceptional in her way, open as a meadow and every bit as lovely.

I cleared my throat. "I saw Miss Woods."

"Oh?"

The sound was pitched high enough that I could practically taste the fear in her throat.

"Yes."

"Did you . . . find out anything?"

"Yes. Then she knocked me cold with a whiskey bottle."

Ellie Abell gasped, covering her mouth with her hand. "I'm so terribly sorry, I never . . . My *God*."

"I didn't mean to ketch you."

"No, I'm snug, it's just . . ." She made an effort to steady her breathing. "Well, it's *dreadful*, isn't it?"

"You're the one said she might be violent," I observed mildly.

She shook her head. "I mean, I didn't *know* it before, not for absolutely certain, and heavens, to think she was my closest friend and now it's come to—oh, Mr. Wilde, you seem like an honest sort, and that's awful. Are you all right?"

"Hale enough. I wondered if you could help me with something, though."

"If I can, of course I'll try."

I reached into my frock coat. "Do you know a Miss Dunla Duffy?" I asked, passing her the note.

She stopped walking. Swayed, paper in hand, and I steadied her. Her caramel irises glowed—a fox's eyes, one cornered by hounds.

"Where did you get this?" she whispered.

"From Miss Duffy. We're acquainted. Her house burned down, you know."

"Yes. I do."

We resumed walking. Catharine Market was near enough to the Queen Mab to trigger scuttling, spiderish memories. And close enough to the docks that it's populated by both the hardworking and the criminal, the stalwart and the damned. A ragpicker passed us with his obscenely long hook on a pole, a bag of scraps slung across his shoulders. Dead rabbits with teeth missing and cigars lodged in the gaps cast admiring looks at my companion. The scents of fish and fowl on the wind grew stronger as the light continued to fade.

"Dunla Duffy is an outworker for New American Textiles." She spoke in an odd, untuned-piano tone. "The outworkers and the cutters don't associate overmuch, but Sally's mad scheme got us all . . . twisted. Oh, I don't mean to imply that *I'd* any prejudice against the outworkers beforehand. I mean, *some* of the manufactory molls do. Against popery and such. I was raised Episcopalian, my grandparents were from Yorkshire, and we take a different view on these matters. These Irish lasses might be unenlightened, but how can they help they're raised in ignorance? God, I can't possibly . . . How I *wish* you'd never seen my note." Her hand on my arm had begun to tremble.

"It is yours, then."

She nodded, and a dewy sheen of tears flooded her eyes.

"Miss Abell, seeing as the house in Pell Street took two people up in flames and Miss Woods escaped me, I can only beg you to tell me plainly what's happened."

If I had her pegged for the right keyhole, moral obligation would open her lips when they might otherwise have remained a locked strongbox. And I'm more inclined to use keys than axes. Sure enough, she released a shuddering sigh, a prelude to a story.

"I didn't want to believe it." Her voice shook. "When I think of Sally at Mount Holyoke, all that time we were diarying sonnets and Scriptures and sums, it's as if an *anchor's* been attached to my heart when I try to fathom what she's done since. Might we sit down, Mr. Wilde?" Miss Abell had turned an unlikely shade of ashen, a color so wrong on her perfect skin that I didn't think I could forgive myself for painting it there. "I'm feeling a mite—"

"Of course."

We'd reached the borderline of Ward Four and Ward Seven—Catharine Street. The market buzzed with Saturday-night wanderers flitting in and out of the torchlight and the few scattered gas lamps like so many mayflies. We passed eels in open barrels slithering, glossy and snakelike, over and under and over each other, passed mounds of salted mackerel and pyramids of leeks, to a vendor who boasted a table with benches. Once we'd seated ourselves beneath the lank-haired cook staring out of his booth, I realized I'd no notion when last I'd eaten.

"Two plates of corned beef with the fat, and mustard, and some rolls, and two glasses of whiskey. My treat," I added. "And if you don't want whiskey, Miss Abell, you'll overlook my having two, I hope."

"Oh! How generous. I *do* want it, though, I'm afraid." She pulled a kerchief from her skirts, drying her still-quivering eyes.

I busied myself with payment and carrying plates, feeling about as ready to hear her tale as she was to deliver it to me. Which is to say less than entirely keen. Seating myself, I tilted my drink to her with a nod.

"Thank you. I think of Sally at school, and *oh*, the hijinks we'd get up to." Cutting the corned beef and shoving it into a folded bit of roll, Miss Abell tucked into the peck like a first-rate Bowery girl.

"What kind?"

"Nothing too sordid, but she was the sort of person it seemed impossible to refuse. I mean . . . well, it certainly wasn't *my* notion to sneak out of the dormitories at midnight to put indigo in the laundresses' tubs where the linens were soaking and turn everyone's drawers and petticoats blue, but I went along with it, didn't I? Sally was a heroine for weeks afterward to all save a few stick-in-the-muds. None of us ever planned on being *literal* bluestockings, but . . ." She trailed off, smiling ruefully at the memory.

"Miss Woods implied she was considerably less refined than you."

"Oh, she was decisive and clever in a way I've never dared to be—all her words were bullets and her sentences cannonballs." As if seeing the imagery she'd just summoned, Miss Abell stopped with a haunted expression. "I never—"

"You couldn't have known."

I commenced smearing mustard on bread. Oftentimes when people suppose I'm not listening, the listening grows considerably more profitable. My graft is to sit there, scarred and sympathetic, whilst they shovel information like dirt onto a corpse.

"Sally was . . . I admired her so," Miss Abell breathed. "Do savvy that I don't expect you to share my taste in politics. Plenty of good Christian men find they cannot. But whenever a new cause was proposed at the seminary—say, a campaign to defy the postal injunctions against abolitionism, for instance—Sally was the first banging on doors with a pen in her mouth and a sheaf of petitions in her fist, calling, *What ho, sisters! Our voices are needed!* She once raised the funds to buy a *cow*, of all things, for a poor farmer's widow who'd lost hers to a train accident near our school."

"Impressive."

"I thought so too," Miss Abell confessed, skin warming marginally at my praise. "She wasn't like anyone else. And she knew it. And she . . . I honestly don't think she cared a hairpin. When she'd stay up with me in the common room, her playing mad arpeggios almost as if they bored her and me plodding the chords underneath, I felt nearly as special as she was."

Blanks in my canvas filled as Miss Abell spoke. Theirs hadn't been a shallow camaraderie that would turn cold as soon as the winds did—Sally Woods and Ellie Abell had been bloodless sisters. And that sliced away a thin piece of Miss Abell every time she spoke of her lost friend. Whatever had happened between them, the aftermath had been about as merciful as cholera.

And I loathed Robert Symmes more with every passing second.

"After school you came to New York together?"

"Always together, through hell and high water, when we didn't *remotely* understand what either one of those looked like. We were hired at the same time." She swiped a blot of mustard away from her lip with her forefinger. "At the New American, I mean. We shared digs in a boardinghouse in Hester Street belonging to the manufactory. I still live there. Most of us do."

"How did it suit you?"

"Manufactory work was new to us, but it seemed . . ." A pinch of shame marred her pretty brow. "Oh, to think of it now, how ignorant we were. Glamorous?"

"A steady graft, your spoils your own—why shouldn't it have

been? None of us are used to molls earning a living wage as you are, not by half."

"You're kind to say so, but we were fools. When Sally and I were friends, we wanted . . ."

She often paused, I'd noticed, collected stray threads of thought. As if she knew that the slightest misstep would be held against her. That any stray word would render her belief in the rights of women forever invalid, would be hurtled like vitriol in her lovely face.

"I've wanted plentiful untoward things, if it helps," I offered, chasing corned beef with my roll.

Ellie Abell's mouth took on a reluctant expression. Not as if she didn't want to tell me something—as if she didn't want to hear it herself, said aloud.

"I don't . . . I've never thought myself *unlucky*, you see. My father was a university dean in Massachusetts and my mother a painter of landscapes. They taught me everything that sparked my interest—skills to do with keeping house and skills as impractical as my fancies. But . . . I suppose that Sally and I imagined a place where our time was *ours*. I don't mean that in quiet homes filled with their kinchin women don't find joy. I only . . ."

All nonchalant patience, I sprinkled coarse salt over a cut of beef.

"Oh, what's the *use*? I can never put this as well as Sally could," Ellie Abell admitted ruefully. "*She* used to say to everyone who argued with her, if all the men on earth were forced to work out mathematical equations and never fight tigers . . . you see how it wouldn't suit some of them?" She pressed her fingers against her temple.

"Of course. What compelled Miss Woods to fight for higher wages?"

Miss Abell splayed her fingers on the rough-hewn pine. "She

started up talking to Dunla. As if Dunla were some sort of *cause* and not a person."

This was a new piece of the puzzle. "Miss Duffy dropped off her piecework at the manufactory, and Miss Woods . . . what, accosted her?"

Ellie Abell nodded, worrying at a seam in the pine. "At first she only offered her extra food. Dunla looking that lenten and all. Then Sally started up asking *me* whether it was fair, and I told her no, of course it isn't fair, that we could have been in the same straits! But she was desperate and we weren't, and Sally just . . . Oh, the stupid, *stupid* girl."

I settled my elbows on the tabletop. "Miss Woods spent some time palavering with Miss Duffy. Miss Woods developed some strong opinions. Then your employer entered the picture, and Miss Woods . . . imagined she could kill a pair of birds with a single stone?"

Ellie Abell nodded miserably.

"And she kept at it, long after you'd supposed Symmes had no real interest in any cause save his own."

"I don't wish to be ungrateful—I admit it kittles Mr. Symmes to be admired by his underlings, so he'll grant a wish here or there to puff himself up, ensure loyalty, but he loathes being bossed. I *told* her it wouldn't work!" she cried. "But Sally had married herself to the twin notions of having this man she wanted and having a better workplace after Dunla told her she'd recently dined on some trapped rats she roasted over a barrel."

"You haven't told me the important part yet," I said slowly. "How did the strike *end*?"

Miss Abell adjusted her shawl as if it were a chain-mail coat. The shadows in the marketplace had lengthened into bands of flickering torchlight beams and the streaks of darkness between them. Some had begun to eat away at her as the sun abandoned us, turning parts of her hands and torso and face into mere gaps in the gloom.

Exquisitely carefully, as if she were stitching lace onto a board, Ellie Abell told me a story.

The strike had commenced on a mockingly splendid late-summer Monday the previous year. The sort that vanishes in a heartbeat, hinting at autumn and tasting of the last overrich berries still clinging to the bushes. Girls massed before the New American to protest, fresh-faced and hopeful.

Their first day had gone well, save for the glare of Robert Symmes when he arrived, and the bitten-off words that he was "far too poor a man to raise the wages of a passel of pigeons." The second day had gone well save that Symmes broke the ranks of the Bowery girls with a stream of German and Yidisher matrons, marching them into the manufactory to keep churning out trousers for human cattle. The third day had gone well except for the arrival of the out-of-work tailors, many of them union men, who'd started right into catcalls and toxic glares and weighty spitting. The fourth, fifth, and sixth days had gone well excepting the thunderstorms and the fact the tailors had found some tomatoes festering on a shelf before a corner liquor grocery and put them to use against the dissidents' skirts.

Then Saturday had dawned, and the strike had been broken by means of hired thuggery and ended. As if this weren't bad enough, at the close of the day, unlike every other Saturday they'd ever known at the New American Textile Manufactory, no one was paid. And all the while the scissors of the emigrants *snick-snick-snickered* at them from the open windows above Nassau Street.

"I can't think of how Dunla and the other outworkers looked without wanting to cry," Miss Abell said unsteadily. "Oh, we cutters were hungry enough, but we'd saved money for tea and apples. They . . . they'd *nothing* to spare. We pooled our chink, gave them what coin we could, and they used it on victuals a dog wouldn't touch."

"I'm shocked Symmes allowed the strike to continue for a full week."

"Oh. On Friday the article came out in the *New Republican.* 'Rights for Females, Sewing Girls a Busted Flush.' That . . . well, that *more* than settled the matter."

Something familiar caressed my still-throbbing brains. "Was it written by a Mr. William Wolf?"

She frowned, surprised. "That it was. Oh, I'm sure he *meant* it to be fair—I mean, he seemed genteel enough, and I was quoted to good effect, Sally too, but then . . . he talked with *Dunla* for another perspective on female rights, and oh, imagine it."

"She sounded a hair shy of sensible?"

"You could say that. Mr. Symmes was hot enough to *explode* when it came out in the late edition. Said we'd gone and made him a public laughingstock. I think previous to that, our small efforts had amused him, but then . . . It was over the next day. Men were standing there with brickbats when we arrived with our picketing signs. Some of them I recognized as copper stars without their pins. That . . . surprised me."

"It doesn't surprise me," I managed. "But I'm deeply sorry."

"It doesn't matter how sorry you are," she said in a dead-of-winter undertone. "But thanks all the same. Anyhow. It lasted a week, and I never want to cogitate on it again."

Sitting back, I contemplated her. The frozen shoulders and the neutral expression. The hot pulse of living hurt beneath the carefully hammered armor.

"Miss Abell, I can't help but think you're still leaving out the . . . the *most* important part," I ventured gently.

"The most important part is that Sally organized the strike, and that it did *not* go well," she said, voice ringing. "Afterward we returned to work, all save for Sally. I lost touch with her completely. She never so much as sent me a letter. I wasn't worth her while, apparently. That hurt more than . . . more than the rest of it."

My pulse thrummed uneasily. "But you were friends for such a long time before. Weren't you in the aftermath keen to find out why—"

"No." Her tone was dry enough to cure beef. "Sally had delegated me too many . . . hopeless responsibilities. Anyhow, sometime after she was sacked, Mr. Symmes came to me—as her closest friend—with some remarkably disturbing letters. He asked me how he should handle her, and I told him to let her alone. I'd used to care for her so. I tried to protect— I clearly shouldn't have done. I'm sorry, but I've nothing more to say."

She did, though. About an illness she blamed Sally Woods over, one that Miss Duffy was convinced was a pregnancy. About just why in hell she'd delivered a warning to *Dunla Duffy* of all people, when Symmes owned scores of properties and Miss Duffy could comprehend writing about as deftly as she could tact and economics.

So I took a gamble. Speaking as softly as ever I could.

"Miss Duffy mentioned you'd been indisposed after the strike ended."

Ellie Abell rose, adjusting her skirts. Appearing to me, under all the rest of it, lonely. Wholly, despairingly lonely. I've always had a brother. Even when I didn't want one. But there is ordinary loneliness and there is a hollowed-out loneliness like a grave fresh dug. Miss Abell—in a way that sent a pulse of grief through me—looked as if she suffered the latter.

"All the fresh goods will be gone if I dally any longer. Yes, Mr. Wilde, I was ill with a bad case of ague."

"I wish you'd trust me," I pleaded.

"I wish you'd *let me alone*," she begged, bending with the table between us, close enough so I could feel the warmth of her breath on my cheek. "And I need hardly remind you that Dunla is half in her wits and half out of them."

Jumping after her, I stood with my arms spread. Not touching her. But sure enough blocking her, and not proud of the fact. Her eyes gleamed in the spectral light as her hands fisted in her skirts.

"Answer me just one single question more, please, Miss Abell. You warned the Pell Street residents specifically that Miss Woods meant to burn them alive. How could you have known? Miss Duffy certainly seems afraid of your old friend—she called her devil-marked only this afternoon."

"If so, that's the most sense Dunla's ever shown," Ellie Abell hissed. "Dunla was one of several physically *struck* before we finally dispersed. Sally didn't give a dried fig, kept telling us to stay in the circle and the men would stop. She actually said, *It's to be expected people will be hurt in a war.* As if we were an army. Can you *imagine?* Needles versus brickbats."

"Was she always so callous?" I lowered my arms.

She shook her head, eyes swimming. "I hadn't thought . . . Oh, I don't *know* about before. Or what changed her. If she changed. But it oughtn't to have bustled me—she was furious at Dunla over the gammy publicity that ended the strike. Sally never could abide thickheadedness—it had always infuriated her when the rest of us couldn't keep up. If women are to be allowed autonomy, what's to become of the stupid ones?"

"I don't know," I realized. "The same as what happens to stupid men?"

"Maybe. Anyhow. When Mr. Symmes showed me the note about setting outworkers afire, I thought of Dunla at once. He agreed Pell Street may well be at risk, so I did all I could. She and Sally *hated* each other."

"Enough to set an entire house aflame?"

"Have you ever seen what a woman obsessed with vengeance *looks* like when her dreams are obliterated, Mr. Wilde?"

"Yes," I replied. Seeing Silkie Marsh's face before me, smiling like that other breed of angel—the ones who are said to live below us rather than above.

"Then please stop hounding me and *find Sally Woods*," she admonished, drawing her shawl about her shoulders and stalking into the cadaverous twilight.

Seconds later she was untraceable. I'd have had as much luck tracking the smoke that had left the torches five minutes prior. I wanted to follow, sweetly chip and tenderly hammer the truth out of her. But I'm not that man, so I departed the market. Very nearly as ignorant as I'd entered it.

And therefore doing no one in the saga the smallest bit of good.

I headed for my office at the Tombs, planning on taking the proper action of a responsible copper star who's feeling better than half checkmated. I'd used to ignore this key principle in favor of pestering game pieces until they made sense to me. But people have died that way. And I'm a fast learner.

So instead, I asked for help.

"'Tis a waiting game now," Mr. Connell offered, his bluntly plain face troubled. "Now Sally Woods is away from her lair, lackin' the means fer daily coin, she'll buy her last chestnut, get peckish, get careless. . . ."

Connell sat before me where I listlessly presided. Mr. Piest reclined on my desk's edge, sipping the Dutch gin we keep in my cave for ruminative purposes. Mr. Kildare leaned against the wall next to my stacked record books, smoking with his arms crossed.

Kildare's eyes appeared a shade more glazed, his beard a tad less kempt.

Love, I thought, *is extremely unhealthy.* And then recalled seeing Mercy that morning with a sensation like my heart flapping great feathery wings within my chest. Thereby proving my own point.

I sat with a strip of butcher paper before me, listlessly sketching. Later I'd write dust-dry facts about April 21, about suffering Symmes's ire that morning and getting my pate cracked by an incendiary and harassing a beautiful woman. But in the meantime— colleagues at either elbow. Charcoal in my hand. Shapes shifting gradually into the sweet drape of Miss Abell's hair, the daring line of Miss Woods's trousered knee, the pleasant sphere of Miss Duffy's face. Swirls merging into sense, like a sandstorm in reverse.

"Whatever else I think of this abhorrent business," Piest said, "and mind you all that I hold no crime lower than inflicting terror upon innocent bystanders, innocent *New Yorkers* no less, remember, remember the fifth of November after all—"

"We might be rememberin' Catholics trying to blow up the British Parliament a wee bit differently, like," Kildare remarked coolly. "Meanin' no offense t' ye and always bearing in mind that there's more than a bit o' ketchup on yer sleeve there."

"Oh! Please forgive any unintentional offense perceived, my fellow peacekeeper," Piest said hastily, scraping at his coat with his thumb, "but surely—"

"Surely ordinary folk need not be martyred fer some daft notion o' justice, even inside your sad, sorry pate, Ian." Connell shook his head at my ceiling. "Never mind Kildare, he's that addlepated after the Queen Mab. You lot could tweak his nipples clean free and he'd ne'er make a peep save for a lusty sigh."

"McGlynn plays a bigger role in this than we savvy yet," I mused, not looking up from sketching Bird's ear. I didn't know how long I could live with my small friend not speaking to me but felt like I'd mere hours before expiring.

"I'll question him," Connell offered.

"Allow me t' do the honors. I've better cause," Kildare snarled.

"Don't break McGlynn too much," I advised.

"Just enough." Kildare smiled. "And a wee bit extra, like, fer Caoilinn."

"God help us," I sighed. "We break him later, if we have to, when we *must*."

Seeing the point of this, the others made no answer.

"As for Mr. Wilde and my humble self . . . we will separately question all involved and comb the streets in search of Miss Woods, in the name of our fair city," Piest concluded.

"Aye. We'll help t' search everywhere she e'er was or planned to be." Kildare rallied himself to his full height.

"And we watch this Miss Abell, and this Miss Duffy, and this unholy Mr. Symmes, may Christ grant yer brother all fairest weather," Connell said quietly.

I nodded. "Thank you."

Not with any reluctance. I agreed with them, mind.

But I knew, having learnt my own brains more thoroughly than when I'd first started police work, that legwork and muscle weren't what was wanted just then. If they had been, Val could have punched someone in the phiz already and sent the secret spilling, ruby red and precious, out of that person's mouth.

And so I peered at the shapes floating on the butcher paper like the pale scraps of visions. My dreams tend to dissolve within seconds upon my waking—fade into a color or a mood or a whispered word. That sense of reality losing its edges was apparently infecting my daylight hours. Partially realized monsters lurked behind vaporous curtains, hinting at tragedies I couldn't understand.

I stayed in that sorry state of poor spirits and worse police work for nearly four days' time. Clutching at straws, knocking on board-inghouse doors. More or less waiting, for all I tried everything I could think of, for all that my weary feet were afire each night when I blew out my candle and fell into an almost-sleep as tortur-ous as the almost-waking.

It was the second fire that snapped me clean out of the dumps.

14

The factory girls of Amesbury have had a flare-up and
turned out. . . . The girls were told they must tend two
looms in the future, by which they would weave double the
number of yards that they now weave on one loom, and
this without any advance of wages.

—*BOSTON EVENING TRANSCRIPT*, MARCH 25, 1836

SO MANY DISTASTEFUL OCCURRENCES plagued me during the
four days between my parting with Ellie Abell and the second
fire, it behooves me speak of them only in brief.

When I arrived back the night of April 21, none too pleased
with myself, Elena Boehm left off crushing fresh salted butter into
loaf sugar for frosting. She then deliberately smeared my cheek
with a streak of it she'd scooped onto her forefinger. The tail end
of the stripe landed at the outer edge of my scar.

"What are . . . ?"

She shrugged, returning to her mixing bowl. "Nothing to do
with love it has, no great announcements."

"Still," I insisted.

"You mark me on paper with charcoal, I mark you with creamed
sugar. Do not worry yourself."

"So you're marking me because . . ."

221

"Because you finally did the same, marking me on paper and leaving it for me to find, and I am glad, because that is what people who know other people and touch them and talk to them *do* to each other," she snapped. "Mark them. Go away. I am working."

Mr. William Wolf, I discovered on April 23, after scouring Manhattan for traces of Miss Woods and getting predictably nowhere, wasn't merely the author of the New American Textile Manufactory strike article. He was also a ruthlessly intrepid professional who nosed after every crusting blood trail like a prize hound and had recently returned to his incognito work. He'd thus remain impossible to find for the foreseeable future.

"You say you've *nil* notion of where Mr. Wolf might be holed up?" I demanded of Ninepin. Again at Buttercake Joe's, though absent the half-promised Mercy Underhill. Plenty of reasons existed for me to be testy at the kinchin. "And I'm meant to believe you?"

"You truly figure me for a cross-cove?" Ninepin tore his dainty spectacles off and regarded me with the full ire of the New York news hawker. I'm man enough to admit it was daunting.

"No, of course I don't—"

"Because I ain't never *once* played you for a paper-skull."

"I'm sorry, the case is just that much of a manure pile."

"You think I'm a whipster after all, then. Not just some trumped-up lullaby-kid."

"You're fully aware that I respect—"

"But you think I ain't crumey enough nohow to court Miss Daly, is that what's after pestering your pate?"

Opening my mouth, I found it better sport to close it again. Ninepin rose to his full five feet five inches of fifteen-year-old manhood—which admittedly is an inch taller than I am—and shot me a glare that could have felled a six-point buck.

"I'll have the Wolf for you by this time next week," he said bitterly, adjusting what I suspected to be a transformed county-fair first-prize ribbon he was employing as a cravat.

"Thank you. I'll bring—"

"You keep Miss Underhill. I've always said she's an iron insider, and I'd never take it back. But I've other fishes to fry. And I mean that honorably, Mr. Wilde," he amended hastily.

That was a thoughtful clarification. But it didn't make me any more endeared to the poor lad as he strode out of Buttercake Joe's.

As for Bird, she ignored every opportunity I presented her to forgive me my churlishness and go back to being fast mates. But she granted me other concessions. Brief, grave smiles. Allowance of comfortable silences. That is, until April 25, when we were ensconced on our bench outside the Catholic Asylum, sun brushing our faces in passing like an absentminded grandmother, and she asked me a question.

"How do you know if you're in love?"

So close, I thought, *so close and now this.*

I actually considered baldly changing the subject. I'll be ashamed of that cowardly urge until the day I'm a meal for a lusty earthworm.

"There's a mutual . . . connection," I attempted helplessly.

"What sort?"

"Different sorts, depending on the person. People, rather."

"What sort for you, then?"

It was a fair question. "I'm not exactly sure. The sort that feels as if . . . as if they're a part of who you are. If they were gone, you'd miss them like a missing limb."

"That's just as I thought," she declared quietly.

I've never claimed to be a brilliant man. But the following conversation will irrevocably sound the final chip in that tombstone carving.

"Bird, you don't *know* James Playfair. And without knowing a person, you can't really love them the way you might think you do. Trust me."

I was met with a chiseled-ice stare just as I patted myself on the back for not saying to a former kinchin mab—one who'd known men since she was eight, though I don't suppose conversations about the nature of love are ever easy—anyhow, my point is I didn't say, *You're too young* or *He doesn't suit you*, because when did any of her other suitors fucking suit her? Or God forbid, *He's too old for you*, when she'd had far older.

Nor, *He's in love with my brother.*

"I don't know him, fair enough. But that's easily solved," she reasoned.

"How so?"

"I'll *get* to know him."

Pinching my nose between my fingers, I said, "Ordinarily, that would be a flash lay."

Bird's pale face turned ivory hard beneath the freckles. "But?"

"But . . . not in this one."

"And?"

"This isn't something I know how to tell you. It's a touch on the . . . indelicate side."

"Oh," she said softly. A breeze whipped a tendril of mahogany hair against her chin, and she pulled it away. "It's not something a cove would normally talk about with . . . with a kinchin, is that what you mean?"

"Yes."

"But you figure you need to tell me anyhow?"

I gnawed my lip, registering the faintly prickling sensation that I was about to botch it all spectacularly. God knows I am absolutely incapable of botching things in a niggardly fashion.

"You're acting so gingerly because you don't want to tell me that he'd never want someone who used to work as I did," she whispered. "Aren't you?"

Twenty kinds of horrified, I caught her by the hand. *"No,* God no, that—"

Pulling away, she stood up. There's an almost statuesque sadness to her calm, square face at times, a timelessness like a marble figure. But this sorrow was messy. It could have felled me, nearly did, in fact. And I've plentiful practice at grief.

"I don't lie to you anymore—I don't want you to have to lie to me either," she said hoarsely.

Bird used to be a remarkable liar. A masterful painter of alternate scenes, vistas blazing to life as she filled her canvas with near-truths and brazen falsehoods. They were often better stories than the truth would have made. They were often kinder.

"You're *entirely* mistaken," I pleaded.

"Then what the devil were you going to say?"

"He's a molley," I blurted out. "Bird, that's what I was going to say. Not—*nothing* like what you thought."

The tears in her grey eyes spilled over. Brushing them away with her sleeve, face still as a doll's, she shook her head.

"You're not as good a liar as I am," she managed, turning away.

"Bird, it's the truth. Now, for God's sake—"

"I'd rather you not come tomorrow, Mr. Wilde," she answered, quickening her pace back in the direction of the Catholic orphanage and whatever lessons and lectures she'd have to endure that afternoon with a fresh-broken heart.

My hands were shaking, I discovered as I watched her disappear into the school. Pulse going like a spooked tomcat's.

I got to my feet, returned my hat to my head. Started walking. Since I was on Prince and Mott, my boots steered me straight for the Knickerbocker 21.

There was a day I'd never have dreamed of walking *toward*

Valentine Wilde when facing a crisis. But this was a different sort of Thursday, the worst Thursday I could have passed in a year of Thursdays, and my brother is always at his engine house on Thursdays, and he might be the debauched king of the dead rabbits, but he's also fond of Bird and brutally honest when I need him to be.

So I plunged into placid Ward Eight.

Distantly, as if I were peering at a careful model replica of the world, I noted that my brother's ward was plastered with political posters. That was typical—we'd an election May 1, and anyway, slogans of yesteryear keek through rips in today's pet mottoes as if the Democrats and the Whigs had combined forces to spread a brightly scaling rash over Manhattan's skin. We locals scarcely saw them. That is, until I encountered a matched pair of broadsides pasted in the window of a coffee shop skittishly attempting to maintain political neutrality, and I stopped in my tracks.

On the right was a newly printed woodcut of Alderman Symmes. His handsome features and elegant moustache had been elongated to make him look smugly devilish. The text, printed in at least six different fonts of howling capitals, read:

IS THIS THE FACE OF PROGRESS?

ROBERT SYMMES, TEXTILE TYCOON,

HAS BEEN FOR FIVE YEARS

ALDERMAN OF WARD EIGHT

HAS HE DONE RIGHT BY YOU?

ARE PITTANCE WAGES & CRUMBLING

BOARDINGHOUSES PROGRESS?

VOTE FOR

VALENTINE WILDE

WARD BOSS, POLICE CAPTAIN,

SENIOR KNICKERBOCKER 21 ENGINEMAN

AND SPIT IN THE EYE OF HUNKER OPPRESSION

Adjacent was another portrait, this one of Val. His arched hairline curved into a villain's peak, still-boyish face cruel as a schoolyard bully's, the ever-present sacks beneath his eyes etched in malicious smears.

DEMOCRATIC PARTY INSIDER

OR . . . TRAITOR TO TAMMANY?

VALENTINE WILDE—FOR YEARS THE VERY FACE OF:

CORRUPTION, INSIDE DEALMAKING, GRAFT,

AND NEPOTISM!

NOW MAKES A BID FOR ALDERMAN GUARANTEED TO TEAR

APART THE HEART AND SOUL OF WARD EIGHT

VOTE FOR YOUR LOYAL SERVANT

ALDERMAN ROBERT SYMMES

AND TAKE A STAND AGAINST DANGEROUS

BARNBURNER RADICALISM

It was tamer than it could have been. It didn't say anything about *nigger-lovers* or *sodomites.*

Nevertheless.

I set off walking again. The posters were thoroughly disquieting, I grant. But I was so splintered by then I scarce noticed the new worriment—as if a penny had been added to the Tammany coffers or a cup of water poured into the Hudson.

A rich whiff of smoke met my nostrils, and I looked up.

Someplace a few blocks away from me, black soot and white steam poured into the air, gushing like blood from a wound.

For a moment I stood frozen in place.

There are accidental fires in New York every single day, I thought. *This is only another.*

Breaking into a run, I discovered that I hadn't been listening. Hadn't heard the tender hissing, the distant crackle like a sweet caress over satin. Nor the mildly clanging bells and the gentle shrieks of whistles. Men's faint, faraway shouts.

Whereas I'd not been meditating direct on my brother seconds previous, the combination of *Ward Eight* and *fire* was enough to deluge my entire brain with the scoundrel. When I veered south on Spring, the crescendoing half-thrilled, half-terrified hubbub told me I was nearly there. A final quick left on Washington landed me in the midst of the chaos.

The fire was out, it seemed. Mostly. The structure was in a row of low, mean, unkempt lodging houses. Adjacent to the briny western slips where seafarers quit their creaking boats to find cheap temporary digs and cheaper temporary company. The building was still alive, however. Hissing and spitting and steaming, expelling wet smoke and hot ash like snowflakes. A monster taking its last spittle-choked breaths before shuddering to sleep.

A smell lingered, something meaner than smoke. Something leering. It crept down the throat syrup-slow.

But worse—or potentially worse—two engine companies stood before the grim wreck.

One, I saw when I careened to a halt, was Neptune Engine Number 9. Drake Todd stood at the helm of his machine, red fireman's shirt soaked, his hawkish face and the long silvery scar beside his eye making him resemble nothing so much as a pirate at the helm of his ship.

Opposite him—apparently just having arrived to discover a rival fire gang and smoking rubble instead of a fire—stood my brother before his own perfectly polished engine. He was flanked by his volunteer firedogs, their ropy hands fisted on hips or lightly slung over the axes in their belts, braces cinched tight over pugilistic shoulders. Puzzling whether the Neptune 9 crew might be in the market for some friendly smashing.

"Do you pack of scamp-foots mind telling me what in the name of the devil's red arse you're doing here?" Valentine snarled.

My brother looked *terrible*.

Not the way Valentine looks terrible before noon as the morphine sweats out of him, skin grey and slick as if he's made of river clay. And not the way he looks terrible when he's in altitudes on the godless substance, glassy green eyes sharp as broken bottles and laughing as if he has a spear in his side. This was a version of terrible I'd not seen in years. He held his weighted cane cocked over one shoulder, always a weapon if also a crutch when the wretch can't see straight, opposite hand planted arrogantly on his hip. But a tremor below his left eye jumped erratically, his mouth seemed parched at the corners, and the face that normally tempers flinty anger with a gleam of irony didn't seem remotely amused. It was a moonless-midnight expression, one that frightened me.

"What am I doing here? Well, strike me dead if Valentine Wilde himself didn't just ask a stupid question." Todd sounded wearied by his fire-dousing efforts but otherwise unmoved. "Is that building just there smoldering, and am I wearing a red shirt?"

The Neptune men not occupied with spraying down the remnants of a furnace chuckled. The Knickerbocker men cast placid smiles at one another. The breed of smile meaning, *While we are not amused by the previous jest, the odds of knocking some teeth to the cobbles seem to be pleasantly increasing.*

Val swung his stick down and used it to take a step or two forward, his lips curling.

"Pardon, let me rephrase that question," he offered in the sugary tone that meant things were about to go very, very wrong. "Do you pack of scamp-foots mind telling me what in the name of the devil's red arse you're doing here when your engine house is in *Ward Two*, and how in burning blazes you got here so quick-footed, and why in holy hell that building looks to me as if it was torched deliberate-like?"

Catching a brass rail, Drake Todd swung down from the engine, on a level with Valentine. He wasn't nearly so tall—no one is—but his bowlegged swagger and the countless scars on his knuckles were enough to bode ill.

"It looks like a deliberate torch job because it is one." He spat on the ground—not directly at my brother, thankfully, which would have been a cardinal mistake. "White phosphorus planted all through the place. Never saw clearer signs of an incendiary."

"Sick son of a bitch," Val mentioned coldly. It sounded both rote and meaningful, as if it were the amen at the end of a prayer.

"Sick son of a bitch," Todd intoned. "Though from what I hear, 'sick *bitch*' is more likely. You savvy whose building this is, I take it?"

Unable to remain in the shadows, watery knees or no, I sidled up behind my brother. His cronies nodded at me, as did Todd. Val turned, and the brows above his haggard eyes knotted in confusion.

"I was heading for the Knickerbocker and saw the commotion," I explained. "You look like a warmish stiff."

"And you look like a stunted puppy with a face fit to turn milk into cheese," he snapped.

A force beyond my control drew me back an inch or two. Several of the Knickerbocker men muttered under their breath, and one made a few trilling sounds like the ironic chirping of crickets. It was apt enough. No one was laughing.

I swallowed whatever had risen in the back of my throat, which felt like it could have been my spleen.

Val and I have always fought like wildcats. Before I hated him, when I was a kinchin and thought him a king. All the long while I hated him, when I thought him senselessly malicious. After I'd stopped hating him and knew him for courageous and shattered and vicious and steadfast. And I can't remember a time, whether in the honeysuckle meadows of Greenwich Village or sleeping in a turned-over skip, when he hasn't mocked me for my scrawny size. Often it's couched in bizarrely complimentary insults along the lines of *That's my brother—built like a Pygmy, but that lad could have you flat on the ground before you so much as saw him make a fist.* So *miniature idiot* or *fluff-brained little dandelion* or even the memorable *thimbleful of shit* wouldn't have even merited a blink on my part.

My face, though. My face is a wound that looks healed over but isn't. And Val *never* rags me over that. Oh, he'll suggest, *If you keep rubbing at your face like you're kneading dough, I'm putting your pate in my oven* or *How you think you draw less attention to a scar by twisting it like a bloody wine cork I will never understand.*

But those remarks—crude as they are—stem from the fact he seems to hate that I hate the disfigurement. As if I were rabbit enough to fly it like a battle standard.

I'm not.

Something that could almost have been consternation tightened my brother's square jaw.

All at once he turned back to Todd.

"White phosphorus, you say," he resumed. "Casualties?"

Forcing air from my lungs, I reminded myself that I could always break my brother's nose after the present conversation had concluded. And held my tongue.

"Aye, white phosphorus," Todd allowed. "Nary a death this time, we were that quick about it, and the second and third floors unlivable. Actually *impossible* to live in, if you take my meaning, not a cellar with shit seeping through the walls. The flooring had rotted clean through, kept falling on the heads of the residents. Archie! Share and share alike with Timothy Wilde, as he's taken an interest."

Todd's friend Archie Vanderpool, soot-smeared and sweating like the heavily muscled hog he was, approached us. He passed me an open cigar box, angling a disgusted glare at Valentine. I wondered why. But I was livid enough with my sibling to take the object myself and pretend with a will renewed that the smell wasn't making me nauseous. Nestled within the cheap pine receptacle was a chunk of spent fuel, yet smoking, the source of the evil white smoke. It had reddened the eyes of all present, turning already aggressive men to scarlet-gazed demons.

"I take it this is energetic material," I said.

Ordinarily my brother would have jeered at me for not knowing. But he only peered downward. "Phosphorus, all right."

"And this building belongs to Alderman Symmes, I assume."

"Of course it belongs to Symmes," Valentine grated out, drifting a bit sideways but steadying himself with his cane. "What I still want to know is what the Neptune Nine boys are *doing here.*"

"They put out the Pell Street fire too." I glanced at Val as the memory stirred. The too-beautiful engine in the midst of my ward's catholic—and I mean that in both the religious and in the adjective senses—squalor. "That's Ward Six."

As if it were possible, Valentine's scowl deepened. "Are you Neptune coves tired of Ward Two? Can't say as I blame you, manufactories popping up like mushrooms—it would leave me in tears."

My mind tied itself into a truly painful knot. Picking over details as a miner sifts for gold, I recalled our initial meeting with

Todd and Vanderpool, and Mr. Piest's preamble explaining our presence.

It seems that the building's owner has been the target of scurrilous threats, he'd reported.

Threatening letters, you said? Vanderpool had questioned minutes later.

Only Mr. Piest hadn't said anything about letters at all.

"Someone warned you this building was specifically at risk," I realized. "Now. Today."

Drake Todd tipped his head readily. "In the flesh, at our engine house."

"Who turned stag?"

Todd mulled it over in the careful manner I generally associate with reluctant truth-telling. "Never left a name, said Symmes shared his dustier mail with her and she was there on his say-so. Good meat on her, pale brown hair, very comely."

My blood froze.

"Surname of Abell?"

"Maybe so," Archie Vanderpool demurred. "Seemed a good girl, for my money. That's twice she's tipped us—put us onto the Pell Street blaze as well. Symmes told us in person to treat whatever she said as gospel."

I ought to have expected it. Supposing Miss Woods owned even the residue of a conscience, she wouldn't have wanted the city entire to burn for her cause. She'd have given fair warning. And Miss Abell had all but confessed to me she was further involved.

When Mr. Symmes showed me the note about setting outworkers afire, I thought of Dunla at once. He agreed Pell Street may well be at risk, so I did all I could.

And yet I hadn't expected it. Even Val, who's never surprised, blinked owlishly at the rival gang.

"Miss Woods sends Symmes notice a hairsbreadth too late to

stop her," I understood, "and he's arranged for you to race to whichever property was targeted."

"Pays us fair chink for it too. As if dousing stirs weren't our honor-bound duty. Supposing *some* firemen aren't fit for the job, it's the lot of the rest to take their place," Todd finished.

A grim, grainy silence fell. It was punctuated by the American natives and Tammany Irishmen of Val's fire company edging forward. Jack, a fair-haired friend of my brother's with gaps in his mouth like missing fence posts and a pair of gold front teeth, grinned as he advanced. Others contented themselves with gleeful cracking of knuckles and the donning of brass ones.

Valentine tapped the pearly head of his cane against his palm. It's the least often employed and least subtle of the motions he uses to threaten people with the thing. And therefore the most distressing.

"Our engine house is within buggering spitting distance of this wreck. Explain *fit for the job*, if you please," Valentine hissed.

The Neptune 9 men had begun similarly massing. Leaving the last of the spraying hoses and tugging closed the gushing Croton pumps. Sensing atmospheric violence crackling, the way bats can see in the dark.

Drake Todd's wickedly slim lips quirked. "It's no wonder you can't savvy the good the manufactories have done, Captain. Ward Eight didn't *burn* in the 'Forty-five fire. Ward Eight wasn't a *trash heap* and us the men what cleared it."

My brother took a furious step forward as I caught his elbow. He shook me off as if I were a scrap of lint.

"You're taking the snuff," he seethed. "I walked into five sodding blazes on Broad Street and dragged eighteen people out of them, shoveled rubble and ash and baked body parts into barrows the same as the goddamn best of you."

I know what my brother does. And I know why he does it. But it splintered me yet further, the actual hearing him tell it.

"Did you rebuild your own ward after you'd tidied it?" Todd growled. "I did. I did, and so did Robert Symmes, and so did all the other tycoons who turned right around and *kept building.* If you want to fault my loyalties, you can sod straight the fuck off."

"Oh, *loyalties,* my apologies. Just post me, is this a political conversation?" Val crooned. "Or a personal one?"

Todd's entire body coiled like a furious bowstring. "The businessmen of this town keep the whole bloody clockwork oiled, and you cheddar-brained Barnburners are going to shove a wrench straight in the works with your goddamned *principles.* Who gives a shit about slavery when New York can't even feed itself?"

"I funnel more chink toward my voters through Tammany-appointed jobs in a week than Symmes pulls out of his arse for his manufactory wenches in a year." Val's eyes narrowed into brilliantly sparking slits.

Todd merely spread his feet wider. "You're looking at a Hunker firehouse, and the more jobs at *any* pay the better when people rot to death on street corners. But that's neither here nor there. *Obviously,* I'll man up when the closest engine house refuses to put out fires if the buildings are owned by Symmes."

My brother found himself at a loss for words. It was like watching an alley cat botch a landing—unnatural and vaguely embarrassing for the onlooker. He just stood there, staring with leaden pistol-shot irises. The rest of the Knickerbocker 21 seemed similarly winded.

"When the *what?*" I spluttered on everyone's behalf.

"You heard me," Todd scoffed. "These snakes won't touch a Symmes building. Look who their bloody delusional captain is— it's on his orders, no less."

It wasn't true. I didn't even have to ask. My brother would as soon leave a fire unchecked as he'd overcook a lamb chop.

"That is the biggest hummer I have ever heard. My ears are bleeding," Val snarled, swaying like a sapling in a thunderstorm. "Of *course* I never—"

"You did, and any man who disavows protection over certain buildings for his own ends is a disgrace. I'd not waste my own spit in the eye of such a purblind coward as that." Casually, as if donning a scarf, Todd slid a set of brass knuckles over his fingers. His interests weren't merely mercenary—he'd actually swallowed what he'd been fed.

I went very still inside.

"Symmes told you that?" I wanted to know as I pulled my hat and jacket off, slinging them over a handy embellishment on the Knickerbocker engine.

"He did. You want a fight, eh? My quarrel isn't with you, Mr. Wilde. What the hell are you playing at?"

I wasn't sure myself. But firedogs who'd gladly have lain down in the mud and been run over by carriages for Valentine Wilde gathered around me. We were of a sudden hivelike. Buzzing with toxin-tipped tails, swarming in the direction of a mutual foe. I'd never felt such a sensation. Amidst the haze of spite and smoke, I called out, "Val, what do we do with their engine after we've fibbed them black and blue?"

It was a genuine question, by the by. I've helped to quell riots, but I'd never joined a gang brawl previous. I'd have felt more comfortable teaching our local street pigs flight.

Unfortunately, just then my brother chose to slump to the ground as if an avalanche had cracked a mountain in two. He lay there on the wet, ash-coated cobbles. As aware of the world and the impending clash as his own corpse would have been.

A lancing pang of panic told me that it *was* his corpse in fact.

Two Knickerbockers dove for Val's body, dragging the sprawling hulk underneath their engine. If I'd had a better plan, I'd certainly have suggested it to them. But it's difficult to do any masterful mental work when you're gaping in distress at your collapsed brother's boots as they bump and skid along the cobblestones away from you.

And anyway, I was distracted. Drake Todd's eyes shone bright as the brass on his knuckles as his fist made its honey-slow arc toward my face.

15

*Be assured that the "OLD HUNKERS" have drank too
deep at the fountain of power—have been fed and
pampered too long upon the spoils, and relish them with too
keen an appetite, to allow this their last opportunity to
pass without a desperate and tremendous struggle.*

—*NEW-YORK DAILY TRIBUNE*, OCTOBER 27, 1847

THE RESULTS OF THE legendary mitten-mill between eleven
Neptune 9 men and eight Knickerbocker 21s were as follows, as
I wrote in my police report that late afternoon:

*Report made by Officer T. Wilde, Ward 6, District 1, Star
107. Arrived on scene of a quelled conflagration at 510 Washington Street. Determined by experts to be incendiary blaze,
suspected culprit Miss Sally Woods, printer by trade, sworn
enemy of property holder Alderman Robert Symmes. Neptune
9 Engine Company responsible for eradicating fire, having been paid by Symmes direct for protection according
to their senior engineman Mr. Drake Todd. These circumstances, in my opinion, deserve further and most immediate
scrutiny.*

Afterward a fight broke out between the Neptune 9 com-

pany and the Knickerbocker 21, the nearest engine house to the
site geographically. The altercation escalated due to multiple
causes.

I paused. At a profound loss for words.

"Hit a rough patch?" Valentine sneered.

We Wildes sat opposite each other in one of Tammany Hall's
private spaces. Officially, it's a parlor a few corridors away from the
main dining room, concert space, meeting hall, et cetera—all the
blithely populace-friendly façades that convince Manhattanites to
think of Tammany as a benevolent grandfather with hard candies
in his pockets. Unofficially, it's where my brother convinced his
own cronies not to murder me in 1846. The study resembles a
men's club, filled with important books and pictures of doubtless
important politicos and carpeted with important-seeming rugs. I
sat behind a positively magisterial carved desk, awaiting the
powers-that-be who'd summoned us to explain ourselves. Val
sprawled in a leather armchair opposite, being about as helpful as a
genital rash.

Oh, I was still weak with relief he was alive, mind. But that
feeling mingled with the desire to shake him until his head
snapped off.

"Need some suggestions?" he added cuttingly, nodding at the
report.

"That would be so helpful. What part should I scratch first,
then?" I asked him sweetly. "The part where you fainted because
you treat yourself like an open sewer, the part where you weren't
conscious while I was getting punched in the guts with brass
knuckles—which hurts, by the way—the part where you were
asleep when your pal Jack's head was smashed against your own
engine, or maybe the part where you were *bloody unconscious* when
we beat them despite their outnumbering us?"

It had been a quick, nasty thunderstorm of a fight. I'd floored two opponents including Todd—him with a chopper to the eye after landing several other blows and dodging (once unsuccessfully) his gleaming metal knuckles, the other with a doubler to the solar plexus. Thanks in no small part to Val, I'm a feral little fighter. Regardless, when it was over and the hands of the bested shaken like decent men and the field of battle cleared, I'd still had to accost a lady two streets over for smelling salts to revive my disastrous kinfolk.

Shame looks like rage on both of us, scarlet and raw, so Val merely ground his teeth at me.

I stared at the unfinished page I'd half written. Hating it.

"What is the *matter* with you?" my brother snapped. "So Tammany gets wind of a mitten-mill, and they send for us, and they tell you to have the police report *ready*. Jesus, how hard can it be?"

"I *always* hate writing them. They record things I don't want to even think about let alone remember, but I guess I have to diary them, don't I, since you landed me the worst graft in all of Manhattan Island. I really don't thank you for that often enough."

He sniffed. "You were born for police work. And you're a pretty article, forgetting you're literate the instant the Party wants a report from you."

"*You're* a pretty article, swooning in the middle of a free-for-all," I hissed.

"As if I *meant* to do that," he returned contemptuously.

"Oh, you didn't *mean* to do that?" I cried. "My mistake, you should only be held responsible for things you do *intentionally*. Fair enough, did you mean to take so much morphine you keeled over like a newborn deer? Did you mean to mix it with hashish or laudanum or ether or whatever made you so weak your firedogs had to *hide you under your own engine*?"

Val lurched forward in his chair, livid. "I have a political campaign to win in *less than a week*, I have been *working*. Writing speeches, visiting Democratic cronies for handshakes and assurances, fund-raising, running my goddamn engine house, policing just in case it slipped your mind I was a police captain, and let's not forget trying to *find Sally Woods*, which you seem incapable of doing. Or did you track her down during the fire brawl, Timmy?"

At the calculated word *Timmy*, which nickname I despise, I could feel my blood boiling under my shirt collar. Maybe I wasn't capable of finding Sally Woods. But I was capable of making my brother pay a pound of flesh for saying so.

"How's Jim, by the way?"

"What the devil does that self-righteous nancy have to do with anything?"

"Oh, you've not seen him since he left, then. I figured as much," I remarked, realizing only as they left my lips that the words I spoke were true, "seeing as you seem barely capable of so much as dressing yourself without your *wife* to look after you."

If I'd stood up and slapped him in the face, he'd not have reacted any differently. Val's eyebrows shot up, then crashed down again, the veins in his neck quivering with fury.

"Listen to me, you unspeakably obnoxious ant," he bit out. "I have a lot of pals, which is a way of life that's pretty foreign to you, but I don't *need* any of them in particular. It's flash to have a pack at your heels, but I am my own man, and I sure as hell don't require a whinging sodomite who disappears into the ether the instant I most want his support."

"Your cock in his arse is irrelevant to his being a sodomite, of course. You probably didn't *mean* to put it there. You tripped, and Jim was strategically posed."

"Leave it the fuck alone," Val raged, on his feet by now and gripping the other edge of the desk with white knuckles.

I mirrored him instantly, palms on either side of the failed po-lice report, the pair of us facing off with fangs bared like street curs. "Aces, you do plenty more than that by accident. Did you mean to make Robert Symmes so peppery that God only knows what he'll do to us?"

"I meant to serve my city."

"Oh, of course, perfect, you're running on a Barnburner plat-form out of *altruism*. Did you mean to call me ugly in front of two entire fire gangs?"

"I am sorry about that!" he shouted, incensed.

"You're *sorry* about it?" I yelled in disbelief.

"Yes, I apologize!"

"You're never sorry for anything, ever, and you're sorry about *that*? *That* is what you're sorry for?"

"Are you deaf?"

"What in hell is *wrong* with you?"

"Whatever's wrong with me, at least I'm capable of writing a police report."

"No you aren't, not having been *awake to observe events as they progressed*."

He made a grab for the pen. I'd been poking him in the chest with it, in the interest of emphasis. We grappled for the thing, arms straining, pulling and yanking in what resembled a bizarre version of arm wrestling. I hesitate to name it our most dignified exchange.

"I *hate* you," I spat for the first time in years.

"I don't give a solitary, singular shit."

"Yes you do, you thoroughgoing prick."

"No I—"

The door behind my brother opened, and a pair of men walked in. One was George Washington Matsell, a fatigued grey monu-ment in his sack coat with the gold chief's star pinned to the lapel.

The other was a Tammany boss of sufficient importance that I might as well refer to him as God. Not to imply that he boasts impressive moral fiber—merely that when Abraham Kane says *jump*, your boot soles are generally in the air by the time he's finished the syllable. Glancing down to the unfinished police report, I began to regret my shortcomings.

After all, I'd met Mr. Kane on the first occasion I visited Tammany. The involuntary occasion, the one at which Symmes had lusted for my blood.

I'd given Abraham Kane the moniker Scarred Nose when I'd no notion of his real title. But while the scar is striking, it doesn't go very far toward describing a uniquely arresting person. For instance, Chief Matsell is almost as tall as Valentine and about twice as wide. But despite his owning a medium stature, Kane's sheer density makes him appear just as formidable as his colleagues. And then his eyes are remarkable—an ordinary brown but sharp as shivs, with fine feathers of wrinkles amplifying their incisiveness. He dresses like a rich Party bureaucrat. Doeskin trousers, billowing blue silk cravat, and a stovepipe hat. But somehow he doesn't look wealthy, appears oddly more *real* than most people. And as for the small white seam just at the bridge of his beak—the skin might have split there, but unlike many pugilists', his nose has obviously never been broken.

Best of all, he has a way of being amused by insubordination that implies he's reasonable as well as deadly. Or maybe Abraham Kane is simply tickled by the thought that anyone could possibly defy him. If he wants you promoted, you prosper. If he wants you dead, you die. Quick or slow, as he best pleases.

"Is that pen of particular value, gentlemen?" Chief Matsell inquired irritably.

"It would be of signal use if I'm to finish this police report, sir," I groused.

"He ran into spelling difficulties," Val sneered, releasing his grip.

"I'm going to kill you," I told him, resuming my seat as Val did the same, my pen scratching along like a crackling fire. "I'm going to put my hands around your throat and squeeze until you are dead."

"Your hands wouldn't even fit around my throat."

"Don't make me laugh."

"As if that's even possible. You never laugh."

"Gentlemen, my time is at a premium," Abraham Kane announced, pulling up a simple wicker chair and seating himself as if it were a Viking's rough-hewn throne. Val edged the armchair he'd been using to the side, Matsell likewise dragging a comfortable perch into the semicircle they'd formed around the desk where I furiously scribbled. My brother dropped his hat on the floor and, in a gesture I associate with utter frustration on his part, thrust both hands through his dark blond hair until he resembled a caged lion in a zoo.

"Apologies," Val offered the politician with genuine deference. "This week has been . . . taxing."

"I see as much. Drinks, I take it, are in order?" Kane headed for the glassed-in sideboard and its liquor. "I can hear you fine from here, Captain. Start talking."

"It's no secret that Symmes and I have always tugged at each other's hackles," Valentine admitted hoarsely, elbows on his knees. "His politics are slender as a fresh-landed Irish, and he wouldn't even know he had a ward if he wasn't required to live in it."

"If you're implying his fortune is vast and little else interests him, I won't contradict you," Kane mused, pulling down a gin bottle.

"I am at that. But more to the point, he offered me a bleak-mort in trade for getting Sally Woods out of his way, and any cove who'd treat a girl as if she were a carrot deserves to be thrashed. I should have checked with you lot before my play at the Knickerbocker benefit, I'm aware—I did post Chief Matsell here, who I assume passed the news along. But it's been almost three years since I was promoted to police captain, and between the state of the nation and the state of Ward Eight—"

"Captain Wilde, I fear you're characterizing this disintegrating situation as isolated when unfortunately it is all too common," Kane interjected, thrusting a glass of gin in Val's face. Another appeared before me, and Kane returned to the sideboard for his and Matsell's. "The deterioration of Hunker and Barnburner relations is widespread enough that I fear it signals national calamity. Meanwhile, nothing you can say about Robert in particular interests me in the slightest. Nor does Robert interest Cornelius, for that matter."

My pen paused in considerable surprise.

Cornelius, I thought.

He meant Cornelius Villers. I'd once called him Pince-Nez, and along with Kane and Symmes he'd completed the triumvirate of Party aristocrats who'd wanted to throw me in the Hudson. Villers is the merciless brains behind Tammany, the thinking apparatus who sits beside Kane like a grotesque two-headed deity. He has a pince-nez resting on his hooked nose and is cadaverously thin, with a cadaver's affable nature. No one likes Villers, but liking him isn't the point of the man. He's omniscient.

Val dragged a disbelieving thumb along his lower lip. "Neither you nor Mr. Villers is remotely hocused I've set myself against Symmes?"

Seating himself, Kane crossed his legs and took a mouthful of gin. "No. We are not. And we don't have to explain ourselves to you."

"Of course you—"

"But I will anyway," Kane decided, eyes dancing with intrigue.

"Robert Symmes as a tycoon alderman has proved of use to the Party in myriad ways. But Mr. Symmes owns so very *many* holdings, you see, and in so very *many* locales, that he of late has felt it safe to conceal certain information from us regarding his earnings. I prize loyalty above all else, as you know, gentlemen. It has been most distressing to learn we have been deceived by one of our own."

Chief Matsell turned his needle-sharp eyes to the ceiling. "He's meant to cut the Democratic Party in no matter what the venture? In short, you have a deal with the man, and you've found his mathematics lacking."

"Chief, your insights are as astute as ever."

Casting my mind back, I remembered the way Villers and Kane had treated the alderman of Ward Eight when I'd been in a position to observe them. Not having anything better to do, tied to a chair and all. The silences following Symmes's speech, the answers that didn't address his questions. The oblique way they'd looked at the man, as if he were a silhouette of Robert Symmes— property owner, alderman, textile manufacturer—and his actual self had never been there at all. Kane's explanation of just why they wanted me to betray my firmest principles, delivered in an almost sympathetic tone.

Loyalty is important to us, Mr. Wilde. It might even be of primary importance to us. Well, to me, anyhow.

A soft knock sounded. As I glanced up, Silkie Marsh entered, trailing a cloak of rose-hued velvet over her unadorned black satin skirts. She swept it off, revealing its crimson lining, and hung it next to the door.

I glanced at my brother.

He was already eyeing me, a single brow raised in sincere distaste. And severe alarm.

"Ah, Madam Marsh," Kane said cheerfully, pulling up a fourth chair before the desk. "Right on time. Do sit down."

"Many thanks, Mr. Kane. Chief Matsell, Valentine."

Her voice was plumb-line-straight, determined—not the girl-ish tone she employs when she's flamming you. A worm of disquiet commenced burrowing down my spine even as the faint aroma of violets spread.

I've mentioned that Silkie Marsh is a death trap waiting to spring. But as any man of science would tell you, there's a long, lonesome mile between comprehending the nature of a powerful force and proving it. Anyway, her breed of lawbreaking isn't the sort Tammany minds overmuch, it being the variety that rakes in hard cole, which she then showers over all and sundry as if she were a captive djinn. So somewhere in the depths of her Greene Street brothel, Madam Marsh probably has a small collection of Demo-cratic trophies with her name engraved—as opposed to written warnings that vice, conspiracy, and murder aren't generally consid-ered virtues.

Meanwhile, her arrival sent my teeth scraping.

Chief Matsell's face presented an unstudied blank. Abraham Kane pulled out a cigar from a carved ivory box, perfectly at his ease. Of those assembled, he was the only one who *might* not have known her soul to be tissue-thin.

But then again, he might have known and failed to care. It wasn't as if Kane was a stranger to killing things.

"Valentine, my word, are you unwell?" Silkie Marsh exclaimed.

It was honestly asked. She might not care for humans, but as Val's ex-mistress she does at times treat him as a regrettable piece of lost property. I imagine she'd have looked so if a prized necklace had been stolen from her to be cut up piecemeal and fenced. Any-way, Val had been dragged through wet ash and manure and worse earlier, so the query was a sound one.

"Fit as a fiddle," he answered.

I delivered a particularly savage dot of a period to my report.

"You seem a bit . . . fatigued," she continued, pulling her gloves from her fingers.

"Too much business to be done and scarce enough hours to do it in," he answered brightly.

"Yes, I can only imagine that your campaign must weigh heavy on your mind so soon before the election. And despite my other Party obligations, including those owed to my own landlord, I entirely support your cause, Valentine."

My brother smiled. The one that's all canines and no humor whatsoever.

"You really must take better care of yourself in the meanwhile," she insisted.

"He had a short rest. I'm sure that revived him," I muttered.

Valentine would have glared daggers at me. Had he been alert enough to focus his eyes.

"Oh! Mr. Wilde," Madam Marsh said to me affectionately. "Apologies, I didn't see you behind so large a desk."

My eyes didn't so much as lift from the page.

"Now that what passes for pleasantries are out of the way," Kane announced, amused, "the chief and I need a word about the Symmes situation."

"I thought you didn't care if he's reelected," I mentioned, puzzled.

"We don't," Chief Matsell said icily. "We care that his buildings keep burning and you lot have failed to prevent the occurrence."

It was fair. It cut, though.

"Not for lack of trying," I shot back, abashed.

"Of course not, Mr. Wilde. Though I take it you wouldn't mind overmuch seeing my brothel and its residents go up in flames." Silkie Marsh displayed the line of her slender neck as Kane delivered her a glass of gin. "Your sole investigative copper star here has the oddest notions about me, Chief Matsell."

Matsell's grey eyes sparked in a flinty fashion. "Madam Marsh, I'm a Party man to the marrow. Note I didn't say 'Party puppet.'" The deep lines along the chief's mouth twitched at the sides as he studied her, as if the fact of her ignorance amused him. "There's more between my ears, and between my legs for that matter, than cotton stuffing. So you'd best watch yourself. I've been watching you for years."

Amidst the chorus of amens in my head, I caught a small sigh from Silkie Marsh. It was the sound a cat makes when it feels greatly appreciated and curls up to bask in the sun.

I tapped my pen against the inkwell and soldiered on.

"This is about firedogging, then, pure and simple," Val theorized. "You're ketched that your landlord's buildings are under attack. Can't say as I blame you on that count."

"Shall I, Mr. Kane?" Silkie Marsh asked the politico. "They're busy men. I'd hate to waste their time."

"By all means," he allowed.

Silkie Marsh marginally straightened her posture. "I knew Robert as a landlord well before he was involved with the Party. He was always a decisive man—my rent for the building was due quite implacably on the first of the month whether that was comfortable or not. I saw at once that he'd the makings of a determined leader if not a particularly benevolent one."

Her tone was a queer combination of ease and practice. It betrayed nothing.

But that's in itself peculiar. Isn't it? I thought.

I'd been in the midst of writing:

—Why should Alderman Symmes confide so deeply in Ellie Abell, assuming she warned the Neptune 9 company?

But interrupted myself to jot down in the margin:

"a determined leader if not a particularly benevolent one"

"You told me you learned of Symmes's potential incendiary troubles from his property manager, Ronan McGlynn," I said. "Was that the truth, or did you just mean to draw him to my attention?"

I wanted an answer to that query. Something ticklish was running along the edges of my thumbs.

Madam Marsh's brow tilted as if she were smiling at me. "What an intriguing question. Did you speak with McGlynn yet?"

"I did. He said he'd run the Queen Mab—and as the very worst sort of brothelkeeper regarding whether or not the employees *volunteer* for the job, as will doubtless disgust you to learn, Madam Marsh—but it remained Symmes's property. And he gave our firestarter a pretty sparkling motive."

"What motive could possibly justify firestarting?" she asked. Breathless, leaning with her collarbones taut as sails under a heavy wind and her queer hazel eyes alight.

"None. But the chief and I spoke with the alderman thereafter and confirmed that Symmes's relationship with his attacker was . . . intimately personal."

I resumed scribbling. If there's one thing I'm not afraid of, it's telling Silkie Marsh the truth. It baits her, tempts her to revelations both rich and slight. And I was beginning to hear a small, shrill note of discord in our conversations—both with Symmes and about him. So I wanted Madam Marsh to keep talking. She can feign being personable from dawn until dusk, but generally when listening to her I smell greasepaint and clockwork. This wasn't the same. It felt as if she *wanted* me to understand something.

It was highly alarming.

"Ronan McGlynn gave you nothing helpful?" Chief Matsell asked.

"He seemed terribly shocked. He pegged Sally Woods. But helpful? No," I replied.

"Your sources and your Tombs cronies have dug up nothing of use as to where we might find her?" my brother surmised darkly.

"You know how easy it is to disappear in this warren. My men and I've been searching for Pell Street survivors as well—we're to meet tomorrow morning and discuss findings. But so far? Nothing."

"You've seen this Miss Abell and this Miss Duffy, and you've questioned them gently?" Mr. Kane tapped his index fingertips together.

"Yes."

"And you'd not like, I take it, someone *else* questioning them . . . in a less gentle manner?"

I thought of young Miss Duffy's almost poetic perception of the world she could see so dimly, of Miss Abell's innate sweetness. I even thought of how, when I recalled Miss Woods, I wished she weren't a murderess and the woman who'd put an egg on my pate. I wished she were an eccentric who lived in a greenhouse. "No, I'd not."

"You'd not like, for instance, if Cornelius were to take an active interest?"

Rumor has it Cornelius Villers once cut out a man's tongue, fried it like a cutlet, and ate it before his victim. It's not a rumor I've any stomach for investigating further.

"I'd not imagine Mr. Villers would want to spare the time, not when we're so close to a solution," I said slowly, pretending to consider when I could as well have shrieked, *For God's sake keep him out of this*. "I have the best of the star police working with me, and my instincts say this needs delicacy, not intimidation. I'd be obliged if you'd let me see it through."

Please don't collect all the many molls to do with this ugly, ugly thing and make them bleed for the parts they played in it.

"Of course, Mr. Wilde," replied Abraham Kane. With considerable benevolence.

"Yes," Silkie Marsh said softly, beaming at us all. "Yes, Mr. Villers needn't be troubled. I trust in Mr. Wilde's capacity to work it out and to see justice done."

The chief eyed her with unselfconscious surprise. Val's throat tightened. I can't imagine how I reacted to this unprecedented display of camaraderie, being riveted to Abraham Kane—who sat there sipping gin as if he were reclining in a porchfront rocking chair. Utterly unperturbed.

"Symmes is both your alderman and your landlord. You knew Miss Woods personally," I realized.

Silkie Marsh flashed pearly teeth at me. I'd pleased her. "I did, Mr. Wilde."

"How well?"

"Not at all well."

"What's she capable of?"

"Practically anything, in my opinion."

"Something terrible happened. After the strike ended. It involved Miss Woods and Miss Abell, but no one will tell me anything. Do you know what it was?"

Madam Marsh set her gin down. She interlaced her fingers, the picture of a serene, judicious, and—though she repels me—beautiful woman. The blue ring at the center of her eyes darkened to an ocean-deep ribbon.

"Mr. Wilde, you are really rather clever from time to time," she said quietly. "Something terrible happened, yes. I cannot say what, precisely, for I've only suspicions as to the nature of Robert's punishment of Miss Woods for defying him. But I can tell you that he is a pitiless man. He said to me one night at my brothel, and I quote him, *I am going to make that bitch so sorry for humiliating me that she'll wish she was never born.* He did just that, or so I gather. I never knew Miss Abell, and Miss Woods has vanished. So you see, Mr. Wilde, this all has to end very quickly, or there will be hell to pay."

"It really is just about revenge, then," I said numbly. "I couldn't credit it was so simple."

Silkie Marsh walked to the desk, leaning over me. Generally when I look at her, it's like staring into the soapstone eyes of a bust. But this was an oracle's gaze, and a grim one.

"It is about nothing whatsoever save for revenge, Mr. Wilde." She spoke in a low murmur that vibrated through me as if she'd screamed the words. "This matter is *only* and *always* about revenge. Now, see it through, please, before more people are killed."

Silkie Marsh ceased speaking, but her lips remained open, her breaths warm and even. I could see the name *Bird Daly* writ plain as anything across their rosy surface.

"Recall what I said," I advised her softly, with a murder of my own on my mind. "Or you'll come to regret it."

Silkie Marsh was close enough to kiss me, close enough to bite, both of which prospects were equally nauseating. Instead she laughed fondly, straightening as she trailed artistic fingers along the desk's gleaming polish. She went to the door and retrieved her cloak, draping it over her white shoulders. "Good night, gentlemen. Thank you for having me. Oh. Mr. Wilde?" she called back.

"Yes?"

"I can't help but feel you're not through talking to Ronan McGlynn," she concluded just before shutting the door behind her.

The next few minutes, as I hunched over my report and the other men spoke lowly, were hazy. A windstorm had formed in my cranium in which *Symmes-Abell-Woods-Duffy-McGlynn* whirled about like so many scraps of newsprint. *Newsprint.* There was a thought. I needed to find William Wolf, who'd been there just before the close of the strike, who might have heard something, might have left it out of his article, might have smelled danger the way I can smell the faintest traces of smoke.

"Well, I think that's as much as we can accomplish this afternoon," Kane said to my brother, who stared in an unfocused fashion at his trouser leg. "Dinner, Captain? We've matters Democratic to discuss, and the chief and I have a table at the Astor. You may want a change of collar first."

"I'll meet you there," he agreed as they rose.

"I want that police report when he finishes," Kane added to George Washington Matsell.

Hastily, I resumed writing.

"Assuming he ever does finish, it's all yours," the chief returned with a martyred sigh.

Then they were gone, and it was only my brother and me, Val now sitting at the edge of the desk reading upside down as I finished the goddamn buggering police report.

"I don't hate you," I said tightly.

He raised his eyebrows, skeptical.

"Your apology is accepted," I added through my teeth.

My brother's response to this was a derisive snort.

"The scar, I . . . I'd help it if I could," I stammered, furious with myself. "You know I don't mind when you rag me about my size."

"Of course you don't mind that." Val sounded surprised. "Your size is my fault, after all."

Bewildered, I looked up from my writing. "What?"

"Your size." He scrubbed a hand over his stubbled jaw. "It was my doing, so it was my job to make you used to it."

These sounded like plain American words, but the sequence made no sense. "What the devil can my size have to do with you?"

A weary ripple of impatience crossed my brother's brow. "Have you honestly not cottoned to this? Christ. How old were you when we met the Underhill family?"

The mystery deepened. "Fourteen."

"We dined there plenty often afterward, didn't we? When the reverend took a liking to us, asked us to supper or tea three and four times a week?"

"Yes. I don't savvy a word you're saying," I protested, shoving the pen and paper aside.

"Timothy," Valentine snapped, exasperated, "what exactly do you think the effects of severe malnutrition between the ages of ten and fourteen *are*?"

Time slowed to a tortuous trickle as I stared at him. Recalled all the many ways my brother is capable of making a moldering potato palatable, remembered cast-off bread like clay bricks and rare, precious stolen beefsteaks and the memorable occasion the cat that haunted the halls of our wretched boardinghouse went missing and that we ate a passable stew the next day.

Val's eyes drifted sidelong as he coughed into his fist. "I tried. While I was still proving myself to the Party, it didn't always fadge, but. I tried. Anyhow. Enough of this, fill in the gaps over the Symmes debacle for me, I didn't quite savvy everything we just palavered over. I've been busy."

Dead silence. I shook my head, floored. I didn't want this information, *didn't want it*, didn't want any part of knowing my brother considered himself responsible for my runty stature nor that he was probably correct. It hurt unbearably in locked places I couldn't afford to open just then.

"You napped a crate of oranges off the back of a wagon once," I offered hoarsely. Desperate for any way to fix the pair of us and knowing the task impossible. "We were kings for a whole week. Remember?"

After a silent, pained laugh, Val shook his head. It didn't mean he didn't recall. It meant he'd no wish to speak of it. "You dwell on the oddest things. Come on, some of that just now was a surprise to me. Chant the rest of it."

With an effort that just about cracked my skull open, I numbly reached for the pen and drew the paper back to myself. Returned to the subject at hand.

"It was phosphorus both times," I told him. "That doesn't quite explain what the Neptune Nines were doing there earlier, though Symmes paying them to save his holdings is plausible, since they're based in Ward Two near his biggest commercial ventures. They certainly seem convinced you're not inclined to douse Symmes's properties."

"That's a pile of political rat droppings," he said calmly. "Next?"

"Miss Abell is plenty keen to prevent fires, but I wonder why Symmes trusts her so far."

"I wonder that too."

"I'm after a reporter named William Wolf, who I hope can shed light on the strike."

"It all started there, or seemed to. Can't hurt us. And?"

"Bird Daly thinks I told her she's not pure enough goods for a beau." My already tight throat was sore after that admission.

"You *what*?" Val demanded.

I took a deep breath, rallying. "I didn't. I was trying to tell her that falling in love with James Playfair would prove a bit of a wrench."

"You . . . oh," he concluded lamely. "You could . . . ah, make that argument."

"Mercy Underhill is back and living in a boardinghouse off Broadway."

"*Excuse me?*"

"I don't know what to do."

"How about send her a welcoming meat pie and leave her the hell alone?"

"I've been visiting her. My landlady is furious with me."

"Your landlady is not alone, you bottle-head. You should be giving Miss Mercy the berth of a pox ward."

My brother is one of several men who have engaged in casual relations with the love of my life. That fact makes me want to rip my own skin off, so I refuse to ruminate over it. Meanwhile, he's less than fond of her. Seems to think she unduly influences my moods.

"That's not going to happen. You're right, though." Dropping the pen, I pushed my knuckles into my eyelids, seeing multicolored blood pulse starkly against the bone. "I can't think. Or not about . . . any single thing for long enough to make sense of it. I've never felt this rattled. Val, something terrible is going to happen, I know it."

"Look at me."

I did. His lips were pushed into a concrete line.

"Not to *us*, all right, my Tim? I know you're ketched over this Symmes business, but I won't let it touch us. Keep your nets in the water and send me word if you snag anything. Now, finish that blasted police report. And I'm dead serious—stay clear of Mercy Underhill if you know what's healthy for you. Which you obviously don't."

I'd have said, *That makes two of us.* But I hadn't the strength.

He fetched his hat and his heavy stick from his chair. Gave me a brief nod. Quit the room and presumably the building.

Timothy Wilde, Star 107, I signed the report ten minutes later.

I returned the pen to its stand. For a moment I listened to the ticking of the gilded grandfather clock in the corner, stretching my right hand backward with my left. Then a pheasant carcass scavenged from a restaurant's rubbish bin crossed my mind. Unripe apples, tea made from mint weeds and lemon rinds, tomatoes stolen from a churchyard.

Breath faltering, I folded my arms and placed my head on them, and I stayed there. A small man slumped across a large desk in the middle of Tammany. For far longer than I like to recall.

16

I WAS FORCED TO POST notes to my colleagues at the Tombs the
following morning indicating that I'd be missing our scheduled
parley. Not because I didn't need to see them but because Mercy
Underhill doesn't generally slip unfolded sheets of foolscap without any envelopes under Mrs. Boehm's front door reading:

> *I would like to speak with you. If it's nothing then it'll come to
> nothing as everything else does in its due time but if it isn't
> nothing you'll want to know about it even though one day it
> will fade just the same. Meet me at my lodgings for breakfast.*

No one will think anything of it I assure you and anyhow there's
nothing to think exactly is there and the best kippers and toast
I find are to be had at nine o'clock, God not having granted our
proprietress the gift of early rising.

—Mercy

I'd descended the stairs at seven in the morning on April 26, freshly shaved and washed, to find Elena Boehm seated at the ever flour-grainy and butter-smeared table. No matter how many times a day she scrubs that piece of furnishing, it's always blessed by her most recent culinary effort. I've never minded it. The kitchen table smells *comfortable*, in a way nothing else does.

Elena was making a list. I've always liked that she's left-handed, though I've no idea why. Well, I've a hint of one, perhaps. It indicates she isn't a normal person, which makes me that much more easy in her presence.

"She still sounds not very well, your friend," Elena said hesitantly. After I'd gawked like a looby for ten or twelve seconds too long at Mercy's note. I couldn't blame her for reading the thing—it wasn't even folded in half.

"She was better, before . . . Just recently, I mean."

It sounded a miserable protest even to my own ears. Elena squeezed my wrist and went back to jotting down items.

"For dinner. Tonight. Forgot, maybe?" she asked without inflection.

"God no." I dragged myself from the mire of my thoughts. "Bird is coming over for dinner. If she still agrees, mind. She thought I said something terrible to her yesterday."

My landlady waited for me to elaborate. Arms crossed, fingers latched tight over her blue dress sleeves and her strangely colorless eyes pinned to my wreck of a face. I elaborated.

"Ach!" she exclaimed fondly, creasing her wide brow. "The

poor thing. No, no—don't think that. It might have been clumsy, but not ever would I suppose that you would *think* of such untruths, let alone speak them to Bird. You will fix this between the two of you. Bring some things back for dinner?"

"Of course. Which things?"

"A leg of mutton," she said, noting the request with a check mark on her slip of paper. "For the hash. If you can find any fresh parsley, that I would like. I have the dried mushroom powder for roasting. Wine we have, in the pantry. Maybe please some fresh butter? We are low on butter."

"Butter, parsley, leg of mutton. That's all we need?"

"Would not that be a rare blessing."

I smiled. "Anything else?"

She shook her head, wordless.

Something undisguised about her face struck me just then. I realized that never, not a single time in my life with her, had Mrs. Boehm deemed me unworthy of her secrets. On every occasion I'd asked after them, she'd answered me. Hesitant, maybe. But ultimately unguarded. And I understood that her explanations had been caresses, her confessions intimacies. Despite the fact I'd scarcely told her anything, unless I was unspooling like a skein of blood-red ribbon. It ached, when I saw it plain, in a part of me I hadn't known was dedicated to Elena at all. She'd said that people mark each other, and I owned by happy accident a stunning collection of Mrs. Boehm's anecdotes. Meanwhile, I'd never so much as wondered if she wanted to know where I'd been born.

"I want you to know everything, but I keep it from you because I don't want you to be frightened," I said all in a rush.

"Why on earth would I be frightened?" she replied, surprised.

"You think I don't like talking to people, talking to you, but it isn't that."

"But you *don't* like talking to people," she said softly. "People tell you too much. And then you walk away from them with a full mouth and closed lips."

She was right. But she was also mistaken.

"I'm not talking about *people*, I'm talking about *you*. My life is very ugly. I don't want you to be frightened. Not ever, and especially not due to my needing someone to listen to me because I'm already afraid."

I'd her face in my hands before I knew what I was doing, and her jaw lifted for my mouth, and then I was tasting *vanilla*, *cinnamon*, all along the edge of her throat and only hoping that the things I did and the truly stupid things my brother did would lead her to no harm.

She took me by the throat with the flat of her palm and pushed me back. In a friendly manner, smiling. Nothing but warmth in her pale eyes and amusement lifting her pronounced cheeks.

"You like being told to buy fresh parsley," she conjectured. "Or maybe you like me not to be worried?"

"The latter," I said at once, trying to press my nose back into her neck. The act on my part wasn't studied, nor even driven by romantic inclinations. When I think about it, it was affection. A simple thing, the *simplest*, affection.

Or shouldn't it be?

"You go now," Elena said, laughing as she put her arms around me. "You go to this Miss Underhill and see what it is she means to say."

"All right," I sighed against her neck.

Then I let her go. Elena tucked a wisp of hair about the density of a spider's web behind her ear, waving her hand in a comradely farewell. We couldn't have known what would happen that night, read the future in the flour grains on her table. But it's been years since April 26 of 1848, so many years, and when I think about what I ought to have done differently, among all my great errors I nevertheless remember that wave, and that I ought to have kissed her before the gentle creak of the door and the thud of my boots in the dirt marked my departure from what had been—for all its many singular silences—a happy home.

Half an hour later, after leaving an apologetic note to Piest, Connell, and Kildare tacked to my office door, I was seated at a low bench in the public dining space of Mercy's lodging house. It was a longish kitchen, really. A normal one, strung up with neatly braided garlic and onions, flour stacked in the corners. Except that the farthest wall, where not hung with cast-iron pans, was littered with pinned-up theatrical notices on corkboard—calls for actors, playbills, congratulatory notes, flyers as raucous as Tammany propaganda tacked helter-skelter above the cutlery.

As was decidedly not the case with Party publicity, it made for a nice effect, I thought.

The room was done in simple blue and white tiles that made one think of sharing a fresh crust or pouring a beer for a friend. I'd expected the lateness of the designated nine-o'clock hour to mean we would monopolize the meal hall. But a space was warmed by the dwarf at the far corner of the dining bench—Kindling, I recalled—and the waifish blonde with the perfectly rounded-off lips sat across from him. When I entered with Mercy, they waved quite unabashedly, then started up a quiet symphony of whispers and giggles over bowls of hot porridge. It would have been charming had I not known dead to rights the gossip was about me.

"We help ourselves over breakfast, though luncheon and dinner are served to us," Mercy said as she and I collected plates and toast and preserves and some admittedly handsome kippers that lay in a skillet. A carafe of coffee rested on the table, and we sat on either side of it. "I admit, I much prefer it so. Papa and I always did for ourselves or each other, and when I was in London, I supped with my cousin. You can trust cousins, the food they pass you. Here I feel such a stranger that something always looks wrong about meals, the colors and such, though I don't suppose it's very lucrative policy to poison one's lodgers. Is it?" she added anxiously.

Mercy wore a light off-the-shoulder day dress of black-and-white-checked cotton—it was neatly pressed, and the wide band of salmon-colored ribbon she'd passed through her thick black hair was artfully done. But her skin was pale enough to be faintly blue, and she'd been gnawing at her underlip to the point of leaving it raw. I remembered how she'd looked left in an ice bath to freeze to death by her paranoid lunatic of a father and fought the urge to take her heart-shaped face in my two hands and kiss her back to health.

"No." I poured us both cups of steaming coffee. "Though if you want, I'll come over every mealtime and taste your plate for safety."

Idiot, I thought when she smiled knowingly.

"Would you?" She stopped, brows pinching together as if she'd hurt herself. "I'm sorry. You so seldom say to me all of what you mean. It's just . . . fragments, you see, smashed eggshells and broken teacups. So I formed the habit of questioning you further. But you needn't answer that. I've always wondered if death by poison is painless or if it burns from the inside, little rivulets eating through your bloodstream until you're hollow. If it were peaceful, like going to sleep, I'd not mind the idea so."

A distant, unrelated titter from the dwarf followed by, "Oh, you naughty thing," from the actress filled the silence as I absorbed this harrowing sentiment.

Mercy has always been morbid. Always. She'd once, for *Light and Shade in the Streets of New York*, written a short story about an emigrant mother whose child was starving, who'd served her boy black pudding as a last gift before dying. The source of the blood for the black pudding was never explicitly stated, but the doctor upon declaring the poor woman dead remarked how clumsy she'd grown in her last illness, with so many bandaged cuts on her arms.

But this was different. The empty way Mercy's hands rested before her, palms-up on the table, fingers softly curved in over nothing at all.

Your father died by his own hand. He'd been broken by the weight of the world, and that is not allowed to happen to you, never to you, you are precious and living and—

"Anyhow," she said, as if continuing a conversation, "I've been thinking. And talking with Dunla. That's why I sent a street boy with the note before dawn."

"You sounded distressed," I hazarded.

"Did I? I can't . . . It was a dewdrops-on-spider's-silk sort of morning. Eerie. I can never remember those very well after they've passed over. Distressed, you say?"

"There was rather a lot of talk of nothing."

"Oh!" She sipped her coffee, seeming much relieved. "I was reading Shakespeare last night. 'Tomorrow and tomorrow and tomorrow,' you know the speech. It must have gotten stuck. That happens at times now. I couldn't get rid of the voice in my head reading 'Now that the wind and earth and sky are silent' for over a week once, though it was Chaucer reading me his translation and not Petrarch himself."

Smiling, she fell quiet.

It was hardly comforting. But it was in line with her usual daylight madness, so I commenced breathing again. "How are you getting on with Miss Duffy?"

"Very well. She is fourteen, I've discovered, and hasn't a soul left to her in the world. And she's perfectly sensible once you come to know her, though I admit she owns a peculiar turn of phrase. She's a bit like buying the yearly almanac and opening it to discover it's only rather exotic illustrations and no prose to speak of. Eat your breakfast—it's quite the safest meal, as I said."

Only you, I surmised as I sampled a kipper, *would call Dunla Duffy sensible and then describe her as a pictorial almanac.*

"Here's five dollars, by the way," I said, remembering. Dipping inside my frock coat, I passed her the notes. "Courtesy of the star police, since I'm sure you didn't expect a new bunkmate."

She frowned. "Don't you recall I've money of my own now?"

"That doesn't mean you signed up for a half-simple Irish sewing girl."

"You know full well I've always done charity work for the Irish. Anyway, I like her. She's seen unspeakably ugly things and still doesn't care for ugliness."

"You're right. But I'm in dire need of some answers."

"And thus you need fresh Pell Street sources, I suppose?" Mercy dipped a knife into the butter pot and spread it delicately over her toast. It was such an ordinary action, so akin to the sort I wanted to share with her endlessly, it seemed of enormous importance. "Sources who may have seen something unusual and can phrase such things rather more prosaically?"

"Just so."

"That's why we are finding the Witch."

I paused with my fork midway to my mouth. "The woman whose light Miss Duffy was so ketched over stealing?"

Mercy nodded. "At first I thought it a fruitless corridor to venture down, but she looms so powerfully in Dunla's head that I can't help feeling we're being led to her by some force. And of course the rest of the residents have scattered, but since, as Dunla says, witches quite naturally are to be found in their towers with their cauldrons, she'll be easily discovered."

Swallowing my toast presented fresh challenges of a sudden.

"Timothy?" Mercy's lips pursed.

"Do you really . . . think she's *that* sort of witch?"

"Of course. Dunla told me so."

"Yes," I said. The word somehow acquired additional syllables.

"Oh, here she is herself!" Mercy exclaimed. "The poor thing, now she is allowed a little sleep, I can never bear to wake her. Dunla, dear, come sit with us after you've filled your plate and explain to Mr. Wilde about the witches."

And please, in the process, assure me that the love of my life isn't insane, I begged some faceless deity as the sewing girl scouted the buffet.

Miss Duffy sat down, weirdly round eyes pinned to her plate. She'd taken several kippers and three pieces of toast that were now as much piles of berry preserves as they were bread. It struck me with a little jab twixt my ribs as a melancholy business, that she'd so seldom had access to such things. Not to mention the fact she was likely as much preparing for the grim future after she left Mercy's rooms as she was making up for lost meals.

"What about the witches?" she asked with a rather large amount of toast—or preserves, rather—in her mouth.

"You were afraid of the Witch because the other girls said she was mad, granted. But why else were you afraid of her?"

"Oh, sure enough because o' the spells she were after a-casting within the tower." Morning light glinted from the odd mossy-copper braids Miss Duffy had worked into a small bun atop her head.

I confess that this explanation did little to aid my understanding.

Mercy's eyes were twinkling. "Why don't you tell us exactly what that looked like, as you told me yesterday?"

Miss Duffy, between bites, explained in her peat-thick Irish brogue that when she'd first arrived in Manhattan six months previous, staggering into the New World like a shipwreck victim, she'd been greeted by an Irishman at the docks. My neck prickled instantly, but this greeter was no Ronan McGlynn. It was instead a member of the Irish Emigrant Society, which has for a few years now sought to lessen if only by needle-thin degrees the barbarity of our welcoming system—and by welcoming system I mean the process of ships spewing newcomers from the whale's belly to fend for themselves. The Society fellow (she couldn't recall his name but believed he was an angel in disguise) took Miss Duffy to his offices in Ann Street after asking where her kin were and what her plans might be and discovering her slate blank on both counts.

And anyway, after he'd spoken with you, he knew you for a loose-limbed lamb on the slaughterhouse floor, I thought, silently thanking the anonymous gentleman.

Upon arriving at the Irish Emigrant Society, Dunla Duffy was given a bowl of barley broth containing "sure enough real beef and turnips" and a map of the city. As she ate, she was taught that St. Patrick's Cathedral was on the corner of Prince and Mott and made to memorize the address lest she need help. She was told not to bother seeking assistance at Protestant churches (Mercy's cleft chin twitched in familiar repulsion at this). She was admonished that the only respectable trades for Irish girls included sewing, servitude, or—if she was very lucky and personable and quick—serving food in a Catholic-friendly eating house. She was to ask the literate to read employment notices to her from the *Herald*. The cheapest of desperate housing could be found in Ward Six, but there was one address she was to "avoid at all costs as a churchgoer, as it was sinful and perilous." Miss Duffy's savior described it to her.

"And when first I passed by the place, I found he were ne'er slaggin' me neither, fer all the witches live there and huddle over their cauldrons, sure enough," Miss Duffy whispered. "I saw them through the entrance, whenever I dared t' pass it by. But I were that dead on me feet sometimes, so's I had to go through the square or faint dead away, and then ye can't help but see the tower and the hell flames. The door bein' always open and all. The Witch lived there afore Pell Street. I saw her specific-like."

Speechless with delight, I spread my arms wide, leaned forward over the table, and grinned at Mercy Underhill.

She smiled at me with one side of her too-tender mouth. Pleased with herself. As well she should have been. The woman who makes my blood sing isn't simply a talented wordsmith but apparently an investigative genius to boot. I shouldn't have been surprised. She'd given me the decisive clue to the kinchin murder tragedy years ago, when by dint of her charity work she'd introduced me to Ninepin.

"You see why I thought you might take an interest?" she ventured. Letting her blue eyes slide sidelong.

"Indeed I do. Miss Duffy, is the square you speak of in the Five Points?"

"O' course."

"And the tower is an enormous brick building, once painted white but now filthy? With a pair of pointed rooftops? Between the taller peak and the front door below there's a great crumbling arch with three gaping windows, all the glass smashed and then blocked up with oiled paper in tatters? And the doors are always flung wide to the plaza?"

"Oh, aye, ye know it well, then," Miss Duffy agreed.

"I do. Mercy, you're a wonder."

She angled her head at me, smoothing down the curl at her nape.

"Miss Duffy, would you describe what the Witch looks like?"

"Grey hair coarse as a brush, all a-leapin' off her head like, though she ties it back wi' a red kerchief. She has seven queer devil candles what reek like hell itself. Them's what got me in trouble."

I leaned over to retrieve my hat from the bench. "This is too flash to waste any time over. Thank you, I'll make it up to you both somehow. Now if you'll excuse—"

Standing with a steely edge of determination, Mercy pressed Miss Duffy's shoulder warmly. "I shall see you at supper, I hope, Dunla. I found a book on flowers in the parlor, and it's filled with the most beautiful picture plates. I left it on the table for you."

No, I thought.

"Going for a walk, Miss Underhill?" the dwarf called out.

"Of sorts," she agreed as I opened my mouth in violent protest.

"Oh, don't dream of going unescorted, Miss Underhill. I'd *hate* to think of you encountering any ruffians. *Do* say you'll not go alone!" cooed the flaxen-haired actress.

Kindling's face was reddening to a shade not unlike his hair, a laugh trapped in his chest. "Your star-police friend here would oblige, surely? To save us both the worriment over your safety?"

"He'd oblige, I think," Mercy answered serenely. My fingers twitched in helpless mortification as she headed for the door. "He's very kind."

"Do you know, he *seems* so, and I've an extraordinary sixth sense in these matters!" agreed the actress. "Enjoy taking the air, my dear. If you go down the shilling side of Broadway, there's the most *marvelous* display of engagement rings in the window just south of—"

The performers collapsed in chortles as I made a hasty departure from their dining hall. Not because I was shades of embarrassed I'd never known existed in the pantheon of human humiliation, but because Mercy Underhill was walking calm as you please in the direction of the Old Brewery, the most lightless hive of human wretchedness in all of Ward Six.

Y ou needn't be so flustered, you know," Mercy advised, her small hand on my arm. "It isn't as if I've not been here previous, once to distribute medicines and once to help a group of charity workers give a tour to some British reformers—or didn't I tell you about that before?"

"You didn't tell me much," I couldn't help but return in my profound consternation. "Before."

Stifling a sigh, Mercy returned her eyes to the hulking blot of architecture we stood contemplating. Traveling to the Old Brewery in the heart of the godless Five Points had been a mere matter of walking down Centre Street for eight or so blocks, watching hectic sparks fly from the great wheels as the New York and Harlem Railroad was dragged northward by straining, marble-eyed horses, and then turning east on Anthony Street. A stroll of ten minutes had taken us there.

"It hasn't changed," Mercy mused.

"Apart from acquiring a few score more residents? No, I don't imagine it has."

Once upon a time, as Mercy might write, the place where we stood had been a woodland pond reflecting the preening sun's face back to it as if the waters were a handheld mirror. I don't know when Manhattan began its slow creep outward like a cancer, but sometime about fifty years back, a brewery was built on the edge of the sparkling waters. Add a dozen or so other filthy industries wanting a water source to the landscape and we had ourselves a fetid swamp. So we paved over the surface, and the swamp went away. Except it didn't, not really. It festers under the entirety of the Five Points, which is why all the buildings here sag into rot and ruin about a month after they're constructed. As for the Old Brewery, as it's called, it's an ancient nightmare of a place.

And since no one can be bothered to knock it down, people live there.

Hundreds of them. Irish, blacks, and other indigents—like penniless outworkers, I took it—swarm the wreck. Dunla Duffy had been right to be warned away. There's no better place to develop conditions like a shiv in your neck or a constellation of smallpox on your belly. As for witchcraft, she'd been describing the place after sunfall, when human locusts flutter around great scavenged iron pots and cauldrons on the ground floor with fires kindled in them—anything to keep warm whilst keeping the flames from licking at the walls, doors flung wide to the night sky to prevent the meager hearths from smothering every last occupant.

If the woman called the Witch could live someplace else—an oozing cellar, a sweltering attic, a populous apple barrel—she would. But lacking lodgings so suddenly and recently, I'd every hope she might be found there.

As did Mercy. Apparently.

"Are we venturing inside," she wondered, "or admiring the view?"

"This way," I said, turning us aside. "Miss Duffy was right about one thing—there's no way we're walking in there without our own light."

It took me five minutes to convince the corner grocer to lend a copper star a bull's-eye lantern, followed by the selfsame proprietor charging me double the fair price of oil to light it, which struck me as pretty fine style. In we stepped over the threshold of the Old Brewery, its gloom reaching for us like the maw of a descending predator. The front room is cathedral cavernous, designed to house vats of ale. Now it houses dozens of the drunk, the sick, and the simply poor. Hints at upper levels emerged in smudged charcoal lines, echoes of snores and of whimpers reaching our ears. But even in broad daylight, the paper over the windows means the place is too shrouded in midnight to make much of a visual impression.

No, what strikes you first is the smell. Unwashed bodies, unclean refuse, unadulterated woe—sweat and shit and sex and every other uniquely personal scent signaling *Get out.*

"Why do you want to be here?" I asked Mercy, toeing an impressive insect carcass into the piles of broken glass and moldering rags along the walls.

"Because I discovered after my mother died that if I don't do this sort of thing continually, I'll become frightened of it. And I don't want to be the sort of girl who's frightened."

I couldn't answer her. My mouth was too full of *Please, would you please just let me tear off a string of your heart and wind it around my finger?* Anyhow, I was distracted.

The rag piles had started moving. Blinking at the lantern's harsh, concentrated glow. A family of Africans—or at any rate four sets of red-rimmed eyes mounted within skeletons pasted over with black skin—peered back at me from a little heap on the obscenely filthy floor. They'd covered themselves in burlap coffee bags.

"All right," I said to Mercy lowly. "I'm not glad you're here, but I'm . . . glad you're here. I've only been within the doors of this place once, during the riot over the copper stars' forming three years ago. You're more familiar with this terrain."

"Not in any valuable way."

"You've explored it twice?"

"Yes, but—"

"If you were an outworker living in this sort of hell, you'd need somewhere between seventeen and eighteen hours' work per day to keep your blood pumping, yes?"

She considered. "Supposing even that effort proved enough."

"Where's the light?"

"Pardon?"

"This woman seems to have nearly taken Miss Duffy's head off for working from the light of her candles. If there are seamstresses here, they'd forsake warmth preferring free illumination."

"Of course," she exclaimed. "But God, Timothy, I don't . . . Wait, let me think."

"The cellar is out, of course," I reasoned. "The staircases here are a hazardous business?"

"What? Oh, yes. The coming down is hardest. One sometimes feels as if one can *climb* anything, challenges oneself to put a hand on a rotting banister here, a foot on a creaking stair there, but returning . . ."

"Which is just what I mean. Would you so much as attempt it if you were stitch-blind? Or even partway there?"

Ellie Abell and Sally Woods had been doing cutters' work— hardly a fortune involved, but reasonable hours with a weekly pay. Plenty of other females in the textile industry could labor hemming difficult cloth or sewing on buttons or adding fancy stitchwork with no ill effects for decades.

The outworkers, though . . . The only reason Dunla Duffy's eyesight remained keen was that she hadn't been here long enough. Toil enough fruitless hours in meager light, allow hours to bleed into dusky days and then months and then years, and the sense of sight itself revolts against tyranny. Withers and dies.

"I'd never risk it, no!" Mercy assented, understanding me. "This front room admittedly boasts the most windows, but it's claimed by the most long-standing occu—"

"Is there a problem here, little sunbeam?" a sinister voice rasped out of the gloom. "Some of us are trying to *catch a wink of sleep.*"

In a flash I'd averted the lantern and steered Mercy—to my deepest reluctance—farther into this sable sea calling itself a building. Not one of the placeless people surviving in the Old Brewery could outfight me.

But all of them at once? Should a brawl commence? With Mercy on your arm?

As we drew away from the front steps where the sunshine bled through, the Old Brewery grew improbably more grim. I tried not to trouble anyone with the lantern, but few of the sots sprawled along the walls owned the strength to object. Anyhow, my type wouldn't bustle them—copper stars often lead tours of this pit. Rich foreigners hug their arms tight to their waists and mutter deprecations about Americans and feel generally more pleasant about their own slums and pay us bright coins to watch people starve to death. Charles Dickens famously tried it when I was twenty-four. At least he didn't enjoy it. Being . . . well, Charles Dickens and all.

"If I'd only paid more attention," Mercy hissed, following the lantern beam with her eyes. "I could have— Wait, wait, stop."

Avoiding the slumbering bodies flanking an aisle so as not to be trampled, we'd rounded a corner and reached a parallel corridor making a right angle along the wall.

"This way," Mercy gasped.

Dropping my arm, she took my hand.

Through we plunged, and out again into another room stacked with bodies, and then yet another, nearly as large as the one before. Mercy led me with fingertips warm as Bird's rosary beads against my palm toward a little room along the back side of the structure. When my lantern glanced off the entrance, I saw that its door had long since been torn off for firewood and the hinges pawned.

But even so far across the chamber, I could see that a diffuse glow of light emanated. A light made all the eerier by the pitch darkness in which it then drowned.

tere.

ead.

"The office," Mercy said in my ear. "This was where the brewers did accounts. So they wanted daylight, long ago. Before we were born."

We stepped slowly toward the hole of a doorway. Crossing the threshold felt like passing into another world. But we did it. Hand in hand, heart in mouth.

The room contained the following, as I later made note:

—heaps of snipped thread, gathered in a corner for later salvage, presumably for kindling
—piles upon piles of unfinished pantaloons, sleeves, drawers, and handkerchiefs
—fifteen sewing girls in various states of malnutrition

And a single woman with billowing iron hair tied down under a red rag, face deeply scored and tongue thrust between her teeth, working at the cuffs of slave trousers, several unlit but unique candles resting beside her outwork.

"Who in blazes are you?" the crone demanded in a voice like a knife being sharpened on a stone.

She was right to be peevish. I hadn't introduced myself. But I knew, sure as Mercy's hand rested in mine, that I had just encountered Miss Duffy's Witch. And I suspected—as would later prove correct—that, as so commonly follows encounters with witches, events of great magnitude and ugliness lurked behind the horizon of my immediate future.

17

O! Men, with sisters dear!
O! Men, with mothers and wives!
It is not linen you're wearing out,
But human creatures' lives!
Stitch—stitch—stitch,
In poverty, hunger, and dirt,
Sewing at once, with a double thread,
A Shroud as well as a Shirt.

—THOMAS HOOD, "THE SONG OF THE SHIRT," 1843

"I'M TIMOTHY WILDE, copper star one-oh-seven," I said.

Silence. Bony hands continued stitching, ever stitching, actions rote and mechanical, red eyes pinned to the seams before them. Just as I'd surmised, they'd torn the paper from the two large windows, and though houses are packed thick as lice in Ward Six, a golden midmorning glow yet permeated. Tender and innocent-seeming.

Unlike the women.

Not that they seemed ignoble. The mere fact of them being there meant they'd chosen *not* to be somewhere else, as Dunla Duffy had likewise decided. They weren't smothered in chalky powder and crimson rouge, walking arm in arm through the dock-sides and the boulevards, calling out propositions in stark detail. They weren't covered in spangles everywhere save for their bare breasts, leaning out of windows in Ward Four. Neither were they poured like cream into sheaths of satin with lace overlay, waiting to be chosen from a line in a brothel resembling a mansion.

They were sewing. As if sewing were breathing, and in a way it was. But life had been crueler to them than words can convey and, there in that lowest den in the Five Points I saw more fully what Val was talking about when he insisted we couldn't go on as we were.

One of the girls was crowned with blood-crusted gouges along her dark hairline. When I realized that was because she'd fallen asleep with her head uncovered, and she'd been too weary to awaken when a rat started gnawing her mazzard off, I thought we'd do best to build an ark, flood this cesspool of a city, and start it over fresh. No furnishings were visible, though I spied empty grain sacks on which the girls sat, and I presume under which they slept. Outwork lay in colossal folded piles on either side of each laborer. Their lips were chapped, expressions numb, fingers steady as the clock in the cupola of City Hall.

"Brought your lady friend to the zoo, have you?" the Witch sniffed.

She didn't look up, but neither did her companions. There was something almost threateningly *alive* about the Witch, despite her smallness. As if she'd dared the universe to put her out of her misery and the universe wasn't proving up to the task. Her hair was indeed a grey blizzard, barely controlled by the oily kerchief, her face weathered enough for her to have been born during the Revolution. But the bones beneath were strong, even handsome, even vaguely familiar, as if I'd seen her likeness once in a classical painting or a portrait of a beautiful debutante. Her eyes remained a

shocking blue. She'd been forced to sell some of her inventive candles in the desperate circumstance of finding new digs, for Dunla
had mentioned with all her native superstition *seven*. I spied five.

Finally, her outwork's quality—compared to that of the other
molls—was rather appalling. She stitched willy-nilly, tacking down
the edges of kerchiefs as if no one had ever dared to tell her the job
hadn't been executed to his liking. I suspected the lax overseer to be
Simeon Gage of New American Textiles, since I'd first heard of
the Witch living in a Symmes-owned building. But whoever the
weak-handed boss, I could scarce blame the cove.

She was terrifying.

What sent you to this hell? I thought wonderingly. *What deliberate
crimes, what accidental mistakes?*

"My name is Mercy Underhill, and I often perform charity
calls," Mercy answered her readily. "Though I hate the necessity of
visiting the hardworking in times of distress. What is your name,
if you please, madam?"

The Witch, for we still hadn't any more polite term to employ,
dropped her piecework into her lap and *howled* with laughter.

I could see why the Pell Street girls said she was mad. The
mirth was so unbridled, galelike in its force, that Mercy took half a
step back, and I felt my right hand drifting as if to shield her.

Tears forming, the Witch subsided into gusty chuckles. "What
finishing school did this pious seminary bitch come from?"

After that the room turned rather deafening.

"Want to see a lass wi' open sores on her bum from sitting?" an
Irish girl drawled from the corner.

"Won't you sit down for a cuppa?"

"Oh, stop, the lot o' you, they dasn't mean no harm."

"Buy a bloody ticket, there's a sporting girl."

"Are we meant to *appreciate* you realize we're working?"

"And more to the point," the Witch continued, nodding her

head, "why should I feel any better about her staring at me than I should about a reporter here to make a dollar off my life story?"

"I didn't go to finishing school, and the difference is payment," Mercy replied evenly. "If you'll speak with us, I'll give you this lantern my friend is holding."

Everyone froze. Me especially.

"We're not—"

"People *live here*, Timothy." Mercy was quiet but radiating force—a white coal at the still center of the hearth. "We can exit a building without a lantern. What say you, madam?"

The Witch's eyes had fixed ravenously on the lantern, as if the object were real victuals. The rest of the girls hadn't stopped sewing, not for a moment, never dropped a stitch for me or for Mercy's sake.

"Ask your questions," the Witch said.

Then she drew out a longish carving knife.

"And if you don't leave the lantern afterward, I'll make your face look like your beau's."

Miss Duffy was right to be frightened, I realized, flexing my hand.

"How long had you lived at Pell Street when the fire broke out?" Mercy asked.

The tongue appeared again, thrusting between the Witch's lips as if she were a lizard. "A month, maybe more."

"Did you do outwork for Symmes or just live in his building?" I questioned.

"Both. He's a man of importance. I'd call him 'Alderman' if I were you sorry lot."

"How did you come to know him personally?"

"Never said I knew him," she scoffed. "That doesn't mean I'm witless enough not to know he owns half the city. I *work* for him.

Lived in Pell Street, before it burned. That's the whole story, Copper Star one-oh-seven."

"Did you take part in the strike last year?"

"Do I look simpleminded to you?"

"No. But the organizers were hardly simpleminded either."

The same laugh erupted, slicing through the stench. "You think not?" the Witch hissed. "You think that women who defy power are smart? I'll tell you about how smart I was once, so you can kiss my arse and get out of my office. Would that tie a pretty little bow on your outing? Since you're leaving the lantern, you ought to get your money's worth."

"We'd like to learn all you're willing to tell us."

"I was a maid once." The Witch arrowed her eyes at Mercy. "Was I a pretentious, guilt-ridden, coddled smear of dung like you? I was not. Could I say no to the master of the house? Yes. But I *didn't want to*—I supposed he'd throw over his wife for me, you see. Does that sound smart to you? So eventually my belly swells and I'm chucked out after the master blames one of the groomsmen for my trouble. Do you know what's funny about that?"

We said nothing. I shook my head.

"It's funny because I lost this game *once*. And ever since, I've been winning, because I'm not stupid enough to ask the world to revolve in the other direction. I left the baby at the door of a church. I worked at tailoring fashionable undergarments for years. When I lost that job, I kept on as an embroidery specialist. When the detailing dried up, I started outwork hemming. I won't outlive every last person who spat on me," the Witch concluded. "But I will spit on them, I will *spit on you*, until my corpse is dropped in an unmarked hole."

Murmurs of approval filled the room and flew, like a horde of stinging insects, out the open window.

"When you lived in Pell Street," I said, at every kind of loss, "did you notice anyone suspicious?"

"No one. Not a single person."

I balked at this certainty. "You sound pretty sure."

"I am *pretty sure*, you oaf. I lived in the downstairs front room, and how many hours of sleep per night do you think I allow myself? The answer is three, and I sleep light anyhow."

"None of the cutters ever paid a call?"

"What business would that pack of uppity hens have visiting us? You suppose we'd tea cakes to offer?"

This was troubling. Sally Woods could, admittedly, have somehow planted the phosphorus months earlier—but the odds were against it, to my mind. Too much risk of its being discovered, too much time spent between planning a heinous act of vengeance and setting it alight. A week or two, I figured, would be the longest gamble she'd have countenanced.

We were getting nowhere at admirable speed. So in a last-ditch effort, I asked, "Have you *any* information that might help us find the person who burned down your home?"

The Witch stopped sewing. Her eyes lifted. They cut right through a man, sliced the meat from his bones and left him there to bleed.

"My *home*?" she spat. "My *home*, the fellow says. If that was a home, I'm the belle of the ball. Christ, get out of my sight, the pair of you. I didn't think it could get any worse in here. I was wrong."

Aching with disappointment, I stepped forward and set the lantern down. The Witch cackled in glee and dragged the bull's-eye closer, as if it had been a treasure chest.

"What are the candles made out of?" Mercy asked as we went to the door.

"Turned animal fat, the sort that's well past eating." The Witch flicked her eyes up at us. "Why, you want a sip? Jesus, if I could send all so-called *reformers* to Liberia instead of the Africans, I could maybe die with a smile on my face."

Leaving that abyss was a nerve-wracking feat. For all the hugeness of the space, the sounds of countless people waiting to die made it seem as if the walls were closing in. It probably took us three minutes, stepping carefully, moving faster as our eyes adjusted. It felt like a lifetime, though. And when we'd made it through the front door, still blessedly hand in hand, we gasped the marginally fresher atmosphere as if we'd come up from the depths of an inky ocean.

Mercy pulled away and, with her back to me, retrieved a small kerchief from the pocket of her black-and-white day dress. Tugging at her elbow didn't work, so I stepped around her. She'd nearly dried her eyes by then, but a single track remained, and I wiped it away with my fingertips. She smiled shakily.

"Were you frightened?" I asked.

"Yes, but . . . that's not what I . . ." She bit her lower lip, hard enough to hurt. "She was wrong, in a way. About me. But I wish . . . I wish she hadn't also been right."

"No." I cupped my other palm to her face, willing her to look at me. "She was wrong. About every single word."

"How can you be certain?" she asked, fresh tears welling into blue pools.

"Because *I know you.*"

You don't remember, I didn't say, *when you were thirteen and you lent me a little green chapbook of poems you'd written, poems you wanted back when I was through, and you don't know that whilst you were at church, I sat at your father's desk and stole his ink and paper and copied the entire collection out line by line. I know everything there is to know about you, and I'm still here.*

"Yes," she said in a whisper like autumn reeds. "Yes, I think in spite of everything perhaps you do after all."

*Y*ou *comprehensively brick-brained lunatic,* I thought when I arrived at my office an hour later.

Collapsing behind my desk with a large glass of gin, I drained the liquid and deposited my head in my hands. I just sat there for long moments. Feeling the liquor sweetly buzz through my veins like bees. Rubbing at my temples absently. Harder on the side where my scar rippled, unsightly and utterly unchangeable, across a quarter of my face.

Why in hell didn't you just kiss her senseless?

Mercy would have let me, I thought. Before I brushed away the last of the tears and skimmed my lips lightly along her hairline. Before I offered my arm and walked her back to the theatrical boardinghouse. Before I left her at the door, half smiling and composed again.

Anyone would think you're coward, a virgin, or a fucking eunuch.

I slumped forward, the heels of my palms grinding into my eyes.

Knock-knock-knock.

"Come in."

The door swung open. Ninepin stood there with a short, square-shouldered, well-dressed gentleman wearing quiet plaid trousers and a matching brown swallowtail coat, a man with whom I was not familiar. The stranger swept his hat off as they stepped into the room.

"Well, I've brung him at last," Ninepin reported sulkily. "He tumbled to a dusty mob of tobby coves working James Slip—wanted a story out of them, went underground so's he could get one, and then peached to the hamlet of the Fourth. Mr. Wilde, meet the Wolf."

Rising, I extended my hand, and the news reporter shook it

firmly. I knew that Ninepin had just said William Wolf had disappeared in order to procure a story about a gang who by night bludgeoned pedestrians and then tipped them into the river, and that afterward the journalist had duly notified the captain of Ward Four. But I wondered if Mr. Wolf knew it. That had been an impressive run of flash patter, even for Ninepin.

"Timothy Wilde, star one-oh-seven. Thank you for coming."

"Not at all."

William Wolf's voice was deep, his eyes widely set and nearly black. Ninepin and the boys were right, I thought in some surprise. If Mr. Wolf wasn't Indian, one or both of his parents surely claimed Mexican descent. I wondered whether he'd come from the alarmingly large region poised to become an American slave state rather than a Tejano wilderness. His lips were angular, broad, and turned down at the corners, and his glossy close-cropped hair, far shorter than the usual fashion, was dark enough to reflect glints of blue. How in hell he'd managed to become a newsman of note I couldn't fathom, for—legally speaking—Indians hold about as many rights as blacks, which is to say few in letter and none in practice. Most of them, or at least the ones who haven't faded westward into the distant forests or settled in the gaps between cities, sell food or trinkets or do manual labor for a living.

"Have a seat, Mr. Wolf. Thank you, Ninepin." I passed him his money. "You can leave us to it."

"Bloody self-important, noddle-pated . . ." he muttered sadly.

"Ninepin, I'm sorry," I added to his skinny back. "Write to Bird all you want, and best of luck. You're a fly bloke, and I was being a right prick."

Ninepin turned. He pulled his glasses off, predictably, and tapped them with great gravitas upon his chin. "Truly?" he questioned.

"Truly."

"I savvy she's your friend. And a fellow has to look after his doxies and all."

"Well . . ."

"So that's pretty white of you, Mr. Wilde."

"Cheers. Off you go."

"In a second. Share a nip of your sky-blue with a cove and we'll call it square."

Sighing, I poured Ninepin a tiny measure of gin. He drained it, smacking his lips together theatrically.

"Nothing like a quick stop to sluice your gob afore the afternoon stiffs come off the press. Fare thee well, Mr. Wilde. Mr. Wolf, write faster if you please, your work is golden, and I need the extra chink to court a ladybird."

Grinning, Ninepin departed. I quashed warring urges to thank the scamp for appreciating Bird's finer qualities and offering to strangle him if he ever so much as breathed on her person. But since Bird needed just such a harmless distraction these days due to my own stupidity, I held my tongue.

William Wolf had seated himself opposite my desk. His gaze was thoughtful and patient—the perfect expression for a reporter to adopt when questioning a subject—but laced with tart amusement. No, *irony*, I thought. His interest in humans hadn't led to his wholehearted admiration of the species.

"Would you care for a splash yourself?" I asked, going for another glass.

"Why not, as it's nearly lunchtime."

"And already feels like midnight." I poured a pair of drinks and sat down again. "I've been . . . active. You're right, of course, and you needn't accept."

"I always accept," he answered, swirling the tumbler philosophically. "One can never know what would have been the usual order of business in a new environment unless one says yes. You're an intriguing man, a notable man, and your office is new to me. So I say yes."

"To everything?"

"Nearly," he returned. "Not to quack nostrums purportedly made from snake venom being sold out the back of a corner grocer in Ward Seven. It was only colored laudanum, of course, or so it proved, but the prospect was dangerously unpalatable."

I felt my mouth curving upward. "You have a wide range of interests."

"So do my readers. What are the particular interests of the man who solves riddles for Tammany Hall?"

"I'm surprised you've heard of me."

"I'm surprised you're surprised."

Pondering, I linked my fingers together. "I'm working on a problem, and you wrote an article about the key players."

"Was it riveting?" He failed to smile, which somehow lent the question all the more air of droll humor.

I nodded. I'd dug up the edition at the Mercantile Library Association in Nassau Street, where periodicals are archived, digging through rack after rack of print as the city clerks bustled through the quiet reading room, their hair neatly slicked and their collars turned up against their chins. Then I'd found it staring me in the face—RIGHTS FOR FEMALES, SEWING GIRLS A BUSTED FLUSH. It was a colorfully written account of the molls who'd defied New American Textiles. The much-maligned "Frailty, thy name is MAN" sentiment, for instance, was juxtaposed with a blistering portrait of Dunla Duffy, whose grasp of the strike's purpose had been tenuous and was rendered in broad strokes. Miss Woods and Miss Abell had fared much better, but praise for their backbones and the lovely, clever heads those stalwart spines supported hadn't prevented Wolf concluding:

We await Alderman Symmes's decision with interest—but not, let us add, with much uncertainty as to its nature. And thus, like so many other Movements of these cataclysmic times, despite its passionate origins the strike against New American Textiles seems poised to prove so much banging of spoons against copper pots—all sound and feeling, and incapable of any success other than to create its own cacophony. Within that very hullabaloo, however, lies the kernel that so dismays the Conservative—Power has had its nose well and truly tweaked by the Fliers of Petticoat Flags, and though they accomplish ever so little, the din of their voices will not now be easily quelled.

"I want to know your impressions of Miss Woods and Miss Abell."

He nodded. "I want an estate on Long Island with a kennel of racing dogs."

"Do you want anything simpler?"

"The story of your investigation. And how *you* investigate it."

Rubbing my fingers over the upside-down semicircle in my chin, I reflected upon the profound dangers of this proposal.

"I don't know that the details can be made public."

"Shouldn't they be?"

"I try to follow my conscience, but the Party—"

"Oh, I see. You've a fondness for your own good health, as do I. Nothing Tammany fails to approve—just everything else. I'm fascinated by you, you understand. To our health."

William Wolf finished the gin decisively and tilted his head back, awaiting my answer.

I didn't like it. Not being the subject of an exposé and not sharing my all-too-scandalous information. But I needed the fires to stop. Thus I suspected what I really needed was a portrait of the hours between when the "Busted Flush" article appeared and the vicious quelling of the strike the next day. I had to know why two passionate friends were no longer speaking. And why Ellie Abell had once seemed to Miss Duffy to have stars in her eyes when now only the icy glimmer of tragedy lingered there.

"It's a deal," I told him.

William Wolf pulled a notebook from his brown swallowtail coat as I reached for the pad on which I pen police reports and sketch suspects. Oddly mirroring each other.

"How did you come to cover the manufactory girls?" I asked.

"I was already interested in female rights—they accidentally timed the strike to suit me. What do you think of the movement?"

"I think some of the women I know are sharper than I am. Doesn't mean I like to see them jeopardized, but their work should be fairly compensated."

"Ah, a social radical. I take it you're an abolitionist, then, as they go perennially hand in glove?"

"I was antislavery long before the Bowery girls started antagonizing the tailors, yes."

"Your brother, Captain Valentine Wilde of firefighting infamy, is suddenly running on a Barnburner ticket. Do you support his campaign?"

I blinked, not having lent any special thought to this thorny question. "I'm not a bit political, but Val's a hard worker and a Free Soil hero. How came you to write about female autonomy?"

"It's a hot enough subject that anything you say will at least be read if not appreciated. I don't care if people appreciate me, only if they buy a copy of the *New Republican*."

"Ninepin heartily agrees with you. Tell me about meeting the seamstresses."

"Of course. Tell me why you're intrigued by them."

I was beginning to enjoy the rapport of this tit-for-tat questioning. Mr. Wolf placidly jotted notes in jerky shorthand, knee cocked akimbo with his shin resting against his leg. We somehow felt like collaborators after a five-minute acquaintance. I suspected that to be a talent of his.

"Alderman Robert Symmes owns a great many properties, and two of them have been burned by an incendiary using white phosphorus," I replied cautiously. "Threatening letters were sent to him previous. Say nothing of the firestarter in the press, or we'll be sharing the Hudson as a final resting place. But the motive is almost certainly vengeance originating from the strike."

Mr. Wolf looked up from his scribbling in some excitement. "A sewing girl turned anarchist?"

"Do you think it's possible?"

"Possible and then some. Not so far as Miss Woods goes, mind. But Miss Abell? In a heartbeat."

My pate had begun to tilt in agreement before the words registered. When his meaning did land, my pen froze.

"Miss *Abell*?" I couldn't help but exclaim.

Frown deepening, Mr. Wolf repeated, "Miss Abell, yes. I spent three of the strike's six days sporadically interviewing them both, so it felt as if I came to know them rather well. The data is limited to my own impressions, however."

"Will you give them to me?" I badly wanted to know.

He coughed pleasantly, adjusting his waistcoat. "Interesting. My impressions tend to be valued in printed form only, though I am the first to admit that my appearance carries distinct advantages to the undercover investigator—before you sits a man who, when dressed in rags or in feathers, is universally ignored if not kicked down the street. It's terribly useful. I follow the natural flow of the river, you understand, only steering when absolutely necessary."

"If you'd describe the terrain in this case, I'd be indebted."

He smiled, an uptick that drew the corners of his mouth parallel rather than curved skyward. "Mr. Wilde, a single word has taken me further than I had dared hope in this world, and that is the word *yes*."

Settling more comfortably into his chair, Mr. Wolf delivered his account. Following the strike had been uneventful for him on the first day. Two days later, when he returned to collect more quotes and soak up the scene, the tailors had arrived and begun to make their displeasure known by lobbing obscenities and putrid vegetables. Mr. Wolf, whether from sympathy or suspicion they were ripe for a chat (I suspected the latter), asked Sally Woods and Ellie Abell to tea after the day's protests. He'd done so again when he returned for the last time—that was Saturday, the day after the article appeared in the late Friday papers.

"It had already rained all over them on their way to the manufactory," he said, remembering. "Then a pack of hired bullies descended, and it was over in five minutes. Symmes ended the strike . . . definitively, though I can think of other words. There they stood, bedraggled as wet cats, exhausted and bruised to boot, their circle all but disbanded, though Miss Abell and Miss Woods lingered. Miss Woods was scarlet with fury, pacing interminably, while Miss Abell dispensed advice as to injuries among the outworkers. I bought them another pot of tea, as they were short, and wished them well."

"What gives you reason to think Miss Abell could possibly set fire to a slum?" I prodded.

He spread his hands. "Here's my recollection of the pair. First of all, they were thick as any set of thieves. Inseparable. The instant violence threatened on that picket line, their eyes were on each other—reassuring, defending, planning. And the brains behind the planning was without doubt Miss Woods. Her mind, Mr. Wilde . . . I marveled at it. Your women have been talking about equality for decades, but outside of my own people I'd never *seen* it, so I wasn't sure it was possible for whites. She grasped questions of politics, business, housing. Miss Abell worshipped her."

"You don't imagine extraordinary abilities can be used destructively?"

"I meant nothing of the sort. You said you know women who are sharper than you? Well, Miss Woods is sharper than me, Mr. Wilde, and I know better than to burn down a building belonging to Robert Symmes. Another will pop up overnight. When half his businesses disintegrated in eighteen forty-five, did he bat an eyelash? Miss Woods is too keen to make such a dull play."

Baffled, I passed my fingers through my high hairline. "But Miss Woods frightens him. I saw it. Hell, I wasn't exactly easy around her myself."

"The first time we met, she asked if it had been losing my family that led me to abandon tradition for enterprise and congratulated me for defying convention. No one is easy around Miss Woods."

"How did you answer?"

"Since she was right, I told her my parents are Swedes, and very proud of me," he joked.

Half smiling, I topped up our gin. "And Miss Abell?"

Mr. Wolf paused his note-taking, black eyes shining. "Miss Abell is affectionate, trusting, and well intentioned. I can't possibly think of a person who would be more easy to manipulate. That's why she was chosen for the final meeting between parties after the strike ended, I imagine."

I'd been riveted enough at the character study, but this was new information. My pulse sped instantly. "There was a meeting scheduled?"

"Oh, yes. The article had been printed Friday and I brought them copies on Saturday. Brickbats and hired thugs dampened spirits worse than the rain, but the girls seemed hopeful even then, for they said Symmes had arranged a tête-à-tête to settle the aftermath amicably. Not with Miss Woods, mind, who could probably talk circles around the likes of him before calling for fresh rebellion, but with Miss Abell. She'd have made a far more impressionable emissary, or so the alderman must have surmised."

"She was to negotiate with Symmes and deliver the seamstresses his terms?"

"Precisely so. Lacking a victory, they sought a just defeat."

Miss Abell's face drifted into my mind. Her softness, the rushing but careful way she spoke, as if she were frightened her head couldn't quite keep up with her tongue. She wasn't dense by any stretch. But William Wolf was right. She was . . . malleable. And she'd been summoned to a meeting with Symmes. Alone.

A sick, creeping feeling flickered in my guts.

"So what don't I know, Mr. Wilde?" the journalist asked.

I'm not sure why I trusted him, though in retrospect I think it was as vain as the fact he reminded me of the parts of myself I can stand. Anyhow, I needed help in the worst way. So I spilled.

"For one, Miss Woods was having an affair with Symmes."

"Wrong."

"Excuse me?"

"No, she was his mistress, but I did know that. A few remarks from my interview with Symmes himself were . . . telling. Next?"

Parting my lips, I paused. "After the strike ended and the friendship dissolved . . ."

"Yes?"

"I know that something happened between the three major parties, and I know it was vile. Neither girl can speak of Symmes without turning bloodless, and Miss Woods wants him drawn and quartered. Has this meeting between the alderman and Miss Abell any bearing, do you suppose?"

He tapped his pencil on his knee. "It occurred after my last encounter with them. The trio's relations are mighty convoluted, I take it."

"Mystifyingly so," I affirmed, thumbing the edge of my writing pad.

Failing to say, *And I think Miss Abell was once in a family way, and I think she warns an engine company when death is about to strike, and I can't understand any of it* was difficult. But I managed to swallow those facts deep in my gullet. If I was right about Miss Abell, she'd already paid for her errors in blood. And if I was wrong, and word got out, she'd be disgraced if not permanently unmarriageable, thanks to me. Reputations have been razed to dust over lost kerchiefs and paper sentiments, let alone kinchin.

"You thought I might have known what happened between them?"

"I hoped you did." I smiled crookedly. Then it slid off my face, not belonging there. I felt like hell.

"Mr. Wilde, what are you thinking?" William Wolf questioned.

"I'm thinking something is hideously wrong and I want it set right again."

He nodded gravely just as my door flew open and a head with a wild grey mane appeared. Mr. Piest's eyes bulged still more than the usual, his crabbed hands clutching both doorknob and frame.

"You must come with all speed, my friend," he panted.

My feet were already under me. "What happened?"

"It is still happening, I regret to report. Mr. Kildare took it into his head to experiment with rather more extreme measures against McGlynn in the name of evidence gathering."

"Shit," I hissed, donning my hat. "Is it working?"

"If it fails to kill him, it might."

"Come along?" I asked Mr. Wolf.

Inviting him was an intuition, nothing more. But for a whim, it was zealously requested. I know I'm meant to be a star police, and

I know I detest some of our practices, and I know sure as my pulse that the public are meant to trust us. And that we don't always even attempt to deserve it.

"What do you think?" Mr. Wolf gestured to the door. "My motto in all such matters is *yes*. I'm certain whatever is in store for us will be of interest to readers."

He hadn't the faintest idea.

18

WE HURRIED THROUGH CORRIDORS like vast catacombs, Piest
and Wolf and I, the passages chilled though outdoors the April
sun blazed. Passing brutes with iron on their wrists dragged by
brutes with copper fixed to their coats. For all its monstrous size,
the Tombs is always crowded in the afternoons. We elbowed past
bailiffs, witnesses, victims. Bewigged lawyers, red-eyed lovers.
When we missed the turn that leads to the men's lockup, I caught
Piest's bony elbow.

"He's not in his cell?"

"He is in the northwest corner of the yard, Mr. Wilde," Mr.
Piest replied with a terseness uncharacteristic of him.

I groaned. "Damn it all directly to hell."

"What does the northwest corner mean?" Mr. Wolf inquired.

I hastened my pace to match that of my eccentric Dutch friend.

The sunlight as we stepped into the interior yard exploded in our eyes like the blast from a cannonade. The air was warm and faintly hazy, the open square blessedly free of the gallows. But in the northwest corner, I could already spy my friend Kildare lifting a heavy hogshead full of brown river water.

"Wait!" I cried, causing his dark head to pivot.

The fact that the Tombs is a brutal place is a burden I bear daily. I am well aware, however, that it could be still worse. For instance, we're not allowed to whip prisoners, thank every kindly power. Bread-and-water diets with solitary confinement, never for very long periods if I'm honest, is the typical punishment for the raving canary birds we're saddled with. They tend to quiet down after a day or two and stop trying to shiv one another, which is all we were after in the first place. But that doesn't mean we don't have alternative discipline for the absolutely intractable.

It's called, innocuously, the shower bath. If I could light it on fire, I would do, in a heartbeat.

"My God," murmured Mr. Wolf, who could now see McGlynn plain. Or his bruised bare torso and the top of his head anyway.

The shower bath is a sturdy coffinlike box, made quite tall so the prisoner can stand upright when he's stripped naked and put through the front door. McGlynn's hands were both protruding from the walls, forced outward at right angles to his body in a queer adapted version of stocks. Above the arm restraints is a device that looks like a shelf with a fixed bowl resting on it, which also comes apart when a man is subjected to a dousing. Inside this bowl McGlynn's head had been viciously secured by means of a hole in the base, while above him on a second shelf, a nearly spent hogshead of Hudson water trickled onto his pate, spilling over the brimming lip of the bowl. McGlynn was blindly, weakly thrashing in broken little twitches, straining to keep at least his nostrils above the water level, as the point of this charming contraption is that the mouth is submerged and the deluge all but drowns a man. Kildare had clearly been about to switch out the feebly leaking hogshead for a fresh one. His face was a study in cold rage.

"How many *is* that?" I clasped him by his thick arm.

"Mr. Wilde, what a pleasure. T' be sure, I forget now," he hissed. "May well be the third, 'tisn't unlikely to be the fourth."

"*Four* hogsheads of river water?" I cried. "Are you out of your senses?"

"Wilde, ye know who he is and ye know what he was after doin'. I'll not be scolded by the likes o' you, sir, fer all you're a mate o' mine. Let go."

I tightened my grip on his sleeve. "You've made your point."

"Christ, but ye've not stones enough to question a criminal?"

"How in sodding hell are you meant to be *questioning* him? He's halfway to drowned and can't *talk*."

"Your innate nobility of spirit precludes you from continuing this most *alarming* exercise, Mr. Kildare," Mr. Piest pleaded. "Come, you've doubtless instilled in him a most penitent, chastened—"

"Why don't ye leave police work to them as has balls fer it?" Kildare growled.

Behind me, terrified gurgles and wet sniffs emanated from the shower bath. If McGlynn hadn't drunk about a gallon of river water by then, I'd eat one of Piest's boots. I've had nightmares about the shower bath. They don't compare to being locked in it, frigid water everywhere, lungs afire, stripped and shivering and nigh berserk for a full breath. Still.

"Who in hell is *this*, then?" Kildare demanded. He'd belatedly discovered William Wolf, writing shorthand at breakneck speed about ten feet off.

"Oh, don't mind me, I wouldn't dream of hindering you." Mr. Wolf looked up, but not at Kildare—at the shower bath and its miserable occupant. "I record things for posterity."

"A scientist, are ye?"

"Something like that."

"Would ye like t' see firsthand how this works, in that case?"

Kildare's eyes shone with resolve, his arm beneath my clutching fingers trembling under the weight of the full hogshead. My attention shot to Mr. Wolf as a pang of nerves lanced through me.

"Yes." William Wolf's eyes darted to Mr. Kildare, the set of his downturned mouth equally resolved as revolted. I knew then that like Mercy he would stop at nothing, pay any price to see the world as it was. "Yes, do go on."

"This has gone quite far enough, as we are *gentlemen*!" Piest cried.

"Put it down *now*, or we're going to have an argument," I ordered fiercely.

"We're going to have an argument, then, bless yer tender heart," Kildare grated. "And me twice the size o' ye in every place save maybe bollocks, ye mad bastard."

"You know as well as I do my size is completely irrelevant," I snapped with new passion in light of recent revelations.

"By Jesus, Wilde, let go, or I'll—"

"What in the name o' holiness is going on here?" a new voice demanded.

I started breathing again, though I didn't unhand Kildare. Our friend Mr. Connell strode across the yard on angry legs, taking in the scene and the solution in one glance. He stepped straight to the shower bath and released the valve on the boxed-in lower compartment. Fish-smelling water gushed out, nibbling at our boots.

"Switch that back off," Kildare snarled.

"I'll not," Connell returned calmly. "Get a bloody grip on yerself, Ian, for the love o' Mary."

"Dermot Connell, if ye don't leave yer interfering hands off of the prisoner, who's gettin' what he sure enough deserves, then—"

"Oh, aye, *deserves*," Connell shot back. He busily unlatched sliding wood locks, freeing McGlynn piecemeal. "I'd like t' see him hanged, meself. But he'll not turn my best mate into a torturer, and I'll not look at ye, Ian, and see a British soldier wi' a great horsewhip in his hand. Drop the fucking hogshead afore I smash yer fool pate in."

With a furious curse, Kildare tore away from me and obeyed, throwing the heavy thing as far as he could—which wasn't far. It bumped along uneven dirt to a sad halt. Connell opened the box and, reaching up, pulled the neck shelf with its flat-sided quadrangular bowl as if sliding open a dresser drawer. More water flooded free as McGlynn flopped from the shower bath onto the mud. Limp as a guppy and sucking in huge gasps of air.

"New York's defenders triumph again to thunderous applause," I heard Mr. Wolf murmur under his breath.

I winced—at his words and at the razor-wire tangle in my chest. But there was nothing to say. Turning to my friend Piest, I shook my head wordlessly before hastening to fetch McGlynn's togs. They were sopping up liquid and smeared with dirt, but serviceable enough. I might have handed them to our captive. But when I thought about what he'd done, and how many times he'd likely done it, I merely tossed them at the wretched creature.

"Right." Mr. Connell palmed a hand over his fiery red pate. "Now yer in a reflective mood, when ye can breathe, we've a few more queries t' pose by your leave."

Pushing to his hands and knees, McGlynn spat at the ground. His pale skin was bumpy as a plucked fowl's, silhouettes of fists and boots mottled all over his fleshy frame. Only his skinny legs, trembling from fright and cold, remained unmarked by the copper stars.

"Leave me alone," he rasped when he could speak. "Please just leave me alone."

"In a minute," I said. "Mr. Piest? You're been searching for Miss Woods night and day. Anything to ask?"

"I prefer to question fully clothed men, begging your pardon and apologizing for what you might consider overdeveloped sensitivities, Mr. Wilde," he replied mildly. The glare in his protruding eyes he leveled square at Kildare, who glowered back at him tenfold.

"Any actual questions?" I asked Mr. Kildare. "Or was this a spree?"

"There's days as I want to squish you like a wee little spider," Kildare returned. But he sounded exhausted—fraught with love and muddy intentions.

"Fine, I'll start," Connell growled as McGlynn tugged mudsoaked smallclothes up his legs. "We've questioned ye more times than I like t' reflect on, and ye've not explained how a madwoman could ha' planted phosphorus in yer employer's buildings unnoticed. Try again now, there's a good lad. How did Sally Woods do it?"

A half sob escaped the white-bearded wretch, one of seemingly hopeless anguish. It shivered through him afterward. Lingering and disconsolate.

"Please," he choked. "I don't know. *I don't know.* If I don't know, I can't tell you, can I, you brutes? When is Symmes getting me out of this hellhole?"

"A quarter t' never, by my watch," Mr. Kildare spat.

A groan escaped the older man, quickly choked off. He began buttoning his shirt. Still on his knees, still breathing as if he'd been born seconds before—gulping and greedy, unused to the practice.

"He is quite correct, and furthermore the Queen Mab has been abandoned entirely," Mr. Piest felt free to announce now McGlynn had a shirt and drawers on. I felt a surge of affection for his often ridiculous sense of chivalry, his ardent respect for a terrible populace. "It can do you no harm to help us, only the greatest potential good. You knew Miss Woods—where is she likely to be, and how could she have accomplished all she has?"

McGlynn started weeping. Chest heaving, arm covering his eyes with a tattered shirtsleeve. Kildare made a satisfied humming sound, Connell a disgusted noise at the back of his throat.

All the while Mr. Wolf's pencil went *scratch* a few feet away from me.

"I don't know," McGlynn sobbed. "She's . . . devious, brilliant, the craziest bitch I've ever met. I *don't know* and *can't say*. Have a little pity."

"The sort o' pity ye were goin' to show Caoilinn?" Kildare mused bitterly.

"Whatever Irish whore you're on about, don't think her any better than a slut who'll stab you in the back the second she's able," McGlynn muttered.

Kildare advanced, fists clenched.

"Ian," I snapped. "Not worth it."

"Ye've *naught* idea what it's worth to—"

"Mr. McGlynn!" I all but shouted, my palm flat upon Kildare's chest. "What happened the night after the strike was broken? At or after the peacemaking meeting between Robert Symmes and Ellie Abell?"

The oddest thing happened. He didn't want to—tried to stop himself, even. But hell and high water had done their work by that point. And Ronan McGlynn flashed an evil glint of a smile before his face returned to sniveling.

"Nothing," he answered. "She'd an appointment to meet Mr. Symmes, but she never showed."

"I'll have it out of you the hard way," I threatened.

"No," he said, sounding almost bored. "*You* won't."

I'd have proved him wrong, I think. But I was interrupted.

"What building of the alderman's do you imagine most at risk for targeting next?" Mr. Piest wanted to know.

McGlynn's head lifted. He closed his eyes, breathing hard through his nose. He lumbered, disjointed and battered, to his feet.

"I can't," he said, with another pathetic hitch to his breath. "I—"

"If only 'twere the Queen Mab," Kildare muttered.

Everyone froze.

We will not be cowed by those who think us less than human, I thought, seeing the note—the only one I retained, the only one Miss Woods hadn't taken with her when she brained me—emblazoned before my eyes like a brand.

"Mr. Wilde?" William Wolf called out.

I was already half running, Piest at my heels, out of the Tombs.

"Ask them whatever you like," I called back to Mr. Wolf. "Connell, Kildare, put McGlynn back where you found him!"

Then we were out of the courtyard, in the Tombs' hallways, sprinting like fugitives through gaping corridors built to strike terror into the heart of a lawless city.

"It is only a guess, Mr. Wilde," Mr. Piest reminded me breathlessly as we dove streetside out of the prison in the direction of Ward Four.

"It is a very bloody good guess," I shot back, waving frantically at a free hacksman. He pulled to the side, horse whinnying at the sudden change.

"What are you hoping to find?"

"Maybe nothing. Maybe energetic materials. Maybe in the walls, maybe in the cellar, so long as we learn how she's doing it."

Regarding the "she" I referred to, I was no longer certain of anything, I realized as we lunged into the hack. The journalist's voice echoed between my ears. Louder than the cries of the coster-mongers, louder than the blunted roar of the traffic as we turned onto Broadway.

Miss Woods is too keen to make such a dull play.

Miss Abell is affectionate, trusting, and well intentioned. I can't possibly think of a person who would be more easy to manipulate.

"Mr. Wilde?"

Feeling the first hint of pain, I discovered I was staring blankly out the window with my knuckle in my teeth.

"Nothing." I tucked my hands under my arms, suddenly self-conscious. "No sign of life at Miss Woods's greenhouse?"

"I fear not, Mr. Wilde, or so the ever-stalwart Mr. Austin and Mr. Clare assure me."

"The copper stars watching the alderman's buildings since Miss Woods escaped me have seen nothing suspicious?"

"They have not. But, regrettably, we haven't the resources to guard all his properties on a twenty-four-hour period. Searches for incendiary materials have been made but thus far have revealed nothing."

"If Miss Woods truly wanted to harm Symmes, why hurt his buildings rather than his person?"

"A woman, however resolute, would fear attacking a powerful man physically," Piest reasoned.

He's right, I thought.

Then *I'm missing something* clanged like a clock chime inside my head.

Streets passed. Duane, Reed, Chambers. Why should a highly intellectual woman take such risks? I asked myself. And alternately, how could a highly suggestible woman for all her intelligence hatch them in the first place? They couldn't be working in tandem, as they didn't even speak to each other. Supposing that assumption correct, of course.

The hack pulled to a halt, wheels grinding.

Mechanically, I stepped down as Piest paid the driver. I took in the street where everything had started. The chipped bricks, the blocked windows, the vibrant decay of a place devoted to the worst varieties of vice.

"Come," Mr. Piest urged.

We entered the Queen Mab. The hallway with its tragic-seeming pornographic décor was dark and grotesquely quiet. An oppressive, glowering silence. I was struck by how very *empty* the place was. Deserted, in fact, in the absence of Ronan McGlynn. Finding an oil lamp on the table, I reached into my waistcoat for matches. We made for the sitting room where Symmes had presented his offer of fleshy compensation to Valentine. One that, in retrospect, seemed as bizarre as it was cruel.

"My God, Mr. Wilde, I can hardly credit it, though it makes perfect logical sense."

"What?" I turned back to him.

"You were right," Piest replied, on his knees at the edge of the room.

I brought the light closer. My friend Mr. Piest is abnormally good at seeing things. He'd pulled a loose baseboard from the wall to reveal a small gap. Little chunks of a white material lined the space along the floorboards, yellow-tinged and horridly eerie. White phosphorus, it seemed clear.

"How did you see that?" I marveled.

"The dust." He waved his bony hand at it. "This place is in the most egregious state of disrepair, but here the filth was displaced. I look for such things often, you understand, finding so many stolen items lodged in traps and under paneling."

"You've still the finest set of eyes in Manhattan. This means . . ."

"Yes?"

"I don't know," I realized. "I don't know what it means."

Thump-thump-thump sounded shoes on the ceiling above our heads.

It was a good job I'd set the lamp on a table, or I might have dropped it. My eyes met Piest's instantly.

"A squatter taking advantage of an empty house?" I whispered.

"It could be absolutely anyone," Mr. Piest agreed.

Lifting the lamp again, I headed for the upper rooms. I can be pretty stealthy when I like, but Piest's crab legs and ten-pound boots are guaranteed to make a racket, so I didn't bother softening my step. Anyway, the pair of us blocked the exit. As soon as our feet hit the boards and the light streamed up ahead of us, the movement in the chamber above stopped.

"Have a care," I murmured.

"The same to you."

We reached the second-story corridor. The first room was the bedchamber where Caoilinn had held a knife to Kildare's neck. I stepped inside.

Sally Woods stood within, staring at a baseboard likewise pulled from a wall lined with malevolent chunks of white phosphorus.

"Miss Woods, I take it?" Mr. Piest gasped.

"The same," I marveled.

With a startled shout, she ran for the window. But the place had been designed to keep just such creatures locked within, and when she tore the dark covering away, she found it both latched and barred.

"There's no way out," I warned. "We won't hurt you. But you're coming—"

One would think, as I am widely considered reasonably intelligent, that being knocked senseless once by Sally Woods had taught me not to underestimate her.

One would be wrong.

Seeing no possible exit save for the doorway, she rushed at us.

When I moved to catch her, she used her momentum to shove herself against me as Mr. Piest snatched at her with long arms.

I don't know if it was Mr. Piest or Miss Woods who knocked the oil lamp from my hand. I only know that the fuel spilled into a little pool that instantly transformed into a glowing puddle of fire.

All three of us froze in horror.

"Oh, no," Miss Woods breathed, trembling under my fingers where I clutched her fitted jacket.

"Keep hold of her," Mr. Piest commanded, "and go downstairs."

"Jakob—"

"Do as I say, Mr. Wilde! I have this situation well in hand, and you *must* escort the lady out of danger! Whatever she may have done, we cannot risk her life. Go!" he shouted, rushing down the corridor after God knows what.

I did as I was told. Miss Woods, now I'd a solid grip on her, struggled to keep pace with me as we hurtled toward the ground floor.

"What is he planning?" she gasped.

I couldn't say, couldn't even open my mouth for fear my stomach would fall out. Every ounce of determination I possessed was devoted to keeping Sally Woods captive without actually hurting her. In a blessed instant of sanity, I tore the tie from a window curtain before hauling her outside.

"Mr. Wilde?"

The smoke-drenched panic didn't ebb when we reached the street. Not with Piest still in the building, not with the obscene amount of incendiary material within. We crossed the cobbled road, heedless of traffic, ducking between a cart loaded with beer kegs and a gentleman's stately carriage and four.

"Face away from me, please."

She did, arms quivering. I tethered her wrists at the small of her back in an unyielding bind and then wrapped the tasseled rope several times around my hand. We attracted plentiful stares from pedestrians. Though whether that was due to my carefully restraining a beautiful woman's hands or the fact the beautiful woman was wearing men's duds, I couldn't have guessed. I could tell from her pressed trousers she hadn't been sleeping rough, but she seemed thinner. She'd been in a boardinghouse—one chosen for economy and lacking in decent peck.

"Ward Six or Ward Four?" I asked.

"Four. A wretched den on Oliver Street. It isn't what you think, I swear to Christ it isn't. Mr. Wilde? I know it looks—"

"It looks like you started a failed strike, had your heart broken by a despicable man, sent him threatening mail, and then started setting fire to his properties."

Slumping against the building opposite the Queen Mab, I gripped the end of the curtain cord and stared at the house that was about to explode with my closest friend in it and tried not to fall into a thousand sharp-edged pieces. Because I don't like to think of myself as a coward—cannot bear cowards, in fact—and I realized I'd just been expertly manipulated.

Of course he would tell you to get the girl out of danger, of course he would say the one thing that would make you leave him there, of course he—

"Are you arresting me?"

"Of course I am."

Come out, I thought wretchedly. *For the love of God, come out of there and make ludicrous statements about honor that no one save you believes anymore, and next week drink gin in my office with Connell and Kildare until none of us can see straight, and then pop up spry as a jack-in-the-box the next morning.*

311

"Mr. Wilde, I was looking for answers myself just now. You have to credit me—I thought if I could only solve it, then I could go back to my ken. I've no livelihood without my press. I'm not a criminal."

"Miss Woods, you hit me over the head with a liquor bottle."

"If I hadn't, you'd have collared me then!" she cried. "I was sorry to do it, never wanted to do it. Robert has plentiful enemies, if only you'd listen—"

"I'll listen if you tell me something useful for once. Miss Abell was summoned to a meeting with Symmes after the strike ended." Glancing at her, I hesitated. "What happened?"

Her boldly featured face with its high coloring and strong lines, already pale, faded to chalk. She shook her head.

"Come out," I whispered at the Queen Mab. "Come out, damn you."

"Mr. Wilde," Miss Woods said unsteadily, "in the course of your investigation, have you seen Ellie since I . . . How is she?"

"In fine health and poor spirits. She— Oh, thank *God*."

Mr. Piest, looking not the smallest bit singed, strode out of the Queen Mab on gangly legs and stopped to blink at the sun. Spying us, he scuttled across the road, rubbing his hands together as a man will do when he has accomplished a worthy task. He was one of the most gorgeously ugly sights I'd ever clapped eyes on.

"Do not, and I repeat, do *not* play me for a goosecap like that ever again," I snapped, pushing myself away from the wall.

"Mr. Wilde, I have not the smallest notion of what you are referring to."

"Yes you do, you lunatic. The fire is out?"

He nodded, grey wisps floating around his shoulders. "What an ingenious use of a curtain sash, Mr. Wilde. Yes, one cannot douse an oil fire with water, so I simply had to find their washbasin and deposit it upended over the flames. Smothering took a matter of a minute afterward, as I expected. It was hardly a taxing effort on my part."

"I'm going to the nearest pawnshop and buying you a bloody medal of valor," I said seriously.

"Oh, come now, I was merely taking the most obvious practical steps—it was nothing so valiant as all that, surely," he protested, ears pinkening.

I felt a tug at the rope wrapped five or six times around my fist and turned to view Miss Woods. She looked, from the white streak in her hair to the soles of her riding boots, the picture of miserable guilt. That's not mere misery, mind. I've seen it at the back of my brother's eyes a thousand times. It was just as terrible on a comely anarchist. The things she'd done were terrible too, I reminded myself, and I'd all but caught her red-handed.

"What are you going to do with me?" she asked.

Unfortunately, it was a question with a single possible answer.

The women imprisoned at Sing Sing do sewing outwork, their negligible earnings paid over to the State of New York. The molls imprisoned at the Tombs sit on hard pallets, shivering in the winter and sweltering in the summer, praying or singing or screaming as suits their fancy. Struggling not to succumb to despair or something swifter, like dysentery or pneumonia.

I didn't like shutting the cell door on Miss Woods—I wasn't even then entirely convinced of her wrongdoing, despite staggering evidence against her. My conversation with William Wolf had rearranged the puzzle pieces, scattered the fragments of a half-completed board. But I knew she was dangerous, and that she frightened Robert Symmes, and that I needed to keep her close.

So shut the door I did, her eyes boring into me like rapiers.

"I haven't set fire to any houses, Mr. Wilde," she said through her teeth as I turned the key in the ponderous lock.

Slinging my fingers around the bars, I leaned in. "But you did threaten the alderman."

She swallowed. "Repeatedly."

"And you attacked me."

She nodded, wincing. "I'm sorry. People get hurt in a war."

"People *die* in a war. Two women died when you torched the Pell Street slum."

"Mr. Wilde, I've never clapped eyes on the building you're referring to, but if the deaths of two women could end the battle of the sexes and free my gender from slavery, I'd count the cost light. Because plenty more than two will be hushed before we can walk in the midday sun without fear of men," she hissed.

"You're not helping your case, Miss Woods."

"What does it matter," she said flatly. "You don't believe me anyhow."

Needles versus brickbats, I thought, remembering Miss Abell's account of the strike and Miss Duffy's injuries. I wondered whether the reason Miss Woods unnerved me was that the eyes of a colonel fresh returned from the war in Texas stared out of a woman's face— accepting of tragic losses to the point of being mistaken for callous. She ought to have been the queen of an ancient empire, and here she could do no better than cutting slave clothes or printing heretical screeds.

Which brought another item of interest to the front of my mind. "How do you explain this?"

I passed her the only note remaining to me, the only one she hadn't taken from her greenhouse and presumably destroyed. The initial message that had sent the alderman to seek Valentine.

We will not be cowed by those who think us less than human.

She took it, uncomprehending at first. After all, I'd never shown it to her. Then an agonized little moan escaped, and she put her fist against where her heart must have been pounding, reckless and inflamed, against her breast.

"How do you come to have this?" she cried out. *"How?"*

I sighed, rubbing my fingers against the bridge of my nose. "So . . . yes. You printed this."

Closing her eyes, Sally Woods nodded. "Robert Symmes gave it to you?"

"Yes."

With a palsied hand, she returned it. I've never in my life seen anyone fight that hard against weeping. Had I not known better, I'd have supposed that tears would melt her flesh if she allowed them to fall, long-suppressed bitterness scoring deep tracks down her spun-sugar skin.

"Mr. Wilde, will you do a single thing for me?" she asked gruffly.

"Yes," I answered.

She crossed her arms over her belly, pressing as if she were trying not to be ill. "Go back to my greenhouse and search through my archives of odd jobs. You're my last resort, I fear."

"You wrote a manifesto?" I questioned, slowly folding the message and replacing it in my pocket.

"No, I printed one for the Venerable and Distinguished Brotherhood of Tailors. It doesn't quite fall in line with my views, but there was plenty within about the greed of modern tycoons, so I agreed to publish it, and they paid very well. Just find it, please, for Christ's sake." A few tears spilled over, and she wiped them with her sleeve cuff. I passed her my handkerchief. "Then come back for your handkerchief. All right? I have your handkerchief. Promise me."

"I promise. Listen, I'll be back to take your statement anyhow, but before I do, at least consider trusting me. Robert Symmes is a terrible person, and you *want* to tell me the truth."

"I only wish I could."

"You can. Are we clear?"

"I can't. But yes, we're clear." Pocketing the cloth, she thrust her hand through the bars. "You're coming back for your kerchief. You gave me your word."

"I did." I took her hand, if only briefly. "Good-bye for now, Miss Woods."

As I walked away, letting the gibes and the hoots of the jailed stargazers slide over me like so much rainwater, I wondered at three questions:

—Why should a clever incendiary leave the perfect paper trail behind her like bread crumbs through a forest?
—How did the sewing girls—any of them—manage to plant energetic materials?
—Why is Abraham Kane allowing me to do my job?

There were other questions on my mind, to be sure—ones about Sally Woods's desire for me to find a radical article she'd been commissioned to produce. I'd a cautious notion what she might be referring to, and the mere idea that I might be right sent my entire spine tingling. But though much remained unanswered, at least, I thought, the Queen Mab hadn't burned half the city to cinders, nor Jakob Piest neither.

I stopped by my office to write Matsell a note indicating that Sally Woods's full statement would come on the morrow. Going one better, I did it in duplicate and sent the copy to Abraham Kane. Then I glanced at my appointment book, and my skin went cold.

Day after tomorrow would be the elections.

Friday, April 28: Valentine Wilde versus the incumbent Robert Symmes. Hunker versus Barnburner in a potentially deadly mêlée of fists and votes, not to mention the Whigs and the Liberty Party and the American Republican Party. Which meant all copper stars on hand, guarding certain ballot boxes and gleefully throwing others in the East River, as well as a fight if not a riot. I was never called on for such duties. Matsell knew better than to trust in my political enthusiasm. But this situation differed significantly.

I would be voting for the first time in my life, I'd decided. The resolution delivered a small flutter of feathery nerves. Pouring a finger of gin, I raised it in the general direction of Ward Eight and my no doubt hopelessly inebriated brother.

"Go straight to hell," I said aloud, swallowing it down.

By the time I escaped the Tombs, six o' clock had struck and the gas lamps carved long shadows in our unswept streets. The markets in my ward are where foodstuffs go to die, so I hurried to the closest butcher and grocer along Broadway for mutton and butter and parsley, anxious—as if I hadn't enough on my mind—over what Bird would say to me that night. The thought her small foot might not even touch our doorstep was appalling, but, *No*, I thought, *she's braver than you are, she'd never cancel*, and so I added a newspaper parcel of the first wild strawberries to my purchases as the clouds painted themselves violet and orange and a queer cool lavender.

I was right about my small friend if nothing else, for Bird opened the door before I'd even quite reached the bakery, having heard my hasty step in the road. Her hands were sticky with dough, her perfect box-shaped face serene. Elena Boehm—in the kitchen beyond, shaping rolls for our supper, fine hair dusty with finer flour—winked at me, and I breathed easier.

"I still don't believe you, even after what Mrs. Boehm told me," Bird announced, stepping aside to let me pass.

"All right," I said, a bit startled.

"But I'll try," she added, grey eyes steady as granite.

"All right," I agreed, pushing a stray piece of dark auburn hair behind her ear.

Then we didn't talk about it.

I hung my wide-brimmed hat, and Elena kept teaching Bird how to bake, as she'd been doing for nearly three years, and we didn't talk about it. We laughed together. Over me trimming off excess mutton fat and shallowly slicing my finger open, because Valentine has always been a dedicated cook, for reasons I'd always suspected and now knew for an agonizing certainty, and I am an ignoramus who buys shilling oyster sandwiches when my brother isn't providing supper. Over Elena sending Bird into fits with a German drinking song. Over Bird's face when the mutton leg came out, dripping and decadent, and I moved to slice it into cubes for the hash.

"Mr. Wilde," Bird whispered, tugging at my sleeve edge.

I was about to answer her. But at the same moment, there came a knocking. Not at our front door either.

At the back door.

Insistent without being loud.

When I think something is wrong, I am only occasionally correct, but I am always cautious over it.

When I *know* something is wrong, I am perennially right.

At the look on my face, Mrs. Boehm edged herself between Bird and the back door. I retained the carving knife and crossed the kitchen, cursing the fact it hadn't ever occurred to me to put a spy hole at eye level. That was changing, I determined, with Mrs. Boehm's permission. That was changing tomorrow. Meanwhile, I was nigh certain that now I'd arrested Sally Woods and solved his problem for him, I'd a thug sent from Robert Symmes if not the man himself to deal with, eager to teach the Wildes a lesson in manners.

I was wrong about that. I wish I hadn't been, though. Every single time I think about it.

When I opened the door, James Playfair practically fell into my arms as I dropped the knife. Shirtless, his upper body covered in blood, bruises, scrapes, and sweat.

As well as in tar. And in feathers.

19

That old Tammany opposite us, once consecrated to the genius of true freedom, has latterly admitted within its sanctuary, the priest of Baal, but we will purify it; yes, even by a sacrifice offered without the gates.

—MIKE WALSH, *THE NEW YORK HERALD*, MEETING OF THE BARNBURNERS AT CITY HALL PARK, JULY 1848

"JIM?" I GASPED, holding him up.

"I hate to intrude, but—" he attempted, then bit down a moan when I tightened my grip.

Tar, I thought stupidly, even as the gummy material stuck to my waistcoat and jacket. It had been more than ten years since I'd seen anyone wearing the stuff.

A person doesn't generally die of it, I thought next, heart racing.

Not generally.

Only sometimes. When it's heated enough.

The pine-pitch reek flooding the air was suffused underneath with the crueler aroma of burned human skin. Bird, who'd emerged from behind Elena, let fly a full-throated scream.

"Get her out of here," I ordered sharply. "Elena, take the carving knife and don't let go of it, and go next door and tell them *do not open up* for anyone but me, all right?"

"Yes, yes." She lifted the knife, face drawn with horror. "But I will leave Bird and come back here, I will help you—"

"*Do not* come back here," I hissed. "It's too dangerous. Go."

I was already dragging Jim to a chair as Mrs. Boehm took a sobbing Bird Daly to pay a surprise call. I was also thinking. Remembering what I could about medicine. Praying to no god in particular, but with a fervency that would guarantee any one of them listening if they weren't deaf, sadistic, or nonexistent.

A person doesn't generally die of it, I thought, willing myself calm.

When Jim was safely draped over our table, I fetched another kitchen knife and carefully folded his slim fingers around it.

"Symmes did this?" I asked with metal in my voice.

"None other than, though he'd assistance."

"I am leaving you for five minutes," I said clearly.

"Oh, please don't say that," he choked, all pretense at glibness vanished.

"Listen to me—you're going to be fine. I'm filling the hip bath at the pump outside."

"Yes, my apologies, thank you," he said, panting a little.

I went.

As I stood outdoors in the pale, firelit darkness of Ward Six, filling up the hip bath, determined not to grow so enraged I became useless or careless, I let my mind drift over positively murderous thoughts regarding Robert Symmes.

And suddenly I knew.

The outlines were as vague and foreboding as my grimmer sketches, but as for broad brushstrokes—I understood everything. Generally, it feels like falling off a cliffside onto barren stones. This time it was no more jarring a landing than that of a windswept snowflake, seeing as I'd more important things on my mind than solving a crime just then. Nevertheless, a quiet understanding had settled over me thanks to what had been done to James Playfair.

Feeling light-headed, I leaned against the Croton pump and directed a bit of queasy spittle at the ground.

William Wolf, I thought—and correctly too—*was right.*

Muscles straining, I dragged the hip bath brimming with cold reservoir water back indoors. Jim had sat up a little. Still holding the knife, face turning the sickliest shade of green I'd ever witnessed. When I'd pulled the sloshing tub to the table, he made as if to stand.

"I'll help," I said. "Did they get your legs at all?"

"No, merely the visible areas."

It wasn't *merely.* They'd drenched his shoulders and his chest with hot tar, painted his back and crossed round the sides. I'd say it covered forty percent of his upper body, the pale remainder mottled with contusions and sickly sweat, which gave me cause for considerable optimism. Because if the seared flesh encompassed more than half a fellow's surface area, and if the tar was scorching enough—

A person doesn't generally die of it, I told myself fiercely as I lifted the taller man, togs and all, into the hip bath.

"Sink down," I said.

Jim buried himself to the neck in frigid water, wearing a frozen look on his handsome face as if he might crumble apart when touched. I felt all too brittle myself without the excuse of being covered in pitch and chicken down, and Jim is one of the most dignified men I have ever met in all my days, so I reached into the hip bath and started taking off his shoes.

Jim put a hand over his eyes as he shuddered. "Thank you."

"Don't you *dare* thank me. What happened?"

"I was playing the piano at the Hall, and . . ." He stopped, swallowing hard. "Everyone was there, the donors and tycoons and such, worried over how badly the vote will be split day after tomorrow and throwing all the money they can at the dilemma. I'd finished, and they'd paid me, and God knows I've been careful ever since . . . ever since the Knickerbocker Twenty-one benefit, but Symmes was waiting outside with his compatriots."

I removed the second shoe and the stocking beneath. "He'll pay for it, I promise you. Was it in public?"

A person who's been tarred and feathered generally doesn't bother with recovering his reputation. He simply departs. And often enough forgets to pack his name.

"No, I was kicking up too great a fuss. And the rest of the Party likes me—I play for Hunkers as well as Barnburners—so they'd never have managed it on the street. Symmes told his cronies to seize me, four of them, and they'd a barrel of hot pitch in an alleyway. They dragged me back there and . . . well."

Jim was shaking in earnest by then, as anyone would be submerged in an unheated bath. I waited and he waited, meanwhile, for the cold to do him some good.

"Say the word and I'll fetch a doctor," I offered quietly.

"No, don't for God's sake, I shouldn't even be able to look at him. You were the *one* p-person who I . . ." He trailed off, clenching his lean jaw.

"And you were close enough to my ken that I imagine hardly anyone of importance saw you." I paused. "Right. Does it seem to have hardened fully?"

He nodded, blue eyes closed.

"Here."

Offering Jim my hands beneath the water, I pulled him up to a standing position. Cold as a dead fish and nearly as limp. I remembered Jim suddenly, dressed to the nines and playing the piano at his own ken one night, a night when my brother drank only half a bottle of whiskey and didn't take any morphine tonic at all, and I felt my throat constricting.

"Chair," I said, half carrying him over to it. "I'll be right back."

I went for a warm blanket, a paint scraper from the shed behind the house, a jug of kerosene, copious towels, a flask of laudanum, and the whiskey bottle. Setting everything but the blanket on the table, I draped the wool around him. His head lolled a little, and I caught his neck in my hand.

"Jim?"

"Present and among the living."

"Hear, hear. Drink this."

"With pleasure."

I poured more laudanum down his throat than might have been strictly wise. But he didn't object. And he was about to start objecting, I knew.

Strenuously.

I reached for the whiskey and swallowed some of that. To steady myself.

"Jim," I said again, softly.

"I know," he replied with a sigh.

"I don't want to. But . . ."

He looked at me direct, a ripening bruise on his cheek twitching. "I'd rather it was you, Timothy. Truly."

I drew a tremulous breath. "I'd rather it was anyone else."

"If you say no, I should hardly blame you. I'd understand, would never hold it between us," James said, nothing save fondness in his eyes beneath the wracking pain.

"No, I am *not* saying no—who do you take me for? But we'll fetch my brother first. I'll send a street kinchin for—"

"Don't you *dare* send for your brother," Jim snapped. "I'll leave at once if you so much as try."

"Jim, that makes no sense. He's good in a crisis, would never flinch from one, and he—" I stopped myself. "Don't you want him here?"

"No."

"But why?" I pleaded.

"Because I believe in things!" he cried. The tears that had barely threatened a moment previous spilled over, and he swiped them angrily away with his unmarked palms. "I believe in gracefulness, and beauty, and common decency, and . . . oh, I can't even tell you what I believe in anymore, but those were the cardinal points, and I assume he appreciated them, and it would *kill me* if he saw this. Do you understand?"

I took longer about it than I should have. But then I've never pretended to be as brave as my friends are.

"I understand," I said.

Quiet descended like a noose around our necks.

I have to start, I thought. Not moving.

"Timothy," Jim said with all the force he had left, "I'll be *fine.* I'm English. We like a little pain."

He managed to make me smile, which saved the pair of us. I picked up the kerosene and started rubbing it into his skin, damp chicken feathers waving softly in the breeze that my movements created. And after about twenty minutes of depositing the kerosene all along the many edges of the tar, pretending I didn't have to do what was clearly my duty, I picked up the paint scraper.

I will never forget, not until I am the faintest shadow of a memory, that it took a full half hour of peeling his flesh off before Jim started to scream.

L ater that evening—night, rather, for even the moon had fled by then—I walked to Herr Getzler's front door and handed him a large tray of half-prepared foodstuffs.

"Danke," he said, face tense with worry. "Is there a way I can help?"

"Keep the women under your roof safe. If possible, keep them calm as well."

"Yes. This I can do," he replied soberly.

I headed back toward my own front door. "I'm genuinely sorry. It's an emergency—I'd not ask otherwise."

Thereafter I heard drinking, midnight dancing, all manner of normalcy emanating from our foreign neighbors, the babble not flagging until dawn was about to blow its bright whistle. A beautiful bedlam, one designed to keep Bird and Elena from thinking overmuch about what they must have just heard emanating from the bakery.

James Playfair I'd deposited in my bed by then. Plenty of his skin ripped off his person, plenty more of it burned enough to peel away later, but blessedly free of suffocating tar.

He was right. Of course Jim was right, I realized, watching the bedclothes tremble. *Valentine cannot have watched this.*

I'd cauterized the burns with diluted nitrate of silver and wrapped him up in all the linen I could find. I'd changed my togs, unceremoniously dumping my pitch-stained clothing in the street for rag pickers. Never wanting to see them again. Now there was simply a courteous, talented, desperately hurt person bleeding into my sheets as I sat in a chair nearby, watching him with my fingers linked over the cleft in my chin. He managed to sleep fitfully, thanks to the drugs. Would come awake with a gritty, anguished sound, and I'd say, "I'm still here," and he'd force himself silent again. Which had *not* been my goal.

"Timothy, you look as if you committed the original sin," James rasped at a quarter to five in the morning.

"I didn't realize you were awake," I returned, jumping a little.

Meanwhile, the light beyond the window was swelling. Bloating to blue and then a fine faint grey.

"I'll tell you a story, shall I?" he questioned.

It was because he knew me, and accidentally cared about me. And I wanted to say, *No, haven't you enough to bear just now?* But I was frayed past snapping.

I sat there, ears open.

"When you were first hurt in the eighteen forty-five fire, I fear I didn't know what to do," James told me quietly. "Your brother was desperately anxious, and I wanted so to help. But he said to me, after I'd tried as best I could to cheer him, that only you could improve matters, since only you could take the terrible thing that had happened to you and make some sense of it."

I remembered Jim as I'd first met him at the Liberty's Blood saloon. Recalled him saying, without so much as a pause to take in my masked and ruined face, *Of course he's your brother. Look, he's delightful. Hullo, Tim.*

"And you did make sense of it, brilliantly. 'Bright young copper star,' he always calls—"

"If you say a single further word that makes it sound like you're dying, I'm peeling more of your hide off for larks," I vowed.

"No, oh, God, I only intended to remark that your own experience may not have been comfortable either, but Val was . . . he was rather brilliant about it, I thought. The precedent at least leads me to hope he won't throw me over entirely after this regrettable occurrence."

"Did you just call my brother a cad enough to throw someone over due to *a burn injury?*"

He laughed, if only for a moment. I considered it a profound triumph.

"Can I send for him now?"

"No." Jim shifted, wincing. "The entire object of this happy enterprise was to throw him off his stride just prior to the election. If he should find out, Symmes will have accomplished far more than otherwise."

It agreed with everything I knew of Jim's character. But I didn't have to like it, and I didn't know how long I could keep mouse—I'd see Val all too soon, and surely he'd read it on me, see stamped on my brow that something ghastly had happened.

"I can't promise to lie to him," I admitted. "It doesn't generally work, in any case."

"Just delay seeking him out. Please?"

"You're in charge here. I'll be back in ten minutes with fresh supplies."

Brooding, I made up a tea tray with cold broth and cheese and a few of Mrs. Boehm and Bird's fresh rolls, a jug of small beer, a large knife, and the laudanum bottle. When I regained my bedchamber, I pulled the chair over with my foot and set all in reaching distance.

"Can you walk?"

"Let us not attempt feats of skill and daring just yet, but I believe so."

"Are you all right for a little? I'll be back, but there are . . . matters I need to see to."

"I'll be fine here. But don't hurt yourself, Timothy," Jim requested soberly. "Tell me you won't do something reckless."

"I won't do anything reckless," I told him.

I meant it too. For all the good it did.

After locking Jim inside, I shoved a note under Herr Getzler's door requesting he shoot anyone attempting to break into Mrs. Boehm's Fine Baked Goods with his prettily carved German flintlock. As well as another message containing equally plaintive injunctions that Elena and Bird stay with the Getzlers until the day after the elections.

Then I returned home in the thin morning light, rubbing my hands. If *vengeance* was truly the theme, I thought, recalling Silkie Marsh and her frosted-over eyes, I'd officially decided to give the perpetrators a run for their money.

But my first duty was to send a note to Mercy, warning her. Seating myself downstairs, out of earshot of Jim's labored breaths and feeling a downright villain over it, I penned the following message to the woman who so wholly occupies every spare inch of my brains:

> *Dear Mercy,*
>
> *I beg you for my sake to exercise especial care for now, as matters have grown improbably darker. Keep a companion with you at all times. And please, don't think any longer about what happened at the Old Brewery. I recognize you to be among the angels, even if the outworkers have been brought too terribly low to mark the difference between a helpmate and a scavenger. Know who you are, and stand by it. Know too that I will stand beside you, should you ever wish me there.*
>
> *Yours,*
> *Timothy*

Heart pounding like a battering ram in a siege, I hastily folded the note and poured wax along the seam, preventing myself altering a single word. But the hope was wild in my chest by that time, and anyhow the man of reason lurking within my muddled pate is well aware I could have measured every letter of that message like an alchemist poring over a potion and it wouldn't have made the slightest difference.

I'd never have singled out the word that sealed our fates.

I returned to the greenhouse in the enchanted-seeming wildwood, clapping Roundsman Clare on the shoulder and relieving him of guard duty, picking the well-oiled lock on Miss Woods's door with a much-abused penknife. The project that Sally Woods had set me proved much more arduous than locating William Wolf's article at the Mercantile Library Association. I pulled dusty crates into the center of the room as the light slowly filtered through the murky glass, flipping through mountains of badly organized pamphlets and broadsides, silence pooling around me as if I were in a human fishbowl.

After about an hour, I found the sheet in question. It was single-sided, the only publication I could find attributed to the Venerable and Distinguished Brotherhood of Tailors.

Most of the broad page was the usual earnest mewling of men who felt they'd been wronged by the modern system of outwork and by the decline of human decency. But in one column I discovered a short story. The tiny fiction was about a tailor who'd lost his livelihood, a fellow who along with equally shabby workingmen blamed the seamstresses for their misfortunes. Together they wrote a message—a threat, really—with the object of making the rich property owner suffer for hiring wanton females.

It read in this way:

> *Women across the nation are on the rise. As strikes don't move you, we'll see whether vengeance might. Improve the hateful conditions of those who wield the needle as a sword or watch your outwork go down in flames. We will not be cowed by those who think us less than human. You might not weep over the martyrs we will create in the name of justice. But you will mind about your lost pantaloons when they burn.*

It was stamped on the identical paper, naturally, as the rest of Sally Woods's printmaking. Likewise set with the same typeface.

"You're going to suffer for this," I announced with grim satisfaction to a man who was not present.

I tucked the folded broadside in my tailcoat, locked the greenhouse, and headed for the City Records Office under a hazy clamshell sky, expecting to find nothing whatsoever. At times the discovery of *nil* can be very telling indeed. Once within the spotless halls, surrounded by the *click-clicking* of many polished shoes, I attempted to look up the Venerable and Distinguished Brotherhood of Tailors.

The effort proved fruitless in the most bountiful of ways—there was no such thing as the Venerable and Distinguished Brotherhood of Tailors.

Belatedly ravenous, I returned to Ward Six and the Tombs.

As I approached Sally Woods and her cell, the look she darted down the cheerless hallway was one of the saddest I've seen. She might have been a flood victim asking whether any of the neighbors yet retained passable boats. I'd a pair of paper-wrapped ham-and-brown-butter sandwiches in one hand, which made unlocking the cell slightly awkward. But after a struggle I threw the door wide.

Miss Woods stood there, deciphering my mood. I can't imagine what conclusions she must have reached.

"You figured out who was likeliest to have planted the phosphorus undetected," I announced.

It wasn't a question. She nodded slowly. Shifting the key to my trouser pocket, I pulled the tailors' flyer from my jacket and handed it over. Finding the passage in question, she pointed viciously as she held it up to me.

"Isn't there a flasher way we could have done this than bashing me in the skull and forcing me to arrest you?" I complained, taking the paper back.

"There are *many* flasher ways we could have done this," she conceded. "But I apologize again for the . . . bashing."

Nodding, I passed her a fried sandwich, the first real food either of us had likely sampled since I'd arrested her, and we departed. Jeers and obscenities trailed after us like optimistic pickpockets. As we quit the cell block, I sensed her footsteps behind me wavering.

"I just want to know about the Venerable and Distinguished Brotherhood of Tailors," I vowed. "I'll never ask you what happened to Miss Abell again, I swear to you. And I want my handkerchief back."

Smiling, she passed it over. It was a bit damp, to be sure. But a fine token of trust for all that, and equal to the cause of removing butter from one's fingertips.

"Who approached you regarding the Venerable and Distinguished Brotherhood of Tailors and their print job? Sorry, don't— let me guess. Someone you trusted only because you already knew him, someone close to Symmes who pretended to pity your misfortunes, someone versed in tailoring and its woes."

"Mr. Wilde!" she exclaimed. "How can you describe the exact—"

"Damn it, I never wanted to meet him again. Will you be all right going back to New American Textiles?"

"Will it do some good?" she answered, her voice like rusted chains.

"It will do plentiful good," I said, thinking with a blade in my chest of Jim's regard for gracefulness and beauty and decency as we reached the road.

The journey to the manufactory took but ten minutes by hack to Nassau Street. Hardly a heroic quest. Our entrance was impressive, however. I still enjoy the picture—a small star policeman with a dented copper pin, entering a sewing manufactory on the arm of a radical labor organizer. She being tall and shapely, with wildly disarranged hair, wearing a pair of pin-striped trousers.

All the Bowery girls meticulously cutting, be the cloth destined for ever so humble origins, looked up at us in shock.

"What the devil is going on here?" Simeon Gage exclaimed, scurrying toward us.

"I imagine you'll want to ask us that someplace private," I said. Giving the words some heft.

Swallowing, the foreman turned on his heel.

I'd ample time to reflect, as he led us to his office, over just how much I'd initially disliked Mr. Gage. How dismissive he'd been of absolutely everyone, myself included. How settled in himself, how *right*, how complacent, and how very, very uncurious, which to me was the worst of all. And he hadn't exactly improved himself in the interim. Simeon Gage's mouth remained obdurate, his eyes beady and close-set. But at the sight of Sally Woods, his hairless pate beaded as if we'd plunged neck-deep into July, and his prim hands wandered aimlessly.

Once cloistered, he picked up a small sheaf of papers. Fiddled with the edges. Set the stack down, gestured haughtily at the pair of chairs across from him. He wasn't fooling anyone.

"I wanted you to watch this," I said to Miss Woods.

Gage's reptile pupils shot to me. "Do you mind telling me just what in hell you think you're doing bringing a loose woman, a known agitator, and I presume an escaped criminal into this manufactory?" he demanded.

"Why do you presume that, I wonder?" I asked.

The room grew quiet. And Simeon Gage quietest of all.

"First, *loose woman*—you didn't mention she'd been the alderman's mistress when last I saw you. Why?"

"Mr. Symmes is a man of great stature, his peccadilloes are his own concern, and I would never dream of betraying them to a *copper star*," he sneered.

"How noble. Second, I'll give you the *known agitator*, since there you're pretty much dead to rights. Third, *escaped criminal*. I arrested her only yesterday, so you seem mighty well informed to me, Mr. Gage. Who mentioned that Miss Woods had been collared?"

"My employer, of course," he snapped. "Mr. Symmes has been awaiting word the threat was past for well over a terror-filled week now, and so when Chief Matsell sent him notification—"

"He filled in his . . . What did you call yourself? *Secretary?* He has several of those, I imagine, but none quite so loyal as you. You seem less busy with paperwork today than you were when I visited previous."

It was a mild observation, for the desk was now nearly empty. It shouldn't have looked as if I'd caught him with his hand in the till. He froze all the same, licking his lips.

"Did Symmes tell you Miss Woods here had been thrown in the Tombs for lighting his buildings on fire?"

"He did," Gage answered almost inaudibly.

"Did you believe him?"

Swallowing, the foreman directed his attention at his desktop.

"I don't blame you, though you must have been grateful for even that bald a lie," I reflected. "Almost everything Robert Symmes owned burned in the eighteen forty-five fire, I'm told. That's when he built New American Textiles. Right here, on charred ground."

Mr. Gage remained riveted by wood grain, blinking myopically.

"How many new insurance policies were you taking out on your employer's most unprofitable slum residences last I was here?" I asked. "Was it only three or four? Ten? I think you said before that you could *barely keep up.*"

"I . . . I couldn't," he stammered. "But—"

"Did Symmes select the buildings slated for destruction, or did you pick them yourself?"

My profession requires me to see many cornered men. Some look like stray cats—gleefully gnawing at the chicken carcass until it's snatched away. Others resemble whipped curs—cringing, having lived for approval for too long to survive without it. That look always riles me, and Mr. Gage looked like the latter. Cowed, almost sorry.

But only because he'd been caught.

"I was following orders," he said weakly. "Nothing I did was illegal. It wasn't fraud, it was just . . . just business."

"How many structures did you reinsure?"

"Eleven," he admitted, chewing on a thumbnail.

"All through different insurance agencies, none of them local, so no one company would throw a fit and investigate you when their accounts turned to cinders?"

"Yes, but using different insurers was all per Mr. Symmes's instructions, I tell you! He strongly disliked Tammany's relentless scrutiny of his financial affairs. Their interest was positively invasive. Variety of insurers was a boon to his privacy. When I heard the structures had started burning down—"

"You *failed to consult the police.* But I can see why the thought of coming clean might have been a little unsettling, so let's talk about something else. You were a tailor once, you said to me."

Whipping the broadside from my jacket, I spread it on the desk. Gage's eyes lit up with recognition before darting from one to the other of us, perplexed.

Miss Woods surged forward in her chair, viperlike. "I *trusted* you."

"I don't know what you mean," he protested.

"The job I did for you," she spat at her former overseer, jabbing the short column of fiction with her forefinger. "The Venerable and

Distinguished Brotherhood of Tailors pro-labor diatribe. I'd mis-
givings about it from the start, but I was short darby for rent and
the price you offered was aces. You mean to say you didn't know
there was aught dusty about it?"

"There was nothing whatsoever dusty about it! Oh, you've still
plentiful cheek left even after your little revolution failed, haven't
you? The trousers are a nice touch, by the way. I'd love to teach you
some manners over my knee!" he exclaimed.

I held up a hand. "Tell me about this print order you commissioned. Now."

Gage's chest puffed out proudly. "I'd kept up with my fellow
tailors after landing this wretched farce of a job where I produce
nothing requiring skill, make *nothing* of value, and Mr. Symmes
was decent enough to lend me his ear on the subject. I was an *expert
tailor*, my boss knows it, and he knows that this modern system is
tearing fine men apart. He asked if any of my friends had ever
written about the nobility of labor."

"And that didn't strike you as a touch odd."

"The alderman is a civic leader who wanted to know how his
voters felt," Gage growled. "Mr. Symmes approached me asking—
as a businessman and a gentleman, mind—whether I'd like to see
my own side represented in print. And then Mr. Symmes recommended your press to me, Miss Woods. He took an interest. He
took . . . pity, perhaps, after the strike. I thought it a . . . a
noble-hearted gesture of forgiveness toward you."

Miss Woods answered this remark with a furiously clenched
jaw rather than words.

"I did! You printed the broadsheet yourself—I know you found
our points about the degradation of labor apt! Mr. Symmes asked
merely that a short piece another friend of his wrote be placed
within the rest of the material. As it fit, we were glad to include
the tale for distribution amongst freemen. I always supposed the

commission was meant to aid his former sweetheart in your new line of work."

"Oh, the *hell* you did!" Miss Woods cried.

"He might have," I objected. "He idolizes one of the very manufactory barons snatching the bread from the tailors' tables. He's an idiot."

"True enough."

"Go on, Mr. Gage. Anything else you'd like to tell us about your part in a ruthless criminal conspiracy?"

"Criminal conspiracy be damned! I did take out insurance policies for Mr. Symmes," Mr. Gage wheezed, loosening his collar. "And I did create the Venerable and Distinguished Brotherhood of Tailors at his urging, because I was told that it would accomplish some *good* in this upside-down world where women work and men are penniless."

"Symmes paid for the initial print run?" I confirmed.

Gage nodded sullenly.

"And when you asked about producing more issues?"

"He . . . he's very busy just now." Gage's voice dropped, and he scowled at the wall clock. "Mr. Symmes is a generous man, a good and decent employer. He needn't—that is, I'm not surprised he hasn't repeated the favor so soon. Maybe after the elections."

We were quiet for a moment.

"I want a list of the eleven buildings whose insurance payouts you raised," I declared.

"But—"

"Sorry, I didn't mention I wanted that *now*."

The foreman rose, selecting files from a drawer. Twice, droplets of nervous sweat rolled from his shiny brow to land *splish* on the pages. But he obeyed. Gage passed the documents over, eyes pinched.

"Thank you for your time," I said, standing.

Sally Woods made no objection as we quit the building. Nor did Simeon Gage, for that matter. He collapsed back into his chair as we exited, hand fluttering over his breast. When we'd reached the street, Miss Woods's startlingly dark eyes darted to me, bruised and thoughtful, and I took her arm once more.

"Oh, no, I'm arresting him," I vowed. "I'm just not certain on what charge, and I need my hands free at the moment. Anyway, you know as well as I do this wasn't his doing. As I mentioned . . ."

"He's an idiot. Correct."

"You're free to return home, Miss Woods. Meet me tomorrow at the Tombs first thing, seven in the morning. Go straight to the chief of police's office and speak to no one on your way. I'll be there."

She brushed a hand through her tousled hair, dismayed. "What in hellfire can you be doing right now that's more important than this matter?"

"You know that Robert Symmes is running for alderman against my brother."

"Of course," she answered. Curious.

"I have to take care of my brother's closest friend. He's been . . . injured."

Her eyes shifted away from me with a swift flinch. I saw depthless pain in her mouth, in the set of her shoulders. The sort of grief that could have ridden us both on a rail, straight out of New York City and into the wide unknown. Where maybe people are kinder to one another in some cleaner, emptier land.

"The alderman wanted to make a point," she whispered. "But he didn't attack your brother. He thought of a far worse punishment."

I tilted my head in the affirmative.

"I'd not have put it so neatly," I answered. "But yes."

S topping at the Tombs on my way home, I scratched brief instructions to Chief Matsell:

All is not as it seems. The details are too sensitive to discuss save in person, to which end I suggest meeting at a quarter to seven tomorrow with another key player in your office. In the meanwhile, please place copper stars at the enclosed listed addresses, as they are at high risk of combustion.

Hesitating, I twirled my pen. But I was almost certain. No, very certain. So I added:

Here is a sketch of the incendiary. Advise your star police to be on the watch for her, and if they should see her approach a Symmes property listed here, to bring her in for questioning. Lacking physical proof, her capture on the scene will prove most useful. Please instruct them not to hurt her unduly.

Sketching the culprit took me about ten minutes. Hand steady, fingers flying. As if I could use the false image to conjure her presence within the prison walls, could place her safely behind the bars that had once held Miss Sally Woods captive with a few bold vertical stripes of black ink on white paper.

20

A woman is nobody. A wife is everything. A pretty girl is equal to 10,000 men, and a mother is next to God, all powerful. . . . The ladies of Philadelphia, therefore, under the influence of the most serious and sober second thought, are resolved to maintain their rights as Wives, Belles, Virgins, and Mothers, and not as Women.

—"THE WOMEN OF PHILADELPHIA," *PUBLIC LEDGER AND DAILY TRANSCRIPT,* 1848

"TIMOTHY, I really cannot imagine what you are doing down there."

What I was doing was half dozing on my bedroom floor on top of a quilt that early evening. And Gentle Jim, as Val calls the fellow, was keeking over the edge of my bed at me. A bit muzzy from the laudanum, for my money. I'd sure as hell given him enough of the stuff.

"I'm thinking."

"Ah."

"Not effectively."

I'd returned home late that morning and helped to peel Jim's bandagings off, replaced them, and curled up, following the previous night's sleepless watch, wrapped cocoonlike in Elena's quilt.

Watching the swollen shadows as they crept inexorably along the floorboards. Jim was making a bold play of it, but every movement was a torment. My own ancient injury by comparison seemed a fancy I'd invented and not a true hardship at all. As if I'd constructed a paper Timothy, scribbled a scarred phiz on him, and set him up starring in pageantries like one of Bird's dolls. I'd have indulged in shame over that, shame thick and hot and dark as good coffee, if I'd had the energy.

Meanwhile, I marked Jim breathing very shallowly above me. *In-out, in-out, in-out* against my pillow. The notion of leaving him again scared me witless. I'd thought plenty over what he meant to Val.

I'd never noticed what he meant to *me*.

"James Anthony Carlton Playfair, if you die, I will *kill you*. On my honor."

"I'm making an earnest effort not to."

I was up immediately, pressing my palm to his brow. He was feverish, but not dangerously so, not to my paltry knowledge. I wanted so to ease him, to say, *I'll fetch your mother and your sister,* whom he loved more than almost anything else. But his mother and sister were in London presiding over high teas and entertaining parliamentary officials, and none of the many letters James has sent them in four years have merited replies, thanks to his father's wrath— God knows whether they even receive his correspondences—and so I stood there. Useless.

"It hurts," I said. Knowing it true.

"That doesn't matter," he said. Knowing it untrue.

A thought occurred. "Shall we get you as high up in altitudes as Val generally is?"

"Timothy." Jim's bloodshot eyes gleamed, that electric understanding I'd always found fascinating about him. "Are you proposing to raid your own brother's morphine supply?"

I was.

After dusk had seeped like a spill of violet ink across the firmament, after breaking into my brother's blessedly empty digs, I arrived home with all of Val's morphine tonic in a heavy satchel and a resolute smile on my face. Tapping briefly at my bedroom door, I entered following an indistinct welcoming sound. Jim's face was drawn. Frost white and just as delicate.

I sat next to him, careful not to jostle my straw-tick mattress overmuch. "Thank you, that was a spree."

"Delighted you take such joy in sneak thievery," he murmured.

"Most fun I've had in days." I opened a bottle of morphine. "For God's sake, never take to this habitually."

Jim cast an ironic look at me as if I were a mysterious troll lodged under a bridge, unsure of the ways of humans. Next he shivered and then winced at the constriction of his skin, stopping himself from audibly suffering by taking his lip in his teeth. Shaking like a leaf all the while.

I poured him a morphine tonic in a small glass. I poured myself a whiskey. And we drank.

The next morning, the morning of the elections, I arrived at George Washington Matsell's desk clean and orderly in appearance at a quarter to seven. When I sat down, he regarded me with weary walrus eyes, and I momentarily disliked inconveniencing him. There was nothing for it, though. He could see fresh news bulging out of me. Worms gnawing through an overripe pear.

"Do you have an inkling why Abraham Kane is letting me go about my business?" I questioned.

He nodded. Seeming tired, seeming . . . no less powerful, simply deflated. As if a bit of air had been vented from the balloon of his person and now he was sinking, skimming the tops of the trees.

"Alderman Symmes has arranged to light his own least profitable buildings on fire to collect the insurance and presumably erect better ones," I reported. "We've already kept the incendiary out of the papers, and the insurers are based out of town, so I presume he means to keep mouse over the white phosphorus unless they question him—and if they do, paint himself the victim of a monomaniacal firestarter. Easier far than evicting tenants and paying for demolition. Also about twice as profitable, supposing you need a fistful of ready screaves to pay for reconstruction."

"Excuse me a moment," Matsell said, baritone cool as a submerged anchor.

Opening a drawer, he pulled out a manuscript—his dictionary of flash patter, meant to assist coltish copper stars with the local jargon before they found themselves in serious linguistic difficulties.

"Screaves, you said?" George Washington Matsell asked, flipping to a page at the back marked NOTES AND ADDITIONS. "Which I take to mean ready cash?"

"Paper money specifically. Yes, screaves," I admitted, embarrassed.

"Spell it."

I did.

"Thank you."

My chief closed the unfinished tome and returned it to its resting place.

"You're not surprised that Symmes has been torching his own properties," I observed.

"Mr. Wilde, I am about to share with you several personal opinions. Said opinions are not those of our Party. They are mere musings, as if you and I were sitting in a coffeehouse sharing a pot and mulling over the human condition. You'll not repeat them."

My elbows landed on his desk with my fingers linked. "Post me."

Chief George Washington Matsell smiled. A full one, such a smile as I've never seen from him before. It hocused me momentarily. He generally considers smiling at a fellow, decides against it, and the fellow counts the rumination a high privilege.

"There was a time when you'd have been sharp as nettles over keeping mouse for Tammany's sake. You've grown, if you'll pardon my saying so."

I imagine—extrapolating from his deep chuckle—this remark turned my expression moldy.

"Oh, come. You were a man in the first place, but now you're a better one—the needs of the city itself must be taken into our accounting, as well as the needs of its individual citizens. But enough of this. Mr. Wilde, I'd like you to ponder the subject of Robert Symmes and his greed."

I wasn't meant to say anything. So I reflected, and the word that emerged was *bottomless*, and I held my tongue.

"Now," the chief continued, "please mull over the subject of his cruelty."

Insatiable, I thought. Briefly, I cursed myself for listening to a piano-playing pacifist and not sending word to Val. But I'd solve that as soon as I could, I figured, and anyway I'd been pretty heavily occupied at keeping James Playfair alive.

"Finally, reflect over his intelligence."

George Washington Matsell saw comprehension and the morbid sort of awe on my face, the kind of concentration that folk direct at graphic carriage accidents. Crazed incendiaries and dirty politics weren't the half of this sordid affair. Because Robert Symmes was brilliant in a single field: he was merely and only creatively heartless.

"What tipped you?" I asked quietly.

"I knew something smelled heartily of fish following the meeting with Mr. Kane and Madam Marsh. I couldn't put my finger on it. But when you asked yesterday that I divert more copper stars to specific addresses, I compared it to a second message from Mr. Symmes, ostensibly thanking us for collaring Sally Woods. He suggested 'calling off the mongrels haunting my properties now the danger is past,' but I trust your opinion rather further than I do the alderman's."

Of course he'd resented the roundsmen attempting to help him. Symmes wanted those properties gone. Never concerning himself over two charred stargazers who probably knew only a quarter hour's kindness in their lives and then left the world in flames.

"I'd have sent you word, but first I went to Mr. Kane for guidance, and he suggested waiting until after the elections for a full briefing. How did you figure it out?" the chief wanted to know, passing his fingers over his great belly.

"It wasn't . . . I found the right story," I attempted in some frustration.

My chief nodded. Not because that made sense. Because he knew me.

"As for the incendiary herself—"

"I'd rather not speak out of turn just yet," I demurred. "Not until she's caught and questioned."

"She planted the energetic materials herself?"

"No. Ronan McGlynn did."

I thought of how dimwitted I'd been over McGlynn, how unobservant. He'd been stupefied at the news the Pell Street house had burned when I'd confronted him in his cell. Or so I'd imagined.

He hadn't been shocked. He'd been terrified.

Why didn't you notice his reaction was wrong as was possible? I asked myself for the dozenth time. *He might have been angry, yes. Livid? Naturally. But frightened to the point of panic? Of the sort of bluestocking he despises? Of fire, simply because it paralyzes you?*

All McGlynn's protests of his ignorance, his sobbed *I don't know*, his inability to cope with the brutal treatment my colleague had subjected him to, the crushing fear—it hadn't been due to his ignorance at all. The mental torment had stemmed from his knowledge. The key to end his suffering had rested in his hand—gleaming like a beacon, impossible to use. Telling us the truth after the shower bath would have meant confessing to firestarting—or at least to planting incendiary materials, which wouldn't have exactly been greeted with a slap on the back.

Matsell's grey head raised as a knock at the door reverberated. He called the visitor in, and Miss Woods appeared, in her usual attire. Hair pinned up in a great brown briar's bush of waves with a froth of white at the temple, sleepless circles stamped under her eyes.

"Miss Woods, I take it," Matsell grunted. "Chief of Police Matsell, at your service. Please sit down. I thought you were incarcerated."

"I was, sure enough." She sat, glancing at me.

"There exist a great many proofs against you."

"And one proof in her favor." I pulled out the single false threat that had been cut from the Venerable and Distinguished Brotherhood of Tailors periodical and the identical offset quotation in the pamphlet itself. "Symmes secretly paid for this to be printed through an intermediary—inspired by the other threats, no doubt."

Leaning forward, Chief Matsell studied the documents. He steepled his fingers between the deep furrows down the sides of his nose and mouth.

"Very clever," he admitted. "But it is not proof *against* the alderman unless we can show that Robert Symmes sent this to himself. Still. Excellent work, Mr. Wilde. Miss Woods, you certainly made a wide target of yourself."

"Don't I know it," she said dully.

"Might I ask what you were thinking?"

"I was thinking I didn't know how to punish him yet, was still planning what was best to be done, but I could still make him afraid to blow out his candle at night," she replied, knuckles white where they gripped the arms of her chair. "I was thinking if I could teach him what it meant to be frightened, he might learn what it meant to feel sympathy. I was all alone in a greenhouse with a printing press, and I was thinking if I didn't promise him that he'd pay, and promise him often and feelingly, I'd walk into the river."

"His crime against you must have been brutal."

"Brutal I could have managed better, I think," she said thickly. "This was monstrous."

"You've certainly suffered for your frankness."

"I never implied it was *sound* thinking. Neither was bedding him in the first place, for that matter. I want to claw my eyes out just thinking on it."

"Doubtless you own regrets on many fronts. I cannot help but contrast the fervency of your hatred toward him with the fact you restricted yourself to a letter campaign and grow puzzled, however."

"He has something of mine," Sally Woods confessed in a rasp. "Someone. In his power. That's as much as I can say, but he . . . I couldn't risk her. I was explicitly warned. The best I could do was haunt his nightmares and pray for inspiration."

It was as I'd thought, then. I'd once, despairing of a solution to my earliest major assignment, created a list of things people would kill for. *God, politics, defense, money, madness,* and *love* ended up written in an orderly row down a piece of butcher paper. Maybe there are other reasons people slaughter one another, but in my career I haven't encountered any. As for reasons people refrain from vengeance when vengeance is what's called for—that, to my mind, made up a shorter list by far. Sally Woods, who witnessed violence with aplomb and thought nothing of braining star police, would have spit in the eye of threats against her own person. A single force existed in the world with power capable of binding her, locking her in a dim glass cage with her misery and her impotent rage.

Fear wouldn't be up to the task, though it might have cowed some. But love would.

The chief made a muffled satisfied sound. "Miss Woods, please consider yourself confined to your home until these matters are settled to my liking. I will advise the two copper stars who were watching it to return at once. Spirits can often run high before an election."

Miss Woods breathed out slowly, rose, and shook hands with the pair of us.

"Take care," she said to me, turning back at the door. "Once Robert savvies you know . . ."

"Don't worry," I told her. "I'll be on my guard."

When she'd gone, I regarded my chief. "I've nil idea how to bring Symmes to task, as he conducted the entire business through intermediaries. But we have to try. He assaulted James Playfair, you see."

Matsell's canyon-deep frown lines shifted in repulsion. "The Tammany pianist? You're brother's friend?"

"The same."

"Is he alive?"

"Something similar."

"Politics," Matsell told me in a voice that verged upon paternal, "is ugly."

"Naturally. Ugly men practice it. Though when I try to brain-work how Symmes came to be as ugly as he is, I'm . . . I honestly can't fathom it."

"I've studied humanity for decades." The chief waved a wide bear's paw at his bookshelves. "How do gangs form? How can females be expected to rise from their squalor when they are never told procreation is optional? Why do languages hang themselves by the neck until they're so much garbled nonsense? I don't have many answers, Mr. Wilde. But my father ran a bookstore, and I went to sea as a lad and saw things both ungodly and marvelous, and I'll never cease being curious. That's what I like about you, what I liked from the start. You want to understand people."

I respected our chief so by then, even in moments of madness admired him, that I could only incline my head in thanks.

"I've three requests."

Shifting, I leveled a steadier stare at him. "What are they?"

"You will not attempt to arrest an alderman who might be re-elected this very day, no matter how eager you are to do so. We will find other avenues."

It gouged a mighty chunk from my belly. But I nodded.

"You will look out for yourself and for Captain Wilde. I watched Tammany split in eighteen thirty-seven, and we were thrashed senseless at the polls. That's preferable to my best policemen suffering the same."

"Thank you. Lastly?"

"Vote for your brother." Chief Matsell stood, tugging down his voluminous waistcoat. "I don't give a damn you don't live in Ward Eight, make it happen. If Valentine Wilde loses to the Whig Party, not to mention to Alderman Symmes, there will be literal hell to pay."

This is patently ridiculous," I informed Mr. Piest and Mr. Connell in my office half an hour later.

I leaned on my desk as they fussed over me. They'd taken my

grey waistcoat and replaced it with a Bowery one, dotted all over with blue cornflowers. They'd taken my black frock coat and replaced it with a billowing grass-green swallowtail. They'd taken my collar and folded it down over my lapels. Any minute, my transformation into the doll-sized version of Valentine would be complete.

It didn't bear mulling over.

"Where did you even get these togs?"

"Where d'ye think, you tit? The Hall," Connell answered. "Every starving Irishman as can walk goes to the Party costumer the week afore elections so's to look a citizen. You do know how voting *works*, aye?"

"Both citizens and noncitizens bribed by the Party by means of jobs and liquor cast as many illegal ballots as they can in a single day, after which said votes will be either tossed in the river or purposefully miscounted."

"Mr. Wilde does have a certain pithy grasp of the subject, you see, Mr. Connell, despite his notorious lack of political affiliation," Mr. Piest noted, chuckling as he handed me a shocking-orange cravat.

A grave silence fell.

"Are you *trying* to hurt me?" I asked him, eyes wide.

"If ye think that the Symmes camp is going t' be kittled by the sight of Valentine Wilde's famous kid brother voting fer him, I've a handful o' magic beans I wonder if you'd be interested in purchasing?" Connell wondered sweetly. "Put on the damn disguise, ye sow-sucking idiot."

Sighing, I snatched the cravat from Mr. Piest and tugged my own off.

"I'm not famous," I said.

Piest and Connell didn't spare this observation so much as a glance, let alone a reply. Just continued rifling through a carpetbag stuffed to the gills with clothing that seemed specifically designed by my brother to torture me.

"How am I meant to vote in a ward that isn't mine?" I asked next.

"That's no difficulty, Mr. Wilde," Piest soothed, holding up a yellow-and-scarlet-striped pocket square and eyeing it critically before stuffing it into my breast pocket. "The going rate for freemen crossing ward lines is fifty cents per voter. All quite usual, fear not."

My palm was beginning to seem a comfortable haven for my face, so I deposited it there. Beyond aggrieved.

"Where's Mr. Kildare?" I questioned through my fingers, as he's seldom more than ten feet from Mr. Connell.

"Gone a-wooing," the latter replied, winking.

"Truly?" I questioned in not-insignificant shock.

"Aye. If this Caoilinn creature don't kill the fool within ten seconds of being escorted to ice cream and coffee, there's a weight off me, I'm that anxious."

"Let us not unto the marriage of true minds admit impediments," I muttered, tucking my hands under my arms.

"Pardon?"

"Nothing. Best of luck to the man. He deserves a warm bed."

"Hear, hear, Mr. Wilde, and may destiny grant him luck with the object of his affections," Mr. Piest agreed.

Mr. Connell approached me. Warily. He swept my wide-brimmed black hat off my head and replaced it with a towering brown stovepipe beaver.

There are limits to what even the most determined men can endure.

"No," I said, taking the terrible thing off.

"But ye—"

"*No.* The hat stays."

Connell looked at Piest. Piest looked at Connell. Minute shrugs passed along their shoulders like sparks over telegraph wires.

"Fine," Connell sighed. "'Tis yer own head at risk, after all."

"The notorious hat stays, as a point of principle," Mr. Piest assented, beaming.

"Right, then I'll be off."

I'd walked about six steps down the corridor when I heard my door shutting with a neat *snick* and a pair of footfalls shadowing me. One light but sure, with a delicate Irish swagger. The other ponderous, produced by quarter-ton Dutch boots.

"Oh, for God's sake, do I have an honor guard?" I exclaimed.

They didn't bother to answer. Again. Leaving me to wonder, and pretty mightily wonder too, *How often am I shepherded by these fellows without my knowledge?* Because I was beginning to suspect that the answer was *As often as necessary.* And I—who'd been too preoccupied with being hungry to have pals once, who'd been unlucky enough to witness old friends rendered cold corpses destined for colder ground, felt marvelously lucky.

For a moment.

A pril 28 was a clear morning, a bright one, a red tinge of hostility already snaking through the atmosphere as we three marched for Ward Eight. Throngs of men strutted along sporting sashes and corsages and Party ribbons pinned to their coats, shouting partisan mania in a heady crossfire of noise.

SOLIDARITY WITH OUR SOUTHERN BROTHERS was the theme painted on a Whig booth at the broad corner where Lispenard met Broadway, and cartmen fighting the election-day traffic shook their whips at the moustachioed businessmen manning their fortress. A smallish brass band lay claim to Grand Street two blocks north, under fluttering banners espousing FREE SOIL, FREE SPEECH, FREE LABOR, FREE MEN. Across the road from the Barnburner musicians, an enclave of mothers had gathered bearing hand-painted signs reading FREEDOM FROM LIQUOR MEANS FOOD FOR YOUR CHILDREN and WHAT TYRANNY MORE WICKED THAN IN-TEMPERANCE?

I'd always avoided election days—even apart from my horror of voting, they're riots long before the fisticuffs start, hysterical anti-papists jostling against Irish gang heelers with clubs held in slack, scarred fingers. But family members are regrettably nonnegotiable, and I'd only one example of the type.

Thus I would vote for my brother. Even if it killed me.

The ticket booths we passed, where the slips for the candidates were handed out, already boasted disorderly queues of steely-eyed men with flasks in their fists. Some of these lines were well over two blocks long, curving round corners and jutting into inter-sections. When we were a quarter of a block into Ward Eight, I spied the first ticket stall announcing CAPTAIN VALENTINE WILDE FOR ALDERMAN and stopped to gape at the crowd.

My brother's queue was four and five rogues wide in places. Jubilant. Plenty dangerous-seeming. Irish and German and native and even a smattering of British scoundrels, interspersed with plen-tiful local merchants wearing monocles and ready smiles. I'd known Val Wilde for a manifestly popular human. But this bor-dered on the absurd. A thin, sneering fellow in a blue coat met my eye as I studied the crowd and tipped his hat to me with a smirk. My hand shot out, gripping Piest's bony elbow.

"That's Sam Scrivener, the picklock we collared not two weeks back," I hissed in alarm. "He's escaped the Tombs somehow. We—"

"Ah, more probable that he, like many of the more Tammany-minded of our prison population, is voting," Mr. Piest demurred, coughing diplomatically. "See? There's a copper star at his elbow, keeping him under guard. A tour of our prisons would discover precious few inmates this morning. Don't fret, Mr. Wilde, they'll be safe and snug and snoring off the liquor behind bars come morning."

"How many times are ye wanting to vote on behalf o' yer kin, then?" Mr. Connell asked me when I'd stared in amazement at Mr. Piest for longer than he thought reasonable.

"Once?"

My friends burst into such a clattering hailstorm of laughter that I glimpsed people halfway down the block turning to stare.

"No, no, Mr. Wilde," Mr. Piest said when he'd recovered. "One vote would be . . ."

"A token," Mr. Connell supplied.

"A gesture of profound goodwill," the Dutchman added.

"But . . ."

"And I hesitate to appeal to your vanity in this of all matters, my stout compatriot, however . . ."

"*One* vote doesn't mean a dog's fart, does it, now? Ye'd be ashamed to deliver that accounting to yer own brother."

"I would?" I asked. Not surprised, but genuinely horrified.

Thus began my first—and I hoped, by the grace of Providence, *only*—day of voting for an alderman candidate in New York City.

"But the line—" I attempted.

"Star police!" boomed Mr. Connell, shoving through the throng. Moses wielding a staff couldn't have been more efficient. "Make way! Yer ballot-approval inspectors have arrived, and all o' we lawkeepers grateful fer your Democratic support at the polls, freemen! Deliver yer votes and we'll deliver justice to our fair streets!"

When we'd reached the front of the queue, irascible mutterings swarming after us like horseflies, Mr. Piest landed a threadbare elbow on the booth's counter before the Party rabbit behind it could so much as open his mouth. My friend winked at the ginger rascal, flapping his copper star.

"We'll need a large sample of Barnburner tickets to test quality, gentle patriot, and best of luck to you on this auspicious day regarding both your personal health and your good fortune," Mr. Piest announced.

"I don't think—" I began.

"'Tis a fact," Mr. Connell mentioned tenderly in my ear. "Ye *don't* think, do you?"

"Forty Captain Wilde tickets for inspection, then, to assure the police force that nothing underhanded is taking place here, my good citizen?" Mr. Piest asked, sliding a five-dollar note toward the now-pleased electioneer.

"How does fifty sound?" The Irishman licked at a black gap in the line of his none too pearly teeth. "Seeing as ye've none other than Timothy Wilde in your company, though curse me own dead grandmother should I ever reveal such to antagonistic parties."

I blinked stupidly. Which in retrospect was probably what they expected of me.

"There's a stout lad," Mr. Connell trilled.

"What a very generous proposal," Mr. Piest approved.

So began a polling experience that I'll never forget even supposing I could bleach the inside of my skull. But despite myself . . . I saw the sport in it. A sort of rapture in *honestly fighting for something*, even if that meant dishonesty in the execution. Half a second on the heels of that sensation, of course, found me predictably disgusted with myself.

Please may I never vote again, I thought as we passed through trial after bare-knuckled trial, our pockets stuffed with slips of paper bearing my inexcusable brother's name.

At Ward Eight's District Seven polling location, I narrowly

avoided a punch to the jaw when Connell stepped forward—
cleanly, almost pleasantly—and caught a Hunker thug's fist. We
stood in a grog shop, flanked by barrels of fat herring and pickles,
having slipped past the intoxicated guards with sage nods and confident spitting.

"Wrong target," Connell announced.

"You're mistaken." The Hunker leered.

The ensuing mitten-mill enabling me to stuff my ticket into
the ballot box that would likely end up bobbing in river water was
fairly exhilarating. I escaped with a disarrayed cravat. My friends
followed with bruised knuckles, laughing fit to burst their waistcoats. Being well used to the process.

At Ward Eight's District Five polling location, which was a
hotel lobby, I took a hard blow to the gut. Choking on air and falling to one knee. I still voted—doubled over, thrusting the ticket
into the slot. Two thugs lay flat as piecrust behind me, which was
my own doing.

At Ward Eight's District Eleven polling location, a gang of
Symmes's cronies descended on us the instant they spied my face.
This time we'd entered a chophouse that had kindly cleared their
buffet table to curry Party favor and the accompanying elections fee.

Whish went our fists as we struggled toward the prize.

Crack went Mr. Piest's nose as he flailed with ungraceful limbs.

Smash went Mr. Connell's elbow into a Hunker's jaw, breaking it.

This isn't you, my brain weakly protested as I shoved my vote
into the box of Ward Eight, District Ten, in a coffeehouse several
hours later.

I'm uncertain what time it was by then, though we felt fairly
spruce despite the wear and tear. Midafternoon, supposing I recall
the sunlight and church bells aright. We'd stopped for a dinner
hosted by the Barnburner faction, who'd set up shop half a block
from the Knickerbocker 21 engine house. My brother was voting

for himself and starting strategic brawls, I was assured by myriad strangers. I thanked them. A bit dizzy, but none the worse for that, and my companions equally hale save for a black eye that Connell seemed pretty fond of and a purpling bruise along Piest's nose.

Val's cronies dished us fried oysters, crowing of victory. The colored women with bandannas over their intricately worked hair spooned us grainy baked pears from their earthenware pots. We toasted one another's health with numerous glasses of gin. We were men of action, men the gods would not dare to interfere with. I honestly believed that for a radiant moment.

"To yer first election and that right uppercut o' yours, Mr. Wilde," Mr. Connell proposed, tipping his glass to me.

"Hear, hear," Mr. Piest chortled, "and may the devil himself quail before the heroes of the New York City Police Department!"

If I could weave the sort of spell Miss Duffy believed in and thereby stop the story there, having cast fifteen illegal votes for Valentine, I would.

Since I can't, I'll skip to the Liberty's Blood saloon, where I at last found my brother. Everything was moonlight and moonshine by that time. There had been serious skirmishes, reports of the unhealthy sort of knife wounds, too many trivial altercations to mention. The three of us star police were well and truly drunk, possessing approximately the awareness of a blood tick.

"What the *devil* are you wearing?" Valentine wanted to know.

I blinked at familiar green eyes, then smiled crookedly down at my hideous orange cravat. The Liberty's Blood is Ward Eight's low-liquor hell in the comfortable mode, a bastion of Party insiders and the fresh emigrants who fawn over them. Somehow Piest and Connell and I had stumbled into the rear chamber. Beyond the dust-shrouded canopy of American flags, back where hardened men carouse until dawn. A truly regrettable taxidermied bald eagle presides there, wings unfurled, over equally distasteful proceedings.

"Did someone knock you in the pate and dress you like a Bowery swell?"

Valentine, I thought, *is speaking to you. Make minimal sense.*

"Why should you want to know what I'm wearing? Don't you want to know what I'm voting?" I demanded semicoherently, attempting to sit up in a canyonlike armchair.

"Down with slaveholder tyranny! May every last barn burn!" Piest slurred from the low sofa opposite me. Connell snored his agreement to the ceiling.

"You *voted*?" my brother demanded. Deeply perplexed.

Valentine looked healthy enough for the balcony, but certainly not the front row. His face was cleanly shaven and his collar spotless, but he'd barked his knuckles on a set of teeth, and his eyes remained sunken as tombstones.

I remembered what I couldn't avoid telling him any longer, and my breath caught in my throat.

"Valentine—"

"They're counting votes now." Pulling me upright, Valentine steered me toward the door. "We're due at a meeting to discuss amicable settlements. Can't have the Ward falling apart, no matter which way the dice fall once the ballots are tallied."

Something about the phrase *meeting to discuss amicable settlements* raised alarums in my addled pate. They meant nothing good, I suspected. Depending upon who was conducting them, I'd a hunch I felt about them the way I do about bear traps.

"Wait, *wait.*" I tore my arm out of my brother's grasp, half falling on a sot costumed as Benjamin Franklin. Since he wasn't awake, we didn't argue the point. "A meeting where?"

"Where do you think? At Alderman Symmes's house, two blocks hence."

"No." I made a blind swipe for Val's wrist and came up victorious. "No meetings."

Valentine shouted something at the bartender, and seconds later a tepid but nicely muddy tin cup of coffee was in my fingers. I drank it at a go and opened my lips to resume protests.

Only to discover that my brother was already halfway out the front door of the Liberty's Blood.

"Tammany can't afford a riot, and neither can the star police. One conversation and we bury this hornet's nest. Pull yourself together, bright young copper star," Valentine ordered over his shoulder. "It's almost finished."

Let us all go to the polls with a full determination to keep
the peace, but also with a firm resolve to deposit our votes
in the ballot box and enable our friends to do so—or die in
the struggle.

—JAMES WATSON WEBB, *NEW YORK COURIER
AND ENQUIRER*, APRIL 8, 1834

THE MEETING WASN'T what I'd expected. And I'd expected the
worst.

"Val, slow down," I insisted as we exited the saloon, wedging
ourselves past beer-stained revelers.

"Why? We're getting this over with." He swung his stick in a
wide arc, the pearly top glinting in the starlight. "Granted, there
are half a million people in this godless city, and there's not a single
one whose company I wouldn't prefer to—"

"Valentine, *he sets his own buildings on fire.*"

My brother stiffened midstride. Then his hand came down on
my collar, and he dragged me like a still-wet kitten into an alley,
stepping over a pair of drunks wearing more Party-endorsing ribbons than was strictly tasteful. I landed with my back to the bricks
and his fingers digging into my upper arm.

"Say that again. Slower."

"Symmes is the incendiary. Or he hired her, rather. Jesus, Val, let go of—"

"Start," my brother hissed, "at the beginning."

"What about—"

"They aren't listening," Val growled in reference to the cup-shot voters. "*Talk.*"

"Symmes asked one of his secretaries, an equally loyal and stupid one, to insure his slums for copious chink. Then Ronan McGlynn planted the energetic materials—since he was the property manager, if he'd said he was putting down rat poison, the poor souls in those houses would never have questioned it."

"How did you tumble onto this?"

I told Val about finding the woman I knew only as the Witch, about inquiring whether anyone who didn't belong there had visited Pell Street and her emphatic answer of *No one. Not a single person.* I'd thought that strange even then but let it slip my regrettably porous mind.

"That initial meeting at the Queen Mab . . ." Valentine mused.

"Yes, exactly! The alderman—"

"Not yet, and maybe not anymore," Val bit out viciously.

"Sorry, Symmes, then—he called you in that day at the clearinghouse so you'd unwittingly help him frame Sally Woods. His buildings burn, she gets collared for it."

My kin leaned heavily against the wall in what looked a potent blend of awe and revulsion. "How many buildings were new insured?"

"Eleven."

"That sick son of a bitch," Val breathed. "He would've stopped once we'd pinned the bluestocking, then? If Miss Woods is locked up in hock, she can't very well be starting fires."

I shook my head. "I don't think so. He'd been feeding notes indicating what buildings would go up next to Ellie Abell, asking her to deliver warnings to Drake Todd. She's the gullible type, I'm afraid, and believed them to originate from Miss Woods."

"Are you implying that dousing the blazes quick was never civic-mindedness, just part of the pony show?" Val growled.

"Dead to rights. Later Symmes would have made it seem the girls were in cahoots all along, that Miss Abell took over the fire-starting from Miss Woods after her arrest but felt tender over incurring collateral damages and tipped the Neptune Nines."

"That's a piss-poor lay, my Tim. Ellie Abell can't keep delivering cautions over stirs and setting them at the same bloody time," Valentine objected. "Not to mention she'd surely have reliable alib—"

"No, no, no, my theory is Symmes had far worse in mind," I interrupted. "The only two fires to date were set *before* I arrested Miss Woods. What would have happened if Miss Abell disappeared at the same time the warnings *stopped*?"

It required two seconds for my brother to process this question before his face hardened with the swiftness of a portcullis slamming shut.

"The fires continue, this time without advance notice. We firedogs lose more buildings. More locals cock their toes up before their time. Building number eleven collapses, and lo and behold . . ." Val pulled a hand down his face, marring the stony set of his mouth.

"Miss Abell reappears," I supplied.

"Ragged and soot-stained, no reasonable explanation where she's been all the while."

"Supposing Miss Abell was held against her will, Symmes could have blamed those girls for whatever he liked."

"Who really set match to tinder on the days of the fires? McGlynn was already napped when the first broke out."

I told him. Val nodded, dawning horror painting hollows along his jawline.

"Cruelty is something of a hobby for Symmes," I continued. "In fact, that's how I figured— Valentine, *wait!*"

My brother stalked with a lion's swinging strides out of the crevice, over the drunks, and into the moonlit road. The set of his broad shoulders and the quick snap of his cane on the cobbles informed me that someone was about to be severely injured. I only hoped the victim's surname wouldn't prove to be Wilde.

"Whatever you're doing, don't do it," I requested, catching up to Val after dodging an overfriendly stargazer with tinsel dripping down to her shell-thin shoulders.

"I've been summoned to a meeting by Robert Symmes, and it is a meeting I plan to attend." Val elbowed through a knot of New York University types gleefully waving rattles and taking swigs from a jug.

"But Chief Matsell said Mr. Kane wants to delay until after the elec—"

"I don't give a rat's tender arse what Abraham Kane or Cornelius Villers wants at the moment. And in case you haven't noticed, my Tim, the elections are over. Run along home."

"Like hell I will *run along*—you're the one wanted me here five minutes ago!" I protested as I collided with a barrel-chested merchant. "Come back, I haven't told you—"

"You have told me plenty!"

It was like tracking a tornado's path through a maelstrom. All around us partisans lurched through the thoroughfare sloshing liquor onto one another's sleeves. I was yet drunk myself, which turned the revelry nightmarish—a blur of red lips laughing, pagan voices howling at the moon. I managed a quick burst of speed between a hot-corn vendor and a country preacher shrieking that the world was ending.

I believed him. But I wasn't sure what, if anything, I could do about it.

Because when I finally caught my brother by the coat sleeve, I was too late. He'd reached Robert Symmes's broad granite doorstep, where I'd once paid a call with Chief Matsell. The row house towered above us, a five-story stone-and-brick ode to wealth.

"I told you to—"

"You need me here," I panted. "Trust me." Raising my hand to the doorbell, I hesitated.

"Are you going to ring that or simply stare uselessly at it, as if it's a nip—"

I pressed as hard as I could. Twice.

We waited. I cleared my throat. Twin barbs of guilt and reluctance had caught in it like a fishhook.

"I'm sorry," I said.

Val's eyebrow twitched upward. "For what? You look eight shades of green."

"For not telling you sooner. I've managed to keep it quiet, but Symmes—"

Val meant to listen to me. He angled his head down and attended, which meant he might have been warned upon certain subjects. But just then the butler I'd so aggressively summoned opened the door, and we were shown through the marble-floored hall into the parlor of Alderman Robert Symmes. The butler hovered as Val explained our business, afterward departing on silent feet.

Meanwhile, I surveyed the furnishings, somehow still more repelled by Symmes. I'd seen only his office previously. But his parlor was appalling. I'd been in the dwellings of folk who prefer money to people before—I'd solved crimes for them, retrieved their stolen silver and their secretly pawned jewelry. It wasn't that the landscapes on the expensively papered walls were tastelessly selected— on the contrary, I thought, *I'd love to buy such things for Mercy and arrange them in a sitting room where the sunset lingers even in February.* But hirelings had selected every object, never Robert Symmes, and thus it felt like a space belonging to a score of people or even none. The army of individuals paid to decorate that room skittered along my skin like bedbugs.

"For God's sake, what are we doing here?" I pleaded.

"Planning how to ensure the Ward doesn't collapse after the election, of course."

"But—"

"But nothing, let me handle this," Val ordered, adjusting his cravat in a handy etched mirror.

"Gentlemen," Robert Symmes announced, throwing wide the double doors we'd entered through, "welcome to my home. Well, one of them. It's once again a surprise to see you, Mr. Wilde. I thought I'd called for the captain here."

"You won a bonus prize," I said stonily.

Symmes flipped open his pocket watch, announcing his aversion to my presence. His unbuttoned maroon swallowtail coat probably cost more than my monthly rent, but I could see he'd been as active as Valentine that day. Shirt collar torn at the edge. A button missing from his dove-colored waistcoat. I wished I'd been there to cheer every blithe fist hurtling toward his person.

"So you've arrested Sally Woods at last," Symmes drawled, pouring three neat brandies at his sideboard. "Your reputation for competence is greatly exaggerated, Mr. Wilde, but I must confess that pleased me."

"Actually, I—"

"Stamfish!" Valentine commanded.

At first I couldn't recollect the word's definition. Val's eyes burrowed into mine, urgency radiating like the heat from a bonfire.

Then I remembered, and my breath hitched in my chest.

At the Queen Mab, Symmes had harped on my brother's gutter vocabulary. *I asked you to speak plain English, and I meant it,* he'd commanded pettishly, and Valentine had shoveled slang into his ears.

Robert Symmes is an amateur boxer and a spoiled business mogul who bought his way into the Party's graces and fell out of them when he lied about his holdings. He's like a talking silver dollar—zero qualifications beyond money and brutality.

And Robert Symmes doesn't speak flash.

I'd never used the word *stamfish* previous, but it's a warning—it means that authorities are listening and all dead rabbits present should switch to rarefied levels of flash patter.

A sprinkling of sweat materialized along my hairline. I learned flash by accident, hate the fact I speak it, and I'd no doubt that Valentine could add more words to George Washington Matsell's dictionary than our eccentric chief has ever dreamed possible. Meanwhile, I was being asked to demonstrate a complete mastery of street slang, and in about two seconds.

"Miss Woods," Val said in an undertone as Symmes returned the brandy bottle to its shelf. "She's polishing the iron?"

I drew a complete blank.

You're only ketched over this because Val is watching you, I told myself furiously.

Touching my tongue to my lip, I willed my heart to slow and my gin-soaked brain to speed.

Polishing the iron with his eyebrows. The truncated expression was obscure, but the entire phrase was self-explanatory once it came to me—it describes a prisoner bleakly staring through prison bars. Val was asking if Miss Woods remained at the Tombs.

"I turned gigger-dubber this morning—she's quit the boardinghouse," I replied. Meaning I'd played turnkey and released Miss Woods.

"She's leery, then?"

"So are the duo fly-cops at her ken."

My brother nodded, the grim line of his lips growing a shade less taut after I'd informed him that not only was she wary, but so were the two policemen protecting her home. If Symmes learned we savvied the truth, what witness to his crimes would he want hushed faster than Sally Woods?

"The state of the English language in these parts grows more diseased by the second," Symmes sneered, twitching a hand at the two full glasses on his sideboard without passing them to us. He turned away. "Do *pretend* to be educated men. Come along! Up to the roof, so we can see the sooner who won this farcical contest."

Casting a puzzled look at Val, I went for the brandies and handed him one.

"Fireworks," he answered to my unspoken question. "They're counting the returns at the hotel down the street. When they're through, they'll set off a massive blowout—blue if it's Symmes. Red if it isn't."

"You say *count* the returns, as if that's what's actually happening," I couldn't help but dig as we regained the opulent entryway.

The alderman awaited at the top of his grandly open staircase, leaning on the burnished rail. Somehow glaring and gloating at the same time. He whirled his coattails at us as he continued down the hall to the next set of stairs, and we followed apace.

"What's the lay?" I asked with steel in my tone.

"Nab him on the scent."

So we planned to catch Symmes out through his own errors. "What if I can't patter—"

"You patter flash like a goose floats."

Up, up, up we went. As high as I've ever been in New York, come to think of it. There was yet another staircase next to the garret, and this we climbed as well, reaching a little square room containing only a door. Robert Symmes opened the portal with a key.

We followed the incendiary into the sky.

When I set foot on the roof of the soaring town house, I lost my breath a bit. The stars were out, securing the sky high above us with diamond-tipped pins. A prettily worked fence bordered the rooftop, and along its edges wrought-iron benches had been placed facing outward at intervals. Currently they looked down on the orgiastic election-day carousal below. Shouts and guffaws and the popping of firecrackers reached our ears from every direction save for the back area of the mansion. It was the one unique aspect of a painfully blank dwelling, and I couldn't lie to myself.

It was marvelous.

Spread out around us like a feast, Manhattan glowed. Tiny points of light beginning around Thirtieth Street and stretching all the way to the Battery. I could see the grand stripe of Broadway, the stately progression of Fifth Avenue, could see clear across the river to the dark forests of New Jersey, and when I turned, there were the distant winking beacons along Brooklyn's bustling shoreline. For once the air was clear, and we were too high above the cobbles to see the filth in the cracks. I've never liked New York. It's too hard to survive here. But for about seven seconds that night, I adored it. Its power and its scope.

"Welcome to my humble sanctuary!" Symmes said, spreading his arms wide with his back to us.

That's when it hit me.

The man was a special breed of insane. It takes a certain sort of vanity to grow so very fond of oneself that one cannot imagine losing the game. He'd already thumbed his nose at Tammany in his relentless quest for wealth. He'd already grown so addicted to godlike destruction that he preferred torching his own properties to collecting the rent. But Tammany is dangerous. So is Silkie Marsh, whose stitch in the patchwork I'd begun to guess at in Chief Matsell's office.

So too is Valentine Wilde, who stood watching Symmes ignore him with a sort of placid wrath.

"'Humble' isn't the word I'd have picked," Val suggested.

"No, you'd have picked a coarser one." Symmes gave a small shrug of one shoulder.

"I might have, at that. What were you planning on proposing to me, Symmes?"

I could see the clench of disgust grip Symmes's back despite being twenty feet distant. He pivoted, blue eyes frosted with the sort of juvenile choler I'd only ever before witnessed in kinchin who'd been smacked. Say what you will about Silkie Marsh—she's an adult, and a formidable one.

"You will refer to me as Alderman Symmes until such time as I am no longer your alderman, which is a faraway dream of yours," Symmes snarled.

Valentine smiled, the one that trickles snowmelt down a man's neck. "I'll decline that offer, seeing as I've never knowingly taken orders from a pimp, thanks all the same."

He's speaking flash to me and regular American to Symmes, I realized. *Two conversations simultaneously, half everyday language and half unabashed code.*

Which is what flash was created for, I reminded myself, settling into my role.

"Refrain from crude libel, if you please, Captain. These negative electioneering slogans grow so tedious," Symmes requested with a soft smirk.

"I could ask the same of you, or didn't you tell Drake Todd and Archie Vanderpool I'd not so much as piss on your buildings if they were on fire?"

"Oh, yes, that was me. And the *least* I can do to your reputation, I assure you."

"Do you figure it would be much to your credit if Ward Eight knew you for an incendiary? Or didn't you torch your own slums?"

Jesus Christ, what have you done? I thought, edging closer.

Sighing, Symmes took a sip of brandy, swirling the glass. "Your rather stupid brother has been talking with his new arrest, I take it. What did Sally Woods tell you, Mr. Wilde? That I'm a very bad man and must pay for it? If I'd known how much trouble that wench would cause, I would never have allowed her to tempt me into bed."

Val shot me a look.

"She was his peculiar," I owned, identifying her as the alderman's mistress, "though she savvies now he was naught but a rabbit-sucker—"

"God Almighty, how difficult is it for you cretins? *Speak English!*" Symmes cried.

He smashed the snifter against the rooftop. Fine crystal shattered into a jagged spill of mirrored stars. Symmes surveyed the mess and widened his stance as if actually proud of the act.

Valentine sipped at his own expensive spirits, not the slightest bit put off over this infantile display. "Just what did you do to make Miss Woods suppose you a *very bad man?*" he inquired.

No. Do not *begin this subject now, not when . . .*

"Oh, would you really like to hear about that?" Symmes chuckled. "That tart was an amusement to me at first, I'll grant. She could suck a cock and talk female rights out of the same mouth, which only goes to show that it's the lowest of whores who deign to touch that nonsense in the first place. In any event, she provided me some pleasurable hours and then failed to respect my position. For a while her strike amused me, but the business went too far. That merited a harsh lesson in the way the world works—as you can probably imagine, given your own circumstances."

My brother tilted his head, justly puzzled.

"Valentine, measure me," I whispered desperately, demanding he listen close. "Symmes wanted to see you caved, so instead of lioning you direct, he came out dead set against James Play—"

"I will *not* be trifled with!" The politico was practically screeching by this time, his even features distorted into a rictus of rage. "Stop speaking in ridiculous vulgarisms this *instant*. And you know perfectly well what I'm talking about, Valentine. Sally cared for nothing and no one the way she cared for that loyal little bitch Ellie Abell. So when Sally's defiance knew no limits, after I was publicly *humiliated* in the newspapers, I sent for her lapdog."

Val's razor attention had fixed on me. "What has Jim to do with—"

"Meanwhile, I've so *very many addresses*, one of my secretaries must have made a mistake." Symmes smiled lightly with his lips parted, a merry summer's-day expression. "Somehow Miss Abell ended up at the Queen Mab, which as you know was once used for *quite* another purpose than manufactory concerns. I hear that something absolutely appalling happened to her there. We all missed her sunny disposition so, come the opening whistle Monday morning at New American Textiles."

All was as I'd thought, then. Robert Symmes had delegated a rape as he delegated everything else. An arrow quivered in my heart all the same, and I drew an unconscious half step back. My brother, for his part, had gone quite still. When he's intimidating people, he tends to employ small, repetitive movements—the swirl of his stick or the tapping of his fingers.

Not this time. He was as motionless as his own headstone.

"How long did you instruct McGlynn to keep her?" I questioned.

"Oh, only overnight, I assure you. Longer wouldn't have served my purposes. She imagined she'd escaped him, the fool. That wasn't the clever part, though," Symmes crowed. "The clever part was the week *after* Miss Abell disappeared from the manufactory, when I found her cowering in a low den in Ward Six. I told her I'd heard about the truly appalling miscommunication, that I had immediately fired Ronan McGlynn upon learning his true colors. Of course, I simply requested that Mr. Gage oversee the repairs for American Textiles instead, but what she didn't know couldn't harm her. Then I offered her a generous bonus to pay for expenses while she recovered, as well as work without fear of sacking if she returned, even supposing she was with child. Which she was, though she lost the brat, I believe."

The fact that I'd figured as much didn't go far toward settling the inferno in my chest. On the contrary.

"In any case, I was *unprecedentedly* merciful with the creature, as I thought it would pay to keep her close. She proved duly grateful, naturally. Where else could a fallen woman have found employment besides a brothel? I probably saved her life. Meanwhile, I told Sally that if she ever darkened the threshold of New American or tried to see her friend again, bits of Miss Abell would be delivered to her front door."

"What," Valentine said in a perfect monotone that chilled me to my core, "have you done with James Playfair?"

"He's at my ken," I murmured. "Plenty sanguinary, but snug in kip, I promise—"

"You haven't heard?" Symmes laughed, rocking backward on his heels. "I dipped him in hot pitch and covered him in chicken down. No wonder you haven't dropped out of the race yet, and here I thought I'd simply miscalculated. I'd have chosen your brother here, but I needed *someone* to arrest Sally Woods since you defected. Now she's safe behind bars, of course," he added wistfully. "So you can expect a similar lesson in your future, Mr. Wilde. That is, unless Valentine here withdraws from the race *instantly*. Regardless of the election results."

It would be a mistake to say that the alderman frightened me, as I was already too deeply mortified to register animal terror. But he'd *convinced* me, and entirely.

Symmes wanted a reckoning.

"Do we have him to rights—enough to see him scragged?" Valentine asked me under his breath.

I ached to say yes—that I'd collected plentiful hard evidence, enough to convict Symmes of firestarting and assault, and yes, we could watch the most despicable man of my acquaintance swing from a rope in the midday sun. But the fact is that I'd failed us utterly. Symmes had passed out filthy tasks as if they were court favors—I could make cases against Gage, McGlynn, the incendiary herself. But I couldn't promise the alderman would hang, not when my key witnesses were a set of radical females.

Only that a jail door might shut on him—and might open again far too soon.

"I've close to nix," I whispered, ears burning.

"In that case, mizzle," Val directed me steadily.

He was ordering me away. "I can't—"

My sibling lifted his crescent-stamped chin and raised his voice, switching to plain talk. "Alderman Symmes here doesn't want any more of your cheek while we're about a Tammany matter. This is negotiation of terms. Be scarce before he decides to think up something uglier to do to you than he already has."

Robert Symmes smiled and pulled out his pocket watch.

"Val—"

"I said *mizzle*. We've been roped, and if we're to tap the farmer, I need privacy."

Roped meant that Symmes had us cornered—but *tap the farmer* was flash for *arrest the alderman*. Symmes lit a cigar and swaggered off to survey the nocturnal landscape, waiting for me to vanish. The concept of leaving turned my blood to water. But while I knew that Val would never trust a bargain made with the devil, he could trick Satan himself into a trap, which gave me a pale-edged flicker of hope. The principle tenet of my life since birth has been that my brother is cleverer than I am.

So when he insisted that I go, I headed for the door.

"Careful," I warned.

Val winked at me. "He'll be a lag before sunup. See you downstairs."

It wasn't strictly possible for Symmes to be a convicted felon prior to dawn. But if anyone could do it, I thought as I descended, liquor still singing faint arias in my bloodstream, Valentine could.

The click of the portal to the sky shutting reached my ears, and I hesitated.

It had clearly been my brother who'd closed it. So I walked along the hallway past the garret, trotting down the staircase.

I was nearly back to the parlor before I stopped with my foot on a lushly carpeted step, thinking more clearly than previous. Realizing I'd still a full brandy glass in my hand, I set it on the rug with some care.

You're wrong, I thought as a tidal wave of fear flooded my stomach.

No you aren't.

Then I was stumbling back up the endless flights like a man possessed.

Stairs, corridor. Stairs, corridor. Stairs, corridor.

Stairs, corridor.

Flying past the garret, I sailed up the final steps and threw myself at the entrance to the rooftop.

I plunged into the cooling air. All was quiet save for the squeals of the carousers far below, their drums and whistles and off-key bawdy songs. Far above New York, a few thin clouds draped themselves in languid configurations across the inky sky.

Whirling, I shouted for my brother.

Then I saw him.

Valentine had slumped to the rooftop with his back to the iron railing. Eyes closed, fingers of both hands laced tight over his knees. His tall hat was missing and his togs more disarrayed than previous—his scarlet cravat had been torn open, waistcoat buttons all but ripped away.

Numbly, I walked to join him and peered over the barrier.

The pearlescent starshine was faint, my vision blurred. But I could almost make out a broken heap of clothed bones.

Robert Symmes, lying where my brother had clearly thrown him to his death. And the glint of a wicked black pool creeping slowly outward along the stones.

22

On her chain of life is rust,
On her spirit wing is dust;
She hath let the spoiler in,
She hath mated her with sin,
She hath opened wide the door,
Crime has passed the threshold o'er. . . .

—PUBLISHED IN *THE ADVOCATE OF MORAL*
REFORM AND FAMILY GUARDIAN, 1852

I STARED AT THE LIFELESS BODY of the former alderman, my teeth fixed in a vise and my scar throbbing. Hearing in my imagination—which has always been too dynamic for my liking— the final slender shriek that must have woven itself so neatly into the cries of dead rabbits and Bowery girls, another splash of red in a savage tapestry.

I knelt on the rooftop beside my brother.

Val's bare head was bowed almost to his knees, limbs gently trembling like the shimmer of a match. I gripped his shoulder. But he still wouldn't look at me. He brought his right hand up to press his thumb and forefinger hard into his eyelids.

"It was . . . unfortunate that I flammed you, but . . . I didn't want you to see that."

My throat twisted.

"You're disgusted anyhow, for all you didn't watch, I know."

Shaking my head violently because my mouth wasn't operative proved fruitless, because Val continued, eyes still trapped beneath his fingers, "It's fine, you're far too square to condone what just happened, hate me all you like, but I can generally see our way clear out of a scrape, and this—"

"I'm not disgusted," I managed to say.

He hazarded a glance at me. I've seen Val half dead on so many occasions that they live fossilized in my skeleton, but I'd never before seen him look frightened.

It terrified me.

"Aren't you?" he asked.

"No."

Valentine nodded once, as if he understood me. His eyes fell shut again, limbs relaxing fractionally as his head fell back against the iron railing.

"Fair enough. It isn't as if it's my first murder."

I'm reasonably sure my heart stopped.

Val wasn't talking about a shiv in a sawdust-strewn gambling den. My brother isn't—wasn't—a killer, no matter his thug proclivities. He was talking about Henry and Sarah Wilde, and an accidental fire that put our parents under the ground with the roots and the worms a very long time ago. Back when Greenwich Village was filled with brilliantly green cornfields and sheep pens and the sixteen-year-old Valentine Wilde lit a cigar in the barn.

"Of course it's your first murder!" I cried, shocked out of my stupor.

He flinched, startled. Sliced a disbelieving look at me.

"Buggering hell, Valentine, I—of course it is, are you insane? You just killed a man who should have hanged and never would

378

have, the worst man I've ever met, and we'd *never* have been safe otherwise, not in bloody Oregon would we have been safe from him. You did it for me and for Jim and for all those girls he'd have kept tormenting like a cat with a mouse, all because you knew I'd never have the balls to do the same, and now you're sitting here and comparing that to . . . *Of course* it's your first murder!"

"You've said that three times now," Val answered in an oddly small voice.

"Well, are you *listening*?" I shouted.

He swiped his fingers over his eyes once more. "It's . . . ah, of passable interest to me, since I've always thought you felt the opposite. So yes, actually, I am listen—"

One second I was kneeling paralyzed on a rooftop. The next I was crushing my brother, clinging to wreckage like a shipwreck victim, knowing that no gesture I could make would ever atone for the things we'd done to each other. But the inadequacy of gestures, I realized with his coat between my fingers, was a petty and cowardly reason not to make them in the first place. I thought of what Mercy had said, on the night she'd returned to me.

Just because I don't know where my efforts will bleed into offense doesn't mean I shouldn't try them out first.

So I wrapped my arms around Val's shoulders, which confused the blackguard, because he recoiled and then stilled and then chuckled miserably for a spell. Finally he snaked one hand up and pressed my arm. Hard.

I didn't mind.

He sighed. "What's that list of yours again, your tally of my shortcomings?"

"Narcotics, alcohol, bribery, violence, whoring, gambling, theft, cheating, extortion, sodomy, spying, forgery, lying, and now murder."

"Impressive."

"Your *first* murder. Congratulations. Do you fucking under-stand me? Your *very first*—"

"Jesus, my Tim, give a cove some breathing room, supposing you want to have a conversation with him. Tim. I'm serious. Tim-othy, *get off* before I throw you from here to Ward One."

Settling back against the railing, I draped my wrists over my knees. Shattered glass sparkled at us from a few feet distant, look-ing about as broken and as glinting with a strange, unsettled hope as I felt just then. Valentine straightened one leg to the floor and pulled the other shin closer. Seeming no more prepared to move than I was.

"Turns out you're flasher on the muscle than Robert 'Bone-crusher' Symmes after all," I mentioned.

My brother laughed heartily at that, features twisting. He was right. He shouldn't have found it funny. But then I shouldn't have said it, so I figure we were even.

"I warned Symmes I was coming for him," he said when the pained fit of mirth had passed. "The fight was fair."

"I could read that in your togs. You didn't have to tell me."

"Yes," he said flatly. "I did."

We were quiet for a little.

"We should be running out the door," I mused.

"We should be *strolling* out the door, bidding a hearty fare-thee-well to the butler, mentioning in passing that Symmes is too lushy to see straight." Valentine pulled his cravat the rest of the way off, twining it in his fingers. "You'd make a sam-fool assassin. Timothy?"

His voice had dropped, so I listed my head in his direction. "Yes?"

"Just how bad is the . . . James Playfair business?"

"Bad. I'd have sent for you, but Jim didn't want Symmes to stake undue claim on your attention."

"Jim is a flouncing dunce with naught between his ears but maudlin piano concertos, the coded sentimental meaning of every sodding flower sold at Catharine Market, and inexpressibly stupid conceptions of honor." Val wasn't fooling anyone. His tone was equal parts fierce and fraught.

Oh, so my brother does love him, echoed faintly in my pate.

"You've been looking after him?"

"Yes." I swallowed, recalling it. "I robbed your house."

Valentine turned to me, incredulous. *"You're* the figner who pinched my morphine?"

"You'd have wanted to help." Shaking my head, I muttered, "He wouldn't let you, so I stole your morphine."

"Tim, that's a mighty kindness, I—oh, God, don't tell him." Val's hooded green eyes flew wide in alarm. "Jim can't know that I killed a man in cold blood, he'd never—"

"He would," I objected. "And *you* should tell him. But *I* won't. You . . ."

I trailed off when an explosion dazzled our vision. A little to the right of us, emanating from another rooftop. An expert lightning maker had fashioned a blazing barrage of fireworks, rockets cascading into the atmosphere and crumbling into smoke as they floated to the cobblestones. A thunderous cheer erupted from below.

The starbursts were red.

"You're an alderman," I said, awed. "They'll be looking for you both."

Val drove a distracted hand through his already madly disarranged hair. "I can't say as I feel like making an acceptance speech."

"Be that as it may, congratulations. Again."

Val only chuckled, still wincing. "Did you really *vote* for me?"

"Fifteen times."

"Oh, sod off, you unbearable little prick."

"No, I did."

"My God. That's almost touching. No wonder you're dressed like a color-blind Bowery fop."

Lips parted on a peppery reply, my eyes drifted from the scarlet constellations, and I felt the blood drain from my face. At first I thought I must be mistaken. That there had been a sort of catch in the world's clockwork, a fretful tic in the cogs.

Seconds later my brother saw it. He pushed to his feet with some effort, cursing.

Farther down the block and one street past us shone the merest hint of another warm glow on the wall of a town house in Greene Street, one we couldn't have seen save for our higher vantage point. Above the hint of light, smoke trickled upward in a drowsy spiral.

"That's Silkie Marsh's brothel," Val realized as I joined him at the edge of the roof. "I've not seen her all day. She was at none of the polling stations, none of the sprees. It wasn't like her."

We exchanged a look.

There it is, I thought as the panic swooped down, flew with soft wings through my body like a bird coming home to a familiar roost.

My brother and I sprinted down the first two flights of stairs. When we'd reached the lower two, Val caught me by the jacket with a bitten out "Slow down," and I obeyed. By the time we'd reached the foyer and the butler had entered the hall with a raised eyebrow, I'd tamed my breathing.

"Alderman Symmes managed to get a touch hockey," Val mentioned. "He's reflecting over his concession speech, no need to rush, but asked if in a quarter hour you'd be so kind as to bring brandy in a new snifter. Damned if the first didn't manage to give him the slip."

"Of course. Good night, sir," the servant intoned.

We were walking across the street next, still walking, reining ourselves like the riders of high-strung mounts, sliding through

patches of darkness and skirting half-stupefied clusters of election-
eers. Avoiding yellow pools of gaslight as if they would burn us.

"Accident?" Valentine questioned.

"Not a chance."

"Ideas, then?"

"One. Symmes found out she'd played him cross. Is there anything Madam Marsh loves more than that brothel, after all?"

"How do you mean, she played him cross?"

I pondered the nature of Symmes's designs—the finest ways to
hurt people threaded into an immaculate plot like a square of lace.
And I knew, as I'd only guessed in Matsell's office, that the over-
grown child spreading havoc like a stray dog pissing on Croton
pumps, all his energy channeled toward dominance, had owned
such a passionate love of suffering that a single snipped thread
could have unraveled the whole and left it a silken tangle.

As, indeed, had happened.

Stepping round the corner at last, we ran hell for leather in the
direction of Madam Marsh's establishment. The single building
that, about a week previous, I'd been asked to protect.

"Offering you a girl to abuse that day at the Queen Mab was a
pretty dense mistake, for all your hooliganism," I pointed out. "As
if someone who knew you intimately had planted a notion guaranteed to explode in Symmes's face."

"What are you saying?"

"I'm saying that Symmes has been Silkie Marsh's landlord
since before he was an alderman. And I'm betting that she didn't
like it."

My suspicions weren't based on the fact Silkie Marsh had
known so much about the fire in Pell Street so quickly, or had been
aware of Miss Woods's shackled enmity. Considering her stargazers with their wide ears and her Party insiders with their wide
mouths . . . Madam Marsh might as well have been the bricks in

the walls, the creak of a stair just when a man supposes himself alone. All the Tammany schemers confided their machinations to her, and Symmes might have proved no exception.

No—the blindingly obvious clue was that she'd *known* that Val would announce his candidacy that night at the Knickerbocker 21. When I thought of the transparency with which she'd first approached me at that soiree, not in the least amazed that Val of all people had defied Tammany, I could only curse myself for not having seen the vendetta being played out before my eyes.

It comes as no shock to me that Val rebelled against Robert's leadership, for lack of a more apt term, she'd said.

As if that weren't enough, giving me all the story I could ever ask for, she'd said during the uncanny meeting at Tammany Hall:

It is about nothing whatsoever save for revenge, Mr. Wilde.

She'd been telling me the truth. I just hadn't realized she'd been referring to herself.

"You're thinking she suggested to Symmes I solve his Sally Woods problem and mentioned I'd like something unusual in the way of a bonus. Meaning Silkie didn't want me on the incendiary case so I'd be duped after all," Valentine said, comprehending me.

"She wanted you on the incendiary case so you'd expose her landlord and made sure to drag me into it as well, not knowing I'd been at the Queen Mab by chance. It's almost flattering," I panted.

"It falls a hair short."

We stopped before her brothel, hearts pounding. Val regarded the scene before us with an expert's canny eye. Meanwhile, my usual affliction asserted itself, my stomach shrinking into a stony pebble.

Part of the first floor was ablaze, dainty yellow and sultry crimson flames licking upward like dragons' tongues from the windows of the receiving room I'd visited on too many grim occasions. People darted hither and thither, shouting for an alarm to be raised, though every volunteer fireman in Manhattan that night must have been neck-deep in lush and seeing in triplicate, delaying their arrival.

Which is why it nearly killed me when Valentine continued walking toward the building.

"Don't," I snapped, following.

"I told you, I've not seen Silkie all day." Val paused, looking up. Perfectly calm. I've always loathed him for that, though I know it's wrong. "I can't smell white phosphorus, so that's to the good."

I myself could hardly breathe, for all we were still safe in the road. "But you don't have any of your gear, just a walking stick. You—"

"I'm the senior engineman of the Knickerbocker Twenty-one for good reason, do you savvy that? I'll be fine. Leg it on the double to the station house for help."

"You can't risk yourself for her of all people!"

"This isn't a question of who *she* is," my brother mentioned while shedding his frock coat, as if we were discussing the weather conforming to everyone's best expectations.

"No, it's about you, it always has been about you, and I know exactly who you are, and you will *not* do this to me," I attempted in desperation. "I realize she doesn't glut on torment like the alderman did, she simply doesn't give a damn one way or the other what people suffer, so long as she profits, plays vicious games for amusement. But this isn't bravery, it's *suicide*. Without any tools—"

"Without any tools, waiting until the blaze spreads doesn't fadge, does it? When the Knickerbockers arrive, tell them they owe me a champagne toast."

Val marched up the short flight of stairs, tried the unlocked door, and disappeared in a sickening gush of smoke.

Had the circumstances been different in the smallest degree, I'd never have managed it—knees knocking as they were, sweat beading along my spinal column, more frightened than I've ever been. And I am frightened shamefully, unmanfully often.

Nevertheless.

I retched at the ground. Shook my palsied hands out and breathed into them a few times. Dropped my coat on the ground next to Val's. Closed my eyes and counted to three.

Then I walked inside a burning building.

It was every bit of the nightmare I'd imagined, unfortunately.

The familiar front hall with the portrait of Silkie Marsh was empty save for a suffocating screen of charred air. I entered the front saloon, where the smell of a hundred gaslights being ignited assaulted my nostrils. Flames skittered along the walls like devilish insects, reflected a thousandfold in the Venetian mirrors. I hadn't made it two feet into that hell before my brother shoved me out again.

"Are you completely brainless?" Val demanded in a ragged voice. "Get the living fuck out of here, Timothy."

"Either you come with me or I come with you."

Pressing his lips together, Val strode for the staircase. The icy sweat down my neck was now a sweltering stream, rank fear resting at the back of my throat. When my brother knelt to examine the carpeting, he swiveled toward me with a pensive expression.

"I thought it was just the front room. But this entire place is soaked with lamp oil."

I ignored the cowardly throb this caused in my chest, ignored the ash settling into our skins as the temperature skyrocketed and the hideous crackling behind us grew louder.

Val rose to his full height. "Walk out that door," he ordered, pointing. "Now."

Gripping the staircase newel as a wave of dizziness threatened, I shook my head.

Val muttered a lavish string of curses and cut past me. Our boots squelched in the fuel-doused carpeting as we hurried up the stairs. The lights in the seemingly empty house were all weirdly ablaze, but despite that I could scarce see five steps ahead. Already nauseous, I catalogued new sensations—a lance like a spitted fowl through the back of my pate, a gong pulsing behind my corneas.

When we reached the hall, we found a chair propped against the knob of a door. Val threw it aside as if it were made of matchsticks and tried the handle. Locked. Kneeling, he deftly pulled his knife from his pocket.

"That won't work." I coughed.

"Why not?"

"It's the wrong size. Bird picked one of these doors with a hairpin."

I watched Val approach a portrait on the wall and smash it with the head of his stick. He wrapped his untied cravat a few times around the thumb and forefinger of his right hand, picking up a slender shard of glass.

"Breathe through your shirtsleeve. It'll help."

Shoving my nose into my elbow, I complied.

Mere seconds passed, moments thin and destructible as paper, before Val had the door open. All the while I saw my friend Bird before my stinging eyes as she'd been at age ten—terrified, setting lies adrift as if they were toy ships and watching them founder, freckles blooming all over her square face.

I vowed to myself, *If you live to see her again, you will make her understand that no one is good enough to marry her, and not the other way round.*

The comfortable bedchamber Val revealed was likewise suffused with light. Silkie Marsh sprawled on the corner of a disarranged mattress, dressed in a rich black gown, gagged with a strip of linen, both wrists bound behind her to the bedpost. Her eyes gleamed through the haze like a feral cat's, golden hair wrecked with the force she'd been using to attempt escape.

"Hello, darling old shoe," Val said dryly, throwing the splinter of glass away and whipping out his pocketknife again.

A rolling, roiling sound like the tide of the ocean rumbled beneath us as the ambient temperature began to sear the inside of my nose. Valentine cut her bonds and unloosed the gag from her delicate mouth, which released a single spat invective. I briefly noted blood crusting under her fingernails, bruises along her bare forearms.

"My heroes," she said, equally mocking as grateful.

"Anyone else in the building?" I wheezed.

"No. I was alone."

I strode back the way we'd come, scouting our escape. When I reached the railing, my heart turned over.

A golden midsummer field of flame had sprouted between the parlor and the entrance, continuing its rapid growth along the fuel-saturated carpeting. Whirling, I returned to the bedroom.

"Not that way?" Val questioned, eyebrow raised.

It was growing difficult to speak. My mind felt corroded, blasted with the poisonous heat. "That window, there. Bird tied stockings together and—"

"Do you really think I didn't have bars installed thereafter, Mr. Wilde?" Madam Marsh hissed, reeling past me. The firelight set all her edges ablaze at the room's threshold, turned her into the silhouette of a beautiful devil.

We dogged her to another staircase. Another rooftop, another battle, only this house was but three stories tall and disintegrating like so much tissue, reports like gunshots sounding in our wake as the downstairs dissolved.

"What happened?" Valentine demanded.

"We were all engaged for the evening's festivities at Tammany, and I gave the servants a holiday. When our escorts arrived, they sent my sisters along in the carriages while another begged a private word. After lashing me down, he appears to have set my home on fire."

The three of us crested the staircase, chests heaving as if we'd run a mile in the desert. It felt like I'd hot sand in my mouth, sand in my throat. The physical flames hadn't yet crawled voraciously into the upper floors, but they would.

Very soon.

"Valentine, find something to serve as a rope and meet us on the roof," Silkie Marsh commanded, waving a white hand down the hall at two blank doors. "Mr. Wilde, you're with me."

As if I wasn't already trapped in a loathsome enough hallucination, we now appeared to be taking orders from our mortal enemy, for Val turned on his heel whilst I pursued her in the opposite direction.

Silkie Marsh threw open a plain wooden door to reveal an attic, steps in its corner leading to a hatch that fed onto the rooftop. We were surrounded by boxes. Stray trunks. Cloth-draped chairs meant to be mended but ultimately forgotten. The usual detritus accumulated by dozens of people living in a single residence over a number of years. Crossing the room, Madam Marsh snatched a piece of burlap off a massive chandelier. Its crystals were missing, its brass unpolished. She'd obviously replaced it with a finer one, and here the original lay.

"I can lift it, but I can't carry it very far," she breathed, nodding at the trap leading to the roof. "You can, though."

Seeing her mind, I dove for the thing. It was indeed light enough for her to hoist with a single effort, but far too unwieldy for her to haul up to the roof. My body was so weakened by then, skin dripping like a midsummer glass of iced tea, that I borrowed a trick from my brother and tore my cravat off, wrapping it around my damp palm before clutching a branch of the fixture.

"Get the hatch open," I husked, nearly suffocating.

When she'd thrown it wide and scrabbled topside, I breathed a fraction easier. Knowing that hesitation meant none of our ashen corpses would even require headstones, I set one hand to the stair rail and dragged the metal beast up after me.

My fingers were numb when I'd finished the task, my breath coming in parched gasps. But I managed it, depositing the chandelier at the roof's edge next to the little decorative fence that all the town houses in this row featured.

Then I more or less collapsed on the roof of Silkie Marsh's goosing-ken, sucking down air, as she sat with her fist tightly clenched before her mouth. Both of us staring at the roof opposite. Both awaiting Valentine, on whom our lives depended.

"Did Symmes confide in you, or did you tumble to his incendiary lay yourself?"

Not looking at me, Silkie Marsh wiped her fingers over her lips. "Robert may have suggested to me that Miss Woods meant to turn firestarter, and he may have shown me notes to that effect. I may have found the notion patently ridiculous after he'd boasted he was expanding his textile empire threefold, and it's possible I reported my suspicions to Mr. Kane and Mr. Villers."

"Symmes discovered you'd peached to his betters?"

"I can only assume so," she answered, waving a hand at the floors below us.

"How long have you been plotting his downfall?"

Silkie Marsh didn't even mull it over. The tale was perched at the end of her tongue. "I was short on rent about a year after moving in, and he found a convenient way for me to repay him. In my new parlor. In front of all my sisters. After I'd said no. As a—"

She stopped, turning to face me. Eyes blown black, grime coating her skin and hair as it did mine. Furious beyond any raw emotion I'd ever seen her produce.

"I hate you," she said clearly. "Your kindly, sad, *interested* face, your knowing irony, your virtue, your . . . your everything. I *detest* you, Timothy Wilde."

"I detest myself plenty often," I admitted. "And I loathe you entirely."

She inclined her head, as this was no surprise.

"Val is your new alderman. And Symmes is dead, by the way."

Silkie Marsh's lovely lips parted. For a moment she sat there quite still. Then delicately, she tipped her chin back and laughed at the stars.

"Mr. Wilde, how *marvelous*. I'd hardly dared hope for so much."

The sound of Valentine ascending the narrow steps reached us. When his head emerged, he heaved great breaths of night sky as he escaped the cauldron into the witching hour. He'd taken a set of maids' blouses and tied them wrist to wrist as he went. Seeing the chandelier, he smiled regretfully and pulled himself the rest of the way up by his forearms.

"Val?"

"I'm fine. Pass me the frilly grappling hook."

Silkie Marsh and I shoved it to him. He tied one end of the makeshift rope to a brass arm. As the roof itself began to simmer beneath our skin, my brother eyed the structure fifteen feet distant to the east of us and hoisted our last chance in his fists.

The triumphant smash of broken prisms sounded as the fixture hooked itself to the opposite rooftop's railing. Valentine—his face the color of moss, bags beneath his eyes eroded into craters—braced himself against the short iron barrier with his foot and began to tie the sleeve end to a sturdy finial.

"You first, Silkie," he said.

Eyes streaming, I watched her as she traversed the thin line between the houses. Hand over hand with her small ankles fixed tight around the improvised rope. She faced a perilous moment at the opposite edge as she left the tether, but she clawed her way up and over the rail by hooking one arm around the chandelier.

Then Silkie Marsh was facing us, the fixture in her hands, eyes glowing like fireflies in the darkness.

She considered untying the rope and being done with us. Throwing the chandelier into the alley for good measure. I could see it. My tongue felt swollen and clumsy in my mouth, my lips parting on a *no*.

For several seconds she stared, panting.

You always knew the pair of you were going to die in a fire, I thought.

Then she steadied the thing, pushing it into the rail, and shouted, "What are you waiting for?"

"You're next," Val ordered, exhaling hard.

Arguing would have been futile. I leaned over, swung myself around, slung my legs over the tiny bridge, and set to.

It was terrifying. A lifeline made of shirts, a drop to death or crippledom beneath me, Robert Symmes drowning in a lake of his own blood fresh in my mind. But I was heading *away from the fire*, and anyway I couldn't afford to think about it. Not with my fingers nearly slipping on the sleeves, lungs straining for air.

Silkie Marsh doesn't weigh nearly as much as you, I thought about halfway across, when my ear caught the first hint of a creak emanating from one of Val's knots.

I froze, numb with dread, and took a long breath. Swaying a

little, the starscape dizzyingly far above me. The ground seemingly miles below.

Tilting my head backward, I glimpsed Silkie Marsh upside down about eight feet distant. Worlds away.

She raised a mocking eyebrow.

I kept going.

The slickness of my palms was worse than physical torture, the cloth's groans like shrieks in my ears. But I managed it. When I reached the other side, I faced the same struggle as Silkie Marsh had in wrangling myself onto the roof. Save that a slender, ashen hand helped to pull me up.

"I'm pretty sure I dreamed this entire day," I gasped, landing on my back. I saw the first arcs of Croton water spraying, heard the yells of the firedogs.

"Whatever else you think of me, surely you'll own I comprehend the concept of favors for favors," she retorted. Gradually, her expression shifted to one resembling triumph. "And you . . . reported my landlord's demise, shall we say? Come on, Valentine, *move*."

Val's walking stick landed to our left with a thunk. He eyed the rooftop, rubbed his hands together.

Valentine weighs over two hundred pounds if he weighs an ounce, I thought.

Shifting on limbs reluctant to do my bidding, I flung my arms at the chandelier. Pressing it, as Silkie Marsh was, into the solid iron. It wouldn't do any good, wouldn't stop a knot from slipping or a hand from losing its grip. It was a prayer, nothing more.

But it was all I could do.

My mouth, under the charred taste, turned sour with dread.

Valentine caught at the rope and twisted round, ready to pass hand over hand as we had done. When his feet left the opposite rooftop, the thin line sagged mightily, and I turned for several moments into stone.

But it held, and then Val swung an arm up, deftly pulling himself across.

Watching my brother perform the high-wire act I'd accomplished seconds previous was one of the worst sights I've ever been subjected to, but it proved thankfully brief. The sheer length of his limbs more than made up in speed what the impromptu rope lacked in tensile strength. And when he'd reached the edge, Madam Marsh and I leaned over and dragged his massive bulk up to safety.

Slowly, I lifted my burning eyes.

The brothel was still standing, but its interior was a furnace. I could see ceilings falling in operatic descents, rapturous coils of smoke ascending.

We lay there, the three of us. Watching in awe.

"I have to help them keep it from spreading," Val coughed, rolling to his feet.

He offered Silkie Marsh a hand, but she didn't take it. She slowly rose, brushing at her soot-drenched skirts. Staring at her life going up in flames.

"Why should Symmes have switched accelerants?" I asked, thinking more clearly now that cool wind ruffled my hair.

"I don't like it either." Val broke the padlock on the door to the attic with a savage tap of his cane. "Who lives here, Silkie?"

"A family of Presbyterians who are less than endeared to me," she answered with satisfaction. "Let us allow them to bless God by assisting the least of these."

The Presbyterians—all wearing homespun nightshirts and thick dressing gowns and knitted caps in their downstairs hall, arguing over whether to flee—were startled to see three cindery strangers walking down their stairs and out their front door. But we didn't pause for conversation, so I'll never know what they thought about it.

When we'd reached the road, however, a fresh shock awaited.

I'd supposed my stockpile of anxiety drained entirely by then. But a thrill of paralyzing alarm shot through me nonetheless, and my brother and his former mistress froze at the same instant.

Across the roadway at a safe distance, a pair of men stood placidly smoking cigars. Adding tender little curlicues to the reek of incineration.

Mr. Abraham Kane and Mr. Cornelius Villers.

23

Think it no hardship, ladies, that public opinion excuses
you from appearing on the arena of political conflict, or
from saying at the ballot box who shall be our rulers,
or from standing forth as God's commissioned ambassadors
to treat with a dying world. . . . It belongs to you to form
the characters of those who are to occupy these high places.

—ADDRESS DELIVERED BY WILLIAM B.
SPRAGUE AT THE OPENING OF THE BROOKLYN
FEMALE ACADEMY, MAY 4, 1846

THE QUEEREST THING about seeing Abraham Kane and Cornelius Villers standing on that sidewalk, mulling over the fire that
raged before them, wasn't that they didn't belong there.

They did belong there. Clearly.

But it's not the usual way of the world for the puppet masters to
emerge from behind the curtain. Addressing their audience with
subtle smiles and practiced bows.

"Miss Marsh! So you've made it out after all!" Kane exclaimed.

Pasting a look of perfect neutrality on her face, Madam Marsh
approached them. My brother hung back as if he'd other business.
Which was true enough, but neither did he want to confront the
unquestioned dictators of his Party just then. He raised a confident

hand in greeting toward Villers and Kane whilst muttering, "You talk to the Democrats, I douse the stir."

"But—"

"You just walked into a house fire. I'm pretty sanguine you can handle Tammany Hall."

Valentine strode toward his engine company. Red-shirted men swarmed about the doomed building, quelling the rogue sparks that threatened to expand the blaze. They'd already drenched the surrounding structures, and the brothel now better resembled a monstrous manufactory engine vomiting smoke and steam.

"You're enjoying yourselves, gentlemen," Silkie Marsh observed with clinical dignity to the Party leaders. "Would you care to tell me why?"

Kane smiled—not maliciously. But with a certain satisfaction. He was clad in hearty election-day finery, broad shoulders squared under a blue velvet swallowtail. His partner was dressed, as ever, in a black fitted tailcoat that conveyed the impression he'd just either murdered or buried someone. I'd not seen Cornelius Villers in months, had been overjoyed to miss the man, who stared down his clifflike nose at Silkie Marsh, pince-nez obscuring ruthless eyes. The lenses glinted with cunning and reflected firelight. Neither man paid me the smallest particle of attention.

"It's not personal, Miss Marsh," Kane began.

"Surely it cannot be termed *impersonal* precisely," Villers corrected his counterpart, tapping the ash from his cigar with a long finger.

"Oh, come, Cornelius, it was always a possibility that one of our more daring fire laddies would intervene, and surely we've made our point."

"Robert Symmes didn't set this fire," I said as understanding brushed its pointed nails along my neck. "He'd been using white phosphorus, probably had a tidy stock of it. Your emissary used the first thing he could lay hands on, which turned out to be lamp oil."

"But *why?*" Madam Marsh thrust the query at the politicians as if wielding an ice pick, cheeks coloring beneath the grey residue coating us. "Dear God above, what can you possibly mean by it? I'm a major source of campaign funding, of information, I'm a charming hostess, I'm—"

"Dear me, Miss Marsh, this isn't about what you are at all. Please put the thought from your head!" Kane exclaimed.

"Quite so." Villers angled his hooked nose at her. "You've approached the problem from the wrong end. This is about what you are *not*, you see."

"And what *aren't* I?" she cried, stunned.

"You aren't Tammany Hall."

Swaying on small feet, Silkie Marsh regarded the men who had ordered her tied to a bed and her house set aflame. Her eyes were wide with shock, the blue circles within the hazel of her irises shrunk to nothing save a band of hammered steel in the moonlight.

Villers ground out his cigar on the brick wall behind him. "Robert informed us of your . . . assistance over the regrettable Sally Woods situation in which he found himself entangled. He *thought* you most helpful. But we were well aware that you had been materially *unhelpful*, and Robert was simply too impressed by his own schemes to realize the fact. Now we no longer care for Robert Symmes or his rather elaborate insurance concerns."

"God no," Kane echoed with a rueful sigh. "Not when he deliberately failed to include us in them. Did he honestly suppose we'd not discover his intentions?"

"I cannot imagine, but wherever he is, I look forward to his concession."

"And please do convey our well-wishes to *Alderman* Wilde," Kane said to me with a friendly wink.

"But we asked ourselves—or I asked myself, owning the more suspicious nature—whether it was quite safe to include you so deeply in our designs when you could betray us at a moment's notice, Miss Marsh," Villers declaimed. "Since you so blithely sabotaged our friend Symmes . . ."

"Not that we blame you for that exactly," Kane amended.

"I asked myself whether you were capable of drilling further holes in the ship of state. And reached the conclusion . . ."

"The *regrettable* conclusion that you were not to be trusted entirely, since you can hardly argue with the fact that you are *not* Tammany Hall."

"*Know. Your. Place,*" Villers snarled savagely, snatching the pince-nez off his nose and tapping them thrice against Silkie Marsh's slim shoulder.

The grotesque two-headed god of New York fell silent, eyes drifting back to the now-hollow house. Abraham Kane thrust his hands into his pockets with an air of finality. Cornelius Villers returned his pince-nez to his Roman nose, a calculated smile sharpening the edges of his thin lips.

"You meant to murder me," Silkie Marsh said numbly.

"Well, there was always the happy chance that wouldn't happen," Kane concluded, "and relations between us can continue cordially now we understand each other. Are we through, Cornelius?"

"I am content." Sweeping his tall hat off, Villers made an abbreviated bow to the two of us, a cruel scythe of reflected light gleaming from his hairless pate.

"Mr. Valentine Wilde's presence is much desired over at the hotel, but he can hardly be accused of shirking his duty under the circumstances." Tapping the side of his scarred nose twice, Kane gave me a nod as he followed his departing partner in crime. "Tell him he's expected, would you?"

Silkie Marsh and I stared after the Party leaders as they exited.

The hubbub from the firedogs quieted, and the cinders made themselves known, powdery and vile, prickling in the damp pores of our skin. Breathing yet presented a challenge, so I tossed my ruined collar away and unbuttoned my shirtfront a little. Uncaring of appearances, still sans frock coat, taking the air with a ruthless murderess after having voted fifteen times while dressed as a Bowery monkey that afternoon.

There seemed nowhere lower to sink.

"Are you all right?" I asked.

Silkie Marsh contemplated the remains of her brothel as if identifying a loved one at the morgue. A smear of charcoal marred the architectural line of her cheek. I found myself madly wanting to pass her my handkerchief. The world had reversed itself, a dizzying inversion—stars sparkling at our feet in the clean water runoff and filthy earthen ashes strewn across the sky.

"I'll live," she said quietly. "I've accounts at five of the best banks in Manhattan, my sisters and servants were spared, and I've a new and entirely preferable alderman. That isn't the question you ought to be asking."

"What is, then?"

"Is this over, Mr. Wilde?"

She indicated the two of us with a graceful flick of her fingers—dancers who'd been locked in a bloody waltz for nigh three years.

"Could it be?"

Silkie Marsh smiled. A silken-soft curl of her lips as if a pink ribbon had been tugged.

I'd never forgive her, I knew. For what she'd done to Bird, to me, to my brother, to my friends. But the events of that night had exposed the workings of my heart for dissection—I couldn't throw a man from the roof of a building, nor could I tie a soulless woman to a bedpost and set her aflame.

Here was an alternative. One I might not be offered again.

"I do want something of you," I informed her.

"Oh?" The smile disappeared, replaced by a businesslike expression of interest. "What might that be, then?"

"Never," I said clearly, "bring Bird Daly into this. Ever again. You said favors for favors. That's what I want."

Silkie Marsh pursed her lips in thought. Gave a little laugh, tucked a fallen lock of hair back into her irreparably damaged coiffure with one of its remaining pins, and nodded a single time.

"Then she is yours, to do with what you will. Good night, Mr. Wilde." Madam Marsh retreated, smoothing her skirts. "We shall see more of each other, no doubt. As to the nature of those encounters . . . well, that depends upon our own best pleasures, does it not?"

She walked away with her disarranged crown of golden hair held high. I'd no notion whether we'd ever stop trying to destroy each other. Nor if I wanted to or not. But she was the reason my brother and I were still alive, and whether that counted for a week or a year or a single night . . . it still counted.

I watched Silkie Marsh depart Greene Street, my lungs burning in my chest.

When I approached the remains of the fire, Val's cronies were already clearing debris. One wall had crumbled, spilling bricks into the adjacent corridor. My brother's pal Jack whistled as he wielded a great shovel, more Knickerbockers shooting streams at the quelled beast as if ensuring the fire wasn't merely sleeping.

"Was that what I think it was?" Valentine jumped down from one of his engine's rails.

"If you think it was a lesson, yes. Their hired thug is off nursing his wounds somewhere, if Madam Marsh's fingernails are any indication. And of course we could never trace it back to them."

Val blew out a vexed puff of air. "The lamp oil wasn't the only hint. My rabbits tell me they were tipped just after we entered the place. For better reasons than the Neptune Nines were posted, it seems clear, though I can't say as I'll sleep any snugger for that."

I nodded. The tipped-off Ward Two fire company had served conspiracy, not altruism, and Kane and Villers had meant their example to be an isolated one. Still. When I considered Tammany's capacity for wanton destruction, a shiver ran through me.

"Can we do anything about it?"

"Other than keep our mouths shut and bide our time? Not if we want to live aboveground."

"In that case, Val, you're wanted at the hotel."

Wincing, my brother drew a flask from his pocket and took a sharp pull, returning it to his waistcoat.

Had it been liquor, he'd have offered me some. Thus it was morphine or laudanum. He doesn't usually indulge when he's about Party business. But then he hasn't usually just murdered anyone.

Suddenly I couldn't bear it anymore. The not-knowing.

"Did you start because of me?"

"What?"

"Poisoning yourself." Another person was talking. One about a hundred years older than me, with a voice like the creak of a moldering coffin lid. "Did you start poisoning yourself because I was a merciless bastard to you for seventeen entire years after you—"

"No," Val answered, eyes wide.

"If it was because of me—"

"I said *no*, it wasn't."

"How do I know you're not lying?"

"You don't," he said fiercely. "You'll never know, because I'd go to my grave before telling you a thing like that. It's true all the same."

Knuckles bruising my lips, I nodded. It had been a fair answer. It had hurt nevertheless.

I'd long supposed the only fatal flames to be the physical variety—the sort that destroyed my parents, ruined my livelihood, snuffed the life from the stargazers trapped in the Pell Street tinderbox. But there are plentiful killing phrases, I was learning, words that sear a man and leave snakelike scars, I'd been an idiot not to realize it, and whether we're perishing instantly or by inches, the results are the same. The worst death New Yorkers have ever managed to come up with is slow burning, a fate reserved for rebellious black rioters and traitors to the natural order. And I have said *I hate you* to Valentine more times in my life than I have said to him *Good morning.*

How my brother has managed to survive me for so long, God only knows.

Val took half a step away. "Listen, my Tim, I'm about to make the shortest, most inspiring speech in the history of the National Democratic Party, and then . . . I'll visit your ken, if you don't mind."

"Let's be off, then."

"Aren't you for the Tombs?" A line formed above Val's nose.

"Whyever would I go there?"

The line vanished, replaced by an intrigued twitch in the bag under Val's left eye. "The lads just told me—police arrested Symmes's firestarter when she broke into the Queen Mab tonight. In the act of setting a fuse. They want you to question her."

The world swayed a bit. My bones were turning cottony, a collection of threads ill suited to keep me upright.

"Steady on," Val said, frowning.

That was indecently alarming, as generally he insults me into action. "What's her name?"

"Nell Grimshaw." He paused, puzzled. "You told me all about

her. Hell's bells, you even sketched the woman for Matsell. You didn't diary her moniker?"

I shrugged as I turned toward Ward Six. "I never learned it."

The smoke coated my skin too thickly for me to catch its scent any longer. I could feel it nevertheless as I strode toward the prison. Grime in my teeth, grit caking my eyelashes. I longed for a bath. A river, a tide pool, an ocean. Something big enough to wipe me clean of torturing my only kin for almost two decades. A way to cleanse my nostrils and ears of caked ash and of Val's saying regarding our parents' demise, *It's of passable interest to me, since I've always thought you felt the opposite. . . .*

Ruthlessly, I shook my pate. Dwelling on the night's other trials wasn't going to help me.

Not when I was headed for a rendezvous with the Witch.

The gathering in my office at four in the morning, held during the uniquely metropolitan time that's neither night nor day but a hybrid nothing, a lightless in-between period both ancient and capricious, consisted of the following:

Me, behind my desk. Mr. Piest, nursing one of the three coffees he'd bought after being similarly summoned, seated to my left.

And one Nell Grimshaw, firestarter, alleged Witch, facing us from the room's only other chair.

Her steely hair had escaped its kerchief in her struggle to escape the star police. I saw scratches at her neck, and her lip bore a crimson split. But she didn't seem anxious to bolt. They hadn't restrained her before my arrival—she sat with her hands folded, eyes branding my soiled skin. If I hadn't known better, I could almost have credited her with supernatural powers. Dressed in rags, with a ramrod posture, smiling as though she'd invented the four elements, Nell Grimshaw looked like she could have simply pointed her forefinger to torch stone as if it were paper.

"Mr. Wilde, forgive me, but are you certain you needn't seek medical—"

"I'm only tired," I assured Mr. Piest, though despite the coffee I felt moorless as a cigar butt discarded into the Hudson. "Do you have the preliminary report?"

He nodded, pressing his chin into the small folds of his neck. My friend passed the document to me.

"Mrs. Grimshaw—"

"Don't try to be *gentlemanly*. I can't bear that sort of swill," Nell Grimshaw sneered. "I was never married."

"Miss Grimshaw," I corrected myself. "So you were entering the Queen Mab clearinghouse when the copper-star guards arrested you. I want to know—"

"Did you truly draw a picture of me and give it to the pigs?"

Her face had changed. Luminous, riveting, almost . . . almost the person she really was. Not due to the avidity, mind. I'd known her for a force of nature already. This was my flattery of her prowess taking effect. Miss Grimshaw's lined blue eyes shone, and her queenly jaw thrust forward in her eagerness to learn just how famous—or infamous—I'd rendered her.

"I did. I'll find it and give it to you if you answer a few questions. We have you dead to rights anyhow, for trying to burn down the Queen Mab."

She shrugged, smoothing her thunderstorm hair back ineffectively.

"Miss Grimshaw, if you could please recount this evening's events in your own words, we would mark you most attentively," Mr. Piest requested.

"What have *you* to do with it?"

Piest shifted his weight forward, tugging his shabby coat sleeves down. There was a splash of beer from our earlier exploits staining one paper cuff. "Mr. Wilde is my colleague."

Miss Grimshaw nodded. She seemed queerly pleased by her surroundings. The incongruity of her enjoyment struck me as another quicksilver glimmer of lunacy.

"How did you find me out?" She turned her attention back to me, blue eyes keenly focused. "I was never seen setting them."

I saw no harm in answering. "For one thing, you aren't a seamstress. You told me that after being fired as a domestic, you worked stitching fashionable smallclothes. Then doing embroidery, and finally as an outworker. I'd have maybe trusted your obsession with proper lighting as the reason your eyes are still so finely tuned, but that wasn't it at all, was it?"

She snorted. "Plenty of seamstresses are smart enough to know they can't win in the long run by gambling away their eyes at dusk."

"True. But they're much better at it than you are and can thus afford such niceties as light. Your work hemming something as simple as a kerchief is appalling."

I remembered the jagged way her needle had pierced the cheap cloth. As if stabbing someone, every seam drunkenly listing along the scrap's edge. Aggressively incompetent. I'd been stupid enough to think the likes of Simeon Gage intimidated by her when he could never have overlooked blatant ineptitude.

"What were you in actuality?" I asked, intrigued.

A proud smile resembling a snarl appeared on her once-handsome face. "A girl from a family that lost all their money. And then, as I told you, a maid. But for decades after my child's father sacked me, I'd no need of employment. I was one man's kept mistress, then another's. Even toured once, in a company of dancers, from here to Charleston. Bluffed my way into a nannying position when I couldn't dance any longer, if you can believe so much. That held for another twelve years. When their brat grew up, I was tossed out with a pittance. When they left for Oregon to seek fame and fortune, even the pittance vanished."

"You're too canny not to have saved funds. Some calamity befell you," I surmised.

"Calamity is common. What do the details matter?"

"Curiosity. I've lost everything myself once or twice."

"Influenza." Miss Grimshaw shook her head. "Bloody *vultures*, the lot of you."

"So you'd no money left, no intimate friends, and ended up in the dire position of stitching outwork at the Old Brewery. But you were terrible at it, not being used to the task nor the hours. Is that when you made the candles? They were remarkably creative, by the way."

"Any emigrant bitch fresh off the estate could hem a straight line, and you're right enough, they were quicker at it than I was." Nell Grimshaw adjusted the assortment of rank threads that served as her shawl. "I needed extra time. I bought cracked cups with the last of my chink and filled them with the rotten fat a cookshop had discarded. Then it was just a matter of finding some scrap twine."

"You used them for fuses, didn't you, when you set the buildings alight? Put them near some white phosphorus with a fat-soaked bit of string trailing, pretended to take the air, and walked clean away."

Her eyes gleamed at me wickedly. "You're a shade less brainless than I'd figured, Mr. Wilde."

"I can count, that's all. You'd seven, a Pell Street witness was sure of it. After the first two fires, when I saw you at the Old Brewery, you'd only five. However did you conscience it? Two of your Pell Street neighbors died in agony."

I shouldn't have marveled—the Witch had reveled in her own

malice. Miss Duffy had offered to pay for the stolen light the next day and received an open threat in return, though I'd not supposed Miss Grimshaw's answer serious when first I'd heard of it.

By tomorrow, she'd said, *I'll have every last one of you roasting over a spit.*

"As questions of conscience are unlikely to advance our discussion, let me interject, if you please." Mr. Piest raised his palms to our prisoner, the picture of reasonableness. "Your being reduced to the extremities of poverty I can both comprehend and regret, Miss Grimshaw, but as for the firestarting itself, I confess myself at a loss. How came such an extraordinary step about? How did you not simply starve, as so many others have done?"

Passing my tongue over ashen lips, I glanced at my fellow copper star. "If she'd neither kith nor kin in New York, she could easily have died so. As it happened, she'd given up a son on a church doorstep long ago."

"Oh, Mr. Wilde," Piest gasped, one knee jerking akimbo. "Mr. Wilde, I must say, even beyond the inferences to do with her profession, that is *masterful.* I've never had reason to defame the eyes in my own head, mind, but your skills as a portrait artist simply *must* have been at work here."

"What are you yammering about?" the woman I'd known as the Witch snapped at the Dutchman.

"You looked familiar to me when I first met you, madam," he answered gravely. "I could not place the reason. Mr. Wilde proved the superior observer."

He was wrong. I'd done no better than Piest upon initially meeting her at the Old Brewery. I'd thought her—beneath the age and the spite at least—an archetype of a classical beauty or the echo of a belle's silhouette framed upon some unremembered wall.

"Had you always tracked your son's progress?" I questioned. "Or were Robert Symmes's successes previously unknown to you?"

If I'd expected a flinch or a quaver, I'd have been destined for disappointment. Instead she laughed again, her late child visible in flashing blue eyes and a mocking lift of the jaw. Nell Grimshaw hadn't raised her illegitimate offspring, granted. He'd been his mother's son all the same. I couldn't deny Miss Grimshaw's dark history—but recalling her expert marksmanship when taunting Mercy, neither could I help but recognize that the artist painted with the family brush.

Was I a pretentious, guilt-ridden, coddled smear of dung like you? she'd asked. And Mercy, who'd been reviled by countless unfortunates in her life, had taken the poison straight to heart.

"I used to watch him through the church windows, even dress myself in rags so as to sit in the beggars' pew and catch closer glimpses," she breathed with a mother's blind pride. "My bright boy. He was all golden curls as a lad, same as I was. There was none of his faithless father in him. He led the other kinchin about the yard like a general—could outtalk them, outfight them."

I could well picture Robert Symmes terrorizing his schoolyard population with petty vengeances. "He was adopted, I take it?"

She nodded dreamily. "The Symmes family had railroad money—if they were to take in a foundling, they wanted the *best*. They saw him educated, placed among the right people. I heard rumors of all this later, naturally—when I'd returned from touring and was changing dirty nappies for someone else's colicky parasite. But my Robert was never lost to me for long. He was too much in the public eye."

"Had you not lost your position, would you have remained a secret to your son for good, Miss Grimshaw?" A gentle crinkle edged Mr. Piest's pale eye. "That seems very hard to me, for a mother as passionate as yourself."

"When I listen to men, I wonder how the species survived this long," she jeered. "Of *course* I didn't seek him out, you pathetic creature. A respectable widowed nurse they thought me, after I'd bought enough false references. Neither an unwed mother nor a swell's ladybird nor a dance-hall kate. I'd three meals a day and a bed with no one else in it—you think I'd have risked all that on the slim chance an alderman would believe I was his *mother*?"

"But after losing your savings, you'd no choice except to find him." I clasped my hands on my desk. "You wrote to him?"

She shook her head. "He could have been blackmailed, exposed as a bastard. No one knew his origins save myself, the pastor, and the Symmes family. I paid a call at his offices saying I'd news of Robert Grimshaw. He knew his real name, the name I'd left pinned to his blankets at the rectory."

"He was skeptical."

Miss Grimshaw's cheek gained a spot of color. "He'd every right to be."

"Very skeptical. He threw you out the first time."

Rage thrummed in the pulse at her neck. "Not everyone is a gullible dunce along *your* lines, you realize. How did you know about that?"

"I didn't," I sighed, tracing the tide pool on my brow. "But I do know Robert Symmes, and now you've told me. When did he offer you a job?"

"Not a job!" she cried, arcing forward in her chair so quick that both Piest and I startled. "*Not* a job. How dare you suggest a great man would stoop to employing his own long-lost mother. A test!"

A discordant but strident chime of sympathy sounded within me. I'd imagined Symmes had manipulated his mother into assisting him in exchange for money. That would have been plenty distasteful.

The truth was sickening.

"A test," Mr. Piest repeated, eyes darting to me.

"How was the alderman to know she was truly his mother?" I

asked softly. "She'd neither eyewitness evidence nor paperwork. Any nefarious female could have seized her opportunity after learning of his adoption, and powerful men draw parasites like sugar does flies. He wanted . . . loyalty as proof of birthright?"

"My boy was clever as well as cautious," Miss Grimshaw bragged. "And what wouldn't I risk for him? I, who'd done nothing to help him save for give him away? Hang me, jail me, do what you like, I'll claim it was all a scheme I dreamed up with that McGlynn idiot. I'll never testify against Robert."

Piest and I watched her in something neighborly to awe. With a subtle wash of horror marring the finish. I thought of her warning to myself and Mercy regarding the brute who'd been her son and could barely repress a shudder.

He's a man of importance. I'd call him 'Alderman' if I were you sorry lot.

"Think how close we came!" Nell Grimshaw exulted. Then she shrank fractionally. "He was right to suppose he might have been taken in by me. But when I imagine how it could have been afterward . . . He never charged me for the Pell Street digs, you know. I could afford nothing save the Old Brewery after it burned, but none of that mattered. Another month, perhaps, and he'd have taken me home."

It wasn't bearable, frankly.

A flinch must have crossed my face, for Miss Grimshaw glared at me in abrupt suspicion. She needn't have done. I was only recalling her words when I'd begged her to help me find the man who'd destroyed her home.

My home, *the fellow says. If that was a home, I'm the belle of the ball.*

I glanced once again at the initial police report and noticed a curious fact.

"The notes state you'd only a candle when they arrested you," I observed. "Come to think of it, I'm puzzled those men aren't bleed-ing just now. What happened to the knife you carried?"

"That thieving bitch stole it from me."

This wasn't immediately comprehensible.

"Duffy, I think her name was." Nell Grimshaw pronounced the name as if it left bitter grounds in her mouth. "There was a fray at the Old Brewery before I left it."

Duffy, I thought, as the world turned cold.

"A fray? Didn't you get those marks from the copper stars?"

My eyes whipped to the report again. No mention was made of resistance. I'd assumed she'd fought the police during arrest, and meanwhile there she was, perfectly peaceable if poison-tongued, sitting in my office. *Stupid, you are so comprehensively—*

"Ha!" she exclaimed. "Not bloody likely. I was caught in a mob and my knife knocked away. Last I saw was Duffy picking it up again."

"She . . . what?"

Miss Grimshaw's eyes reflected a flinty spark of pleasure. "That self-righteous parasite of a lady friend you were with—she came back to the Old Brewery. Christ knows why, to ease her conscience or just retrieve her damn lantern, I couldn't say. It's clear enough she's a glutton for punishment. I hate that prissy scavenger— I shouted that she carried charity cash just as I was leaving, and . . . well, you can imagine. Pity that Duffy idiot stole my knife. I'd have gotten it back, but the residents were swarming, and it was safer to be done with the place. They were on those girls like rats on a fresh corpse."

The last thing I heard before I reached my door was the quiet, satisfied conclusion: "Robert will buy me another knife. I know he will. I'll need it now, and he is growing to love me, after all."

24

*Here is another query: is it the duty of Society to burden
itself permanently with every vicious woman who becomes
a mother? And is it possible to make such an establishment
of male and female loafers, even with the best
management, anything useful to them or the world?*

—*NEW-YORK DAILY TRIBUNE*, AUGUST 11, 1847

I COULD HAVE RUN for the Five Points, that corroded stain on
the map where last Mercy had been seen. But it was hours since
the attack, and supposing she remained there . . .

If Mercy was yet in Five Points, then there was nothing to do.

Instead I chose the theatrical boardinghouse as my destination. Spearing into Broadway, where every coldly polished window,
every paste-bejeweled stargazer, every hack's gleaming lantern
mocked me knowingly.

Certain of disaster.

As I raced toward Howard Street, fear lodged like a bullet in
the hollow of my throat, I didn't think about Mercy yet alive but
trampled in the muck of the Old Brewery. I didn't think about her
perishing in scarlet ribbons, gazing openmouthed at me from the
straw-strewn cobblestones of Paradise Square. I didn't even think
of her dead—motionless, curled into herself like the whorls of a

polished seashell. Fearing the worst as I did, the world glimmering with a sickly certain doom, I could think only about the past as I scattered pedestrians who stared after me with wondering eyes.

Because in those few minutes . . . I didn't know anything. And that meant Mercy was alive.

If only for a little while longer.

I put my head down and ran, clinging to ignorance. I didn't deserve the luxury. Elena had been right all along. It wasn't just that I wanted to cautiously sink my claws into Mercy and leave them there so she'd never commence hemorrhaging. I also wanted the impossible—for my mark to have been made when she could conceivably have wanted me back.

I wanted to do that to the seventeen-year-old Mercy, the eighteen-year-old Mercy.

Every individual Mercy except for the one three years ago who thought it better to leave me behind.

I reached the quiet brick street, the iron lamp on the corner cracked yet fitfully flickering. Knocking would have been courteous. And impossible.

I burst through the door.

The foyer was empty. Firelight flickered in the parlor beyond, light at the wrong time for theatrical types. Light where all should have been the pale charcoal darkness of the tenuously waking city.

"—argument is moot, don't you agree?" came the voice belonging to the regal actress who'd delivered the bawdy song the day I met them. "It isn't as if we've the means to treat her ourselves."

"Come, come, that was never my proposal," scoffed the baritone of the portly gentleman who'd worn the blinding-pink waistcoat. "But what's a little kindness when the burden is spread amongst us all? She has money already. What she needs are friends."

"We are none such. Would you wish harm to come to her due to the very brevity of our acquaintance?"

"Of course not! I wish *no* harm to come to her at the hands of greedy relations or medical quackery."

At my footfall both looked up. The beautiful and grandmotherly actress wore a once-fine robe embellished with emerald velvet at the wrists and the neck. Her potbellied friend sat beside her on the sofa, a crystal decanter of spirits between them and cordial glasses held in practiced fingers. They ought to have been shocked at the sight of me—painted liberally with cinders, shirt gaping, sans coat, looking like a man invited to dig his own grave.

They weren't.

Setting their glasses down, they hesitated. The grande dame of the stage pressed her palms together, and the portly fellow, wearing a fez and a pair of half spectacles, rose to greet me.

"Very glad to see you, sir," he assured me. "It was Mr. Wilde, wasn't it? Yes, I thought so. We'd have sent word had we known your address, but I see you've heard the news despite our incompetence."

The actress, white hair turned a gentle gold in the glow from the hearth, stepped forward. "She's been asking for you, you know."

"Mercy asked for me?"

She paused. "No, Miss Duffy asked for you. Repeatedly. Miss Underhill is sleeping at last, with Cynthia attending her. You've met the lovely blonde waif who sings comic opera at the Olympia Theatre? Cynthia is a most gentle nurse, and Kindling—I believe you've met our dear little friend Kindling as well—is guarding the door."

When I could make no reply, the rotund thespian announced, "You've passed a hard night already, my good man. It doesn't require a policeman to see that. I'll take you through to Miss Duffy. She's still . . . quite shaken. She said she wanted to look at the moon until you arrived, and we left her to it."

Mercy is alive, I thought as I watched my feet progress through the combined kitchen and eating hall to a scullery leading to the back area. I thought nothing more, the fact washing over and over and over me like the lapping of colorless water at a creekside. When the actor had opened the back door, he turned with a sympathetic grunt and departed.

The ripe smell of the chicken coop wafted toward me, and the spring vegetables in their small patch whispered in the predawn breeze. But a pretty wooden table had been set up next to these necessaries—one surrounded by chairs and carved with many names and sentiments. All the best-loved phrases and the monikers of the people who'd uttered them spread out in knife gouges for those who came after.

Dunla Duffy had moved a seat to the center of the yard and sat gazing at the moon. A pair of perfectly round faces, studying each other quizzically. Her sleeve was torn, and I could see bruising at her wrists. But otherwise she seemed unharmed. That didn't mean she wasn't covered with blood, mind. The stiffening blemishes just couldn't have belonged to her, left alone and content as she was. The moonlight had been smoke-stained and wasted in Ward Eight. Here it shone pure silver like the bowl of a spoon.

I drew up a second chair and sat opposite her.

"There ye are at last," Dunla Duffy said, smiling. "I wanted to see ye."

"I heard." My voice was mere sandpaper by then, scoured by ash and regret. "What happened at the witches' tower?"

The gravity of her expression was only deepened by its simplicity. Miss Duffy looked as a kinchin might when about to expound upon a broken doll or something equally devastating. She smelled of pig shit and death.

"Ye'd not understand it afore I explain about the letter earlier. 'Twere from you, Mercy said afore she read it out to me." Dunla Duffy leaned forward conspiratorially, crooking her finger. "I'm right glad ye wrote her those words, seemin' a man who knows his business and all. I knew her fer what she was beforehand, mind. But it were grand t' have the proof of it."

"What is she?"

"An angel."

Seconds passed as I searched for her meaning, placed each word on a microscope slide. Then it was all so simple that it split me in two. I'd written Mercy following the attack on James Playfair:

> *I recognize you to be among the angels, even if the outworkers have been brought too terribly low to mark the difference between a helpmate and a scavenger.*

"After, I knew I was right to think her an angel." Miss Duffy's eyes reflected light the color of tombstones. "I asked whether she were the true Angel o' Mercy, and she said aye, she *thought* so, though she struggled at times t' recall heaven. I felt that sorry fer her, not rememberin' the hosts and all the saints, and losin' her wings. When she said that she had to bring the truth to the witches, I knew I had to help. Can ye imagine the shame of it? If an angel should need *my* aid and I were found lacking?"

Crossing herself, she smiled at the collapse of the man in front of her.

"You went to help the witches together," I said.

"First we stopped at a market and bought wee candles. Dozens o' them, hundreds. Mercy said that would help t' ease the outworkers and break the witches' power, and that were true as Gospel, for I'd meself much need o' light afore I came here. Then we carried them to the door and went inside, though it were so dark I was half frighted out o' my wits."

Closing my eyes, I saw Mercy as she'd been for most of my

life—walking toward fear and through it, a basket slung over her forearm. Her tiny wrist cocked just so, a few tendrils of black hair escaping the thick braided knot at the base of her neck.

"We passed along candles, all hizzy-tizzy, so many candles I could nary believe my own eyes." Miss Duffy rubbed her nose regretfully. "I'd thought her aglow so bright they'd ne'er dare touch her. But the angel needed me after all."

"The witch who frightened you at Pell Street shouted something. You were attacked."

Miss Duffy nodded as if in a trance. She was only fourteen, I thought. A lifetime for some, an instant for others. Her grassy hair glinted in the moonlight, curling like the snakes Medusa's crown had sprouted.

None of this is her fault.

I couldn't have known she'd be my saint and my executioner—that she'd have both encouraged Mercy's fit of madness and saved her from it. All I knew was that if one of Gotham's gods had truly been responsible for the events that night, then I wanted an explanation. An accounting of just what good this could possibly serve. I touched the edge of a curl where it shone.

"It weren't always so," she told me shyly. "Once 'twas yellow-red, like me mam's. After our cow died, it turned queer. There were a coppersmith next door, and when I grew too weak t' walk to the stream, I washed in his barrels. I thought maybe he cursed me, but he'd always been kindly. It were a *púca*, I think, as done it. The goblins were always terrible mean-spirited in those parts."

A coppersmith's barrels and an emigrant with fern-green locks. So there was another mystery unraveled, or at least for me it was. I stroked along the edge of her hair as I stood. Miss Duffy beamed up at me, a soft glow playing about her mouth.

"Mercy bein' an angel and all, I'd not have taken the knife up when they came at us if not fer you, sir," she whispered. "She could ha' gone back to heaven that much faster, but I recalled she were yer *gealach lán*. Did I do right?"

"Exactly right. What happened when you'd fought them off?"

"We ran," she said eagerly. "No one stopped us after I'd used the Witch's knife. I'd not thought to meet an angel, and I'd ne'er thought to *help* one, but God's designs are mysterious. I've always been foolish, but Fate didn't care that I couldn't understand. It used me despite my thickheadedness. The moon seems far off and all, but the tide still comes in. Don't it, now?"

I looked at her. Wanting to answer, I found myself inadequate. As I so very often prove.

Nodding farewell, I returned to the house.

Murmurs yet emanated from the parlor. They were deciding what to do with Mercy—these bawdy, warmhearted almost-strangers who knew her to be balanced on the edge of a precipice, facing either *greedy relations or medical quackery* or both. I'd have stopped to reassure them but could delay no further over seeing Mercy herself.

So I climbed the creaking stairs, the conversation behind me pausing briefly and then resuming its liquid murmur.

The dwarf called Kindling dozed in a cushioned chair. A violent gust disturbed the ends of his vibrant red moustache as he started awake.

"Mr. Wilde!"

"Don't be alarmed. I've just seen Miss Duffy. With your permission—"

"No, please, go right on in." Kindling drew a patterned satin dressing gown tighter about himself as he shivered, and I was struck again by just how taken with Mercy these people had been. "Cynthia is watching her. When I think . . . *Oh*. Mr. Wilde, I'm so sorry, I—"

I turned the knob. For a moment I puzzled over whether to

tread gently or to stamp my feet and announce my presence. Then a lamp brightened with tremendous care. When it had reached a quarter strength, I could see that Cynthia was likewise wrapped in a robe—lying next to Mercy in the bed, the singer above the coverlet. Swinging her legs to the floor, she blinked at me with her unrouged Cupid's-bow lips dissolving in distress.

"I knew you'd come. We've done all we could without a real doctor. Mr. Wilde, *please* forgive us, but we didn't want anyone to think . . ."

. . . *That she's mad*, I supplied. *And take her away somewhere nothing good could ever happen again.*

"I'm grateful. How bad is she?"

"In no danger, though some pain despite the tonic. There are bruises. None of them threatening, in my opinion. Mr. Wilde, I couldn't *bear* if you thought me to have treated her with any of my usual . . . flippancy. Please—"

"I think nothing of the kind. My thanks to you, and to the others."

Cynthia had abandoned a chair before lying exhausted on the bed, and I pulled it where I wanted it. There is a tangible poetry in particular injuries. An arm twisted by a kinchin adventuring in a tree, a tooth broken in defense of a friend.

Other hurts are senseless, and thus doubly unbearable.

Dunla Duffy had done a heroine's work of defense. Mercy was nowhere braced into splints, I discovered after a few careful sweeps of my fingers above the quilt. Her eyebrow had been split and carefully bandaged, though, and a bruise bloomed upon her cleft chin. A set of starving fingers had clearly torn the earring from one of her ears, for the lobe was swathed in cotton. As I watched her, she stirred fitfully. Smelling smoke and rightly mistrusting it.

"You're all right."

It was the smallest of exhalations, yet she flinched as if I'd shouted at her. The backs of my fingers brushed at the severe curve of her cheek.

"Mercy, you're at your boardinghouse. Your friends are here. I'm here too."

Her hair was a sable vortex on the pillowcase, her smile cracked from worrying it with small teeth. The familiar line creased her brow as she began to bite her underlip, and I couldn't stop myself any longer, couldn't keep my hand that was already on her face from gently tugging at the edge of her lip with my thumb until she released the abused flesh.

Mercy's eyes slid open. I watched as she understood, finally. It felt rather like dying, though without the calm that's meant to follow after.

"I hope you can forgive me," I said. "I was always too careful with you, and then . . . then I wasn't. You weren't meant to go back there."

A few drops of moisture spilled from the edges of Mercy's lashes. Tears of neither pain nor the lamp's glare but of frustration, I thought. Fear, perhaps. My head fell forward, selfish and insistent, and cradled itself in the hollow made by the curve of her waist beneath the bedclothes.

"You must think me very stupid," she whispered.

My cheek brushed a seam in the blanket as I shook my head.

I thought her so many things—a poet and a poem. A beautiful mistake. As incapable of happiness as I was, perhaps. As eager for others to achieve it in our stead. I knew Mercy Underhill to be a thousand and one separate things, one of which was the reason my heart kept pulsing when I was failing to mind the useless organ. I thought her too valuable to prop a word against and call it the right one.

"When I think of Dunla . . ." Mercy shoved her fingers between her eyes. "Just how badly have I hurt her? Is she alive?"

"Happiest I've ever seen her."

"Are you lying to me?"

"I wouldn't dare. She thinks saving you was a holy crusade."

It isn't going to be quick or easy, I thought, looking up at her from my prone position. The thespians had been right to speak in practicalities. Her mother had died untimely, her father at the end of his own noose, thinking himself the local Hand of God.

It's going to be like wedding yourself to a butterfly or an unpublished sonnet. You'll never fully have her, and you'll bleed for it daily.

I wanted it anyhow. I've never loved anyone else.

"Were you in *another* fire?" Mercy asked hoarsely, brow wrinkling.

Startling myself, I smiled at this. "Yes."

"Are you all right?"

"Not even singed."

Her eyes drifted to the ceiling when she realized I'd speak no more on the subject. "I thought I was doing some good all that while. In London. Before. When in truth . . . parts were real and parts, I think now, were only a dream."

Reaching, I tucked her fingers against my mouth, breathing them. Lemon soap and candle wax and noble gestures and every other thing that smelled like Mercy, wedged prayerfully under my nose.

"I've written so many fairy tales that living one shouldn't be such a shock to the system," she added, laughing darkly.

"Apart from the rest of it, I should have been braver for you," I said against her fingerprints. "It might have helped. I'm sorry."

"This isn't your fault."

"That's a bald lie, love."

"Anyhow, not everyone is meant to live one entire *single* life. I've been thousands of people. So I suppose it's fair my own time should be shortened. I only hope I'll remember you. I've been for-getting things, you know, people too, pieces at a time. It's like read-ing a play with all the character names erased."

"You don't have to remember me."

Mercy blinked disbelievingly, her other hand lifting to pass through my hair. "You say such *terrible* things, Tim. You're my closest friend. You always have been. For whom else am I meant to stay alert, stay myself? Aren't you remotely ashamed of the fact I'm delusional? Did you ever expect *anything* of me, if truth be told?"

Shaking my head, I lifted myself by the forearms and leaned down, leaving a single kiss just at the edge of the mouth that had asked me so many impossible questions. Mercy was right. Madness was a humiliating ailment, a wicked one, a disease that sent previ-ously respected citizens to skulk in closets, shun their own kinfolk. Disappear entirely. It competed with abject poverty for the most disgracefully ironclad proof that God loathed the sufferer. Mercy was wrong, though, in another way.

"I never wanted you perfect," I told her. It had been years in coming, and about a decade too late. "I love you. I only wanted you mine."

For an hour, perhaps, we stayed like that. Knowing the worst—that her mind wasn't hers anymore, no more than it belonged to me. That her thoughts had been captured by some other spirit, a creature gentle and malevolent by turns. I held her hand in my keeping. Nothing further. She still didn't love me, the way I fig-ured the landscape.

I didn't care.

After dawn broke and the spell with it, while Mercy slept on, I paid a call on the now-four-person vigil being held in the parlor. I told them, in broad strokes, our story.

And I told them my plan.

D r. Peter Palsgrave is a physician residing on a medically prestigious stretch of Chambers Street—a road chock-full of *brothers
of the bolus*, as flash patter terms doctors. He was initially ketched at
the sight of me, as I know him to have indulged in some plenty dusty
practices years back. Dr. Palsgrave is a solidly good egg, though, for
all his huffing and puffing and his corseted waist, his queer amber
eyes, and his equally rich silver side-whiskers. He's a physician spe-
cializing in kinchin. He's also an alchemist—which means he's a
genius, and a simpleton, and a chemist, and an anatomist. When
Mercy was a girl, he was an intimate friend of the family.

Mercy blinked at the house a few times when I helped her out
of the carriage. Then she gave a crooked little laugh and rapped the
doorknocker herself.

"This isn't a social call, is it?" she asked.

I shook my head.

"I'll consider living here, then, if he allows me to? You imagine
that would be safer than my being alone?"

"Of course he'll allow it. He's a lonesome narcissist who adores
you. And there are advantages to living with a doctor who's cared
for you all your life, aren't there? It's perfect."

"No it isn't. That's the problem, don't you agree?"

A servant, recognizing Mercy with a start, showed us into the
study. It's a grandly eccentric space. Half laboratory, table thick
with cobalt-glass jars and small burners and apothecary bottles
with tight wax seals. Half library, the shelves stuffed with gilt-
leafed medical texts, the warm scent of crumbling paper underlying
the vague antiseptic atmosphere. I'd been there only once. But I
remember thinking it a wonderful place, and I wrote after seeing it,
*With all the magical discoveries already unearthed, what else in the
world silently waited to be fully understood?*

Dr. Palsgrave sat erect behind his chemistry equipment. Scribbling away in a massive notebook, scowling in hearty choler at our footsteps. The lilac light of dawn christened an illustrated human heart before him, arteries curving away from it like serpents, looking wholly as ominous as that apparatus is in fact.

"Whatever my imbecile of a butler may have told you, I haven't the *slightest* intention of seeing any patients for at least another half an hour."

"Didn't you once say I could presume to call on you at any time?" Mercy asked, amused.

Dr. Palsgrave sprang from his chair, dropping his pen, his hand flying over his chest. Rheumatic fever had ravaged his heart at an early age. But to my mind it doesn't help matters that he owns the disposition of the edgier variety of lapdog.

"Mercy Underhill," he gasped. Dr. Palsgrave stroked his palm down his waistcoat, a self-settling motion I'd not seen in years. "By the Lord, you've just taken several years off my life, dearest child. What on *earth* are you doing here? And who is that with—"

Dr. Palsgrave paled at the sight of me. Poor fellow, I know far too many of his secrets. I swept my hat off apologetically.

"I was just escorting Miss Underhill." Smiling at him, I took a step back. "It's good to see you, Dr. Palsgrave. Any progress with the elixir of life?"

He huffed out a breath of relief, the shawl collar of his impossibly tight jacket receding and swelling again. "I am on the scent at long last! *Electricity.* Electrical galvanization can be applied to certain compounds to produce— No, no, it's *much* too complex for the neophyte to grasp. Mr. Wilde, between the pair of you, I wonder I'm not in the midst of complete heart failure. How *wonderful* to see you again."

Dr. Palsgrave wrung my hand, and then, beaming, the doctor embraced Mercy so enthusiastically that her feet left the carpeting.

When he'd set her down, Mercy quirked a smile at him. "I've missed you, Dr. Palsgrave."

"Missed me, missed *me*, she says. What utter nonsense. Young folk are the most charming and shameless liars. But what the *devil* has happened, my dear girl? Are you all right? Tell me what's befallen you, and we'll make all well again."

"It will take . . . it will take some time to tell, Doctor."

"As ever, I am *wholly* at your disposal, Miss Underhill. Do sit down."

"I'll leave now. Will you be all right?" I asked her.

"I think so. How can I thank you?" Mercy inquired, angling her face in my direction.

"You've nothing to thank me for." Tipping my hat to Peter Palsgrave, who stood cocking his head from one to the other of us like a bantam rooster, I turned to go. "And I'll be back soon. I promise."

Remarkable, in retrospect, how calm I was. How level about it all.

Remarkable too that my voice was so even when I left her there.

Remarkable that only afterward—in the street no less, walking with fierce strides away from the doctor's residence and consulting rooms—that the stinging at the back of my eyes turned sharp enough to blind me to the streets of New York.

I'd always recklessly assumed, seeing as I was still breathing and all, that I survived the 1845 fire. Minus a portion of my face, but otherwise intact.

But it had been fatal.

I had allowed hope to perish, to crumble in so many feathery ashes, and by the time I missed it, it had already scattered to the four winds.

25

*Woman is man's partner, not his rival—the complement,
not the double of his being. It is not to her dispraise to deny
her what would add nothing to her worth, while it would
destroy her fitness for her place in a perfect order of
society—the mental energy, the creative power, the
sustained strength of reasoning which distinguishes man.
She is not fitted for public life.*

**—NEW YORK CHRISTIAN ENQUIRER,
NOVEMBER 2, 1850**

"THAT WAS JUST ABOUT THE MOST AWFUL—" Bird Daly cut
herself off, shaking her head.

I'd stopped at a public bathhouse on my way home from Dr.
Palsgrave's. Stupid with hurt and stinking of fire. I'd viciously
scrubbed myself, scrubbed as if I could deny my own existence or
reverse the effects of time ticking solely in one direction. Destruction lingered in my hair yet. Then I'd gone home to our German
neighbors and the two people on earth I wanted to see most.

Elena had pressed her lips to my cheek and vanished, citing an
urgent need to visit the market for her business's sake. *Soon you will
tell me what happened,* she'd said. *Soon, Timothy.* So instead I'd told
Bird, in vaguest fashion, what had happened. She'd turned white as

429

powdered sugar and flung her arms around my waist in a frenzy to make all right for me again.

That wasn't what she meant by *awful*, though.

No, now Bird and I were clearing up the carnage of our ruined dinner, she scraping pots and I scrubbing them spotless in an aching, violent sort of fashion. Queasy with exhaustion. And my brother had just departed.

Not alone.

"It was awful at that." Sucking in a breath, I unfairly directed my rage against a crusted bit of shriveled-up mutton.

I'd been talking with Bird at the squalid table when Valentine arrived. My brother had nodded at the pair of us, jerked his high-browed head toward my second-floor chamber, and wrenched his face into a question mark. I'd said, *Yes, he's awake*, which was the most positive accounting of the situation I could offer, and Val had vanished soundlessly up the stairs.

Bird and I had stared at each other. Equally at a loss. Only muffled voices reached us, indistinct sounds like the murmured repetition of Catholic prayers.

Then Jim Playfair had walked downstairs under his own power with Val's fist supporting his elbow. Not fully dressed, not by half, but wearing an untucked shirt and trousers and socks and boots. He looked as if he'd either died already or was about to on the spot. Greyish sweat stood out along Jim's hectically fevered brow, the scent of delirium flooding the air, and he took a long moment before speaking. As if not entirely certain where he was.

"I am eternally in your debt," Jim had said to me.

"You're nothing of the kind," I'd protested as one of the proudest men of my acquaintance turned away from me without understanding fully who I was.

"Have you ever watched a hanging?" Bird's voice emerged above the scrapes and clatters as she passed me the roasting pan.

"Yes," I admitted. "Not by choice. At the Tombs."

"I've never seen one, you savvy that," Bird said with the odd extravagance of explanation that kinchin use when they don't want to be told their remarks are stupid. "But I read a story about a hanged man once, and when I pictured it, the convict's expression standing there on the trap, he . . . he looked like Mr. V just did."

It was about all I could do not to flinch from that. Because she was dead right. And I hadn't heard my brother say a single distinguishable word during the entire ghastly interim.

"When we're knocked down, we get up and keep walking," I reminded her. She hovered uncertainly while I struggled with cast iron. "We'll be all right."

"Yes," she said unsteadily. "Just, I gunned Mr. V as they left, and I know they'll come out swinging, but . . ."

"But what?"

"It isn't *fair.*"

I couldn't help it. I dropped the pan in the washtub and hugged her close with soapy fingers and said, "I know, I hate it. It isn't fair."

When Bird tensed, I let her go at once. The moment my arms dropped, she walked deliberately away from me, putting the table between us.

A glacial chill descended.

"I want to tell you that you can stop being mates with me if you like," Bird announced with a tremulous lower lip.

Wiping my hands with a rag, I studied her. A little girl who ought to have been carefree. Or as carefree as a kinchin can be, savage and pregnable as they are.

"Why do you say so?" I asked with tremendous care.

She glanced away. "Because I thought you'd told me a real hummer about Mr. Playfair, and I was beastly to you, and then you only meant to be kind, but I called you a liar when *I'm* the liar, and then I saw them. Together. I never thought . . . I met a molley once, at the Madam's, but he was dressed all in sequins. So I didn't understand before. And I insulted your honor."

She ceased speaking for a few seconds.

"So you and I can split out, if you like," Bird informed me in a very quiet voice. "Stop being pals."

It took me a long while to formulate my response.

"Bird," I said.

Her head shifted.

"I don't care what you say or don't say to me. I don't care how you act or what you do. Well, none of that is quite true, but you're sharp enough to savvy what I mean. Provided you don't decide I'm useless, my tombstone will say 'Timothy Wilde, friend of Miss Bird Daly.' Unless you've a different last name by then. Which you will have, supposing I live long enough."

When Bird's face gradually broke into a smile like a sunbeam cresting a wall, I remember thinking only in weak relief, *That was too easy.*

And afterward, *No.*

It wasn't.

Some parts of life are difficult. Too many.

With Bird it was only a matter of being myself right up until she couldn't stand it any longer. She walked back up to me, and I pinched her chin in my fingers as if nothing had happened between us.

We resumed washing dishes.

I daydreamed as I scrubbed that there existed a monument that had watched us—some sort of landmark witnessing our pact. Knowing even as I craved permanence in New York City, that want would never come to pass. Very few noted our presence here, and fewer still cared that I thought every day about Bird, fretted over whether she would fall into some drudgery or other, or else marry the wrong person. It was palpably clear to me how slender her list of options was. The pair of us would live for as long as we could.

As well as we could. That was all.

Then we'd blow away like wishes made on dandelion heads.

I slumbered for a long time that afternoon after taking Bird back to the orphanage. Distantly, I heard customers knocking. I'd have roused myself to reassure them that Mrs. Boehm's Fine Baked Goods would be open tomorrow but found my blood replaced with sludge incapable of propelling me to the door. Soft nightmares haunted me that would have brought me awake under most circumstances. Instead my mind drifted through scorched empty battlefields as if I'd fallen in Texas and my corpse were left to simmer. The smell of charred weeds all around me.

When I awoke, discovering that my hair still reeked and the afternoon sun through my window was full on my face, that grew more sensible.

Elena wasn't baking when I arrived downstairs. She clearly had been, though. The kitchen I'd left spotless as the smallest possible gesture of apology for disrupting her life was chalky with flour, and the oven blasted warmth. Generally when I happen upon her relaxing, she's reading. Something lurid and lovely, like Mercy's short stories were. Before. Nothing magnetizes people like a shared taste in disgraceful fiction.

This time she sat with a small glass of gin, as she favors. Hands wrapped around the simple cup, a tasteful engagement ring on the fourth finger of her left hand.

It was her left hand that passed me a cup of coffee whenever I forgot to ask for one. Her left hand that wrote me notes whenever she wanted fresh oysters. Her left hand that flapped whenever she was disgusted with a customer who'd just departed and she was about to imitate the poor soul.

It would have been admirable to have been surprised. I certainly ought to have managed that much. But I hadn't fought for her. Not once, not a single time, and she knew it. We two were easy, friendly. I'd have jumped into the Hudson to save her from drowning, but it would never have occurred to me to ask if her parents were yet living or how she felt about keeping a dog.

The wedding ring she'd always worn as the widow of Franz Boehm had been so familiar to me, though. Seeing the new one, the band with the single small stone, Elena sitting there as if the jewel belonged on her finger—it unnerved me. It shouldn't have done. She'd never been mine, and I'd known it.

Still.

I ought to have been, even in the depths of my melancholy, surprised.

"I was so dazed earlier. You wore it to the market, didn't you? I don't like to picture you with him," I admitted when I crumpled opposite her with my own glass and the gin bottle between us. "Herr Getzler is a good man. I mean no offense. And I've been terrible to you, practically a curse on this house. I'm sorry for it. I just feel . . ."

Elena passed a wrist over her brow, inadvertently drawing a clean streak through the wheat dust. "Feel how?"

I winced, baffled at myself. "I know you deserve someone who wants to carve your name in every tree he ever encounters. I'm going to congratulate you, I promise. Please don't let the delay make you think ill of me."

Elena frowned, puzzling. It's one of my favorites of her expressions. One I wouldn't be seeing anymore after she'd become a local purveyor of immaculate baked goods with the name GETZLER painted on the sign and not an intimate friend. It was the oddest circumstance and not one she deserved, but in the aftermath of knowing Mercy mad for a fact and watching Symmes's postmortem blow to my brother as it landed, I couldn't begin to feel happiness or sadness or anger. She might as well have been talking to an onion.

"*Soon*, I said. Now you tell me what happened to you," Elena prodded gently. "But slow."

"Your engagement is much more important than—"

"*Nein*. Tell what you've been doing."

It was neither pretty nor ugly. My eyes were dry the entire time, because I felt like a safe that had been cracked open, its contents plundered, and that I was empty.

Elena had seated herself atop the table before me by the time I'd finished. If circumstances were ordinary, I might have brushed my fingers into the crook of her elbow to feel the supple texture there. I might simply have deposited my head in her lap and seen where that might lead. As matters stood, I held a glass of oddly tasteless gin in my two hands and strove to feel *something*, for her sake if not for mine.

"You think all is changing because of you, your mistakes, and it is not so," Elena said, leaning with her wasp's waist down toward me. "Will you listen?"

I was capable of nothing else and therefore nodded.

It had transpired, Elena told me, that after they emigrated, Franz and her son, Audie, had worshipped America with the sort of abandon reserved for visionaries and lunatics. They'd stopped to sample every doughnut and refused to keep a reasonable pace when passing a brass band. This enthusiasm for immersing themselves could have led to their being at the tragic cattle drive up Broadway that took their lives, but Elena wasn't prepared to swear it. The loss of them had devastated her, however, rendered her a third of the woman she'd been the day previous.

"When I met you—how best I can say this?—I was still small pieces," she explained, gesturing with strong fingers, pale blue cotton skirts brushing lightly against my wrist where it rested on the table. "A very long time it took to get more of myself back, but I did. And then I realized that this life, for me . . . it is not what they would have wanted."

"How so?"

Elena tugged a sleeve down, reflecting. "When we came here, it was an adventure. I love adventure. Never they thought I would be left alone to run a bakery. So lucky, *so very* lucky I was that Franz made clear it was mine, but I am no baker. Baking I am good at, I don't deny, but am I a *baker*?"

I gave her a ghastly smile, said nothing, and she wisely continued.

"We ran from my family together and made our own, and now they are gone, but *I* haven't changed." She thumped her gaunt chest. "Josua Getzler is silly, but he loves me and wants to take me to California. Someone found gold there in January, and he thinks there is more of it. I think that is rubbish. Men can be stupid when they hope for something too hard. But I think very fine is his beer, and if more people go west, they will be thirsty."

Draining my gin, I nodded. "I've still made a hash of us, haven't I?"

She rubbed her palms together. "You meant well to send me away with Bird when Mr. Playfair was injured. But that is not who I am. A person to be sent away to safety. And Josua . . ."

"He knows it."

"He suspects," she corrected, looking almost wicked.

"You're one of the most remarkable women I've ever met."

"Now," she said flatly, "you are being again ridiculous. Sit there and I will bring *držkovský* with butter when it comes out of the oven. I cannot say to you how sorry I am for the time you passed. No one deserves such, least of all—"

"I'll miss this place so much," I choked out, my fist wedged against my teeth.

Mrs. Boehm turned back to me, her lovely colorless eyes deepening nearly to blue in her shock.

"I apologize," I forced out, pressing the heels of my hands to my streaming eyes. "Forgive me, please. I've never left here, you know, never past Brooklyn or Harlem, and I hate it, I *hate* what New York turns people into—this city makes the best of us no better than the rats—but I'll never leave, will I? I can't. I have a horrible job I'm inexplicably talented at, and I flatter myself Bird needs me, and if I take my eyes off Val for so much as a second, he'll manage to finally kill himself. If I could marry you in earnest feeling and take you to California . . . I'm sorry. I'm a disastrous person, I know, but I needed a new home, and I found one here. Scouting out another will be . . ."

Elena kissed me to shut me up.

If she'd ever made a grander gesture for charity, I couldn't think of it. But she was about to outdo herself. Just after she'd sweetly pulled my lower lip into her mouth and then shifted to kiss me sideways—parallel, chaste. As if we were making a cross, her hand in my hair all the while.

"Your brother, he is always saying you are stupid," Elena breathed. "Teasing is what he is doing, but sometimes I wonder."

"Why would you wonder about that? I *am*—"

"Listen to what I am telling you, *bitte*. Josua has great savings for California—for all his brewing, he is yet very careful. Money I have as well, a great deal, much from baking, much from hosting a lodger. A friend. You say you will miss this home? *You* will miss it? Audie was born here, Franz built that table *with his two hands. I* will miss it, and strangers will not live here."

I didn't understand. Her nails on my scalp I could fathom, the tender drag over skin, but her words? She might as well have been speaking Bohemian. Or German. Or both.

"Not everything I've taught her yet, but enough." Elena pulled away to glance around her. "I think Bird is a better cook than a baker, but if that is what she wants, the ovens are large and your brother, maybe he can tutor her more. He is very apt at cooking."

Comprehension trickled, leisurely as a drop of tree sap, from her voice to my ears and into my skull.

"In two months I will go west." Elena stood, brushing a thumb over my mouth where she'd reddened it. "We can talk plenty before. But this will all be for the pair of you. Bird, she will be finished school at the orphanage soon. I once needed nothing more than a place and a purpose. I hope she never needs the same when I could have given it to her. She is like my kinchin to me. Money enough you have, Timothy, to settle our accounts."

Elena Boehm speaks excellent English, in a slightly guttural accent that blends German and Bohemian. Somehow I still couldn't follow her.

"Timothy," she said—exasperated, hands on her prominent hip bones.

"You mean to sell me this place?" I marveled finally. "But it's . . . Good God, how much is it worth? What's your price?"

Elena skimmed her finger along a bowl's edge, tasting sweet clotted cream thoughtfully. "Three questions. So many. Yes, I mean to sell you my home. Your home. Second, it's worth several hundred dollars. What was the third? Newly engaged people, notoriously they are distracted."

"What's your price?" I repeated slowly, smiling.

Elena Boehm grinned wider, sampling the leavings from the spoon before passing it to me.

"I don't know. How much do you have?"

Four days later, my hair yet smelling of lamp oil but no longer of Armageddon, I was walking toward Sally Woods's Thomas Street greenhouse on a disturbingly cheerful spring morning when I caught a shock in my peripheral vision.

The young hawker screaming out headlines from the *New Republican* could probably have done a side business fighting fires for all the spittle he was producing. I momentarily quieted the din as I traded coin for news and then settled myself on a splintering park bench on the north side of Duane Street. Not out of earshot—that would have meant a pilgrimage to Canada. But at least out of the line of fire.

I turned up to the article that had arrested my attention.

STAR POLICE: FRIENDS OR FOES?

GRUESOME SECRET PRACTICES OF THE

COPPER STARS REVEALED

By Mr. William Wolf

Reading the copy took me all of five minutes, after which I didn't know whether to dissolve in laughter or in tears. None of it was strictly untrue, mind. On the contrary. And I liked William Wolf considerably. But the contents ranged from:

As the Reader has gleaned from the brutal nature of tactics used by the "coppers" to elicit information from men who imagine themselves drowning and are in fact near to it, and with apologies to the Sensitive for the detailed nature of my description, I wonder whether it is possible to trust any Organization so eager to torment an unarmed New Yorker.

Which would have been bad enough without:

A singularity clear and true as the Polestar within this rabble is found in the person of Mr. Timothy Wilde, Badge 107, whose dedication to the unraveling of mysteries seems secondary only to his acumen—or so the gentleman would like us to think of him, for this reporter suspects that Mr. Wilde's candor reaches no further than do his immediate loyalties.

This highly readable claptrap continued in like vein at such length, painting a light-and-shade portrait of the copper stars with me as their tainted champion, that I quickly allocated it to the gutter. Or rather the bench, where someone might want it for a blanket. I'd rolled it up to shove between the slats when another item entirely caught my eye, at the back nestled amongst the obituaries, and I flattened the paper on my lap again in gaping disbelief.

We learn with sadness that Mr. Cornelius Villers, a longtime Democratic Party leader, Wall Street tycoon, and distinguished member of the New York Lepidopterist Society, was discovered untimely dead at his home yesterday. It appears that, following a meeting at the Tammany Wigwam, Mr. Villers suffered stomach complaints and retired to his home only to decline still further. The gentleman has long been a sufferer of the severest allergic reactions, and we can only sur-

mise that he met with some accidental misadventure of the
culinary variety. The coroner has confirmed he died of natural
causes, and no other guests were similarly afflicted.

I sat there, merely and wholly stunned, for about three minutes. Reading the notice over again. Picturing a brothel mistress with striking hazel eyes and ethereal blonde hair.

Then I slapped the paper against my knee, lodged it in the pine bench, and was on my way again.

For all Silkie Marsh's faults, and they are exhaustive if not global, I've never liked Cornelius Villers.

Or bullies.

Or incendiaries, come to that.

The Thomas Street landlady received me with her usual enthusiasm, but I was nevertheless happy to see that her mumps had improved. Approaching the quiet greenhouse, the symphonic riot of spring tendrils brushing my wrists as I crossed the yard, I heard the incongruous clicking of typesetting and knew that Sally Woods had returned to work.

She answered my knock warily but brightened at the sight of me. That was a relief, as I'd not been certain of welcome. Miss Woods was still in male costume, but one I hadn't seen before, wearing brown checked trousers with pink-collared shirtsleeves and a brown velvet vest. Her coat was tossed carelessly over a chair, and a gem of sweat glistened on her temple.

Miss Woods smiled at me.

Effortlessly, I smiled in return.

"I shouldn't be any too kittled to see you, but I told you I've terrible taste," she jested, though her tone was weary as she elbowed the door open.

Stepping inside, I rocked my hat on my fingertips. "I've arranged for you to have a better guest in an hour, but if you don't mind a quick chaff in the meanwhile, there've been developments."

Sally Woods was already pouring the whiskey. Despite the alarming attire, I now felt free to admit to myself: I thought she was marvelous. I liked her and admired her the way I'd esteem a newly discovered species of jungle predator, perhaps. The sort I didn't understand but knew to be formidable.

"What guest? You're never this cagey." Miss Woods tossed her head, carelessly pinned hair flying.

"Have you been reading the papers?" I redirected.

Her hand froze in the act of recorking the liquor. "No. I've been cloistered here at the behest of the star police. And I've been up to my ears in missed print orders. And scant enough on chink to care. And . . . a damn coward, if I'm honest with the pair of us."

"Robert Symmes is dead."

Sally Woods sank ever so slowly into the nearest chair.

I tried to be as considerate as I was efficient. But I needed to tell her all manner of things. That I knew what Ronan McGlynn had done to Ellie Abell at the alderman's vile behest. That I knew Sally Woods had been told it was her fault entirely, and she was wrong if she'd ever believed so. That I planned to see McGlynn hanged, that I'd arrested Simeon Gage on the charge of falsifying documents, that Miss Abell may have been falsely grateful to Symmes for employing a ruined woman, but the reign of terror was over and New American Textiles had passed into the hands of a Symmes cousin currently en route from Boston. That Symmes, in his despair over the unexpected humiliation of losing the election, had apparently leapt to his death, mortifying his prestigious family.

By the end of the hour, the whiskey bottle was half empty and my handkerchief soaked, wrapped like brass knuckles around Sally Woods's fist.

"I can't believe he's really gone," she said thickly. "It's as if God

Himself struck him down. I wanted to quiet that bastard so many times. With a shiv, with my bare hands."

"You would have," I said, believing it.

Sally Woods flapped my own kerchief at me, blinking swollen brown eyes. "All I did was write useless letters."

"You didn't want Miss Abell to come to further harm."

"For my own sake? Certainly. I adore the girl. For hers? Yes, still more so. But that hardly speaks to the favor of a self-proclaimed revolutionary. I wasn't strong enough to kill him, Mr. Wilde," she concluded, every limb tensed.

"Even if that were true, and it's not, it would have been no poor reflection on you, Miss Woods," I confessed. "Neither was I."

A small knock sounded.

Ellie Abell pushed the door open. She wore a simplified version of her Bowery finery, just a blue-and-white-striped spring frock with a jaunty red jacket. There were lavender moons under her light brown eyes, and her lily complexion was mottled from crying.

I'd never wanted to harm her. She'd experienced the unspeakable already as the pawn of a power-mad monster. But I'd written a short, direct letter anyhow, one pointing the finger at Symmes more than it alluded to her own hurts whilst still making all clear to her. Because the way I saw it, now Symmes was dead and the storm passed, if Ellie Abell and Sally Woods still didn't have each other, didn't try to patch back together the sisterhood they'd once forged . . .

That wasn't the right story. And when I can alter endings to suit me, I do.

"Ellie?" Sally Woods cried, rising.

My hat was already in my hand and I was almost to the door. As I passed Miss Abell at the threshold, she caught my hand.

"I don't like to conjecture what your opinion of me must be," she said hoarsely.

443

"I think you a very brave woman," I supplied.

"Thank you for the letter. Hullo, Sally," she added, attempting a smile.

"What ho, Ellie." Sally Woods emitted a laugh like a cracked bell in a church tower—broken but pure as hymns. "Oh, Ellie. I've missed you so."

They didn't need an audience. Continuing out the door, I paused only to say, as a sympathetic man would say, or so I imagined, "Atop everything else, I'm deeply sorry for your loss, Miss Abell."

For a moment she looked puzzled. Then her brow cleared and a spark of cold stone appeared in her eye. I wondered what callous creature had summoned it.

"You're sorry I lost that animal Ronan McGlynn's baby?"

Hesitating, I studied her.

"Because *I'm* not," she concluded without the smallest hint of uncertainty. Entering the greenhouse and closing the door behind her.

That afternoon I examined my bank account.

It wasn't spectacular, but at least it existed. Mrs. Boehm had insisted repeatedly in the face of my dense disbelief that I could give her a dollar or a hundred dollars and it would make no difference. But I wanted to do right by her. So I took out a small loan, one that I'd make up within six months' finding lost things with the aid of Mr. Piest's vision, and drew a cheque in her name.

Then I went home and boiled myself a cup of coffee and began writing this story.

It's taken me years to complete it. To separate the truth from the facts.

Sometimes I think about the Timothy Wilde who lives in the

three manuscripts about his life as a copper star, the third nearly finished now. The sheaves of parchment are connected in my mind to the smell of charcoal as I draw crime scenes or suspects. Or my own history or my dreams. But these almost-books . . . they aren't the same as the pictorial exercises in dread I roll into a great ball about every other month.

No, I picture the pages, their two dimensions, the words themselves and their finite number of letters written in my obscenely neat penmanship. Then I look down at myself, and I'm real. Corporeal. A lean, short copper star, but one with a rib cage nevertheless. A backbone. I think how hard I tried to make the paper Tim resemble me.

When I'm in a certain humor, I think he's a better man than I ever was. In other moods I think myself a saint compared to that scoundrel. But Mercy was right, as I always suspected her to be.

None of it was real until I'd written it down.

Epilogue

*Independence I have long considered as the grand blessing
of life, the basis of every virtue; and independence I will
ever secure by contracting my wants, though I were
to live on a barren heath.*

—MARY WOLLSTONECRAFT, *A VINDICATION
OF THE RIGHTS OF WOMEN*, 1792

EIGHTEEN FIFTY-FOUR, I reflected in April of that year,
scowling at my thirty-six-year-old reflection in the glass as I
struggled manfully with my green silk cravat, was new-minted as a
fresh golden eagle and already about as capricious as the tossing of
that selfsame coin.

I'd three hours previous copped a gang of palmers—as we star
police call thieves who make a great show of selecting fine jewelry
and then quietly napping a display item or two. Chief Matsell had
been ragging me to collar them for weeks, but a solid conviction
couldn't be had unless their cache was discovered.

It was bully Mr. Piest and Mr. Connell and I stormed their lair
down Vesey Street area. It was even pretty marvelous that Mr.
Kildare hadn't joined us, being distracted by his wife, Caoilinn
Kildare, giving birth, heaping invective on the lucky fellow whilst
breaking every finger in his hand for the fourth time. That was all

aces. But Kildare's absence meant it was three against five, and the palmers hadn't been particularly eager to visit the Tombs. And while Connell is a man on the muscle, Piest is about as good in a fight as a tinned herring. Which meant that my right eye beneath my scar was now a bulbous, eggplant-colored mass.

Just in time for the wedding that afternoon.

The wedding.

The wedding that turned my palms watery and sent my pulse clacking away like a train. The wedding that just now made me unspeakably clumsy as I wrestled with the slippery sodding cravat. The wedding that was probably going to cause me to collapse like a wet kitten the instant I crossed the church's threshold. Supposing I ever made it there in the first place.

Snarling, I undid the blasted neckerchief and made a fifth attempt.

It had to be perfect.

Well. Saving my face, which was never close to perfect but was generally slightly less terrifying than at present.

I heard a distant knock from the ground floor followed by the door of the café opening and quick, sure steps hastening upstairs.

"Do forgive my tardiness! My tailor was making a few last-minute alterations, and the estimable chap simply couldn't manage to—oh, *Timothy.*"

A very finely clad James Playfair stood in my bedroom doorway, holding a brown paper package I knew contained a spray of flowers for my lapel. Slender lips wide, dark brows aloft. He seemed to me, underneath the shock produced by my truly spectacular black eye, to be making a valiant effort not to laugh.

It turned me peppery, I'll own as much.

"This is the most important day of my life and you're going to stand there sniggering over the fact I took a slim in the daylight?" I growled.

Jim folded elegantly against my doorframe, covering his mouth with his hand. Realizing he was hiding nothing, he pulled long musician's fingers down the back of his neck. "Of course not. That is . . . a *little* sniggering. If *slim in the daylight* means a walloping great punch in the eye, then I sincerely regret to say yes."

"You are a deeply unfeeling person," I announced with dignity.

This remark caused Jim to burst into such a fit of mirth that I soberly considered matching his face to mine.

"I take it back. You're a pitiless cad."

"Wholly callous to the finer sentiments," he gasped, bending as he rocked with laughter. "Everyone says so. The deficiency has caused me no end of trouble as a musician."

"I'm sick to my stomach, my head seems twice its usual size, don't ask how my eye feels, and I've now tried to tie a cravat *five* times," I snapped, tearing the damn thing off again. "If all you can contribute to the proceedings is mockery, Jim, leave the flowers on my table and I encourage you to jump out that window there."

Breathless with amusement, Jim set the box down. He crossed to where I stood before the mirror and plucked my cravat from my hands. Still chuckling, he passed it round my paper collar and commenced tying it himself.

"I don't need—"

"Oh, but you *do*," Jim purred. "You most certainly and emphatically do, bright young copper star."

"You don't have to—"

"Timothy, cease fidgeting, I beg. I am making an effort to execute a Napoleon knot backward, which is a business for neither the fainthearted nor the distracted. You are welcome."

Sighing, I rubbed at the edge of my scar. A short time passed with Jim fussing over silk while I contemplated severing all personal ties and emigrating to India. Then he took me by the shoulders and spun me toward the mirror.

I looked . . . I looked like a thug from one of the nastier East River gangs. But my cravat looked outstanding.

"Thank you," I said belatedly.

"Not at all."

"What flowers did you choose?" I asked by way of apology.

Smiling, he retrieved the package and unwrapped it.

Whatever remaining pique I'd felt toward my brother's friend vanished. The miniature bouquet was beautiful . . . delicate, perfectly arranged.

"Lilac, which translates to first love. Honeysuckle, love's enduring bonds. And trefoil, which I grant isn't typical for weddings, but I thought the yellow accent would look so well with your coloring, and it stands for life, which I find appropriate to both you and to the occasion."

"The possibility exists," I said, pinning it to my dove-grey swallowtail coat, "that you are not a pitiless cad after all."

He winked at me in the mirror.

My front door below us flew open without preamble and slammed shut again.

"Light a fire under it, my Tim!" Valentine's voice boomed. "Or are you planning to stand the poor girl up?"

"Yes, thank you, eighteen fifty-four, that is exactly what I need just now," I hissed under my breath. Snatching up my hat, I headed for the landing.

Val stood at the bottom of the stairs holding a frothing champagne bottle, a cork fixed between his teeth, grinning like a privateer. When he spied my mazzard, he spat it out. Howling with laughter that made Jim's earlier outburst seem like a weak smirk.

"It isn't fucking funny," I snarled as I descended the stairs two at a time.

Wrenching the champagne bottle from his careless grip, I

drank what probably amounted to a quarter of it in a single swig. I needed it. Badly. Valentine wore a new waistcoat inhabited by a populous cote of embroidered turtledoves done in silver thread.

I desired keenly to slap the man.

"Yes it is." My brother could scarce speak and was wincing as if splayed on a rack. "It is very, *very* funny."

"Are you *already* drunk?"

"Of course I am, you witless little titmouse."

"I honestly have no idea what you see in him." I passed the bottle to James Playfair, who cheerily took a long pull.

"I don't either, I assure you," he said fondly, handing it back to my horrible sibling. When Val could manage to drink, he tilted it down his throat and made an about-face.

"Oh, I needed that. *That* smeared the icing over the cake. Thank you for taking a punch in the face, Timothy, it brightened me considerable. Our chariot awaits, hop to it."

As we rattled along in the hack, Val and Jim gently ribbing each other while I stared fretfully out the window at the passing strangers and slums, I couldn't help but reflect over the peculiar miracle my life had turned into.

If the 1845 fire hadn't incinerated my hopes and dreams, I'd likely be long married by now, I considered. Supposing Mercy had said yes all those years ago. I'd certainly been about to pose the query. Maybe I'd have kinchin of my own, kinchin with midnight-black hair and sweet, sideways smiles like hers. Maybe I'd be tending bar at Nick's Oyster Cellar with a Julius Carpenter who was still alive, maybe owning my own ferry boat just as I'd dreamed in those days. Standing at the helm with the scent of seaweed flooding my nose and waves slapping my prow, smiling into the indifferent sun.

I thought about the star police forming the same year I'd lost everything, about the flowers Jim had chosen for me. About life and Kildare's new baby, all the infants born so thick and heedless around the globe, and that when I'd started there wasn't a name for my singular profession, but nowadays people were calling me a *detective*. A child born in the year 1854 could not only grow up to do the same sort of work I seemed so inexplicably to excel at but could now put a name to the occupation. Maybe even be proud of it.

Who could say?

And I realized that despite tragedies both minor and monumental, I didn't regret the fate that had befallen me.

Not a single second.

"Stop brooding, you look like a cow." Valentine slapped my arm so hard I'm sure it left a mark. "We're there."

Stepping down from the hack, I peered up at the familiar church spire, blinking in disbelief at what was about to happen. The weather was cool for April, chill enough to be bracing, a grey-and-blue sky watching with detached interest as I took an enormous breath.

"Ready to face the cannonade?" Val asked, dropping a large paw on the back of my neck.

Swallowing, I nodded.

"Forward march, then," Jim decreed, adjusting his tall black hat.

"There you are," Ninepin hissed as I entered the dimly illuminated door. "You're late, Mr. Wilde, and I was that ketched, I thought— Jesus Christ, who's given you a fibbing?"

"No one you know," I sighed.

"A national hero," Val drawled, finishing the champagne bottle and setting it behind a vase.

"Get your arse in that pew," I snapped, pointing furiously. My brother and his friend obligingly disappeared.

"She's here, I take it?" I asked Ninepin lowly.

He nodded his flaxen pate, looking about twelve varieties of sickly. I figured I looked the same, but with an eye swollen shut. The lad was dressed in the better of his two sets of togs, the solemnity of the attire marred somewhat thanks to the monocle he'd adopted when someone finally told him his spectacles were designed for a moll, and by the most hideous Bowery necktie that had ever blinded me. It would have been uncharitable to criticize his tastes, however.

"You've seen her?"

Ninepin shook his head, resting his palms on his kneecaps. His real name is Francis Garvey. Exactly zero people call him that—not his old paper-selling mates, not his fellow journalists at the *Herald*, not the tutors he bribed to teach him to read when he learned ambition, no one. But the pomp of the occasion would certainly call for it today.

At the front of the half-full cathedral, I saw Father Connor Sheehy emerge from a side door I knew well. He lives behind St. Patrick's Cathedral. Tends to its grounds and its flock with equal care and a liberal dose of Irish sagacity. Smiling at us, his bald head crowned with a formal velvet hat, he waved a hand.

"I'm going to hash my guts out," Ninepin groaned.

Feeling no better, I gave him a small push. "All men on deck."

"No, honest to God, I—"

"Ninepin, *get up there*," I growled, shoving the poor fellow harder.

He made it to the dais without fainting, though I'd have called the odds dead even he'd keel over before the end of the ceremony. He'd not been in position two minutes, meanwhile, shifting restlessly from leg to leg, when I heard the small *snick* of the door behind me opening.

A head keeked out, wearing a woven diadem of spring blooms.

Bird Daly was dressed all in white lace. The gown had a round neck, and she'd tied a red velvet ribbon about the gathered waist. Her wine-colored hair was pinned up like a lady's. Now, at age nineteen or thereabouts, it suited her. Perfectly. Her square face had grown with her, every chiseled surface still dotted with reckless freckles, and I loved every one of them, each spot and speck that made Bird herself.

Love like a weight in my chest, a painful press of devotion.

"Mr. *Wilde*," she gasped softly, covering her mouth with her hand.

"You have my abject apologies."

"What for?"

Making a vague gesture of reproach at my face was the only response possible.

Unexpectedly, Bird giggled. She emerged from the door's shadow and put her arms around me, still sufficiently shorter that I nearly got a mouthful of blossoms. Instead I kissed the top of her head and held on.

"Don't speak flash on your wedding day," I advised hoarsely. "And remember your fiancé's actual moniker."

"It's Ninepin," she said, pulling away. "But I'll behave, Mr. Wilde."

"I am completely terrified just at the moment," I admitted to my friend ruefully.

Bird smiled, one of her dimples appearing. She owns several smiles—all of which are precious to me and several that do not look like happiness but rather separate feelings woven over and under one another. This one was an open book. Print-clear and joyful. The rarest of her expressions. She couldn't have given me a better gift if she'd conquered nations in my name.

"Lean on me, then," she said, taking my arm as I readied myself to walk her down the aisle. "I'm not afraid."

I've tied all three of the manuscripts about my time as a star police with kitchen twine. They're bulky objects. Marred by crinkled edges as I hastily turned the foolscap during some periods. Gritty with dust on what was once the topmost sheet when I couldn't bring myself to look at them during others.

I've decided they don't belong to me any longer.

This afternoon at four o'clock, I'm due at Dr. Peter Palsgrave's residence. He's an old man now, alive despite his ailment, though he must be pushed about in a wheeled rattan chair these days. His nurse, Arthur, one of his former students, attends to the task when Mercy Underhill cannot.

But she'll be herself today, sure-fingered and contemplative. I'm certain of it.

Once a very long time ago, Mercy escaped New York City. She departed in hopes of being a writer, and I wanted that for her, wanted her to draw a map of her mind for me so that I could navigate her sinuous shoals, wanted a book of fiction I could study to delineate all her currents and her cliffsides and her lighthouses. She didn't manage it. Couldn't manage it.

After she came back, I began to understand that I'd had it backward. Typical of me. What was needed wasn't a volume to help me understand Mercy. I already love her, after all.

When I arrive there this afternoon, Mercy will be reading in the medicinal herb garden behind the town house with a cup of tea at her elbow, laced with rum if she and Dr. Palsgrave are feeling adventurous. They often are. After telling the pair of them all about Mrs. Bird Garvey's wedding yesterday, I'll wheel the doctor into his study, where he loves to putter about as the evenings lengthen, and when I return to the yard, the slanting sun will render Mercy's face still more angular, and her lips will slide up at my approach. Her whitening hair will waltz with the shadows of the overhanging trees, and she'll know me this time. She doesn't always, not anymore.

But she will today. And if she doesn't, then she will again soon enough.

As the lights are fading to dusk and the fireflies rise from their sleep, I'll give her these three stories. I'll lean down and kiss her, as I often do, and take my leave again. And when she is herself, *whenever* she is herself and not one of the many sorts of spirits that inhabit her mind now, she'll study the maps I've made. She'll read these nearly-books and then she'll know who I am. That's a lifelong dream of mine.

And to think it only took me a little over two decades to work out how to achieve it. We so stubbornly speak to each other in our best pet languages. When really, how much simpler would it be to speak to the listener in his or her own?

This isn't everything I've ever wanted. It's a sliver like the moon that will be rising as I walk back to Elizabeth Street, eyes on the cobbles and on the streetlamps and on my thousands upon thousands of neighbors.

But it's the fraction we were dealt, Mercy and I, and these outpourings of ink I intend to give her will complete the picture of a life sincerely if partially lived.

Time is a tyrant, words our last and only weapons.

—Timothy Wilde, April 16, 1854

HISTORICAL AFTERWORD

The road leading to the American Civil War was a notoriously long one. Acrimony and bitterness over the Peculiar Institution—not to mention the utterly debased nature of the Institution itself—were ripping America apart at the seams long before seven Southern states formed the Confederate States of America and shots were fired upon Fort Sumter in April of 1861. Tammany's rancorous divide between the Hunker and the Barnburner factions was echoed throughout the entirety of the industrialized Northern metropolises. It was widely thought necessary to end slavery, yet potentially devastating to attempt this in fact. Meanwhile, Congress's efficacy as a governing body foundered in the wake of such weighty moral dilemmas—many of which, one must allow, were treated as matters of economy rather than of liberty and justice for all. The conservative bargainers and would-be pacifists were correct if only in a single sense: hundreds of thousands died tragically in the War Between the States. The fact that still-undetermined millions of Africans had already died horrifically and were still dying in slavery, meanwhile, is undisputable.

The acquisition of massive territories in Oregon and Texas deeply exacerbated this already festering debate. David Wilmot, a fiery New York Barnburner whose career I followed closely to ready myself for this tale, recalled an incident that well sums up the problem the country was facing, in a speech delivered in 1847 and re-printed multiple times thereafter. He reported:

> An intelligent member of Congress from the South, in con-versing with me upon this subject, and remonstrating against my course, said, "if you succeed in your efforts to prevent the extension of slavery, and confine us to the territory now oc-cupied by it, in less than a century we will have a population of thirty millions of blacks, with less than half that num-ber of white population in their midst; and, said he, then the terrible alternative will be presented: we must either aban-don the country to them, or cut their throats." Would you, he said, bring such a calamity upon us?

Needless to conclude, Wilmot was unimpressed by the unnamed Southern politico's arguments.

Feminism in various incarnations has existed for as long as fe-males, but as a concerted effort in a modern Western cultural con-text, the 1840s marked a distinct change in organization and tone. Abolitionists of the antebellum period failed at first to embrace another burgeoning "infidel" cause, as the female rights movement would not gain significant traction for decades to come. The indus-trialization of America and its complete lack of social infrastruc-ture had already rendered the most comfortable of lives precarious; and when women began pointing out that they were not allowed to work in positions anyone could see they were well suited for (book-keeping is a ready and early example, as few would have dared to suggest that women were mentally capable of being doctors or law-yers or heads of state), they were roundly dismissed by reformers and conservatives alike. Zealots like Frederick Douglass were the exception rather than the rule. The first Woman's Rights Conven-tion took place at Seneca Falls in 1848, and Douglass accepted his invitation to attend with enthusiasm, stating in *The North Star,* "All that distinguishes man as an intelligent and accountable being, is equally true of woman. . . ." This was a shockingly anomalous opinion. Elizabeth Cady Stanton and her partner-in-reform Lucretia Mott were deeply gratified by Douglass's approval, but they met with ferocious opposition from strangers, friends, and family. Stanton's father, Judge Cady, wished, in fact, that she "had waited until I was under the sod before you had done this foolish thing."

It should be noted that the motivation behind the female rights movement was far more one of survival than of pique or pride or even social progress. When the women went past claiming equal intellect to mentioning that they were not allowed to inherit property fairly, or that they must work or perish, or that the only way to survive destitution was moral ruination (specifically in the sense of entering the sex trade), they received replies such as this one from the New York *Christian Inquirer* in 1850: "Rights imply duties, and freedom from certain duties is one of the most precious rights of women. The immodesty and rashness with which duties not assigned to them are sought by some women, give poor indication of any appropriate sense of the difficulty and importance of discharging those distinctly imposed by Providence." The fact that countless women starved to death as a result of being denied such indecorous "duties" was mainly addressed during the time period by way of assurances of heaven and a just reward in the halcyon afterlife for humble maidens who embraced suffering in a duly Christlike manner.

The stigma against mental health problems, as terrible as it remains at present, was still worse in the nineteenth century; I've endeavored to make not only mental illness but its accompanying ostracism as historically accurate as possible, which proved challenging. Additionally, I often lacked clinical vocabulary when describing various problems (it took me quite a long time on Valentine's behalf to discover, for instance, that the contemporary slang for "high" would have been "in altitudes"). While I'm not an author who thinks that my after-the-fact opinions of my characters have any bearing on how readers view them, on an academic level, it may be of interest to know that I imagined Silkie Marsh as a sociopath, Robert Symmes as a sadist, and Mercy and her father the Reverend Underhill to suffer from hereditary paranoid schizophrenia, an illness which has a definite and tragic genetic component.

Throughout the Timothy Wilde trilogy, I have endeavored to show all due respect for the NYPD's ideals and practices, but I have never pretended their record is spotless, and to do so would be not merely coy but asinine. Heroes and villains and plain misguided men and women often wear the same uniforms. The shower-bath scene in which Ronan McGlynn is interrogated in the Tombs courtyard by roundsman Kildare is taken directly from a nineteenth-century woodcut illustration, seeming by its subsequent description to explicitly describe an early American form of waterboarding. Whether one defines such measures as "enhanced interrogation" or simple torture, one cannot doubt that deep pockets of grey existed in our early law-enforcement practices, as indeed they do to this very day. To acknowledge such is not to dishonor the countless heroes of the NYPD, and one hopes only that history will judge every man and woman according to their deserts rather than their reputations. One shudders to think what a contemporary biography of Captain Valentine Wilde would look like.

During the first ten years I spent in New York, I lived a few blocks away from where Chief of Police George Washington Matsell is buried at the idyllic uptown Trinity Cemetery in Washington Heights. The gate was often locked, so I visited infrequently (though I borrowed piecemeal several wonderful character names from tombstones). But Matsell and his preoccupation with language and his *Rogue's Lexicon*, his passion for understanding people and their motives, the murky bits of his history and accusations of his being a Party bully as much as a reformer and a wildly liberal apologist, are the reasons I was able to infuse these books with the language and the ethos of their time period. Here is to, unabashedly, *The Secret Language of Crime,* and may many more such lexicons be produced during times of tremendous struggle and social upheaval.

ACKNOWLEDGMENTS

Writing this book was an enormous struggle. I have always been what authors term a *pantser*, a charming "seat-of-the-pants" term the hopelessly disorganized call themselves so they don't feel like crying into their Top Ramen bowls and whiskey mugs at four in the morning when the words won't come. To every single one of the friends and family who relentlessly, stubbornly believed in me during that process, I thank you. I'm not ashamed to say there were moments stretching into days when I thought this manuscript wouldn't happen. And I am actually proud of the fact that, after the horrid mess topped 150,000 words in its first draft, you all applauded heartily as I trimmed its length with gentle chain saws.

My gratitude to my editor, Amy Einhorn, for supporting Tim Wilde—and, in every fashion her copious brain can come up with, me personally—is immense. Additionally, I'm in perennial awe of her ability to induce me to tell the *right* story, and at the *right* moment. Thanks to her and thanks most sincerely to her brilliant team, including but certainly not limited to Elizabeth Stein, Lydia Hirt, Katie McKee, Kate Stark, Alexis Welby, and all the other lovely powerhouses who keep me afloat.

The team of completely metal, hard-rocking ladies at William Morris Endeavor, who are the reason you might be reading this book, deserve far more than my simple thanks, for I owe them a